# SEA TIGERS & MERCHANTS

## A New American Generation
## Salem Stories, Book 2

# SANDRA WAGNER-WRIGHT

**WAGNER WRIGHT**
ENTERPRISES

Sea Tigers & Merchants: A New American Generation/Sandra Wagner-Wright—first edition.

ISBN: 978-1-7354132-4-2 (Paperback)
ISBN: 978-1-7354132-3-5 (eBook)

*Cover portrait: Privateer Mount Vernon by Michele Felice Cornè*

# CONTENTS

# CAST OF PRIMARY CHARACTERS

Crowninshield Family

- Captain George Crowninshield (1734–1815)
  - Husband of Mary Derby Crowninshield (1737–1813)
  - Father of
    - Edward Crowninshield (1765–1793)
    - Captain George Crowninshield Jr., a.k.a. Geordie (1766–1817)
    - Captain Jacob Crowninshield (1770–1808), married to Sarah Gardner (1770–1807)
    - John Crowninshield (1771–1842)
    - Benjamin William Crowninshield, a.k.a. Benj (1772–1851)
    - Richard Crowninshield (1774–1844)
    - Mary Crowninshield, a.k.a. Molly (1778–1835)
    - Sarah, a.k.a. Sally (1784–1847)

Derby Family

- Elias Hasket Derby (1739–1799)
  - Husband of Elizabeth Crowninshield Derby, a.k.a. Eliza (1736–1799)
  - Father of
    - Elizabeth Derby West, a.k.a. Betsey (1762–1814), married to Captain Nathaniel West, a.k.a. Nate (1756–1851)
    - Martha Anne Derby, a.k.a. Patsy (1763–1832)

- Anstiss Derby (1769–1836), married to Benjamin Toppan Pickman Jr. (1763–1843)
- Captain Elias Hasket Derby Jr., a.k.a. Elias (1766–1826), married to Lucy Brown (1771–1855)
- Ezekiel Hersey Derby, a.k.a. Zeke (1772-1852), married to Hannah Brown Fitch (1777-1762)

## Outside the Two Main Families

### Silsbee Family

- Captain Nathaniel Silsbee Sr. (1748–1791)
  - Husband of Sarah Becket Silsbee (1750–1832)
  - Father of
    - Captain Nathaniel Silsbee, a.k.a. Nath (1773–1850)
    - Sarah, a.k.a. Sara Silsbee (1777–1840)
    - William Silsbee (1779–1833)
    - Zachariah Fowle Silsbee, a.k.a. Zach (1784–1873)

### Gardner Family

- Captain John Gardner (1736–1815)
  - Husband of Sarah Derby Gardner (1747–1774)
  - Father of
    - Sarah Gardner (1770–1807)
    - John Gardner (1771–1847)
    - Richard Gardner (1774–1836)

Elizabeth Rowell, a.k.a. Lizzie (1770–1862)

# CHAPTER

## Lizzie Rowell

*January 1790*
*On the Road to Salem*

Lizzie shrank into the stagecoach's corner with her canvas bag tucked beneath her feet. She kept her eyes steadfastly focused on the window, though there was little to see as the twilight dimmed.

"Probably another couple hours afore we reach Salem," the grizzled man sitting across from Lizzie said. "Ya goin' on ta Boston tamorrow?"

The stranger stank of stale tobacco and rum. Lizzie pulled her shawl closer and ignored his question.

"You awake, girl?" The man kicked Lizzie's ankle.

"Leave 'er be," the stranger on the opposite end of Lizzie's bench said. "You kin wait till mornin' to find out."

Lizzie clutched the window shade as the stage wove around the deepest ruts in the road.

"So, yar awake," the first man said and kicked Lizzie's ankle a second time.

"Ouch! What's wrong with you?"

He snorted. "Been tryin' ta talk ta ya."

"Well," Lizzie replied as she drew herself up into a straightened sitting position, "I don't feel like talking."

The stranger stretched his long legs until they reached Lizzie's bench. Her heart pounded. Surely, the stage would arrive at Salem soon. They left Haverhill at three o'clock that morning, and it was about twenty miles to Salem. The stranger continued staring at Lizzie, who avoided his eyes.

After what felt like the longest hour in Lizzie's life, the horses slowed to a stop in front of the tavern Traveler's Rest.

*Salem!*

Lizzie waited for the men to disembark before she moved toward the door, where the unwashed stranger loomed in front of her. She shrank back down on the bench, unsure what to do.

The stage driver stuck his head inside. "Ye have to get out now, miss."

Lizzie glanced out the door.

The driver gave an understanding nod. "I'll walk ya inside. Is someone meeting you?"

"No." Lizzie shook her head. "She doesn't know I'm coming."

"Who doesn't?"

"My cousin Anna Shipman. She runs the—"

"Ship Tavern at the top of Derby Wharf. I know it well. Wait inside by the bar; I'll walk down with you after the stable lad takes the horses. Young woman like yerself shouldn't walk alone after dark."

Once they acquired pints of ale, the stranger and his companion seemed to lose interest in Lizzie. There were certainly enough unattached women on the main floor to catch their eyes. Eventually, the stage driver appeared at the door and motioned Lizzie to join him. Clutching her bag, Lizzie adjusted her cloak and stepped into the darkness.

"Name's John. I do the stage run from Haverhill to Boston and back again." John tucked Lizzie's arm under his elbow. "Salem's a nice town. Busy. You say yer cousin runs Ship Tavern. She know about you?"

Lizzie hesitated. John seemed nice, but it probably wasn't a good idea to share too much information. "Yes. She's expecting me," Lizzie lied and decided to change the subject. "I've never been near the sea before."

"Bit different from Haverhill. We started walkin' from Traveler's Rest on Essex Street, and now we're walkin' down Orange Street to Derby Street. An' Ship Tavern is just on the corner. So if you cross Derby Street from the tavern, you'll be on the wharf. Ye'll get yer bearings soon enough."

Lizzie saw several young men walking in both directions on Orange Street and was glad John had taken an interest in protecting her. She'd be terrified traversing the street alone in the dark. As they neared the corner, Lizzie saw light streaming from the tavern door as it opened and closed. Sounds of laughter spilled into the street.

"This is it," John said, opening the door.

Coming in from the dark, Lizzie paused for her eyes to adjust to the light emitted by the large fireplace on the opposite side of the great room and stamped her feet to avoid tracking any more mud than necessary inside.

"We'll go ta bar an' ask after Anna."

John guided Lizzie through the entryway to a long bar with a selection of glass decanters holding various spirits behind it. A lad who looked to be about twelve years old stood behind the bar polishing glasses.

"What'll it be?" he asked.

"I'll have a cider, and the young lady . . ." John turned to Lizzie. "Perhaps a small glass of Madeira?"

"Yes, please. Is there anything to eat?"

"Supper finished a while ago. I kin get you some bread and cheese."

"We'll both have that," John ordered. "Bring it to the table in the corner."

"Wait," Lizzie said. "I'm looking for my cousin Anna Shipman. Do you know her?"

"I should. She's my mam. I'll let 'er know yer lookin' for her. Take yer drinks ta table."

As they made their way to the corner, Lizzie eyed the busy room with apprehension. "How long will the tavern stay open?"

"Prob'ly till midnight or so," John replied. "Once I know yer in good hands, I'll shove off back to Traveler's Rest. We leave at three o'clock in the morning tamorrow."

"It'll be a short night for you, then." Lizzie twirled the wine in her glass, wondering what she would do if her cousin didn't accept her.

A woman of medium height and light hair streaked with gray came to the table with a basket of bread and a plate of cheese.

"My lad said you want ta speak ta me?"

"Are you Anna Shipman?" Lizzie asked.

"I am, and who might you be?"

"I'm your cousin Lizzie Rowell. Well, it's Elizabeth, but everyone calls me Lizzie. And, um, my mother—your aunt—died last week. She told me if she didn't pull through, I should come to you."

In the far corner, a shout went up as a game of darts concluded.

"They'll be wantin' another round!" Anna shouted to her son. "So, Lizzie, how old are you, and what do you think I can do for you?"

Lizzie licked her lips. "I'm nineteen, and I need a place to stay. I'm happy to work for my keep. I'll turn my hand to anything."

"If I let you stay, you'll be behind the bar when we're open and otherwise do what needs doing. But no funny business with the customers. The Ship caters to sailors but is respectable for all that. Mr. Derby doesn't allow debauchery so close to his wharf. So mind none of the young men who pass through here sweep you off your feet. Understood?"

"Yes, ma'am."

"When you finish your meal, my son will show you where to wash up and take you to a room in the attic. It's cold in the winter, but you'll be busy down here most of the time."

In the predawn darkness, an errant piece of straw pierced Lizzie's thin mattress cover and scratched her face. She woke with a start in the dark room and took in her surroundings. The room was small, furnished only with a broken chair, a dressing table with a porcelain bowl and pitcher on the surface, and the rope bed Lizzie occupied, with its thin straw mattress and thinner blanket. She drew the blanket back over her coat.

*I wonder if Cousin Anna has extra blankets or if I have to make my own quilts.*

Lizzie sighed. She hadn't expected luxuries, but the accommodation in her father's barn was better than this. At least the cow and horse had provided some heat.

*Better get downstairs and start working before Cousin Anna changes her mind.* Lizzie shivered and swirled her chestnut hair under a mop cap.

Downstairs, the girl skirted frozen puddles to the outside privy, grateful her sturdy shoes kept her feet dry. Finishing her business, Lizzie added a chamber pot and warmer clothing to her list of items to get. *Maybe there's extra from the guests' rooms.*

Inside the kitchen, Anna's son added logs to the cook fire.

"Yer late," he said.

"It's not light yet."

"Don't matter. Ye can't wait fer sun in winter. I'll come up an' bang on your door tamorrow. There's a mess of vegetables on the counter. You need to chop 'em for the stew."

Lizzie eyed the iron cauldron that was probably the stewpot. *That will be a lot of vegetables.* She sighed. "Is there meat to add?"

"Salt pork's already in the pot. Fill up the rest with potatoes and such. I'll help ye add the water. Well, don't stand there gaping. Start chopping or we won't be ready for dinner."

Lizzie lifted a basket of potatoes onto the top of the wooden kitchen table and started peeling. After an hour, she finished the basket and started in on the carrots, which she didn't need to peel. The boy moved to the other side of the table and began chopping onions.

"I'll help you now, but tomorrow you'll have to do it all yerself."

Tears started streaming down both their faces.

"You never told me your name," Lizzie said, wiping the tears away with her sleeve.

"Most people call me Matt," he replied around a hiccup.

"Thank you, Matt. I've never done this kind of work before."

Matt snorted. "Yeah. By the time we get the stew going, Samson'll be here to take care of breakfast, and we'll go set up the bar. I'll show you how to serve. By then, folks'll be comin' in. You can shadow me today. Tomorrow, ye're on your own."

Lizzie nodded. Not all her tears were from the onions.

# Captain George Crowninshield Jr.

*Crowninshield Counting House*

Geordie disliked his father's counting house. He found it drafty and dimly lit. Uncle Derby's warehouse was a more comfortable place, but he didn't sail for his uncle anymore. While his brothers continued to command ships for Hasket Derby, Sir had pulled him into George Crowninshield & Sons as the family's primary shipmaster. Sitting in front of his father's desk, Geordie rubbed the back of his neck and placed his right leg over his left knee so he could admire his new jockey boots. He liked the more casual look of the boots, with their turned-down tops. He picked a piece of lint off his breeches.

George looked at his son and smiled slightly. "You've done very well with the *Richard & Edward*. It's a good cargo, and we should get good prices for it.

We may have to portion out the coffee a bit. Twenty-six-thousand pounds of beans can't be moved quickly."

Geordie shrugged. "We have a large warehouse, and it'll keep until you have buyers. The raisins should move quickly."

"Humph."

"Do you have something you want to say, Sir? If not, I've arranged to meet several acquaintances for cards at Ship Tavern."

George steepled his fingers and leaned forward. "I'm wondering . . ."

"Yes?"

"Have any young ladies caught your eye? If your mother has anything to say about it, your brother Jacob will soon be courting your cousin Sarah Gardner."

Geordie snorted. "She's so shy, she barely speaks. I don't see how he can court her if she doesn't converse. And I've never seen her dance. But good luck to him."

Geordie uncrossed his leg.

"And whom do you fancy?" his father pressed.

Geordie suppressed his urge to squirm. "I'm scarcely in Salem long enough for anyone to take my attention. I've been at sea since I was eighteen, a situation hardly conducive to close friendships. Why the sudden interest?"

"I want to see my heir married first. You're well liked and could make a good marriage alliance."

"Sir, I must inform you that I have no interest in a business marriage. If I find a woman to my liking, I'll pursue her. And if I find someone I wish to marry, you'll be the first to know. But at the moment, I'm busy sailing our ships and will be for the foreseeable future. Besides, Jacob won't be in a position to marry for several years. He's only twenty, and Sarah must be younger. Who knows what the future holds?"

At his father's silence, Geordie picked up his leather gloves. "And now, I have a card game to attend. I'll see you at home, Sir."

Bundled up in his greatcoat and shaggy hat, Geordie made his way to Ship Tavern. *I wonder why Sir brought up marriage.* He shuddered, and not from the cold. The last thing he wanted was a respectable wife. He enjoyed meeting women on his travels, and that was enough for him. He didn't require permanent female companionship and the responsibility that came with it. Once his brothers established families, Geordie envisioned himself as an eccentric uncle.

Arriving at the Ship, Geordie stamped his feet inside the doorway and left his greatcoat on the rack near the door. He wore a double-breasted coat underneath. Geordie unfastened a few buttons.

"Welcome, Captain Crowninshield," Matt called out. "Come meet our newest family member."

Geordie shouldered his way over to the bar and dropped his eyes to see a young, flustered woman with dark-brown eyes. Her chestnut hair was slipping out of her mop cap.

"Lizzie," Matt said. "This is Captain George Crowninshield. He just came in from Isle de France on the *Richard & Edward* with an exotic cargo of luxury goods. Captain Crowninshield, this is Lizzie Rowell. She just arrived last night."

"Word travels fast." Geordie nodded. "And call me Geordie, as I've told you before." He shifted his gaze to the young woman. "You as well, Miss Rowell."

"You kin call 'er Lizzie. We all do. She's Ma's cousin, come to join our family."

Geordie fixed his attention to the new girl. "How long have you been in Salem?" he asked.

"She just arrived. I been showin' her the ropes, so to speak."

Geordie looked at Matt. "I was speaking to Miss Rowell."

"Yes, sir." Matt handed Geordie a pint of ale. "Will you be playing cards at the back table again?"

"I will. Have any of the lads shown up yet?"

A blast of cold air came in from the door, and Geordie swiveled his head in that direction. "Looks like they have now," Matt said.

"Eben, Samuel," Geordie called out, "get a drink on me and head for the table at the back over there."

Matt began setting up glasses of rum.

"You can call me Lizzie, sir," a soft voice said.

"And you must call me Geordie. I don't care for formalities among friends. And I insist we become friends."

Lizzie blushed.

"Come by the table later. No doubt we'll want to order food and more beverages."

# Lizzie Rowell

Captain Crowninshield walked toward the back table with a confident stride, though he stopped frequently to chat with men he passed before moving on with a laugh and a clap on the shoulder.

"I can't believe he said I could use his Christian name," Lizzie whispered to herself.

"He didn't," Matt said. "Geordie's like a nickname, and you don't speak to him unless it's ta ask if he needs anything."

"You're on good terms with him."

"I try to be, and I hope he'll put me in his crew in a few years. But he's not for the likes of you. His family is one of the richest in Salem. His uncle's Hasket Derby. Keep well away from 'im unless you're serving drinks. Speaking of, take these tankards of ale to the men playing darts."

Lizzie took the long route through the great room so she could pass near the back table by the fire. Two more men had joined Geordie's game. They glanced at their cards and swapped stories as they played. Geordie called Lizzie over and nodded at the tankards she carried.

"Where are you taking those?"

"To the men playing darts."

Geordie smirked. "You do know there's a more direct route from the bar to the dartboards."

Lizzie's heart pounded. "Um, well, I wanted to pass by the fire to warm up a bit."

"Come back with more rum for the table. Eben lost the last hand, so he's buying." At that, raucous laughter broke out at the table.

The men continued playing cards until the fire burned down and the only people in the great room were those who had rented rooms. Eventually, even they began making their way upstairs.

Lizzie cleaned up the other tables before making her way over to the table at the back.

"I'm sorry, sir," she mumbled. "The tavern is closing. You'll have to leave."

Geordie smiled. "I don't think so."

"It's true, sir. We don't allow people to stay in the great room overnight."

"I'm not staying in the great room. I have a room upstairs. Didn't your cousin tell you? I keep it when I'm in Salem."

Lizzie felt her stomach drop and shook her head. "No, sir. She didn't mention it."

"My name is Geordie."

"Yes, sir . . . Geordie." Lizzie wiped the table around the area where Geordie held his glass.

"Would you like to sit down?"

Lizzie stopped wiping. "I have to be in the kitchen for five o'clock tomorrow morning, so I need to, uh . . . I need to go to my bed."

"If I arrange for you to start work at seven o'clock, would you chat with me tomorrow night? I'd like to know you better. And I could tell you about my voyages." Geordie flashed another smile.

Lizzie glanced at Matt, who had stopped sweeping the floor and was watching her. He shook his head. Her aunt already told her that she was not to associate with the customers.

But Geordie was so handsome and had such a nice smile. And he was important. Surely, she shouldn't offend him by refusing to have a conversation with him. And they would be in plain sight, so nothing untoward could possibly happen.

"If my cousin allows me to start later in the morning, I would like to know more about your travels. But for now, I need to get some rest."

"Until tomorrow evening, then," Geordie said.

"Tomorrow."

When she walked past Matt, Lizzie refused to meet his eyes. Her new relative was young, but he wasn't unobservant.

# Captain George Crowninshield

*March 1790*
*Captain George Crowninshield's House*

George paced the cupola at the top of his mansion overlooking Salem Harbor. When he got to one side, he raised his spyglass to sweep his gaze over the beach next to Derby Wharf. The tide was out, making the blocks his brother-in-law's men were placing over the sand clearly visible.

"Damme!" George muttered before pacing back to the other side of the cupola to raise his spyglass and sweep the shore from a different angle.

"Blighter!"

"Who, Sir?" Jacob stood at the head of the stairs.

"Your blasted uncle. Do you see what he's doing? He's laying down a keel. Just look how long it is! And that Enos Briggs . . . see if I have him build any of our ships! How large do you reckon she'll be?" George asked his son.

Jacob raised his own spyglass. "Looks to be over a hundred feet."

"Damme and blast!" George snapped his spyglass shut. "If we want to compete, we need bigger ships. The *Richard & Edward* is a good schooner, but she doesn't carry enough cargo. We need more ships, and they need to be bigger. We can't let Hasket keep the lead over us."

Jacob lowered his spyglass and gave his father a rueful smile. "As Mame says, we must build slowly to build well. Geordie looks out for our interests while sailing the *Richard & Edward*, and I sail for Uncle Derby with an eye to our adventure cargo. By the way, I'm off to Isle de France and India with the *Henry* next week. Uncle Derby's cargo is almost assembled, and with my adventure and your consignment, we should make a good profit."

"You miss my point. I don't want you sailing for your uncle. I want you and your brothers sailing for George Crowninshield & Sons until we earn enough for you all to establish yourselves as merchants working together to advance our business."

Jacob rubbed his jaw. "We are like-minded in that. Come, Sir, such weighty conversations deserve a tot of brandy."

George motioned for his son to descend the stairs before him as he continued to mutter about his brother-in-law. He despised Hasket for his arrogance and his refusal to treat George as an equal. He hated the fact that he didn't have enough ships to employ his own sons and had to send them to Hasket's counting house. And he resented Hasket's wife, his sister Eliza, who ruled Salem society and never missed a chance to snub his own wife, Mary.

In the drawing room, Jacob poured his father two fingers of brandy in a cut-crystal glass.

"To our success." Jacob raised his glass.

George tossed back the amber liquid, relishing the burn. "It's a bit early in the day for toasts, don't you think?"

"Mame!"

"Jacob." Mary Crowninshield nodded. "This is why I ask your father not to spy on my brother's ship. It raises his temper when he sees Hasket's shipbuilding investments."

"Shall you join us, Mame?"

"I'll take a sherry. Now then, what is the source of this disquiet, besides the workmen on the beach by Derby Wharf?"

Jacob quirked an eyebrow. "Sir is impatient."

Mary patted her husband's cheek. "Were your father not so impatient, we wouldn't have George Crowninshield & Sons. But it is equally true that my father built the foundation for the success Hasket now enjoys. Your father stands on his own, with his sons beside him. Jacob is right, Husband, success will be ours, but only if we are patient. Rest assured, Hasket will overreach. It is his nature. Shall we sit?"

Mary arranged her skirts while the men took nearby wing chairs and stretched out their legs.

Jacob cleared his throat. "We need to think about more than competing with Uncle Derby in business. We need to challenge the grip he and his associates hold on Salem's political and social life. President Washington won't be in office forever. When he steps down, there will be a political struggle, and we are well placed to lead the opposition to Uncle Derby's party."

George chuckled. "You don't subscribe to the fantasy of political unity, then?"

"Whether I do or not, such a fantasy will not happen. Every man has his own opinion of government. Uncle Derby and his faction have controlled Salem and Essex County long enough. It's time for new blood. Once I establish my household, I shall put myself forward for political office. In the meantime, I shall recruit like-minded men to our cause."

"A household? Are you finally keeping company with my niece Sarah Gardner?" Mary asked. "Your cousin is a lovely girl, well deserving of your attention. And nothing would please me more than to bring my sister's daughter into our family."

"When I'm in a position to establish my own household, I shall ask to court her. Presently, we're good friends, as we always have been."

George slapped his knee. "Success in business, politics, and wooing—what a lot you have on your mind. Careful your head doesn't swell to encompass your ambition."

Jacob shook his head and chuckled. "I'm sure you won't allow me to increase my hat size."

"I seem to remember a certain zestful young man with large ambitions," Mary observed.

"And see how well that turned out," George responded. "We are a family of substance, soon to replace the Derbys as the leaders of Salem."

"Perhaps." Mary smiled. "Jacob, do you happen to know if Geordie has similar ambitions to yours? Is there anyone who has caught his attention?"

"He keeps his own counsel, for the most part. He's never mentioned politics to me, nor anyone of the fair sex. I think Geordie enjoys his present seafaring life. In my opinion, he has no particular aspirations."

George grunted. Geordie was his namesake, but it was Jacob who would lead the family forward.

Alone in his small study, George considered his good fortune: a wife he loved as much as the day they married, six strapping sons and two lovely daughters, as well as a substantial place in Salem society. But it wasn't enough. His ambition wouldn't let him rest until he bested his brother-in-law. *May the day come soon.* Jacob had a good head on his shoulders, along with the social polish needed in this new age. *That'll be his mother's influence.* But as for Geordie—there was something unsettled about him. The lad kept his own counsel.

George gazed out his study window and dipped his pen. Son John would be nineteen in a month. It was time to send him the customary advice he gave each of his sons as they sought their living on the sea. Advice his own father had never seen fit to share with him.

*Son John,* he wrote, *here is my advice to you respecting your behavior as a man of business and representative of our merchant house.*

*Mixing with men is essential, but remember to keep your own secrets just as they do. Ask advice from the best merchants of the places where you are, even if you don't need it. And be sure to thank them for any favors, no matter how small. This is how to build a network of men who support our merchant house.*

George sprinkled sand over the parchment to set the ink. He would leave the letter in case Jacob wanted to add anything. George chuckled. Six sons, but all so different in disposition and temperament. Unlike Jacob, John often jumped into a situation without looking. Perhaps he would take his father's advice to heart, but probably not.

Satisfied he'd given due consideration to his sons' talents, George went in search of his wife. She was sitting near a window in the drawing room with sewing in her lap, while his daughter Molly was attempting to help her younger sister, Sally, with needlework.

George looked at Molly's sampler. "What's today's subject, then?"

"I'm still working on the brick house. I don't think I'll ever get to the roof."

"You will if you work on it every day," Mary admonished. "You spend too much time playing games."

"And you, Sally?"

George's youngest daughter furrowed her brow. "I'll never finish, Sir. I can't get past the first letter. I keep making the top of the *A* square instead of pointy."

"That's because you don't pay attention," Molly charged. "You'll tear the linen if you keep having to take out the stitches."

A tear rolled down Sally's cheek.

George held out his arms. "Come sit with Sir."

When the child settled, George tipped up her chin. "I grant you, a capital *A* looks better with a point, but would it be such a terrible thing if it was square instead? Perhaps you'll start a new fashion. I suggest that tomorrow you leave *A* and go on to *B*. It doesn't have any points."

Mary laughed and then covered her mouth.

"Mame, don't let her get away with that," Molly complained.

"I think it's time you and your sister put away your needlework and went upstairs. We'll talk about the alphabet tomorrow."

George nodded toward his wife as the girls curtseyed and left the room.

"Tell me, Mary, did you have trouble stitching the letter *A*?"

"As a matter of fact, I did. Points are challenging when you can hardly hold an embroidery needle. But it's not about the letter as much as patience and perseverance."

"And did you eventually succeed?"

Mary giggled. "I don't remember."

"I'm sure you do. I'm convinced you have never forgotten anything since the day you were born."

"If I have, I don't remember."

George chuckled and handed his wife a glass of Madeira. "To our girls," he toasted.

"Our girls." Mary took a healthy swallow.

"I've just written a letter to John. His birthday is in a few weeks. I advised him to practice politic behavior."

Mary put her sewing away and banked the fire.

"It seems to me," Mary murmured, "all our children are impatient. Just like their father."

George came up behind his wife, putting his arms around her waist and placing his head on her shoulder. "Shall I tell you what I'm impatient for now, Mary?"

"Your bed?"

"Certainly, if you share it with me."

Mary laughed and led her husband upstairs.

# Hasket Derby

*March 1790*
*Derby Counting House*

Hasket Derby stood at his office window and angled his spyglass for a better view of the beach next to his wharf. Workmen busily lined up the blocks that would hold the keel of his new ship.

*Blast! I'll have to go onto the wharf if I want to see better.*

Hasket stormed through the counting house area on the bottom floor of his warehouse. He motioned to one of the clerks to open the door and secured his hat against the sea breeze.

Hasket stood at the edge of his wharf, observing the men below. *What the devil is Briggs doing?*

"Matthew, find Enos Briggs and bring him up here."

The lanky youth, still in his shirtsleeves, ran down to the beach. Hasket watched him grab one of the workers, who pointed farther up the shoreline. He continued to watch the workers, the wind whipping his cloak around him.

"Mr. Derby, sir? Is there a problem?"

Hasket looked at the slightly stooped man standing before him and motioned Matthew back into the warehouse. "Why is the keel being laid so low? It's practically on the beach!"

"Those are only the blocks, sir. The keel will rise higher."

"Not on those blocks she won't. We're building a five-hundred-ton ship here, not a fishing schooner. Have you ever built a ship this size?"

Enos Briggs took a breath and squared his shoulders. "I am a master shipbuilder, Mr. Derby, and I do not take kindly to criticism from a man who has never built a ship."

Hasket felt anger building at the base of his belly. He took a breath and kept his voice level. "I don't have to be a shipbuilder to know the tides and waters of Salem Harbor, or that if a keel is not laid at the proper height, the ship will not be able to launch properly. As your employer, I am asking you why the blocks to support the keel are not higher."

"And as an expert craftsman, I tell you I know what I'm doing. Your ship will be completed and launched exactly as planned." Briggs spread his hands. "You can, of course, replace me with another builder."

Hasket expelled a breath. Enos Briggs was possibly the best shipbuilder in America, and the man knew his worth.

"I'm investing a great deal of money in this ship and her potential. If she is successful, I will build more ships this size. I expect every aspect of her construction and launch to be of the highest quality."

"Rest assured, sir. You will be pleased with your ship." Enos put out his hand.

Hasket grasped the man's hand and clapped his shoulder. "Well, then, you'd best be about your business."

Hasket turned back into his counting house.

"Only time will tell which of us is correct," he mused to himself. "I'd rather the ship launch smoothly than be right about the height of her keel."

# Captain Nathaniel West

*June 1790*
*Captain Nathaniel West's House*

Standing in his dressing room at the front of his three-story house, Nate waited for his manservant to finish tying his cravat. Though perfectly able to dress without aid, Nate preferred to keep a servant whose sole occupation was to be sure his employer was turned out perfectly. Hiram held up Nate's embroidered silk waistcoat so Nate could slip his arms down the sleeves before closing the front buttons.

Nate held up his hand. "I'll wear my banyan until I leave the house."

"Yes, sir. I'll have it ready in the drawing room."

Nate made his way downstairs to the back parlor. His wife, Betsey, sat at the head of the small dining table with a newspaper in front of her. She glanced up at him and took off her spectacles.

"Would you like tea, Captain West?"

Nate nodded and accepted a cup. It seemed the distance between them lengthened several inches each day. *No doubt I'll soon breakfast in the barn.*

"How are you this morning?"

Betsey pursed her lips. "With child, as is now readily apparent. Will you see my father today?"

"Yes. He's signing ownership of the *Peggy* over to your brothers Elias and John, to Anstiss's husband, Benjamin, and to us."

Betsey narrowed her eyes. "Us? Will my name be on the papers?"

Nate shrugged. "What's mine is yours."

Cook came in with buttered eggs and a fresh pot of tea. Nate felt Betsey's eyes on him as he spooned eggs onto his plate.

"I shall call on my mother today," Betsey said. "I'll take the children and their nurses."

"Why?"

"She asked to see them. It would be easier if she called on me, but ... Well, our house is hardly up to her standards. And she never misses an opportunity to remind me I should have selected a different husband." Betsey tapped her chin. "Someone like my sister's husband. Father took Mr. Pickman under his wing while we were in Boston. You have amends to make if you want to become part of Father's business affairs."

Nate drew his mouth into a solid line. "I told you when I agreed to our return to Salem that I have no desire to become part of your father's business. I have my own firm and invest when and where I will, with whomever I choose."

Nate glanced at his pocket watch. "I must leave if I'm to meet your father and the others at ten o'clock." He rose and lifted his wife's hand to his lips. "I love you now as much as I did the day we married, even if I no longer meet your expectations. Be patient a bit longer, my sweet. In time, your station will rival your mother's."

# Betsey West

*October 1790*

Betsey pushed herself up in the four-poster bed. A chilly breeze blew in from the window.

"You should close the window," Eliza said. "You'll catch your death from the wind."

Betsey held her breath for a minute until the cramp passed.

"If you're going to order me about, you can leave, Mother."

"I gave birth to nine children. I think I know a thing or two about the process. You need to keep the room warm."

"This is my fourth lying-in. I know what I'm doing. And I refuse to suffocate in an overheated room." Betsey winced.

"Don't hold it in. Your husband should hear you downstairs. He needs to know you're suffering." Eliza picked up a vase and held it out to her daughter. "You should throw something."

"I don't find it as helpful as you did." Betsey grimaced. "*Ooof!* That was a strong one."

"Shall I tell you a secret? I didn't throw things because it eased the pain. I threw them so Hasket could feel my anger. Why should I be in pain while he drank brandy with our guests? I wanted to embarrass him."

Betsey groaned and caught her breath. "Did it work?" She gasped.

"Very little embarrasses your father. It became a sort of joke between us. And, he always gave me more porcelain for later use. Now then, perhaps you'd like to walk around a bit. The midwife will be here soon, and then things might be over quickly."

Betsey let her mother support her as she walked. It was nice having her mother with her for her lying-in. Her other three births happened in Boston, and Eliza hadn't attended her daughter because she disapproved of Betsey's husband. But since their return to Salem, her mother had been polite to Nate.

The midwife tapped on the door and came in with a maid who had her arms full of clean linens.

"You're looking well, Mrs. West, considering the circumstances," the midwife said. "We'll put her in the birthing chair now."

When Betsey was settled, the midwife put her hand up Betsey's chemise.

"Och, I feel the head. A few more good pushes and the babe will be out. Let's get started. Let the pain wash over you as you push."

Betsey growled while she pushed. Eliza wiped her daughter's forehead.

"Good girl. Keep going," the midwife said. "One more good push and you'll have your baby."

Betsey took a deep breath and expelled the child.

"You have a daughter." The midwife cleared the baby's nose and mouth before handing her to the wet nurse hovering near the door. "Mind you, wipe her down and wrap her well while I clean up her mother."

Eliza handed her daughter a glass of wine. "You've earned this. If you don't mind me saying so, I think it's time for you to close your womb. Four children in five years are quite enough. Don't you agree?"

Betsey sipped her wine. "I suppose."

"Good. I'm glad you're being sensible about it."

Nate knocked as he opened the bedroom door.

"I understand there's someone here I haven't met yet." He winked at his wife.

"Yes, Captain West." Betsey waived her hand. "Your daughter is with the wet nurse over there."

Nate walked across the room and opened his arms to receive the infant. "She's beautiful like her mother. Don't you think so, Mother Derby?"

Eliza sniffed. "She won't look like anyone until at least a week."

"Mother," Betsey said. "After Patsy was born, Captain West and I decided to name our next daughter Elizabeth, for you. We'll call her Eliza. What do you think?"

"How very thoughtful," Eliza said while peering at the new baby. "Now that I look again, I agree with your husband. She does look like you, Betsey."

Nate passed around three fresh glasses of Madeira. "A toast to the three Elizabeths. May they always be bound by love."

C H A P T E R

# Captain Elias Derby

*January 1791*
*Hasket Derby's House*

Elias burrowed deeper under the bedcovers. He'd just arrived home last night, and after spending so much time in Isle de France and India, he wasn't accustomed to Salem's harsh winter air. He could hear whispered sounds near the door, followed by an insistent rapping.

"Come in," Elias bellowed as if he were still at sea.

The door cracked open to reveal his brother Zeke's face.

"Are you rising, Brother? Or will you lounge under quilts all day? If so, you should know Father expects you in the counting house before noon."

Zeke opened the door wider to admit a servant carrying a steaming pitcher, the contents of which he poured into the blue porcelain bowl on the dresser. Two more servants brought buckets of steaming water, which they spilled into the hip bath standing in the far corner, with a screen to provide shelter from drafts.

"I took the liberty of ordering hot water for your shave and a bath. Mother would be most displeased to see you again in your present rough state."

Elias swung his legs over the side of the bed, slid his feet onto the floor, and wrapped his arms around himself. "You might have brought coffee up," he groused.

"But then you'd have no reason to come downstairs for breakfast. You're expected at the table for ten o'clock."

Elias chuckled as he picked up his razor and began to strop it. "I take it Mother still requires strict punctuality."

"No more so than Father." Zeke opened the wardrobe. "Since your luggage won't arrive early enough, I leave you my second-best suit and linen. Also shoes. I suspect you may have to order new clothing for Mother's entertainments, but this should get you started."

Elias slid his razor down the left side of his face, admired the effect, and began shaving his chin.

"I'll see you downstairs, then," Zeke said. "It's good to have you home again."

An hour later, freshly bathed and wearing his brother's clothing, Elias stood to the side of the dining parlor doorway, observing his mother. Eliza sat at the head of her mahogany table with her back ramrod straight. She wore a white muslin morning dress with a paisley shawl on her shoulders. Her dark hair, now sprinkled with gray, was pulled up into loose curls held together by a blue ribbon. Eliza held a blue-willow-patterned china teacup up as she talked to her daughter Patsy and waved her free hand in the air for emphasis. Elias noted that his mother's frenetic energy was unchanged since he had left over three years ago.

"We'll have an informal supper party and dancing with family and friends at the end of next week," Eliza said. "Be sure to invite John's fiancée, Sarah, and her family."

Patsy nodded. "Yes, Mother."

"And then in the spring," Eliza continued, "the weather will be better, and we'll have a more formal event."

"Why such a hurry?" Patsy asked.

*Why indeed?* Elias wondered.

"We cannot be too careful," Eliza stressed. "After all that time in Asia, Elias will be swayed by the first pretty woman he meets, no matter how inappropriate. We must ensure he meets only suitable young women. I'm hoping John and Sarah will help make introductions."

Elias strode to the dining table, winking at Patsy as he pulled out a chair across from her.

"I've only just returned home. It's too soon for you to find me a bride."

"Elias!" Eliza placed a hand over her bosom. "You gave me a fright. Come and give me a kiss."

Elias kissed his mother's hand, sat, and reached for the bread basket.

"After arranging our business affairs in Asia, I'm quite sure I have enough discernment to find a suitable bride."

"Of course you do," Eliza agreed. "I'm simply making sure you have an appropriate selection to choose from. Now then, so much has happened since you left, I scarcely know where to begin."

"Tell me about my sister's wedding," Elias suggested.

"She was the most beautiful bride in Salem. Her dress—"

"More beautiful than Betsey?" Elias interrupted with a smirk.

"Betsey was hardly a bride," Eliza sniffed. "Her marriage vows were just short of an elopement, and her husband, entirely inappropriate."

"From what I understand, Nate's done well for himself in Boston."

"Only because at the time they married, despite a connection with our family, he couldn't establish himself here in Salem."

Patsy rolled her eyes. "Mother, they married years ago. They came home last year."

Eliza shrugged. "And have already reproduced again. Never mind, I'm no longer concerned with such matters. Though I'm pleased our family is reunited now that Elias is home. Elias, you must take care. Hasket spends time with your brother John as well as your brothers-in-law and has given them ownership shares in a few vessels. In fact, he gave them a ship last year."

"Did he indeed? Well, I can hardly begrudge my sisters their means of support." Elias smirked and smeared raspberry jam on his bread. "You were going to describe Anstiss's wedding?"

"It would have been the highlight of the season if President Washington hadn't visited our town a week later. Honestly, of all times to decide to visit Essex County! And without any notice! I shall never forgive him for over-shadowing our Anstiss."

"It's a shame you didn't meet the president, Elias," Patsy interjected. "He's a most charming and humble man."

"He led our troops and now he's the president. That is hardly the mark of a humble man," Eliza commented.

Elias raised his hands and chuckled. "You must start at the beginning. When, exactly, did Anstiss marry?"

"It's been a year and a half since her wedding," Patsy said. "I don't know why the Pickmans didn't postpone the date. We could have hosted the wedding after the president left. But Anstiss had her heart set on it, so we went ahead. She and Mr. Pickman married October 20. I'm sure that was the date. It was a Tuesday, and the president arrived the following week, on the Thursday."

Eliza stood with a scrap of lace clutched in her hand. "I can't bear to listen. That man completely upstaged our daughter, and I shall never forgive him."

Elias stood until his mother left the room and then resumed his breakfast.

"So." Elias raised his eyebrows. "Tell me more about this state visit."

Elbows on the table, Patsy leaned forward to face her brother. "Well," she began, "it was a singularly notable event. Even Father was unsettled, and Mother . . ." Patsy rolled her eyes.

"Father said President Washington made a wise decision when he decided to visit New England. That we have a federal constitution and need to stop thinking of ourselves as independent states. We're a nation of business and commerce." Patsy pulled a serious face.

"Obviously." Elias smirked again. "For successful trade, we need a strong government behind us."

Patsy tossed her head in annoyance at her brother's interruption. "Yes. I just told you Father said so. You won't believe it, but when the president visited Boston, Governor Hancock called at his lodgings. And he was unwell."

Elias raised his eyebrows. "Not with a fever, I hope."

"I think he had gout. Well, something that affected his legs. The newspaper said his legs were wrapped in bandages, and servants carried him inside the inn. I don't know why the president put our governor to so much trouble. He didn't seem that officious when he was here."

Elias chuckled. "Politics, probably. So what happened here?"

"Mother, of course, was beside herself. She and I had to have new frocks for the Assembly."

"Wait." Elias put up his hand. "Tell me how he entered Salem."

"It was so exciting!" Patsy grinned. "About one o'clock, when the president was a couple miles outside of town, our artillery fired. We could see the smoke from the courthouse. And then every church bell in town rang for the longest time. Everyone scurried to get in line for the procession to meet him.

"He rode his horse when he came into town. It was the most beautiful pure-white stallion. And he had on his uniform, and his boots gleamed in the sun. It was incredible."

Anstiss's eyes glowed with the memory.

"Did Father join the procession?" Elias asked.

"Of course. All the merchants were there. Father wore his best suit and a new hat. And he had his walking stick with the brass handle. You should have been here, Elias."

"I was a bit busy on Isle de France at the time."

"I know, but still. Anyway, at the courthouse, everyone gathered in the square cheering and waving their caps." Patsy paused. "But even though it was crowded, you could still see the president. That's how tall his horse was. Then our officials took the president inside the courthouse, and he came out onto the balcony. And everyone started cheering again. It was such a sight! Oh, and there was a special gallery on the side with Persian carpets and damask curtains."

"Whatever for?"

"It was for the singers. There was a special ode for the occasion. It went on forever."

"Do you remember any of it?"

"Only the chorus: 'Loud, loud, proclaim, the Hero's come. Proclaim aloud, Great Washington.' He seemed pleased by it, or maybe he was just being polite. I suppose he hears special odes frequently. And after everyone quieted down enough to listen, Congressman Goodhue read our city's address to him, saying how pleased we were that he took the time to stop with us and that everyone was grateful to have him as president. And then the president said he was grateful for his reception and that he would discharge his duties faithfully. And then he wished us every happiness."

"I suppose everyone cheered again." Elias chuckled. "Did he go back inside then?"

"Yes. He gave a deep bow and went inside but didn't stay long. The officials took him to Joshua Ward's house, where he stayed."

Elias raised his eyebrows. "How did that come to pass? Surely, Mother invited the president to stay here."

"Oh, yes." Patsy nodded. "But Mr. Ward's house is far more grand. It's the new brick mansion on the west side of town. I heard the president requested accommodation there because it would be on his way out of town. Mother was beside herself when it was announced that the president would stay with Mr. Ward. She didn't come downstairs for two days. And now she demands Father must build her a new house that will be the talk of Essex County, or perhaps the entire state. I forget."

"She might have done that even without President Washington's visit."

"Possibly, but she's definitely on him about a new house now."

"What does Father say?"

"He changes the subject. Usually, he asks her to plan a dinner party." Patsy flicked a loose curl behind her ear. "After the president had a chance to dine, Father and some other gentlemen called on him to talk about commercial opportunities, and why we need a strong navy. I'm not sure it will make any difference to the president. He has so many other things to think about. But Father is concerned about hostilities between France and England. I'm sure he'll talk to you about it."

Patsy picked up her teacup. "Ugh, the tea's stone cold."

"I'm not surprised. You've talked nonstop for at least half an hour."

"Well, you wanted to know what happened, and Mother only cares about where he stayed the night."

"Did she at least enjoy the Assembly?"

"Yes, I think so. When he arrived at Concert Hall, people set off rockets. It was spectacular to see. All the important Salem women were at the Assembly in their finest gowns, and their husbands as well. Mother says it's a pity she couldn't commission more elaborate new gowns for us than she did, but I thought we turned out rather well.

"Inside the hall, Washington greeted everyone and then stood a bit out of the way with his aides. There were fireworks again at the end. And then he went back to Mr. Ward's mansion for the night. And that was that.

"About nine o'clock the next day, the president mounted his horse and crossed over the bridge on his way to Beverly. Father went with other gentlemen to say farewell."

"So, the president only stayed a day and a night."

Patsy shrugged. "Salem isn't a very large town, not like Boston."

Bundled up against the cold, Elias walked rapidly toward the Derby counting house. Late-morning sunbeams cut through the fog but didn't provide much warmth. Turning down Derby Wharf, Elias opened a door on the warehouse level.

Two clerks bent over tables, compiling lists of cargo inventories and comparing them with statements of customs duties.

Zeke looked up, his face breaking into a grin. "You made it before noon. If you go straight up, you'll be on time with a minute to spare."

Elias chuckled. "I always arrive in the nick of time."

Outside his father's office door, Elias adjusted his neckwear, rapped twice, and waited.

"Enter," a deep voice called.

Hasket pulled out his pocket watch. "Congratulations. You are exactly on time, I'm pleased to say. In future, I expect you to keep earlier hours. I, for example, am out of the house by nine o'clock in the winter. We keep fires in the counting house, after all."

"Yes, Father, I'll keep it in mind."

Elias winked at his brother John, who stood smirking by the window.

"However," Elias continued, "whether I keep the same hours as you remains to be seen." He sat down without being asked.

"Even so, I'm surprised you didn't make your way here sooner this morning. Your brothers and I walked down together." Hasket raised his eyebrows.

"I had to settle into my new billet. Mother is putting me on the marriage market and wants a new house."

"Ha!" Hasket barked. "She's still smarting that President Washington stayed at Joshua Ward's place."

"So, will you?"

"Will I what?"

"Build Mother a new house?"

"In due course. I'm busy building the new *Grand Turk* at the moment. Thanks to your work at Isle de France, I've determined our future lies in India and the Spice Islands. You brought in a total profit of ten percent. I'm very pleased."

Elias allowed himself a moment to preen.

"Have you decided to abandon Canton?" he asked.

"For the most part. There's too much competition, conditions change too frequently, and I presently have a warehouse full of enough tea to satisfy demands for some years."

"What about the ginseng?"

Hasket winced. "I'll sell it to merchants still trading with Canton. It's still a good item, just not good for us."

Elias gazed over his father's head. It wasn't often Hasket Derby made a bad business decision, but the ginseng had been a mistake. That decision had bordered on reckless. Elias picked bits of lint off his sleeve. His brother was not as careful with his clothing as he was, it seemed.

"Will you be sending someone to stay on Isle de France?" Elias asked diffidently.

Hasket chuckled. "Don't worry. If I do, it won't be you. It's time to bring you further into the business. You've more than proven you're ready."

Elias's head shot up. *Thank God!* "Yes, sir. I'm ready to be a full partner in our family enterprises. And I'm planning to acquire a few ships of my own."

"I think the first step is to introduce you to my thoughts. Isle de France is only one piece of the puzzle."

"I presume the port of Bordeaux is another," Elias guessed. *Is he sending me back to France?* "It's a good transshipment point for European and Indian goods. Is it time to set up an agency?"

"As I've said before, we don't need a permanent presence there. It's an unnecessary expense."

Elias thought back to the first time he had broached the idea. Before he went to Isle de France. His father had dismissed it out of hand.

"You look perplexed, Elias. Were you hoping to go to Bordeaux?"

"Actually, I'm hoping to stay in Salem, work in our business, and start a family. I've had enough of being without a home and eating bad food."

Hasket steepled his fingers and stared at Elias, who began shifting in his seat.

"Is there a problem, Father? You look as if you don't recognize me."

Hasket shook his head. "Just thinking about the adventures you've had. I've hardly been beyond Essex County."

"I thought you didn't care for sailing."

"I'll never know either way. But I do know I like making money, and that's what I intend to do. I don't know if you've noticed, but Enos Briggs is building a new ship by our wharf."

"I saw it from Derby Street, of course, but I haven't looked closely at it yet. It's hardly decent weather for strolls on the beach or even the wharf."

Hasket cleared his throat. "Well," he said, giving his son a disapproving look. "If you can spare the time and inconvenience, you will see that Enos Briggs is building a magnificent ship. She'll be the largest ship launched into Salem Harbor."

Elias picked up his father's spyglass and joined his brother at the window. *By Jove!*

"It must be over a hundred feet long," Elias exclaimed. "What kind of ship are you building?"

Hasket allowed himself a small smile. "We're building a merchant vessel capable of carrying more cargo than any other ship we have. Our warehouses will be bursting with goods. The new *Grand Turk* will launch our business as merchants of the East."

"Calling her *Grand Turk*, eh?"

Hasket shrugged. "To continue the tradition the first *Grand Turk* started before you sold her at Isle de France. It's an auspicious name, don't you think?"

Elias shrugged. "Tell me about our new giant ship."

Hasket stood beside his son with his arm around Elias's shoulder. "Enos Briggs has designed a vessel of five hundred sixty-four tons with three decks. She's one hundred twenty-four feet long and thirty-two feet across her beam. We hope to launch her in May. I'm open to your thoughts on the cargo for her maiden voyage to Calcutta. And with the profits she brings home, I shall fund my wife's new house."

"Mother will be pleased to hear it. Has she selected the location yet?"

"I haven't told her she's won her argument yet." Hasket gave his son a rueful look. "Please don't spoil the surprise."

"I wouldn't dream of it." Elias looked out the window again before returning to his chair. "Have you thought about a master for this vessel, for it surely won't be me."

Hasket's eyebrows rose. "You've no interest in taking out the finest vessel in America for her first run?"

"None at all, Father. As I told you, I'm for hearth and home now and for the foreseeable future. But . . ." Elias smiled. "I'm happy to go out on her shakedown cruises."

# Captain Nathaniel Silsbee

*March 1791*

*Aboard the* Betsey

Nath lowered his sextant and noted the angle. The *Betsey* was firmly on course. Placing the instrument back in its case, Nath thought about how to phrase his report to Mr. Derby. The voyage, though not a failure, was less successful than it should have been. He hadn't completely disposed of his outward cargo until the previous November.

Nath wondered if his father's recent bad luck would haunt him all his life. Before he shipped out on the *Betsey,* he and his eleven-year-old brother William had gone with his father on a coastal sail to Maine. The tired schooner, with its loose sails, was the last piece of property his father owned. The man hoped to collect debts but had to accept wood and boards instead of cash, which was a disappointment. His father sold them on to a vessel heading to the West Indies.

"What shall I do?" William had asked. "I'm not clever enough for Mr. Derby's counting house."

"Sure you are. I'll put in a good word for you." Nath had tousled his brother's hair. "And after the voyage I make on the *Betsey*, you'll be old enough to come with me."

It seemed a reasonable promise at the time. How had it gone so wrong?

Nath's pen scratched across the thick parchment paper. *I arrived at Madeira in the* Betsey *after a passage of 23 days from Salem . . .*

# Madeira

*March 1790*

It seemed a perfect day to begin his career in trade as a ship captain. The wind easily filled the schooner's sails, and the bay at Funchal was beautiful, with its clear blue waters. Confident of success, Nath considered the adventure cargo consigned to George Crowninshield & Sons. His friend Jacob Crowninshield, another former apprentice in Hasket Derby's counting house, had made arrangements with his family's new merchant house for Nath to carry ship's stores and foodstuffs that were sure to sell, if not at Madeira, then at Isle de France. For some inexplicable reason, Jacob had taken Nath under his wing after Nath's father abruptly took him out of school and placed him in Hasket Derby's counting house. Nath would be forever grateful for his friend's patronage.

Nath shrugged at his random thoughts before inhaling the salty air and lifting his spyglass. His gaze fell from the green hills of the volcanic island to the port's wharves and warehouses. The sight of so many vessels in the bay gave him pause. Were they all American, and did they carry the same cargo he did?

To Nath's chagrin, the answer was yes on both counts.

Leaving orders for his mate to take on fresh water and whatever fresh food he could find, Nath walked for fifteen minutes until he reached the town center. Bits of palm leaves littered the streets, occasionally shifting in the breeze to release what looked like small flower petals. Glancing around the sunny square, Nath identified the tavern most likely to serve the men he needed to meet.

The swarthy barman's appearance revealed a man who had been in his share of brawls.

*"Um copo de vinho madeira, por favor. Fala inglês?"*

The barman poured reddish liquid into a pottery goblet and nodded. *"Sim."*

Nath raised his glass and took a healthy swallow. The sweet beverage erupted in his mouth, making him gag. He convulsively swallowed to clear his mouth as the barman broke into hearty laughter.

Nath grimaced. "It's not that funny."

The barman passed him a towel and held out his hand. "Manuel."

Nath shook Manuel's hand. "Captain Silsbee."

"Excuse me. I thought you were English. They like new wine." Manuel exchanged a second goblet for the first. "Americans drink this."

Cautiously, Nath swished the new liquid with its fuller taste in his mouth and smiled. *"Obrigado.* My ship just arrived. Who do I talk to about selling my cargo and taking on trade goods?"

"This week? No one. Everything closes for Passion Week."

"And that ends?"

"Monday, the day after Easter." Manuel chuckled. "Disappointed, I see. Cheer up and enjoy our beautiful island. Walk through the vineyards. Visit the winepresses. You might find a new cargo." Manuel winked.

Nath swirled his wine. "And might I find buyers for my goods?"

Manuel shrugged. "What did you bring?"

"All manner of ship's stores sourced from New England pine forests, spermaceti candles, saddles. All the basics." Nath grinned.

"Talk to *meu amigo*." Manuel gestured to a table in the shadows and shrugged.

Two weeks later, Nath steered the *Betsey* out of Funchal Bay, catching the wind south to Africa. His hold still carried too much of the original cargo from Salem, with the addition of large pipes of wine Nath hoped to sell at Isle de France. The added weight dipped the schooner's waterline into the ocean. When the *Betsey* arrived at Cape Town, the port was not open for trade, so Nath took on fresh water and continued on to Isle de France.

To his dismay and disappointment, conditions were much the same as those at Madeira. Twenty American ships sat at anchor at Port Louis, all with wine for sale, as well as the same trade goods.

Standing in the harbormaster's cramped office, Nath presented his ship's papers for his arrival along with exit papers. There was no point remaining in a glutted market. He would head on to Bombay, where he hoped to move the wine. The clerk glanced at Nath's papers.

"*Je suis désolé. Embargo jusqu'en Août.*"

Nath drew his lips into a firm line in an effort to control his temper.

"What embargo?" Nath asked through gritted teeth.

"*Non partir jusqu'en Août.*" The clerk stamped *Betsey*'s entry papers and returned the unstamped exit document.

"August! But that's nearly three weeks."

The clerk tilted his head and spread his hands.

In the following days, Nath made good use of his time but could move only ninety pipes of wine. Realizing the likelihood most of the ships in port would head to Bombay as soon as the embargo lifted, Nath plotted a course for Madras on the Coromandel Coast.

Arriving after a month at sea, he met the same trading conditions as before. Nath's high hopes for the voyage plummeted. He sold a hundred pipes of wine and much of his outbound cargo, freeing up space in the *Betsey*'s hold, but prices were low, and he only added some of the area's blue cloths for a homeward-bound cargo.

"Six months!" Nath chastised himself. "And I have nothing of value to take home. If I go to Calcutta, the situation may well be the same. I need something different for the Calcutta market. Something that will give me leverage for sales."

*I am mortified,* Nath wrote in his personal log, *and filled with anxiety. Bad prospects continue to increase. My disappointment is too great to think about.*

Nath stared at charts showing routes through the Bay of Bengal to the south and east. He decided to take a risk. Instead of going north, to Calcutta, he would take the *Betsey* south, to the free port Pelu Penang. Hopefully, he could sell more wine and purchase pepper for his return cargo.

*October 1790*
*Pelu Penang*

Approaching the harbor area at Pelu Penang, Nath smiled with relief. There were only two ships in port. Then he frowned. *How can that be? Am I too early to trade—or too late?* Boarding the jolly boat with three crewmen, Nath pulled on the oars to reach the shoreline. Ships anchored as close as a hundred yards from George Town, the small village that grew up around Fort Cornwallis, so he didn't have to row long before stepping onto the beach. As he did, a factor walked forward with a wide smile and his hand out.

"Francis Crawford," he announced. "Welcome to George Town. Allow me to offer my services. Whatever you need, I can arrange it for you."

Nath looked at the thin man who clearly spent most of his time in the sun.

"Captain Silsbee." Nath shook the man's hand and followed him into a warehouse. Nath appreciated the building's gloom and small windows that allowed the sea breeze to enter. He was tired of tropical sun on volcanic islands.

"What can I pour for you?" Crawford asked. "You've probably had your fill of wine by now. I have brandy, and also Bengal rum, if you're so inclined. And if you have a pipe, I have some reasonably good tobacco grown on the island."

Nath winced inwardly. Clearly, the man required social niceties before he got down to business. Nath accepted a glass of brandy and a pipe bowl of tobacco and shared his experiences in Madeira, Isle de France, and Madras.

"How is it," Nath asked, "that you have so few vessels in port when every other trading center is a forest of ships' masts?"

"The British East India Company only made us a free port five years ago. Word is slow to travel. I hope you share the news that we are a good place to take on provisions and spices for voyages to or from China. We have lots of products to offer. That tobacco you enjoyed was grown here, for example. And there's pepper, of course, and betel nut, which is very popular in this region. And we are a good place to pick up cargoes we've added to our warehouses." Crawford gave Nath a speculative look. "What brings you here?"

"I have Madeira wine to sell or exchange and blue textiles from Madras. I'm looking for pepper. Can you accommodate?"

"What type of Madeira?"

"Unadulterated. The sweeter version the British and Indians prefer. It can keep in your warehouse until the Indian markets loosen up."

"Any porter?"

"Some. Do you have pepper to sell?"

"Eh." Crawford stroked the gray stubble on his chin. "You're too early for the harvest, let alone properly dried peppercorns. I'll be honest. I have pepper, but it's not good enough for the American market and not worth your time to look at it. But I do have betel nut ready to go."

Nath kept his expression bland and put his empty glass back on the table. "What shall I do with betel nut? It's hardly a product for America or even the West Indies."

"Well, I should imagine that if you're going back to India, you can trade it there for a reasonable price. I'm told it's quite popular in Calcutta and Bombay. It sells all through Asia." Crawford raised his eyebrows.

Nath steepled his hands. So far, he had little to show for his voyage besides an overabundance of wine. And the market in Calcutta might not be any better than other ports in India. But if the betel nut sold, even at a low price, it was better than carrying a hold full of wine and ship's stores no one wanted to pay for.

Crawford poured out more rum and raised his glass. "Shall we come to an arrangement?"

Nath swallowed and clinked his glass against that of his host. "I'm sure we can come to agreeable terms."

*December 1790*
*Calcutta*

It took a month to traverse the Bay of Bengal to Calcutta. A month in which wind and sea conspired together. Either there was no wind, or it blew from the wrong direction. And if the wind seemed cooperative, the current went against the ship's course. When the *Betsey* finally reached the mouth of the Hugli River, Nath had to wait for a pilot to navigate the schooner through the thirty-nine miles of treacherous shifting sandbars to the harbor at Calcutta.

But that was not the worst of it. The pilot, a dour man usually employed by the East India Company, told Nath his destination was overrun with

American ships, and there was an embargo in effect. What if the British wouldn't allow Nath to unload the betel nut? What would he do if he couldn't sell it? There was no place else to take it.

Unable to control his despair, Nath walked away from the wheelhouse and left the pilot to steer the ship. Calcutta would be his final opportunity for a successful voyage, or at least one that wasn't a failure.

At Calcutta, Nath managed to sell the betel nut, but at a lower-than-expected price. In preparation for the return voyage, Nath engaged workmen to careen the ship while the tide was out. Despite the *Betsey*'s protective sheathing, worms had made strong inroads. Almost the entire hull had to be caulked. Once the ship was upright again, Nath loaded her with one hundred tons of sugar, almost more than she could safely carry.

*March 1791*
*Salem*

A day out of Salem, Nath finished his official record of *Betsey*'s unlucky voyage. He hadn't expected to return to praise for his business acumen, nor should his first voyage as a captain have come to such an ignoble conclusion. Nath sighed and dipped his pen in the inkwell.

> After concluding business at Calcutta, I determined
> the best course of action was to return directly to Salem.
> Successful trading proved impossible due to continued bad
> market prospects. After paying all expenses accrued during
> the voyage, I doubt there will be a dollar of profit left. This
> voyage, if not a complete failure, is certainly a severe disap-
> pointment from a business and personal perspective.

Nath put down his pen and rubbed his eyes. Most likely, Mr. Derby would either conclude Nath's career as a ship's officer or, if he was in a benevolent frame of mind, confine him to interminable coastal runs. Nath sprinkled sand over the pages of his report to set the ink and placed it inside his logbook.

When Nath's crew threw out ropes to secure the *Betsey* to Derby Wharf, the unlucky voyage was over. Ships' shadows made wavering designs on the sunlit wharf. At the wharf's head, a new ship as large as the East India Company ships at Calcutta dominated the space. With all his difficulties with the *Betsey*, Nath shook his head at the thought of running such a large ship.

Dockworkers pulled wagons beside *Betsey*'s cargo gangplank. Nath allowed himself a sigh of relief, tucked the bag with his ledger and the logbook with his report under his arm, and strode down the gangplank. Mr. Derby's clerk, Ezekiel Sims, stood at the bottom.

"Welcome back, Captain Silsbee." Ezekiel reached for the bag. "I'll be sure Mr. Derby receives this right away."

Nath gave the clerk a puzzled look. "I thought Mr. Derby would wish to see me."

"He's busy with the new ship. She's a beauty, ain't she?"

"That she is. What's she called?"

"She's not officially christened yet, but word is she'll be the new *Grand Turk*. I'll be sure Mr. Derby gets these so he can review your log and inventory. Call at the counting house tomorrow at ten o'clock."

# Captain Nathaniel Silsbee

*March 1791*
*Salem*

Ducking his head, Nath avoided eye contact and strode up Derby Wharf. As he passed Derby's counting house, his brother William barreled through the door, almost knocking Nath over.

"Nath, you're back!" William grinned from ear to ear and hugged his brother. "I saw the *Betsey* tie up, but Ezekiel—Mr. Sims—told me to finish my work before greeting you. Tell me everything."

William gazed at Nath with shining eyes.

Nath put his arm over William's shoulder.

"One thing at a time." Nath smiled.

"Are you going to see Mr. Derby now?"

"No. Mr. Sims told me to come in the morning."

"That's odd. He usually sees shipmasters straightaway. But then, all his attention these days is on the new ship. Isn't she beautiful? Do you think you'll be able to serve on her?"

Nath shrugged. "I doubt it. Once Mr. Derby goes through my reports, I'll be lucky to catch a schooner to Virginia." Nath turned to face his brother.

"I'll be honest—the voyage was a complete disaster. Prices were down. Competition was fierce. I don't expect Mr. Derby to give me another command. I took my chance, and I failed. I don't expect to have any commissions except coastal runs, if that.

"So, tell me, how is our family? No one thought to send me a letter while I was away."

"Mr. Sims said it was best not to distract you with family news, since there was nothing useful to say. Things haven't changed since you left. We still live with our grandparents. Father picks up a few commissions, but he drinks most of his wages. He gives mother a few coins before he goes out or we would have nothing at all. Grandmother and Grandfather add what they can. Zach and I do odd jobs. But I finished my training and can go out as a clerk now. I was hoping to go out with you on your next sail."

"If I have one."

"Don't talk like that. Mr. Derby is a fair man, and not every voyage goes well."

"Neither does he suffer fools lightly. He took a chance with me, and I didn't rise to the occasion."

"There's no point dwelling on it. You'll find out tomorrow. Come on; I'll walk home with you."

Approaching the house, Nath noticed that most of the furniture was in the side yard, and a rope line had been stretched along the fence. His sister Sara beat a paddle vigorously against a threadbare rug. The fabric emitted billows of dust and dirt.

William cupped his hands around his mouth and shouted, "Sara!"

The girl paused in her work. "William Silsbee, get over here and help me. You . . ." Seeing Nath, Sara threw down her paddle and ran to her brother, flinging her arms around his neck. Nath grabbed her and swung her around before setting her feet back on the ground.

"What's going on here?" Nath asked.

"Just airing out the house. Come." Sara linked arms with Nath. "Mother and Grandmother will be pleased to see you."

"How are things?" Nath asked his grandmother after she brought out tankards of small beer.

Sarah Silsbee ran a hand through her gray hair. "About what you'd expect. Yer brothers take on odd jobs after their lessons. Yer father picks up coastal runs when he can, but with the drink, he's not reliable. Commissions are falling off. He's putting together cargo for a run farther south, but it goes slowly. Did you get your wages yet?"

"Tomorrow, I hope."

"Humph. Yer mother will be relieved."

"No. I'll give some to Father, as is his due, and the rest to you for safekeeping."

"It's good to have you home, lad, but I hope you go out again soon."

A light mist blew over Derby Wharf the next morning. Nath dropped his brother at the counting house and walked down the wharf to check on the *Betsey*. Most of the cargo was unloaded, with a few crates waiting for wagons to take them to the warehouse. Workmen checked her hull. Satisfied the *Betsey* was getting the attention she needed, Nath walked back up to the counting house. Once he'd hoped to take the *Betsey* out again, but that seemed unlikely now.

Inside Mr. Derby's warehouse, laborers placed casks of spices in their places. Nath walked through to the counting house, nodded at his brother, and climbed to Hasket Derby's office. The moment of truth had arrived. Nath rapped on the door.

"Enter."

Nath's stomach fell to his feet as he opened the door. Elias Derby stood by the window. Turning, he extended his hand to Nath, who shook it with relief.

"Captain Derby, sir, I didn't expect to see you."

"Father's attention is on our new ship. Your situation, Captain Silsbee, is, shall we say, less than compelling." Elias gestured for Nath to sit on one of the straight-back chairs facing a large mahogany desk. "My father and I both read your report, and the *Betsey*'s logbook. Father was disappointed by your bad fortune."

Elias pulled out the chair on the other side of the desk with a certain flourish. Sweat trickled down Nath's back.

"My father appreciates your honesty. Someone else might blame circumstances for the poor result of your voyage. You hold yourself responsible."

"The *Betsey*'s success was my responsibility. It was my job to make the voyage a success, no matter the circumstances."

"You are correct. However, Father and I understand that circumstances are sometimes beyond anyone's control. It is our response to them that matters. Seems like the last time I came through, you were still in the counting house. How old are you now?"

"Nineteen, sir. My first voyage out was as clerk on the *Three Sisters*."

"Yes, I remember. Captain Magee spoke highly of your initiative and quick wit." Elias cracked a smile. "He also mentioned you have a good voice for a sea shanty."

Nath felt the tension in the room ease slightly and grinned at the brief change of subject. "Good enough to avoid Neptune's shave."

Elias chuckled briefly before turning his attention back to business. "You may recall, I established our presence on Isle de France and developed markets in India. Such secrets, sadly, can't be kept for long."

"No, sir. As I noted, every port of call had numerous American vessels with nearly identical cargoes."

"And apparently," Elias said dryly, "they always arrived ahead of you."

"Yes, sir. That was more bad luck than anything else. Unfortunately, the similar cargoes deflated prices."

Elias picked up Nath's report. "You demonstrated initiative going to Pelu Penang. Regrettably, it didn't improve results significantly."

Elias folded Nath's report and placed it inside the *Betsey*'s logbook. In his mind's eye, Nath watched his ambitions fold into the report.

"Well, let us move forward. Mr. Sims has your wages, and we will be in touch about your next command." Elias stood and held out his hand.

*Next command? Do I have another chance?*

Nath clasped Elias's hand with enthusiasm.

"Yes, sir. Thank you, sir. I won't disappoint you a second time."

# Captain Elias Derby

*April 15, 1791*
*Enos Briggs's Shipyard*

Elias tied a handkerchief over his face in an attempt to reduce the acrid odor of pine tar that surrounded the steadily rising *Grand Turk*. A cauldron of the sticky substance that kept water from destroying the ship's wooden planks boiled on the beach below. Workers swung mallets to push fibers soaked in the tar into the seams between the planks to keep them from splitting apart. The entire scene was a cacophony of noise and noxious odors.

At the top of the wharf, Enos Briggs and a wood carver from Boston supervised another set of workers who lifted a large bundle wrapped in burlap out of a wagon bed. They stood the bundle upright and began removing the coverings. A pinkish carved knob appeared first. Shortly thereafter, it morphed into a turban and a brown-skinned face with a large black mustache.

Fully revealed, the figure was a Turkish man with folded hands.

Elias chuckled. "A grand Turk indeed."

Elias didn't recall such a dramatic figure on the first ship his father called the *Grand Turk*. Weighing a mere one hundred tons, she had been a good privateer against the British and brought a handsome profit when he sold her on Isle de France. But this new ship, at five hundred tons, dwarfed her predecessor.

"Why did Father resurrect the name?" Elias wondered to himself. "Is it to remember the prizes and profits the first ship brought home? Can the spirit of the first ship imbue the second?"

Elias shook his head and joined a small crowd of men and boys at the head of the wharf. Everyone held their collective breath as workers wrestled the new figurehead onto the beakhead attached to the hull and held it in position while Briggs personally applied the caulking to seal it. Two carpenters completed the attachment. When the Turk was securely seated in his new home, cheers broke out.

Elias glanced up to the cupola at the top of George Crowninshield's house and saw a reflection glint from his uncle's spyglass. *This must stick in his craw. We have a five-hundred-ton ship guarded by a Turk, and he's left with schooners. No doubt my cousins will sail with us for the foreseeable future.*

# Eliza Derby

*May 19, 1791*
*Hasket Derby's House*

Eliza took a moment to admire the way her lawn chemise flowed around her body before donning her banyan. She then sat down in front of her dressing table, with its silvered mirror, tilting her head to judge how much attention her hair would need.

"Flora," Eliza called to her maid. "Come make me presentable."

A young woman holding long hairpins appeared in the mirror's reflection. "How much primping does my hair need?"

With her small hands, Flora smoothed Eliza's mostly dark hair up and away from her employer's face until it blended around the hair bun at the back of her head.

"It's kept very well," the maid mumbled through pins in her mouth. "But the curls are a mess. I have to pull them down and roll them up again."

"Eliza, how are you getting on?" a masculine voice said from outside the door.

Eliza held her head still and smiled.

"Come in, Hasket. Flora is just seeing to my hair."

Balancing two cut-crystal glasses after closing the bedroom door, Hasket walked over to the mirror and held one out to his wife.

Eliza lifted an eyebrow. "Are we celebrating something?" she asked.

"Do you remember when I told you that together we would lead Salem?"

"Of course." Eliza sniffed. "I thought you quite presumptuous."

Hasket winked. "Yet you still took a chance on me."

Eliza smirked. "I wanted the brick house your father built for us."

"I can't help but wonder what it is with you and houses. First, it was our brick house by the wharf. Then a larger house next door. And before that one was finished, nothing would serve but removing to this house on Washington Street, which increased the length of my walk to our counting house. And now you want me to build you the largest mansion in America."

Eliza met her husband's bemused gaze. "You promised me I would lead Salem society. Yet when President Washington visited Salem, he stayed at Joshua Ward's paltry mansion. I was mortified. The way I see it, a mansion of substance is the very least you owe me, especially after all the children I bore for you."

"You are correct, but I haven't neglected you entirely. I've been preoccupied with our new ship. She isn't a house, but she's built like an East Indiaman and is the largest ship in Salem. Furthermore, today you preside over a reception for political and social dignitaries who have come to see such a marvelous sight. The new *Grand Turk* is the key to all your dreams. Her profits will build your new mansion. So, you see, I am, as always, a man of my word. Will you not raise a glass with me to toast our new ship?"

"Excuse me, madam, shall I begin making up your face?"

Eliza glanced at her husband's expectant face and lifted her glass.

"Leave us until Mr. Derby departs, Flora."

After her maid bowed her head, curtseyed, and softly closed the door, Eliza surprised her husband with a broad grin.

She clinked her glass against Hasket's. "To our mutual success!"

"Success!"

Hasket knocked back his glass of brandy, while Eliza swallowed several times in succession before raising her face for a kiss. Hasket lifted her chin.

"We are very like-minded, you and I," he murmured.

Eliza breathed in as her husband's lips touched hers and then pulled her head back. "Be off about your business." She shooed her husband away. "I shall see you on our wharf."

# Mary Crowninshield

*Captain George Crowninshield's House*

"You'll wear a hole in the Aubusson if you don't stop pacing. You're like a dog looking for a place to settle and never finding it."

George stopped abruptly and fisted his hands. "Every day I watched Enos Briggs and his men build your brother's damnable ship. I knew this day would arrive."

Mary peered in her mirror and rubbed some rouge on her pale cheeks.

"What do you think?" she asked. "Is it too much?"

"How can you be concerned about rubbing rouge on your cheeks when I am about to be humiliated before every politician and social leader in Essex County? The shame of this day is beyond belief!"

Mary turned on her stool, then pulled up her silk stockings and secured them with embroidered garter straps just below the knee.

"Pass me my corset, George."

"How are you so calm in the face of your brother's success? Don't you care that he'll be able to crush our business before we even truly start?"

Mary patted her husband's cheek and began doing up her front laces.

"You've been ranting ever since Briggs laid the keel. You know as well as anyone that the sea is a mercurial mistress. One day it's smooth sailing, and the next morning a crushing storm blows the ship back where it came from."

Mary leaned over to lift her bosom above the corset.

"So, yes, today my brother and his wife will lord it over everyone. And when his new ship leaves port, everyone will come to Salem again to see her off. After that, no one will think of her until she returns."

Mary arranged her fichu.

"Hold my dress for me while I step into it."

"Wouldn't you prefer to have your lady's maid do this for you?"

"I can hardly have my maid here to watch you pace and rant. The servants' gossip would be all over town before the launch is complete. My point is"—Mary narrowed her eyes on her husband's face—"Hasket's new ship will soon leave, and whether she has a successful voyage or not, we will prevail in the end because our sons will soon sail in our ships. Together, they will bring home greater profits than Hasket's giant ship. The present is nothing. It's the future that counts."

Mary adjusted a turban to match her green dress and picked up a pair of gloves. "Now, Captain Crowninshield, please escort me downstairs, where our sons and daughters will join us as we promenade over to Derby Wharf. Under the eyes of all, we shall join the crowd of interested onlookers."

George kissed his wife's fingers.

"How is it you always know just what to say?"

Mary smiled. "I just wait until you can listen to me say what you already know. Shall we go down?"

# Lizzie Rowell

*Derby Wharf*

*Rat-a-tat-tat. Rat-a-tat-tat.*

The drum major dropped his baton, freeing the fifes to begin playing "Yankee Doodle" for what seemed like the five hundredth time. Lizzie's head pounded in time with the shrill music.

"I swear, if I had that Yankee Doodle in my hands, I'd ring his neck like a chicken," Lizzie muttered as she slapped six tankards of ale onto the bar. Matt snorted before he grabbed the tankards by their handles and headed toward the back side of Ship Tavern.

"People are stopping at the tables outside." Anna Shipman nodded. "Take some ale out with you and see what else they might want." She tapped her chin. "Better yet, you and Matt walk through the crowd with ale and baskets of bread rolls. They'll be getting hungry. Thirsty too, standing in the sun, especially after a nice piece of bread."

Lizzie eyed the crowd on Derby Street. "We'll be crushed."

"A winsome lass like you? Not likely. Charge them double our usual price. They'll pay it."

When Matt returned to the bar with more orders, he gave the details to his mother and grabbed a handcart so he and Lizzie could fill it with refreshments.

Lizzie wiped her brow. "Who's gonna help your mam?"

"She'll have Flossie cover the tables."

"Didn't know she did anything besides the washing up."

Lizzie and Matt wrestled a small barrel of ale into the cart.

"If there's money to be made, Mam'll put everyone to work, even the chickens." Matt winked. "Did you hear they dug up a tree a couple days ago? Mr. Briggs wasn't happy, cuz they had to clear the tree to keep digging the channel. Come on, let's get started."

Matt pushed the cart into the crowd.

"Bread! Ale!" Lizzie sang out.

Eight hours later, Lizzie wiped sweat and loose hair off her forehead, inadvertently pulling her mop cap off. Almost immediately, her chestnut hair slipped down, covering her shoulders. Lizzie let it fall and bent her head to wipe off the tables. Her feet squished in spilled ale.

"Lizzie," Matt called. "Catch." A crumpled rag sailed in Lizzie's direction. She caught it in the air and dropped to her haunches to clean up the mess.

"Time, gentlemen," Anna Shipman announced and began closing the bar.

Matt circled the room, plucking tankards from tabletops and pointing stragglers toward the door.

The great room sank into darkness as the fire died down to the last coals.

"Matt, Lizzie, you're dead on your feet. Get to your beds," Anna said.

Matt watched his mother count coins. "Did we do well?"

"Never you mind. Just don't be late tomorrow." Anna picked up the money pouch and climbed the stairs.

"I'll go first." Matt winked at Lizzie. "Best to keep the illusion of propriety."

Lizzie nodded, counted to ten, and started up the stairs. At the first landing, she turned left and walked to the end of the hall. Tapping lightly, she opened the door and went inside.

Geordie sat in a wingback chair next to a grate with a small fire.

"Lizzie, I thought you decided not to come to me tonight. Come, sit by the fire. Here, let me help you out of your shoes."

"Thank you. I don't think I've ever been so tired."

Geordie unrolled Lizzie's stockings. "You have a hole in the toe."

"I'm not surprised." Lizzie sighed in contentment. Geordie was so good to her, always seeing to her comfort.

"Your cousin works you too hard. I wish you would let me set you up in a cottage. You could live in Danvers or Marblehead. I'll visit whenever I can." Geordie began undoing Lizzie's corset. When she was in her shift, Geordie began nuzzling her neck.

"I should probably sleep," Lizzie mumbled. "I have to be at work soon."

"You wouldn't if you let me get you a cottage."

Lizzie shook her head. "I don't want my cousin to know about us."

"You think she doesn't?"

"I'm sure she suspects, but she doesn't actually know."

"Mmmm." Geordie began kissing Lizzie's collarbone. "Come to bed. It's too cold to stay outside the blankets."

Lizzie let Geordie guide her to the four-poster bed. "You'll be careful?" she asked.

"Always. You will have nothing from me but pleasure."

# Captain Nathaniel Silsbee

*Derby Wharf*

Nath stood on the wharf with his brothers and other clerks from Derby counting house. The *Grand Turk* should have been away by now. Workers had taken away the blocks holding her in place. The channel was deep, and the tide was in. But the ship wasn't moving.

The fife and drum corps marched toward the other end of Derby Street playing "The World Turned Upside Down."

Workers began attaching tow lines to the ship's stern.

"Who wants to help launch the largest ship in Salem? Come show your mettle!" the call rang out.

Nath clapped his brother William on the shoulder. "That's our cue to get in Mr. Derby's good graces. Follow me, chaps."

Nath led the way off the wharf and joined other members of the crowd already climbing into rowboats to put their backs to the oars and pull the *Grand Turk* into Salem Harbor.

After several hours, the large ship barely shifted. Daylight began fading. "Come back tomorrow!"

But the next day fared no better. More men came to turn a hand. Stout farmers and tradesmen alongside youths who wanted to be part of the great deed. The fife and drum corps spurred them on. The *Grand Turk* shuddered and moved away from the ways, but she couldn't get free.

# Hasket Derby

*Derby Counting House*

Hasket glared at the man standing before him in his office. Enos Briggs was the best shipbuilder in New England. He had designed and constructed a magnificent ship. A ship that had no use if she couldn't launch. Workers came from all over Salem and beyond, and the ship still couldn't move into the harbor.

Hasket was livid. He succeeded at everything he did. He was the richest man in Salem, the most respected for his business acumen. He was about to become a laughingstock. It was insupportable. Hasket continued to stare at his shipbuilder.

Enos Briggs met his employer's eye.

"Mr. Derby, a ship of this size has never been launched from your wharf or, indeed, from any wharf in New England. Some, ah, challenges are to be expected."

"You may recall that I told you when the keel was laid that it needed to be higher. I deferred to your judgment. That won't happen again." Hasket leaned forward. "I have one question for you, and you'd better know the answer. How will you float the *Grand Turk*?"

"She's ready to float, sir. That is to say, she is floating. She just needs more encouragement to move into the harbor. More rowboats to pull her out. We'll pull her farther down the ways and let the tide come up more. Then she will easily float. Be ready to christen her, Mr. Derby. Once she's free, she won't wait for anyone."

# Hasket Derby

*Hasket Derby's House*

Opening his front door, Hasket heard his wife's shrieks from upstairs. He handed his hat and outercoat to the butler, went directly to the sideboard in the drawing room, poured himself a large glass of brandy, and knocked it back.

"Rather a bad day, Father." Elias grimaced. "An embarrassment for us all."

"I'm aware." Hasket poured another glass and sat down across from his son. "I had a word with Briggs."

"I'm sure you did. Maybe the ship is jinxed. Perhaps our Turkish figurehead can't swim and is afraid of the sea. A standard mermaid might have been a better choice."

Hasket barked a laugh. "Leave it to you to find humor in the situation."

"Fie!" Something that sounded like porcelain hit an upstairs door.

"I haven't heard your mother shriek like that since your brother John was born. Any particular reason?"

Elias rubbed his glass between his hands. "Tomorrow will be the third launch day for our new ship. The first day, Mother wore her new walking ensemble. The second day, she wore her second-best attire. Tomorrow will be the third day, and she claims she has nothing appropriate to wear. If the launch goes into a fourth day, I doubt she'll attend, no matter how many politicians are present."

# Eliza Derby

Eliza picked up a porcelain pitcher from her dressing table, drew her arm back, and was ready to hurl it against the wall, until her daughter Patsy grabbed her arm and caught the pitcher.

"Mother, stop it. Breaking all the porcelain in the room is not going to produce a new outfit for you to wear tomorrow."

"Humph! This is Hasket's fault. He knew the keel was the wrong height, but he let Briggs talk him around."

"That doesn't sound like Father."

"Sometimes your father takes a bad risk, like sending ginseng to China." Eliza flounced onto her bed. "What am I supposed to wear tomorrow? People watch me. They know what I wear to public events. I can't wear my new ensemble again until at least September. What am I going to do?"

Patsy tapped her chin. "Do you suppose Betsey might have something?"

"Didn't you notice? She wore the same gown both days. I don't know what she'll do tomorrow."

"Mother, what's wrong with this day dress?"

"Exactly that. It's too informal."

Patsy shook out the almost sheer peach garment. "No, it's perfect. Let me help you put it on."

"It just billows," Eliza wailed.

"Not with the sash, and we'll use matching fabric for a turban. This will be as head turning as the promenade dress. Perhaps more so, with the lower neckline."

Eliza swayed before her mirror. "I suppose it could work," she said grudgingly.

Hasket nudged the door open and stepped over porcelain shards. "May I come in? It's become very quiet up here. Mrs. Derby, you look ravishing." He smiled broadly and lifted his wife's fingers.

Patsy winked at her father. "You see, Mother. I told you this would be perfect."

"You're feeling better, then?" Hasket asked.

"I am not, but at least Patsy found me something suitable to wear."

"More than suitable." Hasket kissed his wife's knuckles.

"Your ship better float tomorrow."

"*Our* ship will head into the harbor to the sounds of fifes, drums, and loud huzzahs."

"Very well. See that she does. I absolutely refuse to set up any more refreshments on her deck."

# Hasket Derby

*Saturday, May 21, 1791*
*Derby Wharf*

Hasket felt an overwhelming sense that his life was endlessly repeating itself. For the third time, fifes and drums marched up and down Derby Street with their incessant screeching noise. Special dignitaries again boarded the *Grand Turk* to be greeted by his sons and wife. The first day, guests went to peer over the stern. Today, they moved directly to the refreshment tent. Much to his disappointment, Governor Hancock sent his regrets. Congressman Goodhue was again present, but without his wife.

*If we don't get her into the harbor today, I'll burn her to the waterline.* It was an empty threat. Hasket had too much money invested to set fire to his ship. Every clerk, dockworker, seaman, and young shipmaster in Hasket's employ manned the rowboats. Builders, farmers, and every day laborer in Salem prepared to assist by hauling the ropes. He spotted Nath Silsbee in a lead rowboat. *He's a good lad with remarkably bad luck.* Hasket decided to give him another ship.

Enos Briggs started the chant: "Heave, Heave, Heave."

The great ship began to move into the channel and descend the ways.

*By Jove! She's going to make it.*

Hasket grabbed the magnum of Madeira his clerk handed him. Holding the bottle like a club, Hasket shouted, in his loudest voice, "I christen this ship *Grand Turk*! May she sail the seas with good luck and good fortune!"

Gripping the bottle's neck, Hasket slammed it into the *Grand Turk*'s bow.

The crowd roared: "Huzzah! Huzzah! Huzzah!"

Hasket raised his eyes to the deck. Eliza stood there looking like the goddess she was. When she raised her glass to salute her husband, their eyes locked in triumph. Once again, he had beaten the odds.

# Captain Nathaniel Silsbee

*July 1791*
*Captain Nathaniel Silsbee's House*

The scene played over and over in Nath's mind, a tableau he was unlikely to forget. He had been between coastal voyages and outside splitting wood when a friend of his father's walked up to his grandparents' house. Nath didn't see him until he turned to reach for another small log to split.

"Nathaniel, is it?" The older man held out his hand. He was stooped and shaky on his feet.

*Must be one of Father's drinking companions,* Nath thought, but paused to wipe his hands on a rag and greet the visitor.

"Nathaniel is my name. It's also my father's, as I'm sure you know. If you're looking for him, he's not here. Haven't heard from him since he took a schooner down south a few weeks ago. If you have business with him, you'll have to come back in a month or so. Give me your name, and I'll tell him you called."

Nath placed a log on the chopping block and picked up his ax.

"Wait. I need ta talk wid you."

"About what? I have no funds to pay any debt he owes you."

"As it happens, yer father does owe me money, but I ain't here fer that. I had word yer father's dead."

Nath snorted. "I'm sure you'll find that's a rumor he started himself."

"Nuh, sir. My mate went south wid 'im and sent word. Yer father sickened and died. They buried him in New York."

Nath froze in disbelief. *This can't be true. Father is in a drunken stupor somewhere. He can't really be dead; he's just hiding from his debts.*

The man held out a pair of bent tin shoe buckles. "My mate sent these. He couldn't sell them."

Nath examined the buckles. The tongue on one of them was bent at an odd angle, like the buckle that had twisted off his father's shoe when he'd tripped over a cobblestone. *If these are Father's buckles, then he probably is dead after all.*

"Why bring them to me?" Nath asked.

"Figure when a man dies, his family should know."

Nath sighed. "You'd better come inside. My mother will want to speak with you."

The following Sunday, Nath sent his siblings ahead of him and touched his mother's arm to guide her into East Church. The square white church with its shake shingles and small diamond-paned windows glistened in the warm sun, but when Nath crossed the threshold, he squinted to see in the shaded gloom.

Sarah Silsbee nodded to people in their box pews on either side of the central aisle.

"Keep your head high, Son," she murmured. "All that we once had, you will bring back to us."

When they reached the Silsbee pew, Nath handed his mother in and sat by the aisle. He would put the box pew up for sale as soon as it was decent to do so.

Reverend William Bentley strode up to the podium, his starched white clerical bands with their sheer edges standing out against his black cassock.

After Reverend Bentley turned over the hourglass and began his sermon, Nath turned his thoughts to his altered circumstances.

After his father lost the family home to pay his debts, Nath began giving his wages over to support his mother and siblings. But his sense of responsibility had not been entirely engaged. Now, Nath was the sole support of his mother's family, the only means for his brothers to establish themselves. Once, he thought that with hard work, he could establish himself as separate from his father. Now, he and his father were irrevocably separated, but though his father's debtors could not legally force him to pay them, if he didn't, he would be forever known as the debtor's son.

Keeping his eyes forward, Nath searched his heart and mind before making two vows to guide his life forward. First, he would keep his mother's family in comfort and provide a good start in life for his brothers. Second, unlike his father, Nath would not establish a family until he could retire permanently from the sea and live with them onshore free from financial burden.

As the service drew to a close, Reverend Bentley offered requested prayers. Nath and his family stood while he prayed for the repose of Nath's father. Sarah Silsbee held a handkerchief to her face to catch the last of her tears.

"You have no need for concern, Mother," Nath whispered. "You will never be destitute or without a roof over your head. Those days are behind you."

# Eliza Derby

*November 24, 1791*
*Hasket Derby's House*

Patsy trailed behind her mother as Eliza walked through her drawing rooms. The train from Eliza's open gown swished softly over her Aubusson rugs.

"Patsy, tell the servants to bring in the bride's cake and complete the table arrangements. Betsey and Anstiss should be here by now. I hope they aren't annoyed that they weren't invited to the Bartons' for John and Sally's wedding. Honestly, their house was so small, our family hardly fit."

"I'm sure they will arrive soon. Elias told me the men were gathering at the Ship before coming to us."

Eliza turned abruptly, bouncing the ostrich feather embedded in her turban.

"I sincerely hope John won't be with them. He and his wife need to be here to greet everyone. And surely, your father—"

"Looking for me, Eliza?" Hasket stood in the doorway dressed in the new fashion of buckskin breeches and riding boots with ornamental tassels. He'd worn the same clothing at the wedding yesterday, and Eliza's breath caught, just as it had the previous day.

"Hello, Father," Patsy said. "Now that you're here, perhaps you can calm Mother's jitters. I'll join you in the main drawing room when John and Sally arrive."

"Patsy," Eliza said, "check on the bridecake and be sure it's exactly in the center of the white tablecloth. And be sure we have enough Madeira for the toasts. And the musicians, be sure they set up in the correct place."

"My dear," Hasket said in a surprised tone. "You can't possibly be nervous about a second-day wedding party."

"It's just, well, Betsey didn't have a real wedding. And General Washington overshadowed Anstiss's and Mr. Pickman's day. John is our first family member to marry properly."

Hasket pursed his lips. "I seem to remember that Anstiss had an extravagant wedding."

"You know what I mean. Betsey didn't . . ."

Hasket put a finger on his wife's lips. "You need to stop dwelling on the past. Though you didn't believe it at the time, Betsey made a good match. Captain West and I have become good business partners. And with the amount of entertaining she's doing, I'm sure everyone speaks of Anstiss's wedding favorably."

"And now"—Hasket lifted his wife's chin—"we welcome John and Sally into the family fold. In fact, I just heard them at the door."

"Hallo! Where are you, Mother?"

"John!" Eliza rushed into the hall. "You're home."

John smirked. "Actually, Sally and I are your invited guests." He kissed Eliza's outstretched hand. "Shall we go into the drawing room and warm up? It's cold outside."

Eliza noticed that Sally was wearing the same round gown she'd worn for her wedding. *I shall have to explain she shouldn't wear the same thing two days in a row, even if it is new. But that's fine. Betsey and I will smooth her out soon enough.*

Eliza greeted her new daughter with a kiss on each cheek. "Come, sit by the fire."

Patsy came in with the housemaids, who were carrying tea and small biscuits.

Next, the Barton women arrived in a flutter of shawls, cloaks, and hats.

"What a lovely home you have!" Mrs. Barton gasped and patted her bosom as if overcome with awe.

Eliza smiled graciously. Like Sally, the Barton women were wearing the same dresses they wore for Sally's wedding. Eliza thought how sad it was to see that the once socially well-placed family now lacked social awareness. *Perhaps I can use my social connections to help them. I don't want John's standards to drop due to the union.*

Betsey and Anstiss entered the drawing room together. Betsey's eyes darted around the room before landing on Eliza.

"Welcome, daughters." Eliza offered her cheek to each young woman to receive the expected kiss.

Eliza beckoned to Mrs. Barton. "You haven't met my daughters yet."

While Eliza made introductions, Patsy supervised the seating arrangement and offered refreshments.

When it was fully dark, Eliza's sons and sons-in-law arrived.

# Captain Elias Derby

"John, you could have joined us, or are you too engrossed in your new bride to share a drink with your brothers? And you, dear sister, look radiant. I hope my brother is treating you well."

Sally blushed and lowered her eyes.

"Elias," Betsey chided. "Don't embarrass our new sister. Now, Sally, Anstiss and I want you to tell us about your lovely round dress."

"Yes," Anstiss echoed. "The print with a floral display is especially fetching. Just the thing for a new bride."

Patsy rolled her eyes and made her way to Elias.

"Would you like tea, or something stronger?"

Elias smirked. "I'm sufficiently fortified at present." He kissed his sister's cheek. "Who do you think will be next? You, me, or Zeke?"

"Neither of us, I'm sure. So that leaves Zeke. After that, though, Mother will be looking to you."

"Surely, no one as fetching as you can remain unattached?"

"Not forever." Patsy chuckled. "But Mother rather likes having a daughter at home to do her bidding. You, on the other hand, are the oldest son. Without Zeke to distract her, she'll set her sights on you."

Servants came in with trays of Madeira.

"Ah," Patsy said. "Father will make a wedding toast, and then the dancing can begin. Will you partner with me in the first set?"

Elias laughed. "You're supposed to wait for me to invite you to dance."

"That would be a very long wait indeed." Patsy winked.

Hasket escorted Eliza to the center of the room.

"John, Sally, please join us."

When the parents and newlyweds were properly assembled, Hasket raised his glass. "Thank you all for joining us as our family celebrates our newest member. Please join me in a toast to my son and his new bride. I present to you Mr. and Mrs. John Derby."

Patsy gave the signal for the musicians to begin tuning their instruments. John led his bride to begin the set. Elias and Patsy came next, followed by Nate and Betsey West, and Anstiss and Benjamin Pickman. The musicians shifted to a lively gavotte.

"We make a handsome family," Patsy commented to her brother before the dance took him away.

"We do," Elias said when the pattern brought him back to Patsy.

Elias smiled and nodded until the dance finished. More guests began arriving for the dancing. Drinking another glass of Madeira, he watched his brother conversing comfortably with sea captains and merchants, while his bride looked ready to collapse from nerves. When his parents were engrossed in their social duties, Elias slipped out of the drawing room, into his coat and boots, and out the door.

The brisk chill brought clarity to his senses. Elias walked into the Salem Inn looking for a game of dice or cards to take his mind off family expectations.

# Captain Nathaniel Silsbee

*December 1791*
*Derby Wharf*

Cold wind and mist whipped over Derby Wharf and swirled around Nath and his sister Sara. Nath wondered what possessed her to insist on viewing the sloop he worked on, the *Sally*.

*There's nothing to see, especially in this mist.* But she would not be deterred. "You never know what might happen," she'd said. "And when you get the advance on your wages, I can take it straight home." So, here they stood on the quay, with a chilling wind and moisture dripping down both their faces.

Though it didn't make any difference now, Nath said again that there was no need for his sister to walk down the wharf. "You'll catch your death. William would have brought my advance home."

Sara clutched her cloak more closely around her shoulders. "Show me the sloop you sail. I hope she's not as small as I think she is. I hate to think of you just bobbing around in the sea."

"It's how I earn a living for us." Nath put an arm around his sister's shoulders. "Come out of the wind."

"No. I want to see your sloop."

"Very well." Nath pointed to a small vessel between two schooners. "That's the *Sally*. She's small, but she sails well."

"Your other ships were bigger," Sara objected.

"They were, but they sailed in open ocean. The *Sally* just travels up and down the coast to Norfolk and back again. I'm never gone more than six weeks."

"The Derbys are punishing you for the bad voyage you took last year."

Nath shrugged. "Possibly, but I had to settle our father's affairs, so I couldn't go on an ocean voyage even if one was on offer."

"Will Mr. Derby ever let you have a proper ship again?"

"Perhaps. Even if he doesn't, I'll earn a comfortable living for our family. And when William gets a berth, we'll have more than enough income. Now, let me escort you up to the counting house so William can take you home. I have to cast off soon."

Condensation covered the counting house windows, casting an eerie light over the desks and ledgers.

"Ah, Captain Silsbee." Ezekiel Sims rose from his high stool. "I have the advance on your wages for you. I calculated your usual days and extended ten percent against your expected wages. I don't have a note about your adventure. What are you taking?"

"Nothing. I don't have the funds."

"Surely, you can use this advance . . ."

Nath shrugged. "It's too late now, but thank you for the thought." Without checking the amount, Nath handed the coins to his sister. "With what I've given you already, you and Mother should be able to keep the wolf from the door until I return. William, Sara will stay here until you can escort her home."

"Of course." William thumped his brother's back. "Come back to us with tales of good fortune."

"Being with my family is good fortune enough. Keep Mother's spirits up, Sara." Nath kissed his sister's cheek. "Describe what a sturdy vessel the *Sally* is."

Turning up his coat collar, Nath strode down the wharf. He needed to cleanse his negative thoughts with salty air. In fact, the *Sally* wasn't sturdy at all. She stuck to the Salem–Norfolk route because she wasn't strong enough to risk heavy seas. Mr. Derby didn't bother to insure her anymore, though that meant that if she sank, her cargo would be a complete loss. Of course, timber, cod, and nails were hardly expensive to replace.

When Elias Derby had first offered him the *Sally*, Nath had been grateful to have any sort of commission, and coastal runs gave him time to organize his father's debts and get his mother's dower rights back in the house his father lost. His family had a secure roof over their heads, even if they were a bit crowded, and he earned enough to pay expenses. But how could he pay off the debts? He didn't have to, of course, but people remembered debts, and he shared the debtor's name.

*I need to get back aboard larger ships for longer voyages. I need money for adventure stakes. But needing and getting aren't the same thing.*

The voyage was uneventful as they passed through the waters off New York, but when the *Sally* neared Virginia, wind from the north increased and fueled higher seas. The temperature began dropping, and Nath ordered his crew to wear oilskins. Better to be prepared.

"Think we're in for it, then?" Micah asked. "Been feelin' my back pain for a while."

"I think we need to be ready," Nath replied. "Robin, boil us up some burgoo and then douse the fire. After that, man the pumps to keep us from sinking lower in the water."

"Aye, sir."

"Micah, you and Thad reef the sails before you eat. Storm's coming up quickly now. I'll take the wheel."

Nath faced the *Sally*'s bow into the waves, set a course to run ahead of the wind, and held the wheel until Robin came up with the watery oatmeal. Nath kept one hand on the wheel while tipping the oatmeal concoction into his mouth. At least it was warm.

The storm was unrelenting, with strong, cold winds and lightning that creased the sky. The waves continued to climb, pushing the *Sally* up to a dizzying height before releasing her down into a trough. Seawater washed across the deck. Nath watched his crew spell each other pumping out bilgewater and strapping themselves to the deck so they could briefly rest.

"I'll hold the course for ye," Micah shouted into Nath's ear through the whipping rain.

"You shouldn't be here. You'll wash over."

"Give me the wheel. Ye've been at this for two days. Take a rest." Micah handed Nath waterlogged hardtack.

Nath nodded, set Micah's course, and sat down on the upper deck with his back against the hull. The hardtack was so soggy it dissolved in his mouth. *I prefer burgoo to this.* Nath leaned his head back. How long would the storm last? Some went on for over a week. Nath didn't see how the *Sally* would make it. A wave passed completely over the sloop. Nath turned his head to the side and vomited. Surely, the storm would blow out soon.

But no sooner did one storm settle than another blew up. One storm or even two, Nath could understand. But the weather remained unsettled for weeks. He gave up any thought of putting in at Norfolk. If he could get the storms behind him, he would sail south to the West Indies, repair the ship, and sail back to Salem with a good cargo.

*Saint Eustatius, West Indies*

Nath lifted his spyglass, almost hesitating to confirm his location. *Yes!* By the grace of God, the *Sally* had arrived at the Dutch colony of Saint Eustatius. Ships of various sizes lay at anchor off the shore entry to the Lower Town. Nath edged his sloop around them, hoping to station the *Sally* near the shore.

A Dutch official rowed out to them, attached his boat to the sloop, and climbed the rope ladder Micah tossed over the side. Once he reached the deck, Nath presented his papers.

The official pursed his lips. "You are a long way from Virginia."

"Not of our own volition, I assure you. We were caught up in a series of nor'easters. I've never seen or heard of anything like it. I reckon we faced heavy weather for about a month. When we finally cleared into better weather, I wanted nothing more than the warm breezes of your island and a place to trade and repair my sloop. Do we have permission to land our cargo and seek repairs?"

The official raised his eyebrows in surprise. "Your cargo survived?"

"We haven't had a chance to examine it closely. When we left Salem, our cargo consisted of nails, cod, cheese, and barrel staves. We broke into the cheese ourselves, but there are still several barrels."

"Well, see what you can salvage and store it in one of the warehouses. You need to take your sloop to Gallows Bay. You'll see ships hauled up on the beach. You might find a place to stay at that end of town." The officer scanned the missing deck boards and frayed ropes. "Good luck to you."

Nath arranged to off-load and store the *Sally*'s cargo before running her down to Gallows Bay. The shipyard was small, and three vessels lay on the beach. Nath decided they would sleep aboard the *Sally* and make arrangements for her overhaul the next morning.

Resting on deck on his damp bedroll, Nath stared at the tropical moon. In some ways Saint Eustatius reminded him of Madeira, probably because both were volcanic islands. But Saint Eustatius was much smaller. While it was easy to careen a ship at Madeira, the small shipyard here didn't look as promising. *Can the shipwrights here actually carry out repairs?*

The shipwright rowed out the next morning. He was short, muscled, and darkly tanned from working in the sun. Standing in his dinghy, he cupped his hands around his mouth.

"Hallo! You da one lookin' to fix yer boat?"

Nath looked over the side. "Aye."

"Swing a rope down so's I can see yer decks." The man pulled himself over the side and nodded.

"Ah'm Todd Duncan. I run the shipyard."

"Captain Silsbee. We've been through several severe storms."

"Ah can see that. I looked at yer sloop above the waterline, an' ah'm pleased to check yer decks, but ah ken tell ye now, this here sloop can't be repaired. Best you ken do is sell her for scrap. She won't bring much. The wood's rotted. An' I daren't look below the waterline."

Nath's stomach fell to his feet. *If I lose this sloop, I'll never have another command. My career will be over.*

"Mr. Duncan—"

"Todd."

"Todd." Nath rubbed the back of his neck. "The *Sally* isn't insured."

"Ah. Then her owner knows she ain't worth savin'. That'll make things easier when you get home."

Nath focused on the words *get home*. If he could get the *Sally* back to Salem with any sort of cargo, he couldn't be charged with losing the ship.

"Todd, the *Sally* doesn't have to be a seaworthy sloop. She only needs to get back to Salem."

Todd lit his pipe. "How much bailin' are ye willing' ta do?"

"Enough so she doesn't sink. The sails should hold well enough. We can replace the vital planks and apply pitch to the seams everywhere else."

"It could be done. I've a vessel I bought for scrap. We could get the planks from there. They aren't the best, tho'."

"I don't need the best. She just needs to get to Salem."

"Your crew needs to do the work."

Nath nodded. "Of course."

"It'll be yer own risk. Ah'm not sayin' she'll weather high Atlantic swells."

"I take full responsibility." *If I fail, I'm no worse off than I am now, but if I succeed, I'll prove myself.*

Todd put out his hand. "We've a deal, then. Let's get 'er heaved on the beach, and we'll git started."

# Captain Elias Derby

*Saturday, March 10, 1792*
*Derby Wharf*

Hasket paced the *Grand Turk*'s length as she comfortably bobbed by Derby Wharf. Waves lapped gently at her waterline. Gangplanks to the upper and cargo decks invited dockworkers to unload their burdens inside the ship. Hasket stopped at the *Grand Turk*'s bow to take in the elaborately varnished figurehead of a Turkish man.

"I still think we should have mounted a mermaid," Elias whispered in his father's ear.

"Too common," Hasket replied. "You were so far behind me, I thought you decided to remain by the fire in the counting house."

"I waited until you stopped before joining you. Mind you"—Elias grinned—"I wasn't sure you were ever going to stand still. Are you committing this ship to your memory?"

"Just enjoying quiet moments with her before she begins her voyage to Calcutta tomorrow. Will you come aboard with me? I have instructions for Captain Hodges."

"Of course you do," Elias murmured to himself. "Complete and with no margin for error."

First Mate Mosely stood at the top of the gangplank. "Welcome aboard, Mr. Derby, Captain Derby. Captain Hodges expects you in his cabin."

Mosely led his employers to the ship's stern as if they didn't already know the way. He stopped to rap his knuckles on the open door, giving Captain Hodges a moment to prepare his greeting.

"Mr. Derby, sir, welcome aboard your ship." Captain Hodges beamed. "And Captain Derby. I've just been going over our route to Isle de France." Captain Hodges glanced at a chart on his desk. "I look forward to utilizing the contacts you made for us there, Captain Derby. Please sit, sirs." He gestured to two wooden chairs.

Hasket cleared his throat and passed Captain Hodges a thick packet of documents. "I've brought your instructions. You may review them at your leisure, but since this is a new venture for us all, I thought it appropriate to also provide verbal instruction. Mr. Mosely, please stay. I'm sure you'll find the information useful."

Elias crossed his right ankle over his left knee and gazed out the stern window. The sun's rays glittered on top of the harbor water. "So much more spacious than the first *Grand Turk*," he mused. But he didn't want to sail the new ship regardless of its superior accommodation.

Mosely took a standing position by the door while his captain sat facing Hasket.

"As you know," Hasket began, "I haven't filled the cargo hold for the outward journey. However, later today, my clerk will deliver several iron boxes to you. These will hold a total of forty thousand Spanish dollars so you can fill the hold with our return cargo from Calcutta. Please keep a strict accounting. I expect to know where every dollar is spent."

"Yes, sir."

"Now, as to the return cargo, I want sugar, saltpeter, spices, textiles. The particulars are in your instructions. Though normal wear cannot be avoided, the *Grand Turk* is a new ship in near-perfect condition. I would say *perfect*, but such a state doesn't exist."

Hasket stretched his lips into a thin smile. The other men gave understated chuckles.

"Fire is our greatest risk," Hasket droned on, "and to that end, I remind you that gunpowder should not be kept anywhere except the magazine on deck. The galley chimney must be swept out every Saturday. A sharp eye must be kept while in port. And, when you unload the ship in Calcutta, order the crew to wash the ship's hold and the lower deck as completely as you would scour a floor. You will find other details in your instructions. One can never fully predict conditions; however, I expect these to be carried out to the best of your ability. Am I clear on these matters, Captain Hodges, Mr. Mosely?"

"Yes, sir," they replied, almost in unison.

"Elias, do you have anything to add?"

*Add?* Elias scrambled. *Father must mean to his verbal instructions. Everything else is meticulously laid out in his written directions.*

"Erm, merely to note that you have a large crew with a total of four mates and eighteen sailors. It is incumbent to keep them busy. As it says in Proverbs, 'Idle hands are the devil's workshop.'"

"I'm aware, Captain Derby. The *Grand Turk* may be the largest ship I've commanded, but she's not the first."

Hasket turned his head to look at his son, and Elias bristled at the implied rebuke.

"Indeed." Hasket rose and offered Captain Hodges his hand. "We'll speak tomorrow before the *Grand Turk* casts off. Good luck, Godspeed, and bring home the largest cargo we've ever had."

"Aye, Mr. Derby, you have nothing to worry about on that score."

The next day, Elias stood with his brothers John and Zeke at a high point of the earthworks comprising Fort Lee on Salem Neck. Together, the three young men lifted spyglasses to watch the *Grand Turk* weigh anchor from Derby Wharf. Catching the tide, the vessel pulled into Salem Harbor. The wind whipped up, and several passengers who expected to disembark at the fort took an early departure.

Adjusting the lens, Elias saw the fife and drum corps standing in place on the wharf to see the ship off. *Perhaps now they can drill somewhere else.* The wind whipped the fort's flags as the *Grand Turk*'s sails filled. Onlookers at the fort began waving their caps and shouting huzzah. Crewmen waved back.

The *Grand Turk* passed by the neck and into the sea. Eventually, she fell off the horizon. Elias remembered departing Salem to enter the endless ocean on the first *Grand Turk* on his way to a destination he'd never heard of before his father informed him he would open trade with the East Indies from an outpost at Ilse de France. Elias shuddered at the memory.

"Hip, hip . . ." Zeke started the chant.

"Hooray," his brothers replied.

"Well," John said, "The *Grand Turk* is away at last. I truly hope she is everything Father expects her to be."

Elias clapped his brother on the back. "So long as she comes back in one piece with a full cargo, he'll be happy."

"For a time," John agreed.

# Mary Crowninshield

*March 1792*

*Captain George Crowninshield's House*

Mary turned the funeral invitation over in her hands, running her thumb over the black sealing wax, with its stamp of a skull and crossbones. She closed her eyes. Mary didn't know the widow very well. She was a Hodges cousin from her mother's family. *I suppose that's close enough for an invitation to a funeral call.*

"I don't want to go," she mused aloud. "Every time George went to sea, I worried the ship would sink, or there would be an accident, or he'd catch a fever. And now I worry for my sons."

Mary read the invitation a final time before shoving it in her pocket.

In memory of Captain Francis Boardman

who recently died at Port-au-Prince,

you are invited to call any afternoon this week

between three and four o'clock

at the family residence on Washington Square.

Mrs. Francis Boardman

*A good man dead; his wife, a widow; his children, fatherless. I wonder how many invitations she wrote. Thirty? Forty? One hundred?*

"Mame?"

Mary turned away from the window to smile at her older daughter. "We'll leave as soon as Benjamin arrives to escort us. You and Sally need to be considerate of the Boardman family. Captain Boardman . . ." Mary cleared her throat. "Well, he won't be coming home again." She sighed. "Molly, you're almost a young woman, and soon you'll attract attention from young men."

"I hope so," Molly said shyly.

Mary lifted her daughter's chin. "Promise me you won't take an interest in any man until he permanently returns from the sea. Accidents and disease surround us, but the dangers men face at sea make everything more uncertain. Do you promise?"

"Yes. Are you asking because Captain Boardman kept taking out ships?"

"Believe me when I tell you there is nothing worse than watching someone you love sail away."

"Mame, look who I found just inside the door." Benjamin walked in holding Sally's hand. "I'm here to escort you to the Boardmans'."

Mary handed her son a black crepe armband to wrap around his sleeve.

"I have another one for your father. Why didn't he come with you?"

"He's busy in the warehouse. He'll meet us outside the Boardman house, and we'll go in together. Are both my sisters coming?"

"The girls know each other from school." Mary adjusted her black bonnet.

Benjamin gestured toward the door. "In that case, let us be away."

The Boardman mansion was on Washington Square, in the newer part of Salem. Benjamin turned onto the recently completed road to the house. Ahead of them, George Crowninshield paced in front of the entryway.

There was a black funeral wreath on the front door, and funeral bunting fluttered around the doorframe in the chilly breeze. A stable boy came out to take the gig while George assisted his wife to the ground. Benjamin handed down his sisters.

Mary attached the black armband to her husband's coat and placed her hand on his arm.

"Shall we?" George asked. "Captain Boardman was a damn fool going down to the West Indies at this time of year."

"*Shhh*, George. You're not wrong, but we don't need to remind my cousin of the circumstances."

George rapped on the door. When it opened, Mary spoke to the footman first.

"We've come to call on Mrs. Boardman, please."

The footman nodded. "Of course. Follow me to the drawing room."

Mary noted that everything in the Boardman house was of the finest quality. Thick Aubusson carpets covered the wood floors. Samuel McIntire's signature carvings decorated the mantel and ceiling moldings.

Mary's heart sank when she walked into the darkened drawing room. She'd been in too many of these rooms, with thick curtains drawn, the fire and candles providing the only light. A platter of wrapped funeral cookies lay on the table inside the door. Mary had no desire for their spicy yet bitter taste.

Mrs. Boardman sat in the middle of a sofa flanked by her four daughters. Her son sat at a separate chair staring at the carpet.

Mrs. Boardman rose so Mary could kiss her on both cheeks.

"Please, make yourselves comfortable. It is so good of you to call." Mrs. Boardman gestured to an opposite sofa. "You know Reverend Bentley, of course."

William Bentley rose from a wing chair by the fire to shake hands with George and Benjamin before resuming his seat and picking up his teacup from the side table.

"I'm here to offer support to Mrs. Boardman. Her husband had such public spirit. We shall miss him greatly, shall we not?"

"Yes." George grunted. "Mrs. Boardman, if there is anything we can do to assist you, please don't hesitate to send us a note. We shall call upon you immediately."

"Yes," Mrs. Boardman said vaguely, as if she didn't grasp George's offer. "I don't think you've met my children. My daughters Mary and Elizabeth go to school with your Molly. And, of course, our two Sallys also know each other. And this is my son, Francis. Francis, shake hands with Captain Crowninshield."

The boy slowly stood, bowed, and offered the stranger his small hand. George gave it a gentle shake. When it was his turn, Benjamin patted the boy's shoulders.

"I begged him to settle ashore," Mrs. Boardman confided to Mary. "But he wanted to have more money to invest." Mrs. Boardman shook her head, and a tear slid down her cheek. Reverend Bentley put down his cup to take his parishioner's hand.

Mary nodded to Benjamin and motioned for him to take the children outside.

"Miss Mary," Benjamin said to the oldest Boardman daughter. "Perhaps you could show us the layout of your garden."

The girl's head jolted up. "Yes! Come along, everyone." She shooed her siblings out of the drawing room, and Benjamin and his sisters followed.

# Benjamin Crowninshield

Outside, shadows fell over the garden pathways. Molly organized a game for the younger children. Elizabeth Boardman stayed close to her older sister. Benjamin felt an odd sensation of sorrow for people he didn't really know. He couldn't imagine what his family would do if Sir suddenly died. Benjamin thought Captain Boardman's death was as tragic as any morality play. He had had a family, and his mansion was complete. He should have retired from the sea and enjoyed life ashore. *I have to sail to make my fortune, but he'd already achieved his. Why would anyone go to sea if he could avoid it?*

Benjamin linked his arms with those of the Boardman girls, certain a brisk turn in the garden would help them feel a bit better. Both of them kept their heads down. After the third turn around the garden, Mary Boardman shook her head. "I can't believe we'll never see Papa again. I knew every time he sailed away, he might not return, but I didn't believe it." Mary bent to look at a group of yellow daffodils.

"Do you have a sweetheart, Mr. Crowninshield?" she asked abruptly.

"Benj. Call me Benj." *What should I say?* "And no, I don't have a sweetheart. I won't consider an attachment before I'm home from the sea. That will probably be years from now."

"Oh." Mary scuffed her shoe on the gravel path.'

Benjamin shrugged. "Um. It will be years before I can leave the sea. I've hardly left the land yet. But, um, when I do come ashore, if you're not otherwise engaged, I would like to call on you. What do you think?"

Mary lowered her eyes. "If I'm still free, I would like that very much."

"And you'll save a dance for me if we're at the same party?"

"I'll save you two, but not together."

# Captain George Crowninshield

*December 1792*
*George Crowninshield's House*

George absentmindedly swirled amber liquid around his crystal glass and gazed at the flickering winter fire.

"The brandy's about to slosh over the sides, which is truly wasteful."

George turned his head toward his wife. "Did you say something?"

"I said, you're going to spill your brandy, which is not only wasteful but will mark the rug. Put the glass down and tell me what's on your mind." Mary snipped the last thread on the button she had added to her son's shirt. "Don't draw your lips into a line. Tell me what's bothering you. Are you still brooding about Hasket's new ship?"

George stood and stretched. "Surprisingly, I have other things on my mind. Tell me, how many sons do we have?"

Mary arched a brow. "The last time I counted, we had six, and five of them live in our house. Which one are you thinking of? Is it Edward or Geordie?"

"Why single out those two? They're all stubborn. They take after you in that."

Mary laughed, the clear sound bringing a smile to George's lips.

"I believe, Husband, they inherited their hard heads from you. What's the problem? Is it because Geordie doesn't want to court a bride yet? He's right when he says you keep him out of Salem too much for him to spend time with any appropriate young women."

As if realizing this wouldn't be a short conversation, Mary put away her sewing.

"Pour us both some Madeira—or brandy, if you prefer—and tell me what's on your mind."

George went to the sideboard for fresh crystal glasses, filled them with Spanish sherry, and handed one to his wife. Mary sniffed the glass.

"This isn't Madeira."

"Astute as always, my dear. This is the Spanish sherry I recently brought in from Cádiz. Try it and tell me what you think."

Mary swallowed and wrinkled her nose. "Well, it's not as sweet. I'm not sure I like it, but the flavor is interesting. Stop changing the subject and tell me what's on your mind about our sons. Are you irritated with Geordie?"

"No. I respect his reasoning, though I think he could attend more dancing assemblies when he's in Salem. Instead, he spends his time flirting with tavern maids when he could be making better female friends. If he gives his attentions to wenches, he'll never settle down properly. I spoke to him about it before he went out last time."

"So you did." Mary tapped her chin. "Jacob already mentioned the Gardner girl. Our younger sons aren't established enough yet to court anyone seriously. And Edward is already married."

George winced.

"Ah, so you're thinking about Edward. His wife isn't our sort, but he's wed now. So that won't change."

"Wed and living in Marblehead, consorting with fishermen instead of sailing for us," George grumbled. "Thus far, he refuses to even ship out as a mate, but I have a proposition for him. William Gray has a ship going down to the West Indies, and he's agreed to send Edward along as a clerk. He's twenty-seven now. He ought to be holding a command for us instead of relying on me to find him a clerk's billet."

Mary put her hand on her husband's arm. "But that's the problem, isn't it? Edward doesn't want our help, and he doesn't want to master a merchant ship. He's happy as he is."

"In Marblehead? Fishing? No, I cannot accept that. We have a company, and he needs to come home to his responsibilities and be part of our business.

I think once he sails as a clerk and understands how things work, he'll throw his lot in with our family."

Mary shook her head. "Does Edward know about your plans for him?"

"Of course he does. Same as our other sons."

"George, if he hasn't come to us by now, he won't. He's a grown man, earning his own way. You can't force him to your will. He's not like our other sons, or any of the young men in our extended family. You have to accept that."

"That's where you're wrong, Mary. I don't have to accept anything. It's time Edward decided whether he wants to be in our family or not. I shall call on him tomorrow. I'll go on horseback so I don't have to navigate a gig through those narrow Marblehead streets."

Mary drew her eyebrows together. George hated to upset her, but enough was enough. He'd been more than patient with Edward.

Mary picked up a chamberstick candle holder and held out her hand. George kissed his wife's fingers. Even when she disagreed, Mary always supported his decisions. George sometimes wondered if he deserved such trust.

*Marblehead*

George guided his horse toward the shoreline. The gelding had done well on the four-mile journey from Salem but needed to rest before the journey home. About halfway down the main street, George saw a livery stable and rode into the courtyard. A young lad who looked to be about ten years old came out wearing a thick coat.

"Tiz a brutal day, sir," he said.

"Aye." George dismounted and handed over the reins. "Take Cicero inside, rub him down, and give him something to eat. I'll call back for him in a few hours. What's your name?"

"I'm Ned, sir."

"And I'm Captain Crowninshield." George gave the lad a few coins so he'd remember how to take care of Cicero.

"Thankee, sir. There's a hot fire in the tavern if you want to warm yerself a bit."

*Not a bad idea.*

George walked next door and relaxed in the blast of warm air from the great fire.

"I'll have a flip to warm up."

An older barmaid started mixing the beverage of beer and gin.

"Follow me ta fire."

She motioned for George to sit at a small round table next to the fire, then grabbed a hot iron and plunged it into the mug. Steam rose to the surface.

"There yar. Pay me on yer way out."

After settling his tab, warmed and sustained by liquid courage, George made his way toward Edward's house. Despite the cold weather, the smell of drying cod lingered everywhere. George passed an India shop, though the shelves looked a bit bare. Farther up, a few mansions appeared in the narrow streets. Bracing himself against the wind, George bumped into several people before arriving at his son's small cottage. The front yard was spare but tidy. Bare shrubs stood on either side of the door. George couldn't decide if the facade might look better in the spring. Probably not. He pulled back the tarnished brass door knocker and rapped.

A young woman wearing a simple gray linen dress with a white fichu answered. Red curls swirled around her white mop cap. Her eyes flicked over George.

"Are you lost?" she asked.

"Are you Mrs. Crowninshield?"

"I am. And who might you be?"

"I'm your father-in-law. I'm here to see my son."

The woman's lips made a perfect O.

"You better come in, then," she mumbled before opening the door farther and gesturing for George to enter.

There was a small entryway with a rack for outerwear that opened directly into the front room, which appeared to also serve as a kitchen of sorts. There was a stewpot set against the fire's coals, and an empty spit straddled the fireplace.

George took a seat on a wooden bench near the fire.

"My husband didn't mention your arrival. Did you write?"

George took off his gloves and slapped them on his thigh. "I sent several notes but received no reply."

The woman nodded and picked up letters from a table. "Are these the notes?" she asked.

"They are. It appears my son didn't open them. If he had, I might not have had to make this miserable journey from Salem."

"That's true," the woman said. "It's a terrible time of year for travel. Um, I'm expecting my husband shortly. He's mending nets, but he'll return for dinner. You've come on a good day. I have a beef stew. Will you join us, sir?"

George gritted his teeth. *If I want to speak to Edward, I either have to stay for dinner or try to find him by the wharves. It's warmer here.*

"Would you like some small beer while you wait?"

"That would be very nice. Tell me about yourself. My son told us he had a wife but didn't share much about you. Just that your name is Mary."

The woman blushed. "There isn't much to tell. My family has fished from here for more than a hundred years. My father and brothers go out for cod during the season. My husband fishes with them now. That's how we met. My husband was a new crew member, and my brothers brought him home. He stayed with my family until we decided to marry. That was two years ago now."

"Does my son have his own boat?"

"He prefers to take shares with my brothers."

"Does he skipper a vessel?"

"Sometimes, but he says he'd rather just keep his head down and fish. Although," she rushed on, "he maintains the boats. So, he's much more important than just a boat hand."

George turned his attention to his beer. *Am I too late to save Edward from his foolishness? Surely, he wants more than to be a deckhand on a fishing boat. How could any son of mine be content with that?*

Edward's wife picked up some yarn and knitting needles and sat by the table. It looked as if she was working on a sock. George shook his head. *I hope Edward gets back soon, or it will be a long journey back to Salem in the dark.*

# Edward Crowninshield

*Edward Crowninshield's House*

Edward stamped his feet and brushed his hands down his clothing in a futile effort to keep moisture from the fog outside the house. He'd worked on the large fishing net in his brother-in-law's unheated warehouse until the light started to fade. Inside, he began taking off his coat and stopped. Something was different. Edward narrowed his eyes and looked around the room. His wife wasn't by the fire, but someone was.

"Let me help you with your coat," Mary said, slipping it over his shoulders. "Your father is here."

"How long?"

"Too long. He arrived about noon."

"That so."

Edward entered the room with his hand outstretched. His father stood to greet him.

"Sir." Edward nodded. "I didn't expect to see you here."

George shook his son's hand with a bit more vigor than seemed necessary.

"If you bothered to read your mail, I wouldn't have had to come. Shall we sit?"

*There he goes, telling me what to do in my own house.* Edward pulled a chair from beside a small table and rested his arms on the back of it. George sat down again on the bench.

"The fire's died down a bit," George said.

"My home isn't a tavern. Since I didn't read your notes, tell me why you're here."

George pulled his eyebrows together.

"I'm curious. Why did you save the notes?"

"I thought they'd make good kindling."

Mary walked up with mugs of small beer.

"Shall I lay another place for dinner?"

"No. My father won't be staying."

"But . . ."

"I said no, Mary." Edward turned his eyes back to his father. "State your business and be on your way."

For the first time, George looked uncomfortable.

"I arranged a job for you on one of William Gray's ships."

Edward kept his eyes on his father while he swallowed some beer. "Not interested."

"The position is clerk. If it goes well, I can probably arrange for you to master boats to the West Indies."

"I told you I'm not interested."

George's face flushed red, and he banged his mug onto the seat beside him. "You cannot seriously expect me to believe you want to live your life as a fisherman. I'm ashamed to call you my son."

"Believe it, Sir. And the shame is yours, not mine. Seems to me, our business is concluded."

"Not by a long shot." George's face turned purple with rage. "Surely, you can see how it looks when my own son refuses to sail with my family business. But to have it be said you prefer to crew on a fishing boat. It is insupportable!"

Edward stood. "You've worn out your welcome."

Mary reached out to grasp his forearm. "Edward—"

"Mary, this is nothing to do with you."

Mary continued gripping her husband's forearm. "But you can't turn your back on your family. It isn't right."

Edward turned to face his wife, whose blue eyes were as big as saucers. "Just hear your father out. Being clerk on a coastal boat sounds like a wonderful opportunity."

*Not for me.*

"Mary, you need to understand. I'm not cut out to master a vessel, and I'm too old to clerk for other men."

"Is that the problem?" George interrupted. "When Geordie gets back from the Indies, you can clerk for him. If you take the position with Gray, you'll be qualified to go out with Geordie. And Geordie will be glad of your help. As it is, he has to be responsible for everything on the voyage."

Mary searched her husband's eyes. "It isn't right for you to help my brothers and turn your back on your own."

"Mary, you don't understand."

"You're right, I don't. I never have."

Edward's shoulder slumped. *I can't fight them both.*

"Very well. Sir, I will accept the position. When do I need to be in Salem?"

"Just after the new year. Why don't you and Mrs. Crowninshield spend the new year with us?"

"No," Edward said with finality. "I'll be there in time to take on the cargo and stay at Ship Tavern."

"Your mother would be pleased to have you at my house."

*Your house is the worst place I could be.*

"That isn't necessary. Explain to Mame I prefer my own arrangements. I believe that's our business concluded, Sir."

George stood as if he were going to clap Edward on the shoulder. Edward put out his hand again.

"It was good of you to stop by. But please don't call again."

George wrapped his coat closely and pulled his hat down.

"Rest assured, I shall never call upon you again," George growled and flung the door open.

Whisps of fog floated into the room before Edward could close the door tightly. Sending his wife an annoyed glance, he pulled his chair back to the small table. Mary set out pewter plates on the table's wood surface and spooned stew into them. She placed a plate of bread in the center of the table.

"Shall I build up the fire a bit?" she asked. "It's cold."

"I'll do it after we eat." Edward lapsed into silence, and the room echoed with the sounds of spoons scraping stew off plates. Mary watched her husband closely before clearing the table.

With slumped shoulders, Edward built up the fire, ensuring that the small flames drew heat from the coals before sitting on the bench. Sparks floated up the chimney.

When Mary brought out more beer, Edward tapped the seat beside him.

"Ask your questions," he said.

"They're the same questions I had when my brothers brought you home and told me about your family. I thought you'd just had a falling-out and would return to Salem. But you kept working for my brothers." Mary placed her left hand on Edward's thigh. "You're a good fisherman, but that's not who you were raised to be. Do you realize this is the first time I've met anyone from your family? Do I embarrass you?"

Edward placed his hand over Mary's.

"*You* can never embarrass me. I'm embarrassed by my family, and by my own choices."

"You don't like fishing?"

Edward smiled slightly. "I do. I like being out on the water and doing useful tasks with my hands. I intentionally turned my back on family expectations. My brothers . . ." Edward paused. "Let me start again. I'm the oldest of six brothers, all of them bolder than I. And you've met my father. Can you imagine trying to live up to his expectations? He came from nothing, but when he was my age, he was running British blockades and married to the daughter of one of the most important merchants in Salem. And Mame, well, there was nothing worse than seeing disappointment in her eyes when my brother extricated me from one of the fights that followed me everywhere. One day, I just walked away and came to Marblehead."

Edward lifted his wife's chin. "Can you understand? I'm not like them. I'm not a fighter. I don't care about status and ships and mansions. The only thing I've ever wanted was your love and to be left alone. And the reason I didn't take you to Salem is that I can hardly bear to be in the same room with any of them. I am a disappointment. A reminder that, unlike my brothers, I'm not willing to hold my ground against adversity. I fish, Mary. I don't want to clerk for my brother or anyone else."

"Then why did you accept the position?"

Edward stroked Mary's cheek and pushed a curl behind her ear.

"I accepted because it was easier than refusing. Sir would have publicly cast me out of the family, and I can't bear the shame it would bring to you and your family, who have given me so much by accepting me as I am. But I must be honest with you. I don't have a good feeling about this voyage. The West Indies are filled with disease. Many men never get home. If I am one of them, promise you will go to my father to claim your widow's portion."

"You can change your mind. I won't think less of you."

Edward drew Mary closer. "I gave my word, and I will keep it. Blow out the candle and lie with me."

# Captain Nathaniel Silsbee

*December 1792*
*Captain Nathaniel Silsbee's House*

"William, are you ready to function as head of household?"

"You know that I am. You've only to bid Mother, Zach, and Sara farewell, and you'll be off to the East." William grinned. "No more coastal runs for you."

"Strange how things turn out," Nath said. "If our father hadn't died, Mother wouldn't have her dower portion of our house. So perhaps it was a blessing after all."

William shrugged. "I doubt she agrees."

In the front room, Sarah Silsbee hugged her seafaring son.

"Godspeed," she murmured.

"No need to fret," Nath said. "I always come back."

"See that ye do. Tell me again about your ship."

"For this last time, I'll tell you that the *Benjamin* is a new ship of one hundred sixty tons loaded with a cargo valued at eighteen thousand dollars. I'll sail around the Cape of Good Hope to the Isle de France and India, sell enough of my adventure cargo to make our family wealthy, and return to you safe and sound."

Nath's grandmother Joanna nodded and wiped her eyes. "Don't fall into drink like your father."

"You know he won't," William said. "Nath is an absolute stick."

"One more thing." Nath handed his mother a pouch. "Here's plenty of money to see you through until my return, but if you need anything else, I've made arrangements for you to apply to Mr. Derby."

Sarah clutched the leather pouch. "Thank you, Nathaniel. Yer a good man an' all."

Nath kissed his mother's cheek. "I'll be off, then."

With a wave to his siblings, Nath strode away from the house. He didn't care for long farewells. Strangely, when he left for a short coastal run, his mother acted as if he would be killed by pirates. Now that he was leaving for a voyage to the East, she held herself to a few tears down her cheeks. Then again, he'd left her plenty of coin.

### At Sea, Aboard the Benjamin

Two nights out of Salem, the *Benjamin* encountered heavy gales and freezing rain. Nath went on deck several times to check the ship's course. A little before dawn, Samuel, his first mate, rapped on his cabin door.

"We got trouble, sir. Ye best come out."

Nath shrugged into his coat and stepped out.

"What's the problem?"

"It's the African cook Robert, sir. He put the fire out as a precaution, but instead of going below, he stayed out in the weather. Now he's frozen through. We took him below and we're warming him up, but there's somethin' wrong with his feet. More than frostbite."

Nath nodded and climbed down the ship's ladder into the crew's quarters. The hammock holding the injured man swung erratically.

"Secure the hammock," Nath ordered. "Someone hold a lantern so I can see what's going on."

Nath put his hand on Robert's shoulder.

"Robert, what possessed you to stay on deck in the freezing rain?"

"Don't like closed spaces."

"Well, let's have a look at you. Someone, bring me a small nail."

Nath felt Robert's face and neck, with special attention to his nose and ears.

"Samuel, cover Robert's nose and ears with wool until they warm up."

Nath continued down Robert's arms and fingers. He lifted each finger.

"Do you feel me when I prick you?"

"Yes."

"Good." Nath glanced at the sailors near him and turned to his first mate. "Samuel, leave Noah with me. You go topside and check our course. Noah, I want wool gloves on this man, and then wrap his arms into the blanket next to his body."

Sweat trickled down Nath's neck. He lifted the blanket off Robert's legs and checked them. They seemed all right. But now the feet.

"Robert," he sighed, "why didn't you at least put on wool stockings?"

"They'd get wet."

*Not an unreasonable precaution*, Nath thought, *but perhaps a foolish one.*

Nath took a deep breath and pressed the nail tip over Robert's feet. On top of his pale soles, his feet had a reddish hue, but he could still feel the pricks. *Now for the toes.* Nath didn't know what to make of them. They were swollen, and Robert couldn't feel them. Nath leaned over to smell Robert's feet. Something wasn't right. He pressed each toe.

"Hold the lantern closer." Nath pressed the ends of Robert's toes again. Beneath the swelling, the tissue felt spongy. Nath stood.

"Very well. Wrap him up warmly and gather all the bandaging materials you can find. Robert, can you hear me?"

"Yes."

"As best I can tell, you have gangrene, and I have to cut your toes off. If I don't, it will spread quickly, and you'll die. Do I have your permission?"

"What'll happen ta me?"

"We'll take care of you until we can put you ashore. Shall I proceed?"

"Ah'm not ready ta die."

"Then we'll proceed. Noah is going to fill you with so much rum, you'll won't feel anything. Do you agree?"

"Aye."

"Noah, get rum and bandages while I find something to cut with. Let me know when he's insensible. You'll need to move Robert to a table. Open the gunport to get light in here, but block the cold air as best you can. Also, find two or three strong men to hold him down. We can't have any sudden movement. And bring more lanterns. I need as much light as you can give me."

Nath stood a moment listening to the ship creak before climbing onto the deck. He took a deep breath of cold, salty air and stood next to his first mate for several minutes without speaking.

"Samuel, have you served with any surgeons?"

"No, sir. I've never been on a privateer. Why?"

Nath rubbed the back of his neck.

"The ends of all Robert's toes are spongy and make a slight crackling sound. I think it's gangrene. If I don't amputate now, it will spread and probably kill him."

"He might not recover from the cut. Maybe we should turn around and go back to Salem."

"We're three days out. We wouldn't get back in time."

Samuel grunted.

"I need a small, sharp knife. I'm going to cut just above the toe knuckle."

"Might do better with a straight razor. Smaller blade. Or scissors, mebbe?"

"Aye." Nath inhaled chilly morning air again. "It looks like the storm blew itself out."

Samuel squinted at the sky. "We should be good for a bit. But don't take too long. Winter squalls come up fast."

Nath ducked into his cabin, knocked back a small glass of brandy, grabbed his razor, and prayed for steady hands.

Back below and sweating profusely despite the cold air, Nath took off his coat and rolled up his sleeves.

Robert lay on a wooden table with one man by his head and two on either side of his body.

"Give him a block of wood so he doesn't bite his tongue. Noah, you'll assist me."

Nath cut five lengths of string and tied each one just above the toe knuckles on Robert's right foot.

"Pour rum over Robert's foot, and then hand me the razor. When I start cutting, be ready with bandages to wipe the blood so I can see. As I finish each toe, pack and bandage it, quick as you can.

"The rest of you, hold him down. Don't let him move or jerk or cry out." Nath turned to the cabin boy by Robert's head. The boy's face was white with terror. "Timothy," Nath said. "Hold Robert's head, and be sure he doesn't bite off his tongue." The boy nodded and adjusted his grip by Robert's ears.

Nath poised the razor over Robert's large toe and began cutting by the string. As the tissue separated, Noah moved in to pack the wounds. Sweat dripped down Nath's face. After several hours, Nath removed the last piece of putrid flesh from Robert's right foot and bandaged it entirely.

"That's enough. Someone needs to stay with him. Noah, figure out a rotation. Give him hot liquid when he wakes up. If he makes it through the night, we'll do the other foot tomorrow. Close the gunports and keep him warm."

Nath put his coat back on and pulled himself up the ship's ladder. Daylight was quickly passing.

"I have the sextant, sir," Samuel said.

"Much obliged." Nath placed the eyepiece and measured the angle to the sun. "I'll check the chart, but we're still on course. You'll need to adjust the watches. I'll need the same men for Robert's other foot tomorrow. And keep your eyes peeled. If you spot a British frigate, flag it down. They usually have a surgeon in the crew."

To Nath's immense relief, Robert survived the night. It seemed cruel to remove the man's remaining toes when he still suffered from the first amputations, but the danger of leaving them persuaded Nath that he had no choice.

Once again, Nath tied the string above the remaining toe knuckles and proceeded to remove the gangrenous flesh. When he was sure Robert was secure and as comfortable as possible, Nath went on deck and leaned over the rail.

*Dear God, grant Robert life. And please don't give such a task to me again.* Nath thought God was more likely to grant his first request than the second, but it was worth asking.

"Samuel, do we have anyone aboard who can cook? We can't eat hardtack until we get to Cape Verde."

"I reckon we can all turn a hand."

"Good. Have someone boil up burgoo. At least it will fill our bellies."

"Aye, aye, sir."

To Nath's relief, the *Benjamin* crossed routes with a British frigate, and the surgeon agreed to come aboard with his assistant. Nath took him below, where Robert rested in a cot secured to the deck. When the surgeon lifted the bandages off, Nath braced himself.

*Are the wounds infected? Did I make Robert's condition worse instead of better?*

"And you changed the bandages?"

"Of course. I couldn't leave him drenched in blood."

"Humph. You did well, Captain Silsbee. The wounds are clean and mending. You say you have no training?"

"None at all."

"Humph. Do you miss your toes, Robert?"

"Not yet. Ah ain't tried ta walk."

"You'll need a cane to balance. Maybe two. But you'll get around. He'll be ready for duty in a week, Captain Silsbee. In the meantime, Robert, start moving around. Get some fresh air on deck. It's putrid down here."

Nath winced at the implied rebuke of conditions belowdecks but felt immense relief that Robert would recover.

# Edward Crowninshield

*January 1793*
*Pointe-à-Pitre, Guadeloupe*

Edward wiped the back of his neck with a kerchief as he watched slaves unload casks of dried cod, furniture, nails, and other necessities of plantation life. Wagons filled with sugar and molasses stood in a line on the wharf ready to be loaded. Edward wiped his brow again. He felt hot. *I shouldn't have taken this job.*

Captain Jarvis came up behind him. "Smatter wid you? Better than shivering in Salem, eh?"

Edward glanced at his boss. "Too hot for me," he mumbled.

"When ye get the cargo sorted, meet me at the taverna. We'll indulge the local beauties. They'll be easy ta please."

"Aye, Cap. I'll be along later."

Edward's vision wavered. *Must be the heat.* He motioned for the slaves to keep unloading, trying to keep his focus on the number of casks leaving the ship. Suddenly, all Edward could see was his wife's face.

# Captain Jacob Crowninshield

*January 1793*
*Captain George Crowninshield's House*

Despite the bone-chilling wind, Jacob whistled as he walked past Derby Wharf to his father's house across the street. Opening the door before the new footman reached it, Jacob tossed him his coat and hat sat on a bench to remove his boots. *Mame will have a fit if I track a mess on her floors, and rightly so.*

"Welcome home, sir," the footman said.

"Thank you, Joshua, but it's not for long. I'm away on the *Henry* in a week. Tell me, have you ever joined a ship's crew?"

"Once, sir. I was ill the entire time."

"Ah. In that case, you're wise to stay ashore."

"Yes, sir. Your mother and her guests are having tea in the drawing room."

"Excellent." Jacob smiled. "I'll pop my head in and grab a biscuit. Don't even think about announcing me." Jacob tapped the door.

"Anyone inside?" he called.

"Jacob, close the door this instant," Mame ordered. "You're letting the heat out. Come join us. Your aunt Elizabeth Derby brought my niece Sarah Gardner to Salem for a family visit."

Jacob raised his eyebrows in an unspoken question.

"They're staying with Sarah's father," Mame said. "Did I forget to mention it to you earlier?"

"No matter," Jacob said. "It's a pleasure to see you again, Aunt Derby." Jacob bowed.

Elizabeth Derby smiled. "I hoped you would arrive during our visit. I believe it has been some time since you last saw your cousin. Sarah, stand and greet Captain Crowninshield properly."

A slender young woman bundled in a thick shawl stood and curtsied. "It is a pleasure to meet you again, Cousin," she murmured. "I'm not often able to travel in the winter. The chill is difficult for my chest."

Jacob bowed his head in greeting. "And I, alas, am usually away when you come to Salem. Mame is kind enough to tell me of your visits."

"No doubt," Sarah said dryly.

Mame cleared her throat. "Jacob, have you time to join us in a cup of tea?"

"Delighted."

"Why don't you take your cups over to the window. You and Sarah can catch up with each other. I'm sure you have much to discuss."

*Let my campaign for Sarah's hand commence.*

"Shall we, Sarah, or will there be too much of a chill for you?"

Jacob reached out to take the cups.

"It's fine, Jacob. My dress is wool, and my shawl is thick. I'll bring a plate of cakes."

Jacob pulled the window curtains closed. "Better to keep out the draft than worry about the light. But I'm happy to open them again."

"No." Sarah smiled. "It's nice to be able to converse without family members watching my every move and whispering behind their hands."

"And do you know what they whisper about?"

Sarah shrugged. "I'm of marriageable age, and my family wants me to have a secure future."

*Does she know I have my eye on her?*

Jacob sipped his tea before asking, "And what do you want?"

"Shall I get us more tea?"

"No, thank you." Jacob stirred more sugar in his cup. "You didn't answer my question."

"Eventually, I want a husband and children. But for the moment, I am content as I am." Sarah dropped her eyes.

Jacob placed his cup on the table and cleared his throat. "You are my favorite cousin, if you take my meaning."

Sarah fidgeted and nibbled a tea cake. Jacob craned his head.

"I do believe you're blushing."

Sarah snorted. "I'm doing nothing of the sort."

"I can't believe it. We've known each other all our lives." Jacob shook his head. "Do you ever think about me?"

"I wouldn't be so presumptuous. Besides, we seldom see each other."

"Indeed. But I have many empty nights at sea and often think of my home and family."

Silence stretched between them. Suddenly, Sarah's eyes danced.

"Do you remember the sleigh rides we had as children? Those were ever so much fun."

"I remember. Next time we meet during the winter months, shall we take out a sleigh? We could make a party with my brothers and sisters. It would give me something to remember during cold nights on the ocean."

"You can invite me next winter, if you're still so inclined."

"Would you accept?"

Sarah dropped her eyes. "You'll have to wait and see. Tell me more about your ship."

Jacob chuckled. "The *Henry* is hardly *my* ship. I sail her to India for Uncle Derby. Business has been quite good, and I've done well on my adventure cargo. I'm hopeful that soon I'll sail exclusively for our family company. We're getting closer to our goal every year."

"I heard your company is doing well. You must be so proud to be part of it, and soon sail as your own man." Sarah's brown eyes glowed. "Will you make a career of sailing?"

"When we're established, my brothers and I can leave the sea to become merchants with our company. I've given some thought to putting myself forward for public office. What do you think?"

"It sounds exciting! I shall certainly tell my brothers to vote for you."

"When I return with the *Henry*, may I call on you?"

"I don't see why not. We are cousins, after all. But I'll probably be in Boston with my aunt and uncle. How long do you expect to be away?"

"It's unpredictable. The *Henry* departs this week, and depending on trade circumstances, I could be gone for almost two years. But I promise to think of you every night." Jacob winked.

"Two years is a long time."

"It is, but we can write letters . . . if you like." *Will she wait for me?* "I can write every day and send them wherever I am. That way, you'll know you're always in my thoughts. What do you think?"

Sally raised her eyes to meet Jacob's. "I would be pleased if you write. You can tell me all about your adventures, and I . . . well, I can send family news."

"I know we haven't spent much time together since we were children, but would it be too much to ask you not to accept an official suitor before my return?" Jacob searched Sarah's face and held his breath. *Please answer before we're interrupted.*

Sarah twisted her fingers in her lap. "I hardly know what to say, Jacob."

Jacob reached for Sarah's hands. "Say that even though you will go to parties and enjoy yourself, you won't accept a suitor until I return. And I promise that when I return, I shall court you properly."

Sarah glanced toward her aunt, who was adjusting her bonnet and putting on her gloves.

"And," Jacob continued, "I shall write to you every day, and I hope you'll write to me."

"Sarah," Aunt Derby said. "I'm sorry to interrupt your conversation, but your father is expecting us. We need to say our farewells."

Sarah extricated her fingers from Jacob's hands and stood. Jacob reached for her elbow.

*I can't let her leave without her promise.*

"Please, Sarah, don't send me to sea without your blessing."

Sarah smiled coyly, revealing a dimple.

"Well, since I'm your favorite cousin, I can hardly refuse your correspondence. I shall look forward to your letters."

*Yes!*

"And shall you accept suitors in my absence?"

"It would hardly be fair of me to make such an important decision before you have an opportunity to present your petition."

"And so, in the spirit of fairness . . . ?"

"I shall withhold any entanglements until after your return."

Jacob smiled broadly. "It's settled, then. I can go to sea with a light heart knowing I have your friendship."

Jacob kissed Sarah's fingertips.

"Sarah, the gig is here. Come get your things."

"Yes, Aunt, I'm just coming." Sarah turned back to Jacob; her face slightly flushed. "Cousin, keep yourself safe, and may you have good fortune on your voyage."

Jacob smiled to himself. *My good fortune has already begun.*

# Captain George Crowninshield

*February 1793*
*Crowninshield Counting House*

"Captain Crowninshield?"

George looked up from the ledgers on his desk.

"This note from Captain Gray just arrived."

"Give it here, lad, and be back at your work."

George turned the note around in his hands. Noted the deep nib of the pen used to address the letter, the precise calligraphy. Clearly, this wasn't a note about business, or even an invitation. It could only be one thing. Edward was either injured or sick . . . or dead. George broke the note's seal.

> Captain Crowninshield,
>
> I regret to inform you that letters received from Captain Jarvis at Guadeloupe bear news that your son Edward Crowninshield was struck down suddenly by a fever and is interred at the cemetery there.
>
> Your obedient servant,
> Captain William Gray

George dropped his head into his hands. Fevers were always a hazard in the West Indies, but to lose his oldest son in what seemed like the blink of an eye was a personal tragedy. Edward could have fallen ill and died in Salem, but the fact that he had pushed Edward to take the voyage made George feel responsible in a way he didn't like.

*It's a damn shame,* he thought, *but life has no guarantee. How will I tell his mother?*

*March 3, 1793*

George guided Mary into the family pew at East Church. She hadn't spoken since he gave her Gray's note, except to ask why God was punishing her again.

Maybe once they offered prayers for Edward, she would come back to herself. *I can't bear it when she grieves.*

Reverend Bentley adjusted his collar and began the announcements and prayers. The congregation prayed for Samuel Derby's wife and family, and then for Edward.

Mary wiped her face and reached for his hand. "George," she whispered. "I don't blame you for Edward's death . . ."

*Thank God!*

". . . though his wife may. But then, he could just as easily have been washed off a fishing boat."

"So, you don't think I sent him into harm's way?"

"You send all our sons into danger without a second thought. Just promise me you'll bring them ashore as soon as may be. I want grandchildren."

"You have my word."

Reverend Bentley stood outside the doorway, murmuring to people as they passed and shook his hand.

"Mrs. Crowninshield, I'm deeply sorry for your loss. We are all in God's hands."

The reverend stroked Mary's hand.

*Let go of her hand! You never even met Edward.*

"We appreciate your prayers, Reverend Bentley. We'll see you later this afternoon at the family reception."

# Lizzie Rowell

*April 1793*
*Ship Tavern*

Lizzie glanced out the window at the predawn stars and traced her hand down the outside of Geordie's jaw. Geordie yammered at her every day about getting a cottage, and today she'd have to agree.

"When I return, I'll set you up in a cottage. Perhaps in Marblehead? I don't like sneaking around the Ship. Matt knows what's going on with us, and I'm sure your cousin does too. She's just been too polite to say anything, but she'll be on you as soon as the *Polly & Sally* leaves port. Actually, everyone who's a regular probably knows we sneak upstairs every night."

Geordie grabbed Lizzie's hand and kissed her fingers.

"Say you agree. Let me take care of you."

"Do you really mean that?" Lizzie whispered.

"Of course. I always mean what I say. Well . . ." Geordie smirked. "Most of the time. But you can trust me on this, lambkin. I don't want you to keep working at the Ship like a skivvy. I want to look after you properly."

Geordie nuzzled Lizzie's neck and lowered her shift below her shoulders.

Lizzie pulled her shift back up, threw her legs over the side of the bed, and rushed for the chamber pot.

"What's wrong?" Geordie sat up. "Are you sick?"

Geordie put his arm around Lizzie's waist and pulled her hair back.

Lizzie retched for several minutes.

"It's passed now," she said, wiping her mouth. "I have to get down to the kitchen. I'm late."

"Come back to bed. I'll tell Matt you aren't well."

For a moment, Lizzie thought she'd be sick again. Her heart pounded out a frantic rhythm. "You can't. He'll tell my cousin, and then she'll know for certain. She already suspects. She warned me what would happen if I walked out with customers. She'll throw me out."

"For what? Being sick?" Geordie drew Lizzie into his arms.

"You really don't know?"

"Know what, lambkin?"

Lizzie turned to face her lover. *This is the part where he leaves me to fend for myself.* A tear slid down her face.

"Geordie, I'm with child." Lizzie gulped and watched Geordie's face fall into sudden shock.

"How can that be? I'm careful, and I know what I'm doing. I've never fathered a child. No doubt you just ate some bad food. It's easy enough to do. Or you have a fever."

Geordie felt Lizzie's head. "You're a bit flushed. I'm sure it's nothing. You gave me quite a fright, lambkin."

"But what if I'm right? What will I do?"

Geordie pulled on his under-breeches and splashed water on his face.

*Bang!*

"Yer late!" Matt shouted through the door. "If ya don't get down quick, Mam will know for sure what ye've been up ta, an' ye'll be out on yer ear."

Lizzie felt her face drain of all color, no doubt leaving her pale freckles standing out like misshapen pebbles.

"It's Matt. I have to go." Lizzie pulled her wool stockings off the chair and poked her feet into them. She tied her stays and pulled on her petticoat.

"Lizzie, wait. I'll talk to your cousin and explain how things are."

"You will not!" Lizzie poked her arms into her gown. "You'll be gone in two days, and I need this job." She passed a slack-jawed Geordie, grabbed her boots, and rushed out the door.

# Captain George Crowninshield Jr.

When Lizzie left, Geordie lay back on the bed, but he didn't sleep. Lizzie couldn't be with child, could she? He was always careful to spill his seed outside. No, she was just upset because he was leaving and being fanciful. This was why he never dallied with any one woman. They became careless and irrational.

On the other hand, Lizzie could be right. *I could have gotten a child on her.*

But there was no need to panic. He'd seen his mother go through enough pregnancies to know women easily hid the truth of things. But if she was . . . Geordie scratched his chin. Well, he'd give her enough money to look after herself if she needed to and check on her when the *Polly & Sally* returned next spring.

Geordie felt his face and decided to forego a shave. He had other things to do. He pulled on his mustard-colored outer wool knee breeches, tucked in his linen shirt, and adjusted his neckwear. Just a simple tie would do today since he would be spending it either in the counting house or on his ship.

Clattering down the stairs, Geordie went into the great room in search of breakfast. The fire cast a cozy glow, though the heat caused the windows to fog. Geordie found a dark corner and kept an eye out for Matt to bring his food. Day laborers came in to break their fast for the day. Geordie waved to the wharf workers who would be loading his ship later.

Matt came over with a steaming cup of coffee, a small pitcher of heavy cream, and a heaping plate filled from the buffet.

"No pork pies this morning?" Geordie asked.

"None left." Matt grunted.

Geordie started to eat his breakfast of potatoes and sausages. Matt stood by his table with a sour face.

"Do you have something to say to me?" Geordie asked.

"I do, sir." Matt shifted his feet. "I used ta hope I could join your crew one day."

Geordie glanced up and smiled. "I'll set you up for training at our counting house before I go. A likely lad like yourself should do well."

"I said I *used* ta hope that."

Geordie put down his knife and spoon. "What's changed?"

"I always thought you were a gentleman, but seein' how you treat our Lizzie, I realize my mistake. Ye're no better than any other rich swell. Lizzie was a good girl when she came, and you ruined her."

*What did she tell the lad?*

"I have no idea what you're on about. We simply enjoy each other's company."

"All I'm sayin' is, when ye come back from yer voyage, stay with your fancy family and don't lodge at the Ship."

"I take your point," Geordie said and went back to his breakfast.

# Hasket Derby

*June 1793*
*Derby Counting House*

Hasket clutched the note in his hand. A fishing boat had spotted the *Grand Turk* off Cape Ann. She should arrive tomorrow, stuffed with her own cargo from Calcutta and what she picked up from Captain Gibaut's *Astrea* in Madras. Hasket spared a moment to worry about his friend's health before returning his focus to the *Grand Turk*.

*Tomorrow, she'll be here. Tomorrow I'll know if the expense and risk were worth the gamble.*

# Eliza Derby

*Hasket Derby's House*

"Do sit down, Hasket. You'll have your answers when the *Grand Turk* docks tomorrow. I told everyone to arrive at First Pier about midmorning as the tide comes in and put word out to the town that she is expected. I'm sure all of Salem will be there. Is Ebenezer organizing the dock men so she can start unloading quickly?"

Eliza looked at her husband's suddenly blank face. "What are you thinking?" she asked.

"You'll be there to share my triumph, won't you?"

Eliza blinked. *Surely, Hasket isn't unsure about the voyage's result.* "Of course. Our entire family, as well as every ship's master and merchant who does business with us, will be at the pier to welcome the *Grand Turk* home. Why are you anxious? This time of year, our ships come in once or twice a week."

"But this is the *Grand Turk*, our largest ship returning from her maiden voyage. And a partial fulfillment of the promise I made you. I promised you would lead Salem society, and the *Grand Turk*'s success is part of that."

"Every ship's success fulfills your promise to me. We lead Salem together in business, politics, and society. One ship changes nothing. But the size of her cargo will doubtless be impressive. Now then, pour us both a whiskey. We need to rise early tomorrow to attend to our business."

# Captain Elias Derby

## *The Next Day*

"Mother, Patsy, I didn't expect to see you awake this early. The *Grand Turk* won't arrive until the tide comes in." Elias eyed the banyans his mother and sister wore over their shifts. "You have plenty of time to dress."

"And I," Eliza said, "am surprised to see you this late in the morning." She spread butter on a slice of warm bread while watching her son. "Your card games at the Salem Inn must have gone on past closing. As I said, your father and Ezekiel are gone to the counting house. I thought you would be with them, but I suppose you have other matters on your mind."

Elias decided to ignore his mother's comments and spooned porridge into his bowl. "I watched Father pacing half the day yesterday. I have no need to see the same behavior today. He won't be at ease until the *Grand Turk* is safely tied to the pier, her cargo hold emptied, and the accounts done. His worry is needless and endless. Our profit cannot be as high as we would like, but it will still be substantial enough to impress everyone."

Eliza sniffed. "You're very cavalier about the situation."

"No. Merely practical. I was not involved in arrangements for the *Grand Turk*. Neither her success nor possible failure has any effect on my standing."

Patsy put down her teacup. "Why didn't you take her out? I know Father hoped you would. Then you would get the credit instead of Captain Hodges."

"You're right. Father offered me the job every day, from the time the *Grand Turk*'s keel was laid until she sailed away from Salem. And every day, I declined. I spent three years at Isle de France and India. I was sick and lonely most of the time. Nothing will persuade me to repeat the experience."

Elias wiped his mouth. "And now, I shall join Father and the well-wishers on our wharf while you ladies prepare yourselves for the day."

When the tide came in at midmorning, all was chaos in the counting house and on the wharf. The fife and drum corps loitered near Ship Tavern drinking tankards of ale until their officer called them into ranks. Small boats waited in the harbor to escort the *Grand Turk* to First Pier. Dockworkers stood nearby with horse-drawn wagons, ready to shift the cargo from the ship to the warehouse. A small tent at the pier protected special guests from the sun.

Elias stepped out of the warehouse, adjusting his coat sleeves while he waited for his father.

"Do you see her?" Hasket asked, approaching him.

"What a ridiculous question, Father. You can see her sails for yourself."

The small boats arranged themselves in front of the *Grand Turk* as if they were pulling her in. Men waved their hats in the air. Shouts of "huzzah" wafted over the water. The fife and drum corps marched down the wharf with their flag waving. One piper tripped over a bit of rope but caught himself.

Elias stifled a chuckle. *You have to keep your eyes open on a working wharf.*

Finally, the *Grand Turk* was at the pier, her Turkish masthead looking slightly worse for wear with a gash in the figure's turban. The crew tossed ropes to secure the vessel. Laborers attached gangplanks to the deck and the cargo hold. Captain Hodges strode down the gangplank with his logbook under his arm. Once he set foot on the wharf, he saluted his employer. The fife and drum corps cut off in the middle of a note.

"Welcome home, Captain Hodges." Hasket shook Hodge's hand enthusiastically as loud huzzahs broke out.

Elias extended his hand, noting that Captain Hodges looked somewhat haggard. "Come, sir," he said. "Mother set up a reception for you in the counting house."

While his father escorted Captain Hodges, Elias dropped back to walk with First Mate Joseph Mosely.

"How did you find the voyage?" he asked.

"The *Grand Turk* is a fine ship, and she handles well. But . . ."

"But?"

"Eh. It takes some time to fill her hold."

## Hasket Derby

*October 1793*
*Derby Counting House*

No matter how he considered the *Grand Turk*'s next voyage, Hasket couldn't come up with an appropriate cargo. She didn't make him any money sitting at First Pier. There was no point sending her back to Calcutta. Most of the *Grand Turk*'s return cargo still filled his warehouses. Hasket's thoughts wandered to the pressing issue: he needed more warehouse space. Perhaps he should accept Nate's suggestion that they join forces to build more warehouses and another store.

"Father?" Elias walked into Hasket's office. "You asked me to stop by this morning."

"I did, and I'm pleased you came before the dinner hour rather than the late afternoon."

Elias sat down, crossed his right ankle over his left knee, and waited.

"I want your ideas. With your experience in the East Indies, what do you suggest as possible cargoes for the *Grand Turk*?"

"You're asking *my* advice? How unusual."

"Only if you can spare time from your other pursuits. I met a couple of your creditors while I was in Enos Briggs's shipyard the other day. I told them you are well."

"Indeed, I am. To return to your question, I wouldn't send the *Grand Turk* back to India. We already have too much inventory that will take time to sell. Besides, we have several vessels in the area already. I think we should try running a cargo to Europe. It's a risk, but also has potential for profits."

"I'm not willing to risk my ship while English and French ships of war and privateers lay in wait to snatch honest traders."

"It's your decision, of course, but she finished refitting a month ago and is just sitting there, collecting dust. It's embarrassing—as if we'd rather be safe than make money."

Hasket ignored his son's needling.

"I'm thinking of sending her on a run to Virginia to acquire tobacco. With the trade embargo in Europe, I suspect supplies there have run low. Tobacco should fetch a good price."

"If the *Grand Turk* arrives."

Hasket shot his son a scathing look.

"And who will take her? Will Captain Hodges bother with such a small project?"

Hasket cleared his throat. "If you paid more attention, you would know he's staying ashore. I'm promoting Joseph Mosely to captain. Hodges recommends him highly, and I know Mosely is a good man. He's also the only man who understands my ship."

"You've decided, then."

"Yes. Oddly enough, our conversation has clarified my thoughts. I'll load the *Grand Turk* with sugar and barreled beef, two items in generally short supply. Our Virginia agent can take care of business, and Mosely should be back by January. February at the latest, which leaves plenty of time to send the *Grand Turk* to her next destination."

"Which is?"

"Probably Europe."

"I believe I suggested that in the first place." Elias grinned. "By the way, I heard something at Ship Tavern you might find interesting. It seems Geordie Crowninshield trifled with the owner's cousin before he left. She's gone into seclusion—at least that's the story."

"I have no interest in tittle-tattle, though your mother might find the information interesting."

"Indeed she will. Two Crowninshield sons making inappropriate connections. One wonders if merchants will do business with men who make such poor decisions about their future. Especially after Mother cuts the entire family."

"I suggest you verify your information before spreading it, lest the scandal blow back onto you. I know the oldest son married a Marblehead woman. But have you any proof about Geordie?"

"Not as yet, but I'll be watching him when he returns next spring."

Hasket raised his eyebrows. "We've wasted enough time on women's gossip."

"Let me know when you have a sailing date for the *Grand Turk*. I'll see if we can engage the fife and drum corps again." Elias winked.

Hasket barked a laugh and waved his son out of his office.

# Captain Nathaniel Silsbee

*November 1793*
*Isle de France*

Nath clicked his tongue behind his teeth and closed his logbook. Strange how quickly life changed. First, the humiliation from his ill-fated voyage on the

*Betsey.* Then the disaster with the *Sally.* The despair in his gut when France clapped an embargo on all foreign ships at Isle de France, which kept him there from March to October. And now? Nath went over his figures again. Now, what had started as a good trading season, followed by six months of idleness at Port Louis, had become a triumph. The Spanish dollars he received in exchange for local currency before the embargo tripled in value. Prices remained low, so Nath filled the *Benjamin*'s hold with coffee and spices. Hardly trusting his good luck, he realized the voyage was a success without going to India. Smiling broadly, Nath went on deck to watch Port Louis recede and set a course for the Cape of Good Hope.

In some ways, Cape Town reminded Nath of Batavia. Both had a canal bisecting the central street. In Batavia, the canal was lined with palm trees; in Cape Town, oak trees provided shade for the promenade, such as it was. Both featured sturdy houses placed in a grid pattern.

Nath snapped his spyglass closed and gave orders to bring the *Benjamin* directly to the wooden jetty.

"You sure about that?" Samuel asked.

Nath shrugged. "We're the only foreign ship here. May as well take advantage to fill our hold with water and fresh food without having to deal with the small trading boats. Between wind, waves, and our wake, they'll be lucky if they don't capsize."

Nath gestured to the dinghies manned by slaves and Chinese laborers bouncing on the slightly choppy water. Disappointed faces looked at the *Benjamin* as she sailed to the jetty.

"Aye. It'll be nice to pipe the water on board instead of pulling it from barrels."

"See to it our water barrels are washed out before you fill them. Fresh water sours quickly. And don't load the fresh food until we're ready to leave."

"This isn't the first port I've been in."

"Aye, but sometimes you load supplies too soon." Nath grinned.

"And sometimes, if ye don't mind me sayin', you order us out of port without prior notice."

"You have me there," Nath chuckled. "I'll trust our victualing to you, then, while I see what's going on ashore."

Nath made his way to the closest tavern. This close to Christmas, there was a discernible holiday spirit among the patrons. Standing at the bar, he noticed a handbill announcing an upcoming baboon baiting.

"You see?" The barman gestured toward the wall.

"I understand the picture well enough. I'll take some Madeira."

"Expensive," the barman grunted. "You just arrive?"

"We're at the end of the jetty. Any trade going on?" Nath placed a Spanish dollar on the bar. The barman smiled, revealing his black gums and missing teeth before sliding the coin into his palm.

"In Cape Town? Always. There's plenty Madeira available. Good prices. You from America?"

"Salem."

"Salem sends plenty ships this way." The barman motioned his thumb toward a back corner. "Those men from Salem."

Nath picked up his wine and made his way to the shadowy corner at the rear of the tavern.

"May I join you? I understand you're from Salem."

"On our way home at the moment. What can we do for you?"

"Depends. Do you have enough cargo space to carry a consignment to Hasket Derby? I may have a proposition for you."

Pleased with his negotiations, Nath walked up the *Benjamin*'s gangplank, whistling an almost tuneless melody.

"Samuel! You still on deck?"

"I am if it'll stop you imitating a dying bird. Let me guess. We're not going home yet. You're going to set a course"—Samuel stroked his chin—"back to Isle de France."

Nath laughed. "If we keep sailing together, we'll be able to converse without speaking. There are two ships bound for Salem on the east side of the harbor. They will take the goods consigned to Mr. Derby. We'll fill our hold with Madeira wine and return to Isle de France to take on more cargo. No sense wasting those Spanish dollars when there's trade waiting to be done. How soon can we leave?"

"I reckon two or three weeks. It'll take a week to fill our water casks. Then we can move the *Benjamin* closer to the American vessels to ferry the goods across in the Dutch company's boats. After that, we'll come back and load up on fresh victuals, the wine, and anything else you acquire. But why? You said we already met our orders."

Nath grinned again and clapped Samuel on the shoulder. "We did, but think how pleased Mr. Derby will be when we exceed them. He wants more than minimum results from his captains, and I didn't start out well with him. This will make up for the loss of the *Sally*. My duty to Mr. Derby is to maximize his profits, and that is what I shall do."

"I'll put the lads to work at dawn, Captain Silsbee." Samuel winked and saluted.

"See that you do." Nath laughed and went to his cabin.

While Nath acquired Madeira wine and ship's stores he could sell on Isle de France, Samuel kept the crew busy. In three weeks, the *Benjamin* was ready to depart, except for some tallow candles that had yet to arrive.

"Shall we shove off now?" Samuel asked. "Not really worth waiting for candles. Sooner we get back to Isle de France, the sooner we go home."

"We'll give it a few more days while I settle up," Nath said.

On shore, Nath made his way to the tavern.

"You still here?" The barman slid a glass of Madeira to Nath.

"Just waiting for the last bits."

"You should go."

Nath narrowed his eyes. "What have you heard?"

The barman shrugged. "You go with tide. I tell your friends settle bills."

The barman picked up Nath's glass and wiped the counter before moving to serve others.

## Isle de France

Standing at the *Benjamin*'s quarterdeck, Nath watched the shoreline as Samuel deftly steered the ship through the channel leading into Port Louis.

Nath mentally congratulated himself on his successful voyage. *After I trade the goods I picked up in Cape Town, the* Benjamin's *voyage will exceed even Mr. Derby's expectation, and I'll have a good profit on my adventure cargo.* Nath rubbed his hands together and smiled with satisfaction.

"Looks like we're the only trading vessel here," Samuel called.

"Excellent. We'll shift our cargo and load up on coffee and spices."

Trading was brisk and profits high. Two weeks after arriving, Nath sat in his cabin doing accounts. Church bells rang from the settlement. Nath chuckled to himself, glad the bells were a reminder of Sunday mass tomorrow and not a saint's festival. Trade had been delayed almost two weeks on his first visit, and then he was caught in the capricious six-month embargo. Not this time, though.

Someone rapped on the cabin door.

"Message fer you, suh." It was Robert, the cook.

Nath beckoned him inside. Smiling, he reached out his hand. "How are your feet these days?"

"They work fine. Ah keep the cane more for looks than anythin' else. People feel sorry for an ole man wid a cane."

"I know I certainly do."

"Ye did yer best, and ah'm doin' fine now. Still on de boat an' not stuck in a strange place." Robert nodded. "Ah'll leave you to it."

Nath shook his head in awe. *The man underwent the horrendous ordeal of my ignorant exertions and lived to tell the tale. God is indeed generous.*

Breaking the wax seal, Nath read the note from his agent ashore.

The council held a meeting last night and decided to post another embargo. *Damme! I am not spending another six months sitting at Port Louis.*

Nath shrugged into his coat, grabbed his tricorn hat, and went topside.

"Samuel, keep it quiet, but we leave tonight. I'm going ashore for exit papers and additional men to prepare the ship."

Nath grabbed two men to manage the tender and steered for shore.

The harbormaster's office was at the front of a small warehouse on the quay.

"Captain Sizbee." The dapper official stood. "What brings you to my humble bureau?"

"Monsieur Martin, I've had a change of heart. I find I can't bear being separated from my fiancée a moment longer than necessary, so instead of leaving three days from now as I originally applied, I want to leave on the next tide."

"You have not mentioned your *femme* before. She must be very beautiful for you to give up trade opportunities."

Nath grinned. "She holds my heart."

"I never took you for a *romantique*. I sympathize, but it is a difficult matter to change the papers." Martin shrugged. "My clerk cannot do it by this evening's tide."

Nath changed tactics. "These are dangerous times for you, are they not, Monsieur Martin?"

"One adjusts with the wind." Martin shrugged again.

"But still," Nate pressed. "One hears terrible things about conditions in France. The Jacobins keep the guillotine busy, do they not?"

"So I am told." Martin gave Nath a speculative look. "It is better to be here than in Paris. The weather is good, and the women are friendly. I am not so fortunate as you. No *femme* waits for me."

"American *mademoiselles* would flock to a man of your education and caliber. But perhaps that situation does not interest you." Nath shrugged.

"How would a humble man such as myself reach America?"

"Many American ships come through Port Louis. One of them could take you back. In fact, since the *Benjamin* will depart soon, you could travel with us."

Nath put his hand into his coat pocket and grabbed a few Spanish dollars.

"Do you think your clerk could expedite my paperwork so the *Benjamin* can sail with the tide? I would be most grateful."

Nath shook Martin's hand, leaving the coins behind. Martin put his hand in his pocket, then withdrew it, and stroked his mustache.

"*Oué.* Let it be so. I shall bring the papers to you on the *Benjamin* tonight during dinner."

"I shall greet you then. It will be a fine night for a voyage."

Outside, Nath let out a breath of relief. If the harbormaster was on his ship, the man could hardly prevent their departure. *Can I trust the man not to go back on his word? It's the only way Martin can get to America on military pay, so he'll keep his agreement. I hope.*

Nath cast his eyes over warehouse workers on the wharf.

"Jacques," he called out to a burly man and reached into his pocket again.

"Capitaine Sizbee, you have work for me?"

"I want you and four of your mates to get the *Benjamin* ready to depart tonight."

Jacques stroked his short beard. "You are clever, Capitaine Sizbee. Did a bird tell you about the embargo?"

Nath shrugged and offered his hand to Jacques, who waved it away.

"Birds are very clever," Jacques commented. "They don't like to leave their nests."

"I've seen them fly out to sea during the day and back to shore in the evening. Do you think they wish they had a boat?"

"Are you thinking a cutter or something smaller . . . for the birds?"

"Seabirds need room to spread their wings." Nath winked. "But a cutter would probably hold them all."

Jacques laughed and held out his hand. "*Bon.* We will fly with you."

Nath rubbed the coins into Jacques's palm. Jacques laughed again and waved to his crew.

The *Benjamin* was ready to depart before the port bell rang to summon people home for dinner. Jacques's crew slipped into the cutter. Martin pulled his dinghy next to the cutter, handed Jacques the dinghy's rope, and hauled himself up the *Benjamin*'s ladder to the main deck.

"You have the papers?" Nath asked.

"*Oué.*" Martin patted his front coat pocket.

Nath gave the signal to slip the cables, and the *Benjamin* noiselessly floated into the channel. By the time the dinner hour was over, the *Benjamin* was on her way to Isle de Bourbon.

*Isle de Bourbon*

"Saint-Denis is a small port compared to Saint Louis," Samuel commented.

"It is," Nath agreed. "But it's still worth stopping here a few days to trade before we head home. We've been out long enough, and we have a solid return cargo, but a little extra never goes amiss. I'll call on the governor before we start trading. I don't want another surprise embargo."

Wearing his dress coat and freshly shaved, Nath strode down the short wharf to the governor's house.

A footman with rumpled livery opened the door.

"Capitaine Sizbee. It is good to see you again, sir. Have you run away from Isle de France?"

"I'm calling for Governor Vigoureux. Is he in?" Nath handed the man his hat.

"*Oué.* He is in the morning room enjoying a cup of coffee. Shall you be joining him?"

"Please."

Feeling at home in the house he had visited at the beginning of his voyage, Nath knocked on the open door to the morning room.

"Jean-Baptiste, are you ready for company this morning?"

"Of course, *mon ami*. What brings you to my humble island? Did you run away from Isle de France?"

"You're the second person to ask me that. I did not 'run away,' as you implied. I simply left during the night."

"Did you secure the proper exit papers so I don't have to detain you?"

"I did better than that. I brought the harbormaster with me."

Jean-Baptiste laughed for several minutes.

"So long as my colleagues don't follow you here, all will be well. How long will you stay?"

"*Merci*," Nath said as the footman brought a fresh cup and poured coffee for him. "I'll stay a day or two to take on provisions and test the trade."

"Can you take your provisions on today and leave tonight?"

"I can if you wish it. Is there anything I should know?"

"*Non.* I simply do not want to see you injured, especially since you are polite enough to call upon me, which most ship captains are not. If harm were to come upon you, it would embarrass me."

Nath stirred sugar into his coffee. "Are you concerned about the new French government?"

Jean-Baptiste shrugged. "I'm always concerned about the government. And also how people respond to it. It would be safer for you to leave tonight if you can. Admiral Saint-Félix is hiding somewhere on the island."

"Do you know where he is?"

"*Non.* Nor do I wish to. He remains loyal to the king. He also annoys the people."

"And you?" Nath asked.

Jean-Baptiste shrugged. "I am loyal to the government, but . . ." He shrugged again.

"These are difficult times."

"*Oué.* One cannot be too careful."

Nath stood. "I'll be on my way, then."

The men shook hands. Nath saw himself to the door and waited while the footman brought his hat.

"A moment, *Capitaine.*" Nath's host pulled him aside. "No one can know what I've said to you."

Nath smiled. "You are a most gracious host, sir." He said his farewells and left the governor's house.

Mentally going over his conversation with the governor, Nath decided to return to the ship. It would be prudent to slip away. When he mounted the quarterdeck, Samuel passed Nath a spyglass.

"We have company."

Nath looked at the French brig bobbing at anchor. The crew didn't seem particularly busy, and the gunports were closed. Longboats ferried men and supplies from the wharf.

"Do you think the ship is here by coincidence, or did she come from Isle de France?"

"Depends how much risk you're comfortable with, sir," Samuel replied.

"At the moment, not that much. Assuming nothing changes, we'll slip out when it's dark. Wrap the winch to muffle bringing up the anchor. But be careful. I'm sure the Frenchman also has a spyglass."

Under cover of darkness, the *Benjamin* again silently drifted through a channel to open sea.

"We're clear," Nath said. "Hoist sails and make haste. Once the brig realizes we're gone, she'll come after us."

At dawn, Nath held up his spyglass.

*Damme!*

"She's following us with full sail. Keep us going as fast as you can."

Nath set a course for the Cape of Good Hope and closely monitored every change in the wind. As twilight dimmed the sky, the brig broke off her pursuit and turned back.

*Thank God!* Nath heaved a sigh of relief and went belowdecks.

# Lizzie Rowell

*December 1793*
*Salem*

The sea breeze hit Lizzie head-on when the wagon turned onto Derby Street. She held her swaddled infant close to her body and covered the small face with her cloak. The farmer guided his horses into Ship Tavern's side yard. Vapor poured out of their nostrils.

"Wait a bit. Ah'll hep you down."

The farmer dismounted, reached into the wagon bed, and pulled out a torn valise wedged around baskets of root vegetables.

"Hallo! What did ya bring us?"

Lizzie's face lit up. "Samson, I am so glad to see you."

"Lizzie? That you? Lemme hep you down."

Samson lifted his arms and stopped. Lizzie moved so Samson could see her daughter's face. "Samson, meet Sophia," she said shyly.

"Well, isn't she a picture? Hold on to her, and ah'll get you both inside."

Samson picked Lizzie up from the wagon before escorting her to a stool near the kitchen fire. "You picked a cold day to visit us," Samson said.

Lizzie looked around. "Is Matt here?"

"In front wid Miz Shipman. They clearin' up from breakfast. I'm sure he'll be here soon. Ah got to help Mr. Jackson unload."

Lizzie nodded. Judging by the almost empty stewpot, with its congealing contents still over the fire, Lizzie guessed the wharf workers had finished their breakfast, and it was too early for late-morning patrons. She clutched her babe. *This has to work!*

Samson came through the kitchen with baskets of potatoes and other winter vegetables that he stowed in the makeshift pantry. The passage door behind the bar opened.

Matt strode into the kitchen, saw Lizzie, and stopped abruptly.

"Lizzie, you're back. I didn't expect to see you again. And you brought your baby. Girl or boy?"

"Sophia." Lizzie passed the baby to Matt, happy to have her arms empty for a few minutes so she could take off her hat and cloak. "She looks good on you. Is Cousin Anna about?"

"She's in front. Are you here for a visit, or hoping to stay? We lost a couple girls, so we need help in the kitchen. I'll tell her you're here." Matt carried Baby Sophia into the front room.

Five minutes later, Anna Shipman carried the baby back into the kitchen.

"Who's a bonny girl?" Anna cooed. "It must be you." Anna passed the baby to Lizzie. "She's starting to fuss. You need to feed her. Matt, go bring down the Moses basket from the attic. So Lizzie, heard from Captain Crowninshield, have you?"

Lizzie hung her head. "No, Cousin. He left me coin, but . . ."

"You've spent it."

"Rent is expensive, even in Danvers. And I had to get things for the baby and keep her warm and pay the midwife." Tears leaked out of Lizzie's eyes.

"I don't know what to do. I didn't listen to you and got myself into this mess, but it isn't the baby's fault. Can't you help me?"

"Why didn't you call on Captain Crowninshield's family? Sophia might be their first grandchild. Maybe they'll take her in."

Lizzie's jaw dropped open. "I won't give away my baby. Can't you help me? Please! Just until Geordie comes back in the spring. I'm sure he'll take care of us."

"He's a swell," Matt said, reentering the kitchen. "Just because he got you into trouble doesn't mean he'll help you out of it. If ye're lucky, he might keep you on the side."

"That's enough, Matt," Anna said. "Did you find the basket?"

"I did," he said, setting the infant carrier on the table. "And I put a soft blanket in it. Mam, we can help Lizzie and ourselves. We need a couple girls to work in the kitchen, and she already knows what needs doing."

"I don't like it. Lizzie will set a bad example for any other girls that work for us. They'll disregard my advice and expect us to help them if they get into trouble."

"Mam, Lizzie's our flesh and blood, and so is Sophia. And we need the help."

Anna stood before the fire, thinking.

*Please, God, let her help us. I promise I won't ask for anything else. Ever.*

"Very well, Lizzie. I'll give you a chance. You can stay until Captain Crowninshield's ship returns. Then, you're his responsibility."

Lizzie jumped up to embrace her cousin, who weakly patted her on the back.

"That's enough. I expect you to work hard in exchange for your room and board. And you'll have to look after the babe. I'm not running a nursery."

"I swear I will, Cousin Anna. I'll be so useful, you won't know how you got on without me."

"Matt, get back to work in front. Lizzie, get an apron off the hook by the pantry and help Samson with the lunch buffet. And you . . ."

Anna looked at the baby. "Try not to cry too loudly. Men come here to relax, not to hear what they come here to get away from."

# Hasket Derby

*January 1794*
*Hasket Derby's House*

"Welcome home, sir. Mrs. Derby is in the drawing room."

Hasket handed his outerwear to his butler. "Is she alone?"

"Yes, sir. Shall I bring refreshments?"

"No. See that we're not disturbed."

Hasket tapped on the drawing room door before slipping inside.

Eliza sat on a damask-covered sofa near the fire. Candles on a nearby table provided just enough light for her to see her needlework. Hasket paused a moment to consider what a picture she made, what a picture she had always made.

Eliza glanced up from her needlework. "Hasket? What on earth are you doing home during business hours?"

*What indeed?*

Hasket kissed his wife's cheek before taking a seat in the wingback chair across from the sofa.

"You missed Betsey. She took her brood home before it was full dark. We're making plans." Eliza smiled in anticipation. "She'll give birth in a couple months, and when we introduce her baby to our circle, we'll reintroduce Betsey to society. We'll use the opportunity to overcome her husband's lower social status and bring Betsey up to ours. She'll be by my side everywhere I go."

Hasket rose and poured himself a brandy from the sideboard. "Anyone who looks down on Captain West isn't worthy of our patronage. Do you care for anything, Eliza?"

"No. Betsey and I had a glass of Madeira earlier. Explain what brings you home at this hour. If you're going to change your habits, I have to reconsider our household routine."

"I need your opinion on something. It concerns the *Grand Turk*."

Eliza drew her eyebrows together. "Didn't you send her to Virginia?"

"I did. I filled her with sugar and barreled beef and told Mosely to bring back tobacco."

"*Hmmm.* She went out last November. Shouldn't she be back by now?"

"So I expected." Hasket poured himself another brandy. "You're sure you won't join me?"

"Will I need fortification?"

Hasket rolled his shoulders. "You might. I've had a letter from Mosely. Trade has not gone as I anticipated. The *Turk* has been at Petersburg over six weeks and only sold half her sugar."

"That could be because the *Turk* is such a large ship. At the time you designed her, I mentioned she might be too large to be efficient."

Hasket felt a flash of irritation. *You're talking about the queen of my fleet.*

He rubbed the back of his neck. "So you did. Will you gloat now?"

Eliza reached for her husband's hand. "It's a bad circumstance, but you'll find a clever way through it."

"It's not just the sugar. If it was, I'd order Mosely back. But the price of tobacco is high, and we've had little luck negotiating a better price. Thus far, we've loaded only one hundred fifty-eight hogsheads. Our agent is going directly to the planters to buy tobacco at a more reasonable price. Meanwhile, Mosely expects to spend the winter anchored in the James River."

"You still could order her home. While she stays in Virginia, we pay her expenses." Eliza narrowed her eyes. "On the other hand, at least she isn't on the high seas, vulnerable to privateers. We haven't earned our costs back on her yet."

"I'm aware of that, but I can't keep her at home just because the French and English sweep the seas. She needs to earn her keep."

Eliza squeezed Hasket's hand. "She will. The *Turk* will be back in the spring with enough tobacco to earn us a fortune in Europe. They'll be in very short supply by then, and Europeans do enjoy smoking Virginia tobacco. Whatever we expend on the tobacco, I'm sure we'll triple it. It's not like you to be so low. Remember, the *Grand Turk* is only a ship, even if she is your favorite."

## Hasket Derby

*April 1794*
*Derby Wharf*

Hasket stood at the end of his wharf staring at the horizon without seeing it. Behind and beside him, he heard the creak of wooden vessels and the muffled shouts of deckhands and dockworkers. The scent of hot pitch floated in the air. Wind whipped up waves in the harbor. Hasket closed his eyes and let the air currents surround him as he ruminated on where to send his ships.

*I'm a fool,* he thought, *to still focus on the way Eliza nonchalantly dismissed the* Grand Turk. Four months later, her reference that the queen of his fleet was *only a ship* still rankled. She was so much more. She was material proof of how far he had risen above his father, brothers, and competitors. He, who had never been to sea, owned a ship the equal of any East Indiaman. *It's only natural for me to protect her from English privateers in case they venture north of the French West Indies. That's why I ordered her home even without a full cargo.*

Hasket's thoughts drifted to the unpredictable dangers his ships faced. French privateers captured the *Lighthouse* on her way to France and the *Rose* on her return from the French West Indies. *What is the point of funding a government that cannot protect its citizens from pirates? Thank God the* Turk *returned safely, but what am I to do with her?*

Hasket patted the letter inside his coat pocket. It was from his agent in Hamburg. He'd read it so many times that the thick paper was creased and the ink partially smudged. As Eliza had predicted, the European market clamored for tobacco, as well as coffee, sugar, indigo, saltpeter, ginger, cotton, and wool.

Hasket ordered Captain Mosely to assemble the cargo, and two months later, he stood with his son and a festive audience by the *Grand Turk*'s pier. Fair winds filled the sails as men tossed the last mooring lines off the ship. Hasket took a deep breath and considered his calculations. The *Turk*'s cargo should fetch enough profit for her to sail from Hamburg directly to Saint Petersburg, where she would obtain ship's stores for his warehouses and some personal items for his family—bed ticking for new mattresses, and sable furs to make muffs and stoles for his wife and daughters. And for himself, two pairs of Russian geese and two pairs of ducks to create flocks at his Danvers farm. The ship and half her cargo were insured. God willing, all would go well.

Hasket raised his arm in farewell.

"Missing her already, Father?" Elias asked.

"She's a ship like any other," Hasket muttered. "Providing she doesn't sink in a storm or fall to privateers, there's nothing to miss."

# Captain George Crowninshield Jr.

*June 1794*
*Union Wharf*

With his logbook under his arm, Geordie sauntered up the wharf to his family's counting house. It was good to be back in Salem. He'd supervise the *Polly & Sally*'s overhaul and familiarize himself with the family's new ship.

"Geordie! Get in here."

Geordie's younger brother Richard barreled out the warehouse doors and pulled him in for a hug. Geordie clapped him on the back a few times and pulled away.

"I forget what a swarthy fellow you are." Geordie laughed.

"Well, we can't all look like a haystack. Some of us have to look like Mame. It's good to have you back. From your letters, it sounds a successful voyage."

"It was. On your behalf, I brought back sixty-eight thousand pounds of sugar, thirteen thousand pounds of pepper, and fifteen hundred pounds of coffee. Mind you, don't swamp the market."

Richard reached out his hand. "I'll take your logbook."

"Did Sir promote you? He usually wants to see it first."

"He's busy with the new ship. Said I should start the accounting."

Geordie squeezed his brother's cheek. "Guess that means you're a full partner now."

"I always was, you buffoon. See the sign up there? It says "and Sons," not "George the Second and Assorted Others." Come on. I'll drop your logbook on my desk and stand you for drinks at Ship Tavern."

Geordie rubbed the back of his neck. "Not sure I'm welcome there. Had a little set-to with the owner's son before I left."

Richard raised his eyebrows. "Had your way with one of the barmaids?"

"In a manner of speaking. She was the owner's cousin, or some such."

"Who cares? Coin is coin, and Anna Shipman is always pleased to take mine."

Geordie shrugged. "It's probably all blown over by now."

In the lawn area outside the Ship, men gambled and played skittles. Geordie followed Richard inside and paused to let his eyes adjust to the darkness. He spotted his first mate playing cards and nodded. Richard returned from the bar with two tankards of ale.

"We'll take a table in the back, and I'll tell you about our new ship."

"Who was behind the bar?"

"One of the new barmaids—though she's not a maid anymore."

"How would you know?"

Richard waggled his eyebrows. "You're not the only one to taste what's on offer."

Geordie chuckled. "So, did Sir name the new ship yet?"

"It's not official. He likes the name *Belisarius*. Says he wants the ship to dominate the Mediterranean like this general did."

"Huh. What does Mame think?"

Richard shook his head. "She thinks naming a ship for a Roman general is pretentious. She has a point, but Sir is pretty fixated on the name."

"And this ship. Will it live up to the name?"

"Well, she's got a copper bottom, and her hull is pierced for sixteen guns. So, she'll be well protected. As to her reputation, that will probably be up to you. Nothing is certain, but you're the obvious choice as master. She's in Enos Briggs's shipyard. We can walk over there if you like, and you—"

"You're back, then," an icy female voice said. "I heard your ship arrived, but I didn't think you'd show your face in here."

Richard jumped in surprise and spilled part of his drink onto his shirt.

"*Damme!* Don't sneak up on your patrons, woman. And I'm in here most days. What are you going on about?"

Geordie chuckled. "I believe, dear brother, she was talking to me. As I mentioned earlier, instead of wishing me a good voyage, her son told me to stay away from the Ship. Yet, here I am, a regular patron back from the sea." Geordie gave her a cocky grin.

"It's a pity you didn't fall off your ship and drown," Anna said.

"I have excellent reflexes," Geordie replied.

"Not where it counts. You left our Lizzie with a memento of your presence."

"I don't know what you're talking about."

"What's she going on about, Geordie?" Richard asked.

"I thought she had the flux or a fever," Geordie murmured.

Richard shook his brother's arm. "Geordie? What's wrong with you, man? You've gone pale."

*Lizzie told me the truth. She said she was with child. I thought it was a play for sympathy or a trick.*

"How is Lizzie?" Geordie asked with a dry throat.

"She's fine, no thanks to you."

"I left her with coin in case she needed it." Geordie held Anna's gaze with an icy stare. "Did you throw her out?"

"I run a respectable house. She knew that when she came here."

"For pity's sake, Geordie, what's going on?" Richard asked. "We're attracting attention we don't need."

Geordie shook his head and swallowed some ale.

"I'll tell you plain what's going on," Anna said in a tense voice. "Your brother, the great Captain Crowninshield, dallied with my cousin. He ruined her and left her without a care while she bore the consequences. And now she works as a scullery maid in my kitchen with her baby in a basket. That's what's going on. Come with me, and I'll introduce you to Lizzie's shame."

"Geordie." Richard tugged his brother's arm. "Just because she has a baby doesn't mean you gave it to her. Don't be a fool."

"Doesn't matter who gave it to her. She's still . . ." Geordie swallowed.

# Lizzie Rowell

Lizzie patted Sophia's back and laid her swaddled infant into the Moses basket before returning her attention to the never-ending stack of pewter plates and iron pots next to the scrubbing bucket. Cousin Anna gave her food, clothing, and a roof over her head, but sometimes Lizzie thought she'd be better off in the workhouse. *Someday, when I'm stronger, I'll take Sophia and run away.*

Lizzie picked up a wet scouring cloth and began scrubbing sand over an iron spatula that was thick with grease. Instead of thinking about her aching back and red hands, Lizzie daydreamed about the farm where she grew up. It would be a perfect place for Sophia. *I could go inland and become a farm laborer, looking after chickens or something.* Lizzie sighed and reached for the next plate. She heard the door to the bar open but didn't look up. No one called her unless plates ran low in the tavern.

"Lizzie? Is that you?"

Lizzie stopped scrubbing. *I know that voice. It sounds like . . .*

"Look in the basket, and see what you left behind," Cousin Anna muttered.

Boots crossed the kitchen. Lizzie winced. *I have to sweep the floor out, and I don't need extra mud.*

"When was it born?" a low voice asked impatiently.

"November," Lizzie's cousin said. "You can count the months yourself."

"Doesn't prove anything."

"She's so small," a softer male voice said.

Lizzie shook her head. *I thought I was done imagining he'd come for me.*

"Don't claim it, for goodness sake," the deeper voice said. "You've no proof it's yours."

Lizzie stiffened. Someone stood behind her. Someone who smelled like the sea. Like Geordie. She plunged her hands back into the hot water and swiped at the plates.

"Lizzie."

A calloused hand pulled her away from the washtub. Lizzie kept her eyes on the floor. *I've lost my mind.*

"Lizzie, won't you look at me?"

Lizzie raised her eyes to Geordie's fallen face. "Go away."

Geordie shook his head. "You don't understand. I'm here to take care of you. I dreamed of you the entire time I was at sea. I saw you in the stars, so near and yet so far. Lizzie, I should have been here. I'm so sorry."

"Stop talking," the other voice said.

"Lizzie. Lambkin. I'm here now. Let me take care of you both."

"The child isn't yours, Geordie. Back away!"

The other man's angry voice echoed in Lizzie's head. *What child is he talking about?* Slowly, she lifted her hand to touch Geordie's face.

"You want to take care of us?" she whispered.

"I've never meant anything more. I'll take care of you both."

"He's lying," Anna said calmly. "That's his guilt talking. He'll never marry you."

"I don't care as long as we're together."

"Are you sure, Geordie?" the lower voice said.

"Will you come with me now?"

A smile ghosted over Lizzie's lips. She left her apron on the table and picked up the basket holding her baby.

Geordie put an arm around Lizzie's shoulders. "Come. We'll take rooms in town until we find a cottage."

"If you leave, you can't come back again," Anna said.

"She has my brother's protection, you miserable woman," Richard snarled before throwing a few copper coins on the kitchen table. They twirled and bounced, until one of them rolled off the edge.

# Captain Nathaniel Silsbee

*July 1794*
*Salem Harbor*

"Home again." Samuel grinned at the *Benjamin*'s captain.

"That we are, Samuel." Nath waved his hat at onlookers on the Neck. *It is,* he thought, *a beautiful day for our homecoming.*

Nath clapped Samuel on the shoulder. "We've had our share of adventures on this voyage."

"Yep. Who knew you were such a dab hand with string and pair of scissors."

Nath grimaced. "Not a situation I care to repeat. But Robert seems fully recovered. I'd say the voyage is a success in all categories. We have a good cargo, high profits, no loss of life, and the *Benjamin* is in good shape after a two-year voyage. Mr. Derby will be pleased."

"Aye. The *Benjamin* is a good ship, and you bring good luck to everyone aboard. I'd be glad to stand you a round at the Ship."

"I accept." Nath grinned. "Now, bring her up to Mr. Derby's wharf. Looks like the First Pier is waiting for us."

Nath went below to finish packing his sea chest. The days of despair were over, the disastrous voyages with the *Betsey* and the *Sally* mere unhappy memories.

Sitting in front of Hasket Derby's desk the next day, Nath watched his employer quickly glance through the accounts while he tried not to fidget. He hoped the fact that Mr. Derby had called him into his office instead of sending him to his son Elias was a good sign. Mr. Derby seldom took time to meet with coastal captains unless they were friends of long standing, and since his son had joined the counting house, he didn't meet with junior captains at all.

"Congratulations, Captain Silsbee. You've made an outstanding voyage. The exact figures aren't tallied yet, but it appears you brought in a profit above one hundred percent. Quite a change from your previous voyages." Hasket smiled.

"Yes, sir. Thank you, sir."

"Have you added up the profits from your adventure cargo?"

"I have, sir. By my calculations, I have a profit of around four thousand dollars."

"Sounds like you'll be investing in your own ships soon."

"I have hopes, but first I have a few family accounts to settle."

"*Hmmm.* I'd like you to supervise refitting the *Benjamin* for her next voyage. I'll be sending her to Amsterdam. Have you been there?"

"No, sir. But after visiting Cape Town and Batavia, I have an idea the city will be full of canals."

Hasket gave Nath a calculating look. "How would you like to find out for yourself?"

Nath caught his breath. "I would like that very much."

"Good. Consider yourself captain of the *Benjamin.* She'll depart as soon as we load her next cargo. And take your brother William with you. He's ready to go out as a clerk."

Nath found himself unable to suppress a grin. "Thank you, sir. Does William know his good fortune yet?"

Hasket smiled broadly and stood. "I thought you would like to tell him." He held out his hand.

Nath grabbed his employer's hand in both of his, almost pumping the man's arm. "Thank you for everything, sir. You have no idea what your faith in me means."

Having Hasket Derby's confidence was a greater victory than outwitting the French.

Nath descended the stairs contemplating the satisfying change in his fortunes. *I thought Mr. Derby would be pleased, but I didn't expect to have a billet for the* Benjamin's *next voyage out.* On the ground floor, Nath turned to the head clerk's desk.

"Captain Silsbee," Ebenezer greeted him with a smile. "It's good to have you back. I have your wages here if you will sign for them. Your other funds will be here once the accounting is complete."

Nath nodded.

Ebenezer turned the account book to face Nath, who signed with a flourish and accepted a combination of coins and banknotes drawn on the Massachusetts Bank.

"Take a few days," Ebenezer said. "Refitting won't start before the cargo is unloaded."

"Very well," Nath said. "I'll just stop at the Ship and then be on my way home. I don't see my brother. Is he here?"

"William is working with the inventory lists. I'll send him to the Ship when he finishes."

"I'll only stay for one drink."

Ebenezer shrugged. "You might want to have words with other seamen on sailing conditions. There are plenty of privateers about."

*If I start that conversation, I'll never get home.*

Inside the Ship, Nath saw Matt wiping down the bar.

"Captain Silsbee! It's good to see you, sir."

Nath reached out to shake Matt's hand. "Thought you'd be at sea by now."

"Not yet. Mam wants me here. What can I serve you?"

"Just some small beer. I won't stop for long."

"Did you run into any Frenchies while you were out?"

"I did." Looking around, Nath spotted a familiar face in the crowd. "In fact, I see one of them now." Nath picked up his drink and headed over to the man. "Monsieur Martin, I see you found your way to the Ship."

"*Oué.*" Martin kissed the barmaid's wrist. "The women are beautiful, as you promised."

The young woman giggled and disappeared into the kitchen.

"Be careful, or Anna Shipman will throw you out."

The Frenchman shrugged. "I will plead long days at sea." Martin put down his empty wine glass. "The wine is sour. Samuel told me about a *pension* where I can stay a few days. I must inquire. I will see you soon, *mon ami.*"

Nath watched the Frenchman walk outside. *I hope he finds his way.*

"Nath! Mr. Sims told me you'd wait for me here."

Nath greeted his brother William with a large hug.

"I was lucky to get away. Your cargo is going to alter all my inventory figures," William said.

"Well, you won't be doing inventory much longer. Though, as my clerk, you'll have to monitor the *Benjamin*'s cargo."

William's jaw dropped. "Clerk? You mean I'm going to sea with you at last?"

"You are. As soon as the *Benjamin*'s next cargo is loaded, we'll be off to Amsterdam."

William's face split into a large grin. "I never thought it would happen. The *Benjamin* is a success, then?"

"Very much so. I have enough to buy back our house and land from Father's creditors as well as part ownership in another ship. We're on our way at last."

"This calls for a celebration. Quick! We have to go home and tell Mother and Sara and Zach. This is huge."

Nath saw awe in William's eyes.

"You've done it, Nath, just like you promised. You restored our family and found me a berth at sea. Mother will be so happy."

# Captain George Crowninshield Jr.

*August 1794*
*On the Road to Danvers*

A flicker of fireflies blinked by the side of the road from South Fields. Geordie gazed at the insects from his gig's seat and absentmindedly slapped Pompey's reins. *Sir certainly enjoys Roman names. Seems like we always have a horse named Pompey. Perhaps I should continue the tradition if I decide to start a family.*

Geordie chuckled. *What an absurd thought. I already have a family,* he mused. Except he didn't. Not really. He would never acknowledge Lizzie or the child. And so far, she hadn't asked him to.

Most evenings, Geordie left Briggs's shipyard on Stage Point, or the family counting house, and took the gig to Danvers, where he leased a small cottage for Lizzie. He liked spending the evening with her. If the baby was awake, he played with her until Lizzie scooped her up and settled her into a small cot for the night. Seeing their faces together, Geordie felt a tug on his heart. But it wasn't strong enough to tie him down.

At the cottage, Lizzie and Geordie sat outside in the twilight. When he wrapped his arm around her, Lizzie put her head on his shoulder.

Every night, she asked him to stay. And every night, he declined and explained that he had to be down at the shipyard. That the *Belisarius* was the best ship the Crowninshields had ever built. That she'd be the real star of the company.

"As captain, I am involved at every stage of the *Belisarius*'s construction," he said. He felt her stiffen in his arms at the mention of his true passion. "I know all her secrets and how to sail her under all conditions."

Lizzie stayed quiet.

"The *Belisarius* is a beautiful ship already—not as beautiful as you," Geordie said, quickly correcting himself. But the compliment felt hollow even to his ears.

"I'm not a ship," Lizzie reminded him.

She began stroking Geordie's thigh. It was almost like their time together at the Ship. *Almost.* But the moment was ruined.

"When do you leave?" she asked Geordie, pulling away from his embrace to look him in the eye.

So he told her the truth. "If we continue at our current rate of progress, she'll launch in October. Then we have to load her cargo. I'm already assembling items in our warehouse."

"Where will you sail?"

"India, of course."

"You'll be gone so long." Lizzie sighed.

*She never sighed like that before, as if I'm disappointing her. When I was young, Mame sighed like that when I didn't live up to her expectations, which was most days.*

Feeling vindictive, Geordie grinned. "We'll be gone a year or so, depending on the trade." He stood, then backed Pompey into the gig's traces.

The color had drained from Lizzie's face, but she stood too, as if resigned to her fate as his hapless mistress. The fire was still in her eyes, though.

"Give us a kiss, then," Geordie said, as if he didn't care. What he meant was, *Don't attach yourself to me. You've forced me into a situation I don't want.*

Lizzie threw her arms around Geordie's neck. Before she could take it further, he kissed her forehead, mounted the gig, and slapped the reins. He knew she watched him leave, but he didn't look back.

# Lizzie Rowell

*I don't know why I wave,* Lizzie thought. *He never looks back.*

Lizzie went inside and lit a candle. The one-room cottage was cozy. It would be snug in the winter. But it was too small for a family—too small to contain Geordie. And the rope bed. *Well, that's too small for him too.*

Lizzie knew that Geordie cared about her and Sophia, but Cousin Anna was right. He might not marry anyone, but he definitely wouldn't marry Lizzie. At the Ship, his brother had looked down his nose at her like she was trash. Geordie didn't look at her like that. But he didn't look at her the way he did before he went to sea either. He was more excited about his new ship than he was about his daughter.

Lizzie stripped down to her chemise and lay on top of her quilt. Outside, crickets chirped loudly. She imagined they were mocking her for being foolish enough to entangle herself with someone like Geordie Crowninshield.

# Captain Nathaniel Silsbee

*September 1794*
*Derby Wharf*

Nath's new first mate, Richard Smith, nudged his shoulder and gave him an apologetic look. Richard was a good man, but it was their first sail together. Nath missed Samuel's ready confidence but understood his friend's decision to stay ashore for his wife's first lying-in.

"We're ready to cast off as soon as you come aboard," Richard said.

"Very well." Nath nodded and returned his attention to his youngest brother.

"So, Zach, technically, you're head of the house now."

Sara snorted and rolled her eyes. "So long as he does what Mother says."

"That's enough, Sara." Nath looked back down at Zach and hoped his brother would have a growth spurt soon. "Our sister is correct, though. She and Mother will make the decisions, but I expect you to keep everything running smoothly."

"Yes, sir." Zach kept his eyes on the ground.

"Look at me." Tears glazed the boy's eyes. "Ah, I see. No need for that. By the time we get back, you'll be the star of Mr. Derby's counting house. You'll be going out with us soon." Nath winked. *The boy has a lot on his skinny shoulders.*

"Do you mean it, Nath?"

"Yes. You just need to grow a bit more." He shook Zach's hand.

Mother Sarah reached for Nath's arm. "Bring William back to us."

"Of course, Mother. I guarantee it. And you've nothing to worry about. The house and lands are yours, and you have funds on account with Mr. Derby." *Not to mention the insurance I took out in case something happens to us.*

Nath flinched slightly when his mother reached out her hand to cup his cheek. He preferred to avoid public displays of emotion. "You're a fine son, and all. God be with you."

Before Nath could reply, Elias Derby stepped forward.

"Don't mean to interrupt family farewells." Elias smirked. "I came to wish you Godspeed on behalf of my father. I have his addendum to your written orders. I presume you know the contents. Follow them exactly, unless conditions require a change, or you discover better opportunities."

Nath gave a casual salute from his hat brim. "I shall read them with interest."

"No doubt. I wish you good fortune, with a quick and safe return."

"Excuse me, Captain Silsbee," Richard said. "We need to catch the tide."

"William," Nath called. "If you plan to sail with me, it's time to board."

William hugged his mother and sister, patted Zach's shoulder, and climbed the gangplank.

Standing amidships, the brothers watched dockhands release the mooring ropes. Nath left William at the rail watching Salem recede into the distance. He remembered the first time he saw the sight, his heart full of fear and apprehension, without a penny to his name. Now he had $2,000 invested in his own adventure cargo, and, unlike the spoiled cod his father gave him for his first voyage, he'd provided William with enough investment for a strong start. With the first part of his pledge fulfilled, Nath could begin achieving the second, enough funds to comfortably retire from the sea.

# Captain Elias Derby

*September 19, 1794*
*Hannah Brown Fitch's Home*

Elias and Zeke stood in a cramped side room while Elias straightened his brother's cravat and patted his shoulders.

"Are you ready to become a married man?"

"Probably not," Zeke replied, "but I'm more than ready to move out of Father's house. Hannah's a pleasant girl. I'm sure we'll make a go of it."

Elias raised his eyebrows. "Pleasant? You want a lifetime of pleasant? Seems like you'd want a wife who could match your wit."

Zeke snorted. "No one in this family appreciates my wit, least of all you. At least she can tell when I'm being humorous."

Elias cracked the door as a young woman passed by on her way into the drawing room. She had the most beautiful chestnut hair he had ever seen.

"Quick, Zeke, who is that woman?"

Zeke pulled the door a bit wider and took a look. "She's one of Hannah's friends. Let me think a minute. She lives in Boston." Zeke scratched his chin. "I think she's one of Hannah's Brown relatives."

Elias pulled his brother away from the door and gripped his shoulder. "Her name?"

"Not sure. It might be Lucy. I'll ask Hannah."

"Promise to introduce us," Elias demanded.

Zeke chuckled. "I'm a bit busy today, what with the wedding and all."

"Promise or you'll have no groomsman."

"You're serious! I shall introduce you before the dancing so you can join the set together."

Someone rapped the door three times before opening it.

"Ezekiel," Hasket said with a stern note in his voice. "The ceremony can't begin until you and Elias take your places. I'm sure the bride is nervous, and I know your mother is displeased with your tardiness."

Elias and Zeke gave Hasket a chance to return to his seat before strolling down the center aisle to the magistrate. Elias scanned the guests' faces, looking for the woman who owned the chestnut hair. She was standing near the front of the assembly wearing a long-sleeved white muslin dress with a blue sash. Her beautiful hair framed a heart-shaped face. Dark lashes framed dancing brown eyes.

Elias couldn't tear his eyes away and hardly noticed Zeke's bride take his brother's hand. Zeke elbowed Elias's arm, reminding him to face the magistrate. When it was time for the ring, Elias fumbled in his watch pocket to find the band lodged in the seam. *This is awkward.* Eventually, he retrieved the ring and passed it to Zeke.

"With this ring, I thee wed and all my worldly goods I thee endow."

Zeke slid the ring on the third finger of Hannah's left hand before placing a chaste kiss on her forehead.

"May I present Mr. and Mrs. Ezekiel Derby," the magistrate announced.

Guests broke out in applause as servants distributed glasses of Madeira.

Elias cleared his throat. "A toast to the bride and groom." He lifted his glass. "May you have a long and happy life together."

"Hear, hear!" Glasses clinked.

"Zeke," Elias muttered. "The introduction."

Zeke murmured something to his new wife and led her toward the focus of Elias's attention.

Hannah embraced the young woman. "Lucy, you look lovely. In fact, my husband's brother is smitten with you."

Lucy blushed and dropped her eyes.

"Don't be shy," Hannah admonished. "Lucy, please allow me to introduce you to my new brother-in-law Captain Elias Derby. You mustn't mind her reticence, Captain Derby. Lucy is very good company indeed."

Lucy's blush deepened before she curtsied in greeting. "It is a pleasure to make your acquaintance, Captain Derby."

Elias bowed. "Truly, the honor is mine."

# Captain Elias Derby

*The Next Day*
*Hasket Derby's House*

"Your mother keeps a lovely garden," Lucy observed.

"Actually, Father's gardeners keep a lovely garden. Mother doesn't know one plant from another."

"Nevertheless, it is well laid out." Lucy shivered slightly. "We'll have to go in soon. I didn't bring my shawl."

Elias gestured toward an open arbor with a bench. "Would you care to sit for a few minutes?"

Lucy allowed Elias to hold her elbow and guide her to the bench. He felt relieved that though there were two other couples in the garden, they were far enough away for him to have a private conversation.

Elias cleared his throat. "How long will you stay in Salem?"

"I'm just here for the week. I couldn't impose on the Fitches any longer. Hannah invited me to stay at her new home, but the last thing a newly married couple needs is an extra relation to entertain. Don't you agree?"

"You're correct, of course. Do you think you might visit Salem again?"

"Perhaps, if I'm invited."

Elias grinned. "I'm sure my brother would be delighted to extend you an invitation. Perhaps for the new year. We could all go sleighing."

"Yes." Lucy clapped her hands. "I love sleighing. There's something about the bells on the horses and gliding through the snow. I think it's magical."

*I think you're magical.*

"I wonder," Elias asked, "would it be appropriate for me to write letters to you in Boston, and perhaps call upon you?"

Lucy smiled, showing her dimples. "I don't see why you shouldn't, within the bounds of propriety."

Elias felt his heart swell. "In that case, I shall open our correspondence next week. Would that please you?"

"Very much."

Zeke shattered the moment with a shout from the doorway. "Elias, bring Lucy inside. We're setting up for the last dance. Hannah wants you and Lucy to follow us."

Lucy giggled. "Well, I suppose our conversation is done. It's been most enjoyable. I look forward to your letters and visits."

*She's looking forward to my letters.* Elias could hardly believe such a lovely young woman could take an interest in him. He rose and held out his arm. When Lucy placed her hand on his wrist, he felt his heart rate increase.

When Zeke and Hannah's second wedding day ended, Elias escorted Lucy to the Fitch family. In the vestibule, the women changed into thick shawls, bonnets, and sturdy footwear. Elias lifted Lucy into the family carriage. Before freeing her hand, Elias risked pressing a kiss to her wrist. *Will she reject such an intimate gesture?*

Lucy's eyes widened in surprise. Then she smiled and withdrew her hand.

"I look forward to hearing from you," she said. "And I promise to answer your letters."

Elias watched the carriage drive away into the gathering darkness. For the first time in his life, he felt like another person might be able to understand the emptiness inside him. *For her, I might be able to give up card games.*

# Captain Nathaniel Silsbee

*September 1794*
*Aboard the* Benjamin, *Texel Island, Outside Amsterdam*

"Hold her steady," Nath ordered. "Release capstan and drop anchor."

"Release capstan and drop anchor," the mate called to the men below.

Crewmen turned the capstan, allowing the anchor rope to follow the anchor from the *Benjamin*'s bow to the ocean floor. The ship shuddered slightly when the anchor gripped the seabed.

"Right, lads. Take in her sails now," the mate ordered.

Nath secured the ship wheel and lifted his spyglass, surprised to see oarsmen maneuvering a small boat around the other merchant ships waiting offshore of Texel Island. The boat came up to *Benjamin*'s starboard side.

Crewmen threw a rope ladder over the rail. A man attached the small boat to the rope ladder. Rowers shipped their oars, and the man climbed onto the *Benjamin*'s deck.

Nath watched the scene with both detachment and curiosity. He knew only smaller ships could enter Amsterdam's harbor directly, but the *Benjamin* was under two hundred tons, as were several other ships bobbing at anchor. So why were they being detained at the barrier island?

William greeted the visitor and escorted him to Nath's cabin in the ship's stern. Reluctantly, Nath joined them. *I doubt he's bringing me good news.*

*"Goededag,"* Nath said slowly. *"Welkom bij Benjamin."*

*"Goededag. Ik ben Herr Hendriks."*

"Captain Silsbee. *Spreek je Engels?"*

*"Sommige. Frankrijk nam Nigmegen. Ze komen snel hier."*

Hendriks looked at Nath expectantly while Nath mentally translated the man's statement. *Frankrijk*—French? *Nijmegen?* A nearby town, perhaps? *Komen*—come. *Hier*—here. Nath rolled the words around his mind.

"French come here?" Nath asked.

*"Ja. Hier. Gaan."* Hendriks made a shooing motion with his hands and abruptly left the cabin.

When Nath reached the main deck, Hendriks had a leg over the side. He made the shooing motion again and climbed down the rope ladder.

"Richard, pull up our anchor. We're sailing on to Hamburg."

"Now?"

"Apparently, they expect the French to attack. We need to leave while we can."

Crewmen began turning the capstan. Looking around, Nath saw several other ships pulling up anchors and unfurling sails. *I suppose we're all sailing to Hamburg. Clearly, no one will be doing business in Amsterdam. Bloody French!*

## *Hamburg*

William lowered his spyglass. "I thought Hamburg would be like Amsterdam, but it's completely different. It's amazing."

Nath chuckled. Seeing new sights through his brother's eyes doubled his own enjoyment.

"You exaggerate. Use your powers of observation. A port is a port is a port?" Nath raised his eyebrows. "What's the same? What's different?"

William sighed. "Why do you make everything a lesson?"

"Because that's the only way you'll learn anything. So, answer my questions."

"Yes. Well." William paused. "So far, it seems like ports are at the end of rivers." He wrinkled his forehead in concentration. "Well, maybe not. We have two rivers in Salem, but our port is really on a natural harbor. What I mean is that Amsterdam is on the Rhine River, and Hamburg is on the Elbe River. But they aren't the same."

"Because?" Nath prodded.

"Well, we weren't really in Amsterdam. We were on a barrier island outside of it, and we had to stay there while they sent their own boats out to ferry cargo and supplies into their warehouse area. I'm guessing that's an added cost?"

"To an extent. But rest assured, Hamburg merchants also exact port charges. And what do you know about Hamburg so far?"

William grinned. "For one thing, we're sailing up the river and we can see the city ahead. But I don't see any piers or quays."

"Look through your spyglass at the water next to the island on your left."

William moved the spyglass around. "Where?"

"Do you see the island?"

"Yes!"

"Do you see ships in rows bobbing beside it?"

William nodded.

"Good. Look very closely, and you'll see that they are moored at what look like vertical logs. That's where we drop anchor and tie up."

William gave his brother a cocky grin. "That's what I said in the first place. Hamburg isn't anything like Amsterdam."

Nath laughed and shook his head. William never gave up a verbal point.

Nath and William took a room near the harbor so they could more easily explore the harbor area and the city beyond. Nath was particularly intrigued by the transfer of cargo. Lighters came to the *Benjamin* to accept cargo and carried it to a warehouse situated directly on the water. A crane lifted the cargo out of the lighter up to the required warehouse level.

"I wouldn't like to be on the crew that turns the windlass," William observed.

"Yet another reason life at sea can be better than other occupations," Nath responded.

His business done and fresh supplies loaded, Nath set a course that would take him out of the North Sea, through the English Channel, and into the Atlantic Ocean for their voyage to India.

After leaving Hamburg's port, Nath and Richard stood on deck watching the North Sea waves grow taller. Above them, crewmen took in the sails.

"Wind's gonna blow up right smart," Richard commented. "Already struck the royal and gallant sails."

Nath grunted. *I don't want another experience like the* Sally. "Reef the mainsail. I'll take the wheel. You can spell me later."

"What about me?" William asked.

"Stay below! I've got too much to think about to be worried about you. I promised Mother to keep you safe, and that means you stay below until the storm blows itself out. That is a direct order from your captain. Do you understand?"

"Yes, sir!"

"Lad needs to learn sometime," Richard said.

"He does, but not today. You have your orders."

Nath went to the stern and attached himself to the wheel with ropes and set a course into the wind. This sea was rougher than it had been the last time he'd sailed the North Sea, and that was bad enough. The waves continued to climb, but the *Benjamin* maintained her position, riding them from their highest point into sickening troughs. Waves washed over the ship, but she stayed afloat.

Endless hours later, the storm blew itself out. Nath computed his probable position and set a course for Dover, where he could assess the damage to his ship.

*Dover, England*

Rays from early morning turned the white chalk cliffs on Dover's headland an ethereal shade of pink. Nath took a deep breath and drew in the view. He lifted his spyglass, checking the harbor's entry.

"Looks like the Royal Navy is building up for war. I hope their focus is on the French and not neutral merchants."

Richard shrugged. "Have you got a fix on the harbor entry?" he asked.

"Aye. Adjust the wheel so she shifts a bit more to port. That'll give us a straight shot into the harbor."

Richard adjusted the wheel. "Those chalk cliffs are something to see. Bet they sparkle at noon. So, what do you reckon? Pull *Benjamin* up to the dock?"

"No. We'll anchor in the harbor. No reason to incur dock fees if she just needs sailcloth. I'll take the wheel while you set up our anchorage."

After securing the anchor, Richard began assessing the storm damage. Nath took William ashore with him to line up ship's stores. Near the shore, the Pier District bustled with sailors and garrison troops. Shops, taverns, and entertainments lined the streets.

"Keep your eyes in your head, William," Nath muttered.

William moved his eyes away from an attractive woman silhouetted against a tavern window.

"We won't be stopping there. I have a good recommendation a bit more into town." Nath walked farther away from the harbor, eventually stopping at the Valiant Sailor. William eyed the brick structure, which included a stable in the back. A rounded wooden sign depicting a sailor standing on a ship's deck with an anchor next to him swung over the door.

"As you continue your career at sea, you will hear about accommodations in various ports. It's good to pay attention, since you never know where you may end up. I'm told the Valiant Sailor is clean, with decent food, which is all we require."

The fish stew at the Valiant Sailor was better than Nath expected, and the ale, refreshing. He was about to lead the way to their room upstairs when William pulled on his sleeve.

"Nath, they're playing some kind of card game. Can we watch?"

Nath glanced toward the corner, where three men sat playing cards and several others watched. It seemed an odd game to Nath, but the only card game he knew was whist, and he didn't play.

Nath waved the barmaid over. "My brother's interested in the card game over there. I saw something similar in Batavia a few years ago but never bothered to pay attention to it. At the time, there were plenty of other ways for me to spend my money."

"You seem like a nice fella, so I'll warn you. The game is called baccarat. Malachi, the man what's dealing, says it's popular in France." The barmaid smirked. "It might be a fair game, or it might not. Malachi usually wins."

"Can we watch, Nath? Please," William said with a winsome smile.

"No harm in watching, I suppose."

Nath and William made their way over to the corner table.

"Ah, good sir," said the swarthy man dealing the cards. "I can deal you in for the next hand. Just need to add a stake to the table."

Nath held up his hand. "Just watching the entertainment."

"But you must join us. If you don't know the game, it's easy to learn."

"We'll watch," Nath said firmly.

Beside him, William bounced with excitement. Nath took in the players' expressions. The one the barmaid called Malachi seemed smug, which caused Nath to conclude he must be winning.

"Eight," the dealer said. "I believe that's my game. Will you play another?"

"No. I've lost three hands already." The sailor placed his empty whiskey glass on the table.

"Come back tomorrow. I'm sure luck will be with you then."

"Nay. We sail on the tide. And you have the devil's own luck."

The dealer chuckled and swept his winnings from the middle of the table. "Who'll be next, then?"

"You should try, Nath," William whispered.

"We're here to watch."

"Surely, someone else wants to have a go?" The dealer scanned the spectators and singled out a young man who looked to be in his twenties. "How about you, sir? Are you feeling brave tonight? I'll start the pool with half a crown. Surely you can afford that much? If you win, you'll double your money."

"I don't know the game, sir."

"It's simple, first one to get eight or nine points wins. Face cards have no points. Aces have one point. I'll deal us each two cards face down. If you think you need another card, you can have it. Nothing to it. Will you play?"

The young man pulled a half crown coin out of his pocket.

*Don't do it,* Nath thought. *Nothing is that simple.*

The youth sat down at the table.

"We should introduce ourselves," the dealer said. "A friendly game is about being friends. I go by Malachi. And you?"

"Thomas."

"Good." Malachi thumped the deck of cards on the table. "Put your money in."

Thomas looked indecisive before placing his silver coin in the center of the table. Malachi matched it. From the top of the deck, he dealt one card face down to Thomas and one to himself and then repeated the process.

Malachi lifted the tips of his cards and returned them to their place face down in front of him.

"Card?" he asked.

"He didn't look at his cards yet," Nath interjected.

"That so? Take a look, then. Remember, you want to get nine points."

"What's the trick?" Thomas asked.

"No trick."

Nath glared at Malachi.

"If your cards are less than five points, you have to take a card. I'll ask again, do you want a card?"

Thomas lifted the corners of his cards.

Nath looked over his shoulder. A pair of twos. Nath schooled his face.

"Yes, I'll take a card."

Malachi dealt him a card face up. It was an eight of clubs.

Malachi didn't take a card. He turned over his cards. He had a five of hearts and an ace of spades. "Your turn."

Thomas hesitated and turned his cards over. To the eight of clubs, he added a two of diamonds and a two of spades.

"That's twelve points, subtract the number on the left for a total of two," Malachi said and pocketed the coins on the table. "I win."

"But . . ."

"You've learned a valuable lesson today." Malachi smirked. "If you don't know the rules, you shouldn't play the game."

William pulled on Nath's sleeve. "Nath, that's probably all he has. Can't we make it up to him? We can afford it."

Nath handed William a crown coin. "Follow him and give it to him outside. No need to embarrass him further."

"Anyone else want to try his luck?" Malachi asked.

"I will." Nath shook Malachi's hand and sat down at the table. "Name's Captain Silsbee. I'm American and I don't carry small coins. Shall we play for Spanish dollars?" Nath threw the silver coin onto the table.

Malachi's eyes popped.

"Or is that too rich for you?"

"Not at all. Give me a moment." Malachi reached beneath his breeches for a money pouch and retrieved a matching coin.

"Very good," Nath said. "I'll be the dealer, if you don't mind."

"I hope you're not insinuating—"

"Nothing of the sort. I simply think it's good to change dealers with each game. Keeps everything fresh."

William rejoined the crowd and nodded to his brother.

Nath dealt two rounds of face-down cards, lifted his cards' corners, and turned them face up.

"How lucky. I have a four of diamonds and a five of clubs, which adds to nine points."

Nath swept the coins off the table. "Do you want a chance to get your money back?" Nath held up one of the Spanish dollars.

Malachi nodded and reached into his pouch to retrieve another coin. Nath passed the deck of cards. This time, Nath pulled a two of clubs and a five of spades.

"Card?" Malachi asked.

"I'll stand," Nath replied.

Malachi pulled a face card and began sweating.

Nath turned his cards.

"Can you top seven points?"

Malachi shook his head, and Nath gathered his winnings.

"Again?" Nath asked.

Malachi nodded.

Over the next two hours, the men played five more hands. Nath watched Malachi become increasingly nervous. After the fifth hand, Nath stretched, gathered his winnings, and stood to shake hands.

"This has been a most profitable evening, Malachi. But the lad and I have an early start tomorrow, so I bid you a good night."

"You can't. You just had a run of luck. You have to give me a chance to recover my losses."

"In fact, I do not." Nath gestured to the crowd of spectators. "These men witnessed every foolish play you made. Luck had nothing to do with it. Good night, gentlemen."

Upstairs, William pulled off Nath's boots. "How did you keep winning?"

Nath shrugged. "I paid attention to my opponent. He had some good hands, but he didn't trust them and took another card, which put him either over or under the points he needed. Remember that, William. Anytime you're in a competition, watch your opponent. It will unnerve them, so they make mistakes. Come get some sleep. We need to be at the *Benjamin* when supplies arrive."

William blew out the candle and crawled into the bed.

"How much money did you win?"

"No idea. I'll count it when the game is truly over."

"When will that be?"

"When Malachi stops playing. Go to sleep."

The next evening, Nath gestured for William to enter the tavern ahead of him.

"He's back in his corner," William muttered. "And he brought friends."

Nath eyed several burly dockworkers, and a sailor Malachi shooed away from the table.

"William, stay close. Let's see if we can just get to our room."

As Nath put his foot on the first step, one of the dockworkers was at his elbow.

"Malachi wants a word wid ye."

"We've nothing to discuss."

"When a man wins as much as you did last night, he owes it to the loser to give him a chance to win back his money."

"I've no time for a sore loser."

"Me and my friends say you do."

Nath squared his shoulders. "Very well. Lead the way."

"Back again, I see," Malachi sneered. "You tricked me last night, but I'll be watching your every move this time. Sit down. And this time, I'll deal the cards."

"As you wish." Nath sat. "What's the stake?"

"My mates and I stand together. I wager the entire pool from last night."

Nath raised his eyebrows.

"Are you sure? By my calculations, that's fourteen Spanish dollars. And you've already lost seven. So, when you lose, you'll be down twenty-one Spanish dollars. Can these gentlemen afford to stake you?"

"I'm good fer it. You playin' or runnin'?"

"Playing, of course." Nath threw a pouch full of coins on the table and gave his opponent a chilling smile. "Deal the cards."

Nath lifted the edges. He had a face card worth nothing and an ace worth one point. He had to take a card.

Malachi took what turned out to be a four of diamonds. Nath's new card was a two of clubs.

Malachi turned over his cards, a two of spades and a three of hearts, giving him a total of nine points. Nath turned over an ace worth one point and a face card worth nothing, for a total of three points.

"Aha!" Malachi chortled, pulling in the pool of bets. "Looks like your luck ran out."

"Indeed," Nath said grimly.

"Play again?" Malachi asked.

Nath shook his head. "I've learned my lesson. Come, William. Let us seek our bed."

William patted his brother's back as they climbed the stairs. "Tough luck."

"On the contrary." Nath grinned. "It was the only way to disentangle myself. Let that be a lesson, William. We take enough chances with the sea. On land, we're better off minding our own business."

C H A P T E R

# Captain George Crowninshield

*November 1794*
*Captain George Crowninshield's House*

"I propose a toast to our ship *Belisarius* and our sons who sail in her. To you—Geordie and John."

Everyone raised their crystal glasses.

"To the *Belisarius* and to us," Geordie said, returning the toast.

"This is also an especially festive evening to welcome Jacob back from his successful voyage on the *Henry*. To Jacob," George said.

"Hear! Hear!" Geordie chortled. "And to besting Uncle Derby."

"I can definitely get behind that," George declared. "And you, my dear?" George turned to his wife. "Do you have anything to celebrate?"

Mary's eyes gleamed. "I celebrate your vision, George. We created a company and built the fastest ship in Salem Harbor. The only one with a copper bottom. With that one decision, you upstaged Hasket's *Grand Turk*. I celebrate you keeping the promise you made to me long ago. I toast our ships and our sons who sail them."

Mary raised her glass and drank.

"Mame! Women can't propose toasts."

165

Mary winked at her older daughter. "Not as a general rule, Molly. But we're family here, so this rare exception does not change social etiquette. Tell me, Geordie, how long will it be before the *Belisarius* departs?"

Geordie smirked at his mother's change of topic. "In about two weeks, I think. Isn't that right, John?"

Geordie's brother swallowed a mouthful of ragout. "Er, yes. We just finished loading brandy and Madeira for Europe. I'll load the other liquors next."

"I trust you're keeping good records?" George said.

"Naturally, Sir. And I note that seventy-five percent of the proceeds go to you and the remainder to us. All for our company, of course."

"Don't forget you have your own adventure cargo as well. You'll make a pretty penny on this voyage."

"We all will." Geordie rubbed his hands. "I'm meeting friends at an inn in Danvers for a game of cards. Do you mind, Mame, if I take a few almond cakes with me?"

George looked up in surprise. "I thought we'd discuss the voyage more after we finish eating."

"I promised to meet them, and John knows everything I do."

Geordie began putting the cakes into a linen cloth.

"Who, exactly, are you meeting, Geordie?" Mary asked.

"Just the lads. We aren't usually in Salem at the same time, and they're shipping out in a few days."

"As are you," George said.

"Yes."

George gave his son a long look. Something was going on with him, but he couldn't figure out what. Mary glanced at her husband and shook her head. George shrugged. *Whatever it is, Geordie won't talk about it before he's ready. He keeps his cards close to his chest.*

"If I don't see you at breakfast tomorrow, I'll meet you on the wharf," Geordie said. "Excuse me, Mame. I need to hitch Pompey to the gig." And with that, he was gone.

"Well," Molly said. "He was in a hurry."

"And he took most of the almond cakes," Sally said with a pout.

"You can have mine," John offered.

"Does your brother have a particular lady friend?" George asked.

John shook his head. "He hasn't mentioned anyone to me, and he's not likely to either. Geordie doesn't like complications. And he once advised me not to leave anyone pining after me when I leave, so I suppose he applies the same advice to himself. What do you think, Jacob?"

"As you say, he's not one to share romantic confidences. However . . ."

"Yes, Jacob?" Mary inquired.

"While I'm in Salem, I shall be calling on Sarah Gardner."

Mary rose from the table. "In that case, it looks like you'll marry before Geordie." Mary grinned. "At least you have someone in mind. Shall we adjourn to the drawing room so the maids can tidy the room?"

George took his wife's arm, led his family into the drawing room, and began questioning John about supplies on the *Belisarius* while his daughters pulled out their needlework and teased Jacob about his romantic hopes.

# Lizzie Rowell

*Lizzie Rowell's Cottage, Danvers*

Sophia pulled on the leading strings that kept her upright.

"Don't pull," Lizzie said. "Walk nicely and we can show your father how clever you are."

Sophia continued pulling.

*She's always in such a hurry, and there's nowhere to go.*

"I know," Lizzie said brightly. "Let's sit on this lovely rug and I'll roll your ball back and forth."

Sophia's eyes focused on the bright yellow ball her mother held out. When she plopped down on the rug to reach for it, Lizzie rolled the ball to her daughter. *She's such a picture. I hope she stays like this when Geordie comes, if he's coming tonight.* Lizzie put Sophia in the dress with leading strings attached at the shoulders hoping Geordie would want to play with his daughter. He usually tried to make her laugh when he was there. But Sophia's moods changed so quickly now. Last week, she cried the entire time Geordie was there. He could hardly wait to leave. *No, I won't dwell on that day. Today will be perfect. He'll come through the door and see us on the rug he gave us playing with Sophia's ball. And he'll smile in that special way he has, with his eyes twinkling.*

Lizzie heard a gig drive around the cottage. *It's him. It has to be.* Geordie whistled as he unhitched Pompey. *Good. He'll stay at least an hour. Maybe longer.*

Lizzie rolled the ball back to Sophia before pinching her cheeks and smoothing her hair. Most of it was in a mop cap, but she'd arranged a few ringlets around her face. Lizzie pulled down her chemise enough to reveal her bosom and remind Geordie how they had once "chatted" in his room at the Ship.

"Is there a little girl at home?" Geordie called.

"Sophia, it's your father."

A smile appeared on the toddler's face. Using her mother for leverage, Sophia pulled herself up and held her hands out for balance.

"Careful," Lizzie said.

Geordie dropped the package in his arms, crouched, and reached for his daughter. Holding Sophia firmly, he stood and twirled around. Sophia shrieked with laughter.

"If you keep twirling her, she'll get sick."

Geordie stopped abruptly, and Sophia started crying.

"Don't cry, angel. I have a gift for you."

Geordie reached into his bag, lifted out a pull toy, and placed it in Sophia's hands. While Sophia turned the toy around, Geordie kissed Lizzie's cheek before nuzzling her neck.

"How are you?" he murmured.

Lizzie's face flooded with heat. She couldn't remember the last time Geordie expressed affection for her. *Oh no! His ship must be ready to leave.*

Lizzie took Sophia from Geordie and placed her on the rug. "What did Papa bring you? Can I see?"

Sophia held out her treasure.

Lizzie looked at the toy. It was a carved wooden chicken sitting on a platform with a thick string attached.

Geordie shrugged. "A friend of mine likes to make wood carvings."

"She doesn't walk well enough to pull anything behind her."

"She can play with it when she's steady on her feet. Oh. I almost forgot." Geordie reached into his bag again. "I brought almond cakes from dinner. I remembered you're fond of them."

Geordie held out a cloth bundle filled with the cakes. Lizzie broke one in half and gave a portion to Sophia, who sniffed the sweet before stuffing the entire serving into her mouth.

Geordie and Lizzie both laughed.

"She's beautiful, like her mother."

Lizzie laughed again. *This is embarrassing. Why don't we ever speak what's in our minds?*

She cleared her throat. "How are things with your ship?"

Geordie reached for Lizzie's hand and began playing with her fingers. "Very well. John is going to be an excellent partner. He's doing all the cargo inventories."

*I don't care about that.*

Geordie gazed at Sophia. Lizzie let the silence between them stretch out.

"Jacob's ship arrived, so we'll be able to work on our business strategy before the *Belisarius* puts out to sea."

Sophia yawned.

"She's tired. Let me put her down so we can talk."

Lizzie quickly tucked Sophia into her cot and sang a short lullaby.

"Her eyes are closed, and she'll sleep soon. Shall I make some tea?"

"Yes, that would be nice. What did you just sing? I remember my mother singing the same song."

Lizzie shrugged. "It's just a lullaby about rocking a baby cradle in the treetops."

"I remember. The wind blows and the cradle falls out of the tree. The words aren't very soothing. Quite the opposite."

"I never really thought about the words."

Lizzie picked up the kettle beside the fire and poured the water into an earthenware teapot.

They sat in silence for a few minutes.

"We need to talk," Geordie said.

"Yes? The tea is ready now."

Lizzie focused on pouring tea into two porcelain cups. Steam curled above the liquid. She added three spoonfuls of sugar to each cup and passed one to Geordie.

"We can sit outside if you like. There's not much wind tonight."

Geordie followed Lizzie to the bench by the front door.

"It's a clear evening," Lizzie said. *This is it. This is when he walks away from us.*

"I doubt I'll have time to call again before my ship sails, but you have nothing to worry about. I leased this cottage for another three years, made arrangements for supplies to be delivered every month, and hired a man to provide wood for your fire. Also . . ."

Geordie reached into his vest and pulled out a purse of coins.

"There's more than enough to see you through until I return."

"See me through," Lizzie said blankly.

"Yes, in case you need things I haven't thought of. But you need to be careful the money lasts. You can't go to my family for help."

"Surely—"

"I'm sorry, but they'll never believe you. And even if they do, you have no claim on me. Sophia doesn't look like me at all." He shrugged.

Lizzie's mouth fell open. *How can you sit there and shrug when you just denied our child?*

A tear rolled down Lizzie's cheek. "You know I have never lain with anyone but you."

"Do I?"

"Yes," Lizzie whispered. "You do. Why else would you bring gifts for Sophia?"

"There's nothing between us, Lizzie. We kept each other warm, but that's all it was. I'm sorry if you thought we had any other connection."

Sooner than Lizzie thought possible, Geordie harnessed Pompey to the gig and drove past the front of the cottage. Lizzie thought about hurling the purse and its coins into the back of his cart but decided to put it in her dress pocket instead. *Coin,* she thought, *is more useful than pride.*

# Captain George Crowninshield Jr.

*On the Road to Salem*

Pompey took advantage of Geordie's inattention to grab grass from the side of the road. The horse tossed his head, but when there was no response from Geordie, he returned to the grass and slowly pulled the gig into the field.

*I'm sorry if you thought we had any other connection.*

Geordie held his head in his hands. He didn't mean to be harsh, but Lizzie was so clingy, and he had to break their connection. He wasn't cut out to have a family. He had no ambition, or any interest in his own household. *It's for the best that Lizzie realizes the truth for herself, because I'm not fool enough to spell things out for her.*

Sunk in his misery, Geordie jumped when the gig's right wheel became wedged inside a deep rut. He lifted his head. Pompey twisted his neck around in apparent curiosity.

"Don't you start," Geordie muttered as he dismounted the gig.

*Damme and blast!*

Geordie built a bed of tree branches in front of the wheel and guided Pompey until the horse could pull the wheel away from the rut.

"Come along, Pompey. Let's get back to the road. The sooner I'm at sea, the happier I'll be."

# Captain George Crowninshield Jr.

*Crowninshield Counting House*

When the *Henry* pulled in a week ago, there were family reunion dinners. Now, they were having a company meeting at the counting house, and Jacob was furious. His long fingers drummed on Sir's desk. John and Geordie sat on opposite ends of the desk, but Jacob's chair was exactly in the middle. Sir had assumed a relaxed posture, but Geordie knew he was trying to calm Jacob down. John and Geordie exchanged glances. They had final preparations to do on the *Belisarius*, but there they sat, listening to Jacob fume. Ebenezer sat near the door to take down any necessary notes. Jacob could have held this meeting without his brothers. The corners of Geordie's thoughts drifted back to Lizzie. *I shouldn't have been so hard on her.*

"Uncle Derby has lost his mind if he thinks I will accept a lower compensation than is my due," Jacob said. "I bring home good cargoes, and he always tries to undercut my earned percentages."

"Son, you are being impulsive. This is a delicate matter that was bound to happen. As soon as George Crowninshield & Sons has enough ships to forego sailing for your uncle, we can shout as loudly as you wish, but until then, we need to keep his business.

"Let us go over the facts again, and I will find mediators who will naturally rule in our favor. Your uncle overreaches, and more than one man wants to take him down a peg. But he is also the richest man in Salem, so we must tread carefully. Tell me again what happened."

Jacob ran his hand over his thin hair, careful not to disturb it unnecessarily. "I took the *Henry* out in January two years ago. Benj sailed on the *Betsey* in tandem with me. As we neared the islands in the Indian Ocean, I sent Benj to Saint-Benoît at Isle de Bourbon and brought the *Henry* into Port Louis at Isle de France. We arrived in April and began to off-load our cargo and acquire items for India. In May, the French decided to keep all foreign ships in port with an embargo. So we sat there the entire summer."

"Did you get that down, Ebenezer?" Sir asked. "Write it in a good hand so our arbiters can read it. What did you do then, Jacob?"

"Nothing. We sat in port. We were able to off-load our cargo, because our factors thought they would have good sales once the embargo lifted and more ships came into port. But it was difficult to find a cargo to take on. Benj made a poor job of the coffee purchase he was supposed to make at Isle de Bourbon. He really isn't cut out to be a merchant."

"Neither are you, Jacob."

"Sir! How can you say that? I've done a good job with my cargoes."

Sir nodded, but his expression dismissed Jacob's claim, and Geordie smiled to himself. He was happiest when one of his brothers took Sir's attention.

"Nevertheless," Sir said. "I have other plans for you that will utilize your—ahem—charming nature. But that is a conversation for another time. Continue. When did you leave Port Louis?"

"As soon as the embargo lifted. We sailed to Madras in January. Then we proceeded to Calcutta to complete our cargo. We left at the end of March and sailed to Bordeaux to trade our goods before heading for home. We arrived back in Salem a few days ago and off-loaded our cargo.

"And now, instead of congratulating me on a successful voyage, Uncle Derby accuses me of inefficiency and refuses to pay me the value of my adventure cargo. Not only that, but he's also given command of the *Henry*'s next voyage to Henry Prince. He's done it purely to embarrass me. I've been master of the *Henry* for four years. To take away my command tarnishes my reputation, and I won't stand for it." Jacob smacked his hand on Sir's desk.

John and Geordie rolled their eyes.

Sir leaned back and steepled his fingers. "Your uncle is a cunning man who squeezes every coin until it squeals. Nevertheless, we shall outthink him. On your behalf, I shall convene a council of arbitration to give their opinion on your complaints. Geordie, what points of emphasis would you advise?"

Geordie snapped his full attention back to his father.

"I can supply the points of emphasis," Jacob said.

"You're too involved in the issue. Geordie, what do you think?"

Ebenezer passed Geordie his notes. He glanced through them and summarized the basis of Jacob's complaint.

"The original agreement was that Jacob is entitled to one-tenth of the stock brought into Salem, and he has not received compensation for it. I, personally, don't think the amount owed is worth all this discourse."

"Uncle Derby cannot be allowed to short me on compensation," Jacob said.

Sir lifted his hand before Jacob could make his case a second time. "Leave it with me, Jacob. I will contact your uncle. We'll appoint the arbiters, and we'll see what they decide. I'm confident they will see things our way, and when they do, we will give your uncle a graceful way to compensate you. Ebenezer, you have the notes?"

"Yes, Captain Crowninshield."

"Good. Sons, let us make a final inspection of the *Belisarius*."

"That's right, Jacob," Geordie said. "You haven't been aboard yet. She's a beautiful ship."

# Captain Jacob Crowninshield

*January 1795*
*Outside Captain George Crowninshield's House*

Jacob checked the harness connecting Pompey and Caesar to the large sleigh. His sister Molly fed a carrot to Caesar while Pompey tossed his head, impatiently waiting his turn.

"We should have a third horse," Molly observed. "This sleigh is too large for two horses."

"They'll be fine." Jacob patted Pompey's flank. "We're not going racing. Are the blankets and foot warmers in the sleigh?"

"Yes. Can we leave now? It's cold standing out here while you brush every snowflake off the seats."

Jacob inspected the seats closely. "I'm not . . ."

Molly winked. "Then why did you look?"

Jacob scoffed. "Get in the second seat. I'll stop by the Boardman house first so Mary and Elizabeth can join you there. Then we can pick up Sarah."

"And she'll sit by you in front. You told me this at breakfast. Boost me up, then, and put the blanket around my legs properly."

"Why can't you adjust your own blanket?"

"Because." Molly batted her eyelashes. "I'm providing you with chaperones so you can go courting. You should thank me for coming out on such a cold day." Molly drew her hood more closely to her face.

"Yes. *Thank you*," Jacob said, trying—and failing—to keep the sarcasm out of his voice.

He climbed onto the front bench, dropped a blanket in his lap, and picked up the reins. "Caesar, Pompey, let's go."

The carriage set off with a slight lurch that jingled the harness bells. When it reached the Boardman house, Elizabeth and Mary were waiting in the front hall. Jacob winced in annoyance as they adjusted their cloaks and bonnets before he boosted them into seats next to his sister. He made sure they had foot warmers at their feet and their blankets were secure. Giggling assailed Jacob's ears, and he turned the horses toward the Gardner house.

Jacob guided the sleigh directly in line to the front door. The girls giggled again as he dismounted, smoothed his coat, and rapped on the door. Sarah's father quickly opened it. Jacob gulped.

"Good day, Captain Gardner. I came to pick up your daughter for a sleighing expedition."

"Captain Crowninshield," Sarah called from farther inside the hall. "I'm just fastening my boots."

Captain Gardner quirked an eyebrow. "It appears all your guests are young women."

"Yes, well, not precisely. The Boardman girls are my sister's guests, and Miss Gardner is mine. It's a perfect day for sleighing. Brisk but not cold. Snow covered but not slushy."

"And where are you taking your passengers?"

"I thought we'd stop at the coaching inn near the turnpike."

"The Eagle?"

"Yes, sir."

"Father, stop interrogating Captain Crowninshield. He'll keep me perfectly safe, and his sister and her friends are with us. You've nothing to worry about."

"Humph. Keep your shawl close so you don't catch a chill."

Captain Gardner stepped aside so his daughter could pass through the door.

"You've nothing to be worried about, sir. I'll look after all the young ladies," Jacob said and was rewarded by the most dazzling smile from his guest. *That smile shall be my undoing.*

"Close the door, Father. You're letting all the heat out of the house." Captain Gardner reluctantly complied.

Outside, Sarah patted Jacob's arm. "Don't worry about Father. He shelters me more than my aunt and uncle do. Shall we go?"

# Sarah Gardner

*Sleighing*

Sarah accepted Jacob's arm as he assisted her into the sleigh. She liked the strength of his arm holding her steady until she was seated. He fussed so much placing the foot warmer that for a moment she thought he was peeking at her feet. But that would be silly. After the foot warmer was in place, he draped a thick wool blanket around her legs, tucking the ends securely beneath her. Sarah blushed from Jacob's proximity and solicitude. But when he withdrew to take his own seat, she missed them.

She turned around to see Molly tapping Mary's shoulder. "It's a pity there's not enough room to seat all four of us back here. Then Jacob would be our coachman and we could command him to any destination—perhaps even New York. What do you think?" Molly smiled mischievously.

"I think I'd rather just go to the Eagle for our dinner. I'm more of a homebird," said Sarah. "How about you, Jacob? Would you like to drive to New York?"

"Not in an open sleigh. Molly gets a bit fanciful." Jacob winked. "But I'm more than happy to take you wherever you wish."

Sarah clapped her hands and laughed. "If we like the Eagle and you're not on a voyage, perhaps we could come again in the summer. And then we can compare the seasons."

Jacob turned the sleigh into the Eagle's entry area. "If we're going to come in summer, you'll need to make good notes so we can compare the two seasons."

"I'll ask the innkeeper for paper, ink, and a quill pen," Molly said.

The Eagle was a sprawling inn with stables and a hostelry. Jacob pulled the sleigh up to the entrance and handed the reins to a stable boy before reaching up to assist Sarah to the ground. For a moment, Sarah stared openly at his eager face. Jacob's deep-set dark eyes flecked with gold danced under thick brows parted by an aquiline nose. Full lips curved into a smile as he held out his hands to grasp Sarah's waist.

Sarah's breath skipped a beat. She put her hands on Jacob's shoulders. He brought her feet to the ground and then released her cloak, which had been caught on the front of the sleigh. Behind her, Sarah heard the girls clabber down, giggling as stable boys helped them balance.

"Come on, Sarah." Molly grabbed Sarah's hand. "Let's get inside and take a table near the fire." Molly's other hand pulled Mary Boardman, who held on to her sister.

"Help ye?" a voice called from behind the bar.

"The young ladies are with me," Jacob said decisively. "We require a small room with a fire. We'll have hot apple cider."

"Jacob." Molly pouted. "It's more fun to sit by the great fire."

Jacob glanced at Sarah, who shook her head. "The small room it is, then."

"This way, sir."

The side room was cozy, with a cheerful, crackling fire and candles on two round tables.

"Sarah?" Jacob indicated the smaller table. "Will you join me?"

"There's plenty of room at this table," Molly exclaimed. "We want to talk to Sarah too."

Elizabeth pulled Molly aside and whispered in her ear.

"Oh." Molly sat with a flounce.

Sarah hung her red woolen cape on a hook by the door and removed her gloves. She took a chair at the small table across from Jacob but knew if she moved her elbow, she would probably connect with his arm. Sarah sat up straight to reduce opportunities for touching.

Jacob gave her a quizzical look. "Would you prefer to sit with my sister and her friends?"

Sarah darted her eyes across to the other table.

"I'm content here. Hot cider is good after being outside in the cold."

"Was it too cold for you? Does your chest bother you?"

It did, but Sarah merely cleared her throat. "It's wonderful to glide along on a sleigh."

The door opened to admit the innkeeper and a boy carrying plates of stew and baskets of freshly baked bread. Inhaling the aroma, Sarah's mouth watered. "What a perfect meal!"

She grabbed a piece of soft bread before her gaze collided with Jacob's. "*Hmmmm.* Jacob, are you watching me eat?"

"No. Of course not. I just . . . you just . . . seem so happy. Does this mean you're enjoying our outing?"

"So much." *Even if I do have to spend tomorrow in bed with a hot brick.*

"Sarah, may I ask you a serious question?"

Sarah dropped her bread into the stew. A splash of gravy reached her fichu.

"Oh dear." She began wiping her fichu.

"Here." Jacob handed Sarah his handkerchief.

"Thank you." She patted her chest several times before realizing Jacob was watching her closely.

"Um. You said you have something to ask me?"

"Well, here's the thing. I have an idea that will bring me a substantial profit. And I'm thinking that if I'm successful, I'll have sufficient funds to establish my own household. Provided everything goes well."

Sarah felt her heart pound in her chest. "How very exciting."

"And I remember that before I left on the *Henry* you agreed not to accept a suitor before my return."

Sarah nodded. *How long will he drag this out?*

"I'll be taking the *America* out in a few weeks. Would you indulge me with an extension of your promise?"

"That I won't take a suitor before your return?"

"Yes. Because when I return, I hope you'll accept me as your suitor."

Sarah swallowed some cider. She'd already waited two years for his return on the *Henry*.

"Did you hear my question, Sarah?"

She raised her eyes. "You're asking me to avoid any entanglement until the *America* comes home."

"I know it seems presumptuous, but if my idea works out, we can marry immediately. And I'll write you every day, just like before." Jacob picked up her hand. "Please."

To Sarah's relief, an older barmaid entered the room with an enormous boiled pudding and syrup, which she placed on the larger table. Molly and her friends clapped with delight.

"Do ye need somethin' else?"

"No." Jacob said. "I'll settle the account when we leave."

The barmaid picked up the used plates and left.

"Shall I get us each a serving?" Sarah asked.

"I'll do the honors," Jacob said.

As Jacob placed a slice of pudding covered in syrup at Sarah's place, his hand brushed her wrist. "I thought you might enjoy extra syrup as much as I do."

Sarah felt her heart pound, but before she could reply, Molly's voice broke into the conversation. "Jacob, look outside! It's snowing. We need to leave before we're trapped here."

"Excuse me," Jacob said to Sarah. "I'm sure Molly is exaggerating, but I'll step outside just to be sure."

Sarah absently stirred syrup further into her pudding as she pondered Jacob's request. *What is two years compared to a good husband?*

Molly shook Sarah's shoulder. "Come and get your things. We have to leave before the snow gets heavier."

"But Jacob isn't back yet."

"I'm sure he settled the account, and now he's probably getting the sleigh ready. Put your cloak on. We need to leave."

Sarah wrapped her cloak around her and followed her companions outside. The snow was steady but light. Jacob helped his sister and her friends into the sleigh before turning to face Sarah, who was lifting her red hood over her head. Jacob settled the covering more closely around Sarah's face, cupping the wool fabric around her cheeks. Looking into his eyes, Sarah realized there was only one answer to his question.

"Forgive me, Jacob. Can you remind me what we were discussing?"

Jacob flushed and reached for Sarah's hand. "If my idea works out, I hope you will accept me as your suitor."

Sarah's face broke into a smile that made her cheeks hurt. "Nothing would please me more."

# Eliza Derby

*February 1795*
*Hasket Derby's House*

The footman added more wood to the fire and poked it until the flames caught. He moved the screen in front of the fireplace so it could catch sparks without blocking too much heat. Eliza rubbed her hands over her arms as she watched the man tidy the floor covering, gather his tools, and leave the drawing room.

"Thank you," she muttered and moved her wingback chair nearer to the fire. *I should have told him to move the chair. That's what he's paid to do.*

"Mother, are you in here?" Elias poked his head around the door.

"Yes, shut the door."

Elias strode across the room and kissed Eliza's cheek. "Father not home yet?"

"You can see that he isn't," Eliza snapped. "Did you leave him in the counting house? What was he doing?"

"Mourning over his ship, I should imagine. Sherry?"

"I'll wait for your father."

Elias shrugged. "As you wish. But you might be glad for preventive fortification before he arrives."

Eliza's face fell. "Can it really be that bad? I saw the cargo list—all solid items from Hamburg and Saint Petersburg. And, just as I predicted, the tobacco sold at a good price."

"Indeed." Elias nodded.

"What aren't you telling me?"

"The long and short of it is, the *Grand Turk* is too big. We have to stay in port longer to sell and buy cargo, assuming the goods are available, and that means more port fees. She requires a substantial crew. She isn't nimble enough for the market. Father kept her for pride, not good business."

"I'll have a glass of sherry after all. Make it a large one."

Elias filled a water goblet with sherry and passed it to Eliza. "Large enough for you?" he said with a smirk.

Eliza's hand shook slightly as she drank.

"You're taking this very hard, Mother, considering your initial impression of the *Grand Turk*'s efficiency is exactly correct. Father and I went over the projected figures all afternoon. We have a net profit of sixteen thousand dollars on the cargo goods. But with the other expenses, including time wasted sitting on our wharf . . ." Elias shrugged. "I left Father to draw his own conclusions."

Eliza drained half her glass. "Your father is a proud man; he won't admit defeat."

"You forget, Mother. When I sold the first *Grand Turk* at Isle de France, it was a business decision. Father's decision will be made the same way. It's no different than deciding to center our efforts at Isle de France and the East Indian trade rather than Canton."

"You've become a strategic-thinking merchant. I didn't expect that to happen."

"You're wrong there, Mother. I'm far too lazy to be a successful merchant. But I know how the business works."

Elias's eyes slid to the mantel when the carriage clock began its tinny chime.

"That's my cue to leave. Father doesn't need my presence when he shares his decision with you." Elias paused. "Mother, if you could be a bit . . . supportive . . . it would help Father come to terms with releasing the *Grand Turk*."

Eliza narrowed her eyes. "Your father and I support each other. Always."

"Yes, but sometimes you tweak his nose a bit first."

Elias kissed his mother's cheek on his way out of the drawing room. Eliza continued staring at the fire. *I should call someone to light the candles.* She swallowed the rest of her sherry and began twirling her glass by its stem. In the darkening room, the mantel clock chimed a second time.

# Hasket Derby

Hasket handed his cloak to the footman, exchanged his boots for house slippers, and opened the drawing room door to a space shrouded in gloom. Frowning, he walked back into the vestibule. "Marcus, get some candles lit in the drawing room. It's like a morgue in there."

"Yes, sir."

"Eliza, what are you doing sitting in the dark?"

Eliza stopped twirling her glass and lifted her eyes. "I beg your pardon. I was thinking of something and lost track of time."

Hasket raised his eyebrows. "Time I can understand, but surely you can see it's dark."

Marcus entered the room, poked the fire, and lit a taper he used to light the candles. "Shall I draw the curtains, sir?"

"What do you think?" Hasket asked.

Marcus nodded and drew the curtains. The once gloomy room now glowed with a cozy warmth.

"Will there be anything else?"

"Serve supper in the small dining room, and let us know when it is pre-pared." Hasket plucked the water goblet from his wife's hand, sniffed it, and put it on the sideboard.

"Elias told me the news," Eliza said.

"And what news is that? I wasn't aware he had any news to share."

Hasket sat down on the opposite wing chair. "Tell me, please. What *news* could Elias possibly have had to share with you?"

Eliza straightened her posture. "You're right, Hasket. He didn't have any useful information. He merely commented that you and he had gone over figures from the *Grand Turk*'s recent voyage, and that profits were not … all we hoped."

"What do I do when a business venture doesn't work out?"

"Usually you absorb your losses and devise a new plan."

"Precisely. I am quite fond of the *Grand Turk*. I was proud to build her, and proud to send her out. And in my pride, I failed to consider the true key to our business."

"Which is?"

"To keep our options open and our investments diversified. Brigs and schooners are nimble. They can move quickly as conditions change, and if we lose one, we still have the other. The *Grand Turk* is the best ship I've ever built, but I shall leave her at New York and sell her as soon as her cargo is off-loaded."

Eliza drew in a startled breath. "Are you sure?"

"Never more so. Now then, I have something else to discuss with you. When we married, I promised you we would lead Salem society, but when General Washington visited Salem a few years ago, he didn't stay at our house. Do you remember?"

"I shall never forget the humiliation."

"And I said I would build you a mansion rivaling any residence in Massachusetts."

Eliza bristled. "So you said, but I've yet to see any progress on that project."

"And yet, my dear, it's been hiding in plain sight all along." Hasket drew a small map out of his vest pocket and laid it on the round conversation table between the wing chairs.

"You may not remember, but during our revolution, the state of Massachusetts confiscated Colonel William Browne's estate because he supported the enemy. Shortly thereafter, I purchased the Browne property from our state. Since then, I've been leasing the mansion." Hasket placed his finger on the Essex Street property.

"The best thing you can do with that monstrosity is tear it down."

"I agree."

Eliza's jaw dropped. "You do?"

"Yes, because if you combine the plot of land next to the Browne estate with the estate itself, you will see the reformed plot of land fronts Essex Street on the north and extends south to Front Street and the South River waterfront. In other words, it's the perfect site for our new mansion estate."

Eliza jumped up, grabbed her husband's shoulders, and soundly kissed both his cheeks. "We'll have the grandest mansion and gardens ever seen in America. And the furnishings will be the very best quality. It will be a showcase! Oh, Hasket, I can hardly believe it."

Hasket chuckled. He couldn't remember the last time Eliza's eyes had glittered with such anticipation. It almost took the sting out of losing the *Grand Turk. If I can't please myself, at least I bring joy back to Eliza's cheeks.*

"I don't want Samuel McIntire to design it," Eliza said. "He builds for everyone in Salem. I want a new design. Georgian, perhaps."

"I'm surprised. Samuel McIntire has designed various parts of all our houses."

"Exactly. I want something new. Different. Something people will notice immediately."

There was a knock on the drawing room door.

"Supper is laid in the small dining parlor," Marcus announced.

"Thank you." Hasket held out his arm. "Shall we go in to supper, my dear?"

"Oh, Hasket, I'm much too excited to eat."

"Humor me."

*This house will keep Eliza's attention for months, perhaps even a year. And then, there will be entertainments.* Hasket assisted his wife to her seat.

"If you don't want to engage Mr. McIntire, were you thinking of a Boston architect? Charles Bulfinch, perhaps?"

Eliza pursed her lips. "I haven't really thought about it. I just want new ideas."

"If that's the case, Eliza, I have an idea that will generate public interest in your project. Write up your plans and put the project out for a design competition. It will generate all sorts of new ideas, and you can select the one you prefer."

Eliza's eyes lit up even more. "I can't wait to tell Betsey and Patsy. This will be the most incredible project Essex County has ever seen."

Hasket smiled and spooned stew into his bowl. *I want Samuel McIntire to design the house, and once Eliza has her pick of designs to choose from, I'm sure she'll select McIntire. She aspires to innovation but generally selects familiarity.*

# Captain George Crowninshield Jr.

*June 1795*

*Aboard the* Belisarius, *Ten Days Out from Saint Helena*

"We've got company." John passed Geordie his spyglass.

Geordie adjusted the lens. A British sloop of war in full sail came into view, and it was on a direct course for the *Belisarius*.

"What do you think? Will she board us or sink us?"

Geordie's mouth went dry. *We're a new ship with a full cargo of coffee, tea, indigo, and cotton.* He swallowed. *My duty is to bring* Belisarius *safely home.*

"She probably wants to board us," Geordie muttered.

"Will you allow it? We're a bigger ship and probably faster. If we aim our guns properly, we can surprise her and get away."

"You really think we can outsmart a Royal Navy sloop?" Geordie shook his head. John was nothing if not impetuous.

"Stranger things have happened. We should at least try."

Before Geordie could reply, First Mate Jonas Anderson joined the conversation.

"Shall I order gun crews ta quarters?"

"Yes," John replied.

"Not your decision," Geordie said in a cold voice. Behind him, Geordie heard nervous conversations among the men. "Order the crew to quarters."

Anderson blew the bosun's whistle, and the crew scrambled to their stations. Some men climbed the ratlines to handle the sails when needed. Gun crews prepared to load the sixteen cannons on either side of the *Belisarius*.

"She's starting to come around," John said. "We have to fire soon, or she'll be too close."

"No. I'm not risking the *Belisarius*."

"What do you mean? A British ship of the line is bearing down on us. We're already at risk."

"She has at least twice our firepower. She'll cripple us, board us, and leave us to limp away."

John's jaw dropped. "You can't let them board us without a fight."

Semaphore flags began flapping from the enemy's deck.

"What do the flags say?"

"She orders us to remain at our station." John sneered. "Surely you won't consider following British orders?"

Geordie's heart thumped in his chest. *It's too late to flee.* The sloop continued closing the distance. Geordie lifted his spyglass. He could see the boarding party massing by the rail. The message on the semaphore flags changed.

"Read the flags, John."

"Prepare to be boarded." He snorted. "We should fire a broadside while we still can."

"Gun crews, stand down."

"For God's sake, Geordie, what are you doing?"

"Saving my ship."

The sloop came alongside the *Belisarius*. Sailors joined the two vessels with grappling hooks and dropped a boarding plank over both their rails. Five British marines crossed over followed by a naval officer in full dress uniform.

"Lieutenant Perkins, HMS *Hornet*. We regret the intrusion, but it has come to our attention you harbor British deserters aboard your vessel. If you would be so kind, please bring your men into formation on the deck."

Geordie nodded to his mate, who gave the order. Gun crews secured their cannons, while sailors came down from the ratlines. Soon Geordie's entire crew stood on the main deck, their faces full of apprehension.

"Be about your duties, gentlemen."

One marine held his musket at the ready while the others walked down the sailors' formation.

"I beg your pardon, but I didn't catch your name."

Geordie kept his eyes on Perkins's face. "Captain George Crowninshield. The *Belisarius* is an American merchant ship, and you have no right to board us," he said in a firm voice. "Furthermore, every man on this ship is an American."

"It appears I need to apprise you of a few legal points," Perkins sniffed. "Firstly, we have the right to retrieve British subjects seeking to evade their duty to Crown and country, and we do not recognize the efforts men employ to disguise their national identity. Secondly, deserters are desperate, devious men. We are, in fact, doing you the favor of removing untrustworthy men from your ship. Besides, you're in no position to oppose us."

Geordie clenched his fists and turned his attention to the deck. Beside him, John's fury radiated in waves.

"Have you found any deserters, Carson?" Perkins asked.

"Yes, sir. Two, sir."

Carson pushed the men forward.

*This cannot be happening. They can't kidnap my crew. But I can't stop them.*

"Those men are Americans," Geordie stated. "You've no right to lay a hand on them."

"I have every right." Perkins turned his attention to one of Geordie's men, Ezra. "You there, state your name and residence."

Geordie looked at the well-built man with sandy hair and blue eyes. They'd sailed together on the *Richard & Edward*. His wife had her third child two weeks before they left Salem.

"Ezra Beck. I live in Salem." He hung his head.

"Beck is American. He's been sailing on my ships for years. He has a family."

"Clearly, the man hid himself well. Congratulations, Mr. Beck. On behalf of His Majesty George III, welcome aboard the *Hornet*." He nodded at Carson. "Take him across."

"No," Geordie objected. "You can't do that."

Perkins ignored Geordie and instead pointed to the other man who had been singled out of the crew, Martin Smith. "You. State your name and residence."

*Leave the lad alone. He's only sixteen.*

"M-M-Martin *Sssssmith*. I l-l-live in *Sssssalem*."

"I know his family," John interjected. "I went to school with his brother. He and his brother were both born in Salem."

Perkins shifted his gaze to John.

"Who are you?"

"John Crowninshield, clerk on the *Belisarius*."

"And you vouch for him?"

"I do," John growled. "He is American, born and bred."

Perkins shrugged. "Very well. He's too small to survive very long on a real ship. Carson, return to the *Hornet*."

"Yes, sir."

The remaining marines crossed the boarding plank. Lieutenant Perkins nodded to Geordie.

"Thank you for your cooperation, Captain Crowninshield. I wish you a safe voyage to your destination."

When Lieutenant Perkins set foot on the *Hornet*'s deck, the bosun piped him aboard. After the *Hornet*'s crew removed the boarding plank and grappling hooks, the *Hornet*'s course turned back toward Saint Helena.

"Jonas, set up the watch and dismiss the men to quarters," Geordie ordered.

By an act of sheer concentration, Geordie entered the captain's cabin with his head held high. He closed the door and pulled out a bottle of whiskey and two glasses. He knocked back the first glass and poured himself another. As expected, John entered the cabin in a rage.

"I cannot believe what just happened. You signed Beck's death warrant and dropped his family into poverty."

"We'll provide his share from the voyage to the family," Geordie said in a wooden voice. He poured himself a third glass.

"And what must the men think?"

Geordie smashed his glass on his desk. "They will think I saved their lives. We could not survive a battle with British marines."

"You don't know that."

"I am captain of this ship, and I order you to keep your opinion to yourself."

For a moment, Geordie thought his brother might strike him. Worse, he thought he might deserve the blow.

With obvious effort, John reined in his temper. "If you require my services, I shall be on deck."

When the cabin door closed, Geordie dropped his head into his hands. Regardless of John's opinion, it was company policy to sacrifice a sailor or two rather than lose a ship. *I did what I was supposed to do.* Geordie sat up again and drank the glass of whiskey he'd poured out for John. Soon he would be back in Salem, explaining the incident to his father.

C  H  A  P  T  E  R

## Sarah Gardner

*March 1795*
*Captain George Crowninshield's House*

The Crowninshield drawing room was as elegant as Sarah remembered. A fire danced cheerfully in the grate. Molly and Sally stood to greet their guest.

"Thank you so much for accepting my invitation," Molly said after everyone had curtsied. "Come, sit by me." Molly patted the seat next to her on the sofa. "At least until Jacob arrives. Would you like some tea and cakes?"

"Yes, thank you." Sarah looked around. "I didn't realize Jacob would be here."

Molly laughed. "He's the one who wanted me to invite you. It's always a pleasure to see you, but, well . . ."

"I understand." Sarah nodded. "Other than needlework, we don't have a great deal to talk about."

"No." Molly shook her head. "Forgive me. I'm being very rude." Molly passed a teacup to her guest. "I may be speaking out of turn, but Jacob wanted me to invite you here and serve as chaperone again, because the *America* will be sailing in the next few days. He wants to talk to you without your father or brothers glowering at him."

193

"My brothers do not glower. My father, on the other hand . . . It's hard for him to accept I've grown up. We haven't seen each other as much as we would like, because he still goes to sea. That's why I spend so much time with my aunt and uncle in Boston."

Jacob strode into the room. "Molly, I didn't realize we had a guest."

Molly rolled her eyes. "I already told Sarah you asked me to invite her. If you'll excuse us, Sally and I will take our needlework over to the window so you and Sarah can stay by the fire."

"That really isn't—" Sarah began.

"Thank you." Jacob sat and poured himself a cup of tea. "It's wonderful to see you, Sarah. I didn't know if we would be able to speak before the *America* sets sail for India."

Jacob's eyes sparkled. "Shall I tell you how I shall make my fortune and become your official suitor?"

Sarah cleared her throat. "That would be most enlightening, I'm sure."

"Here it is, then. I'm going to bring back an elephant from Calcutta."

Sarah's heart lurched. "An elephant! Aren't elephants monstrous big? How will it fit on the ship?"

*I can't believe anyone would be so daring.*

"An elephant," Molly squealed.

"What is that?" Sally asked.

"It's an animal bigger than an ox."

Jacob turned to his sisters. "I'm having a conversation that does not include either of you."

Sarah started to giggle and covered it with a cough.

"If I get a young elephant, it won't take up too much space. What do you think?"

"I hardly know what to say."

"Well, listen a bit further to my plan. When I return, I shall sell the elephant for a large profit so I can ask your father's permission to court you properly. Would you like that?"

"Very much."

"I'm glad to hear it." Jacob smirked. "I don't fancy a long courtship."

"Well." Sarah shook her head. "That's probably up to my father."

"Actually, it isn't. You are of age and can set your own wedding date."

*What does he mean by that?*

Sarah glanced away from Jacob's face. "I'm sorry?"

Jacob grabbed Sarah's hands. "I could be gone two years. I want to marry you as soon as possible after I return. The moment I sell the elephant, we can post the banns. Why waste any more time?"

Sarah laughed softly. "I haven't agreed to marry you yet. And weddings take time to plan. I want my family there. And the bridecake has to mature for several weeks. And . . ."

*Jacob seems so sure about everything, but an elephant? How can it survive the journey? And do I want to marry Jacob? Actually, that's the only thing I'm sure of. But he hasn't actually asked me yet.*

"We'll do what we did before. I'll write every day and send the letters whenever there's someone to take them. So you'll know I have an elephant on board. And when I get to New York, I'll write immediately so you can start your cake. It will take us about two months to get organized, and the cake will be done, the banns will be read, and you'll have a new dress. And don't worry, my parents can host the engagement party, and the wedding can be at your father's house. Nothing simpler. Say you approve."

# Eliza Derby

*June 1795*
*Hasket Derby's House*

"Look here." Eliza pointed to the architectural drawing by Charles Bulfinch.

"We have a massive piece of property," she gushed. "We'll have three stories and a cupola, and huge gardens with walks and sea views, and a conservatory with exotic flowers. It will be a showcase. People will come from miles to see the outside and beg for an invitation inside."

Patsy walked around the drawings. "Do you and Father need such a large house? It seems so extravagant. It's only Elias and I who are still at home, and I'm sure he'll marry the woman from Boston soon."

"Patsy," Betsey replied testily, "how can you say such a thing? It's not about how many family members live there. The servants need space in the attic. And there will be guests and entertainments. Father promised mother she would lead Salem society. Now she'll have the proper setting."

Eliza glared at Patsy. "Thank you, Betsey. I'm pleased you understand the importance of the statement we're making."

Anstiss shook her head. "I'm afraid I have to agree with Patsy. Such a fine mansion will invite jealousy."

"Our very existence invites jealousy," Betsey replied. "In fact, is it possible I detect a bit of jealousy from you? Your husband could never afford to build such a house. Father has been planning this for years. He has the land and money to build a showcase. Why shouldn't he do it?"

# Captain Elias Derby

*Essex Street, Salem*

From their vantage point across Essex Street, Elias and Zeke watched workmen clearing the lot for their father's new mansion. Elias winced to see Reverend William Bentley among the crowd of viewers.

"Trust the good reverend to be here," Elias muttered.

"He's harmless enough. And this is certainly a sight to see. No one tears down a perfectly good house."

"Except our father."

"Did Mother finally select an architect? When I begin building on this lot, I shall select the same man. It will make matters easier."

"How so?"

"I hope to use the same basic design, on a smaller scale, of course. Did she stick with McIntire? He designed our other houses."

Elias rubbed the back of his neck. "Patsy said she finally settled on Bulfinch from Boston. You know how she likes to do things differently."

"Bulfinch, eh? He'll be expensive. But if it's just a matter of scaling down the structure, it shouldn't cost too much."

Elias snorted. "Cost doesn't matter. Father gives each of us a house after we get married."

"True, but I'll provide the furnishings. And, we have no need of a mansion the size of this one. If we want a garden stroll, we'll just cross the street."

The crowd cheered when workmen standing on scaffolds began pounding sledgehammers into the exterior walls.

"I'm glad it's you who will be across the street from Father," Elias said. "I see quite enough of him in the counting house, where I must now return."

"Before you go." Zeke hesitated.

Elias gave his brother a quizzical look. "What?"

"Your creditors came to Father's office before you arrived yesterday."

"He hasn't said anything to me."

"I didn't hear anything from him about it. Perhaps they had other business to conduct. But, Elias, you need to get a handle on your debts."

"My luck will turn. I'm sure of it."

# Captain George Crowninshield

*Crowninshield House*

George and Mary strolled through the garden behind their house on Derby Street.

Mary stopped to admire colorful poppies wearing fresh spring faces before leading her husband through a patch of lavender to a bench under the apple trees.

"Did you know your brother is tearing down the Browne mansion?" George asked.

"Ah," Mary said. "That's why you've been so grumpy this week. Your sister probably persuaded him to build her a house larger than the one she has now. And the only way she can do that is if she builds something completely new. She's always reached beyond her grasp."

"Well, your brother apparently has no objection. Tearing down one house and building another will cost a pretty penny."

"Yes, but he has the pennies to spend."

George barked out a laugh and lifted his wife's hand. "And you, my dear. Would you like me to build you a new house?"

Mary laughed. "Certainly not. I prefer to stay in our cozy brick house near the wharf with our daughters close by."

"I enjoy spending spring evenings with you in our garden."

Mary kissed her husband's cheek. "It's also pleasant to come out after dark to see the stars."

"Can you still find Orion's Belt?" George grinned.

"Come out with me after dark tonight, and I'll show you Castor and Pollux."

"Will you indeed?"

"I much prefer stargazing to house plans. But first, let's go in for supper. Our daughters will be waiting."

# Captain Elias Derby

*August 1795*
*Salem Inn*

Taking a table near the front of the Salem Inn, Elias tapped a fresh deck of cards on its scarred surface. When people tired of watching workmen sling their hammers, they would seek refreshment, and the Salem Inn was the closest to Essex Street. Elias had just enough money in his pocket to stake a game.

Elias sipped his ale and let his thoughts wander. If his creditors visited Hasket's office, they likely wanted surety on his gambling debts, or perhaps one of them was his tailor. *I should have asked Zeke. Surely, Father won't object to my new coat. On the other hand, he definitely objects to my poor investments. It's not as if I control the markets or the weather, and I don't have his deep pockets to cushion the losses.*

Elias called for more ale. A few men came in and nodded to him but didn't pull up chairs. *I'll never be able to marry Lucy if I don't clear my debts enough to furnish a house.* Thoughts of Lucy ignited a deep longing for his own hearth, no matter how simple. But Lucy deserved more than simple.

Elias called for a quill pen, ink, and paper. With writing material in front of him, he thought of the loving, confident support Lucy always expressed for his endeavors. He never mentioned how often his consignments failed to get a good price. That was the nice thing about sea voyages. He could tell her what he sent out and avoid mentioning the result at the market.

*My dear Miss Brown,* Elias wrote.

> For some time, I have been wishing for an opportunity to unfold to you the interest you have in my heart, and the desire I feel to contribute by every manner within my power to the promotion of your happiness.
>
> Today my father began clearing property on Essex Street, where he will build a mansion according to my mother's desires. It fulfills a promise he made to her before they married. And as my mother trusted my father to fulfill her hopes, I hope you will honor me with the same level of trust.
>
> Have you given any thought to coming to Salem next January for the sleighing? I'm sure if I mention your desire to visit, my brother will extend an invitation.
>
> I eagerly await your reply.
>
> Your obedient servant,
>
> Elias Hasket Derby Jr.

Elias folded the paper, called for sealing wax, and held a candle so red wax dripped over the letter to keep it sealed.

When the barmaid brought another tankard of ale, Elias asked her to post the letter on the next stage to Boston.

Three men came to Elias's table. They looked to have modest means, but Elias wasn't concerned about whom he played against as long as they had a stake.

"Care for a game of cards? Take a chair."

Elias began shuffling the deck. "What's your game?"

# Captain Nathaniel Silsbee

*September 1795*
*Aboard the* Benjamin, *Isle de France*

"Congratulations, Richard, you are now captain of the *Benjamin*."

"I'm not sure Mr. Derby would agree."

Nath grinned. "Of course he would. It's the first mate's duty to take charge if the captain can't fulfill his duties. And since I just resigned in order to captain my own ship, you are required to take the position. Just continue the log with my resignation letter, and all will be well. You have a fine crew on a fine ship with a good cargo."

"Doesn't seem right somehow, but you don't leave me much choice."

"None at all, my friend."

Richard drew his eyebrows together. "Are you certain you want to do this? Mr. Derby may not give you another ship."

"I don't need one. I'm part owner of the *Betsey*, and I own this ship outright. We'll sail in tandem until we get to Boston, where you will off-load the cargo while I continue on to Salem."

"Nath," William called up from the tender, "we have to go."

"Are you sure about the crew you signed on? They don't look dependable," Richard said.

Nath sighed in exasperation and put his hand out. "Richard, you're being foolish. It's a straight run from Isle de France to our home port. Shake my hand and wish me Godspeed."

Richard pumped Nath's arm. "When we're all back, I'll stand you drinks at the Ship."

"I'll hold you to it." Nath swung his leg over the rail onto the rope ladder.

"Shove off, William. It's time to put our new ship through her paces."

Nath could hardly believe his good fortune. When the *Benjamin* arrived at Port Louis on Isle de France, trade was brisk and prices high. Not only did Mr. Derby benefit, but Nath's adventure cargo brought enough profit for him to spend $10,000 on a four-hundred-ton teakwood ship, which he filled with coffee and cotton. The only fly in the ointment was his temporary crew, a hodgepodge of sailors who found themselves looking for work. He and William had their duties cut out for them to keep the crew at their tasks, but he could release them at Salem.

"What do you think, William? We have our own ship at last."

"I think you should sell her and invest the proceeds in several ships."

Nath winked. "My thoughts exactly."

# Captain Nathaniel Silsbee

*At Sea Near Boston*

William handed Nath a spyglass. "You need to take a look at this. She started shadowing us yesterday."

Nath adjusted the eyepiece. "What's your thinking?"

"It's the way she sails, always keeping the same distance on the starboard side. And I can't see her flags. I think she's a privateer, and she likes our boat."

"Could be. But we're only a couple days out from Boston. She'd be risking other ships joining the fray."

"Except, at the moment, there aren't any ships near us. The *Benjamin* pulled ahead of us. What do you think we should do?"

Nath passed the spyglass back to William. "Fight, of course. We have six guns and twenty-five men. Hopefully we're wrong, but just in case, we need to prepare for battle."

William put the boatswain's whistle to his lips and piped the call for combat quarters.

The first mate, a towering man of few words, circulated among the watch sections before addressing Nath. "Sir, I regret to inform you that we have five men who refuse to fight for our ship."

Nath pursed his lips. "Any particular reason?"

"They believe that joining your crew did not commit them to combat."

"And what do you think?" Nath asked.

"I think they should defend our ship. After all, if we go down, so do they."

"Well said. Bring me the cowards. Then secure every passageway that goes belowdecks. I won't have them cowering below the waterline."

The mate ordered the dissenters into a straight line. Nath walked down the line, noticing that none of the men met his eye.

"Preston tells me you didn't sign on to defend our ship. Yet you expect to be paid for sailing her. Curious."

Nath gave the men a chance to consider his words.

"Anyone have anything to say? No? I cannot force you to fight, but you're still members of my crew, which means I can order you to repair the ratlines."

"You can't do that," one of the sailors said. "We'll be exposed to their cannon fire."

Nath growled. "I think you'll find that, in the sailing of this ship, I can do whatever I bloody well please." He drew a pistol from under his coat. "Start climbing or I'll shoot you where you stand."

Slowly, the men grabbed onto the rope ladders that would take them to the flapping sails.

The privateer continued sailing toward Nath's brig. When she began turning around to expose her guns, the dissenting sailors scrambled back to the deck.

"Captain Silsbee, permission to defend our ship."

"Granted." William stood at Nath's elbow, awaiting orders. "Prepare to fire."

"Load and aim," William ordered the gun crews.

Men rammed gunpowder and a cloth wad into each gun barrel, followed by the cannonball and another cloth wad. Crews ran the cannon out of the gunports.

"Full volley on my command," Nath ordered.

Nath watched his enemy dispassionately. He didn't want to damage the approaching ship so much as scare her off. *If the discharge isn't enough to impress them, I'll lose time while we reload. Time that could allow the privateer to damage or cripple us.* Nath raised his spyglass, surprised how clearly he could see men on the enemy ship. There were enough to muster a prize crew.

Nath clenched his jaw and held his arm up.

*Wait for it. Wait for it.*

"Fire!"

The order echoed down the line as gun crews ignited the touchholes. Smoke belched out of the gunports. Gun carriages traveled backward from the recoil. Crewmen cleared the barrels and awaited orders to reload.

To Nath's relief, the privateer heaved off from her attack. He looked through his spyglass, but there was no evident damage significant enough to explain his enemy's choice to break contact. *Perhaps she wasn't expecting resistance.* Nath reset his course for Salem while keeping an eye on the privateer until she fell off the horizon.

# Captain Nathaniel Silsbee

*November 1795*
*Derby Counting House*

Dressed in his good suit, Nath left his hat and outercoat on a peg near the door of Hasket Derby's counting house.

"Nath," a voice called out. "Welcome home." Zeke Derby rose from his place on the main floor and came forward to shake Nath's hand and clap him on the back. "It's good to see you again. Richard came in yesterday with the *Benjamin*'s logs, and your success with her trade and cargo is outstanding."

"It was Richard who brought her home."

"Aye. But it was you who took her out and conducted business matters. You'll be happy to know Father is so pleased with your success, he actually smiled." Zeke winked. "So, tell me, are you going to sell the ship you bought at Isle de France?"

"As soon as may be. She represents most of my adventure cargo. Would you like to buy her?"

"Truth be told, I'm more of an investor than a buyer."

Nath chuckled. "You always were clever in business. I heard you married while I was gone. How do you like your new life?"

"I only wish I married sooner. But then"—Zeke shrugged—"I had to wait for my darling Hannah to appear." Zeke inclined his head toward the stairs. "You'd better go up. You know how punctual Father can be."

Nath chuckled again and started up the stairs. Outside Hasket's door, he adjusted his cravat and squared his shoulders. *I'm not the boy with few prospects anymore,* Nath reminded himself and rapped three times on the door before opening it.

Hasket looked up from his papers, smiled with closed lips, and stood with his hand outstretched.

"Captain Silsbee, glad to see you back safe and sound. Your log, accounts, and the *new* captain's verbal report indicate another successful voyage. Please sit."

Nath spread his coattails and sat on the edge of the single straight-back chair in front of Hasket's desk.

"I'm disappointed you resigned your command. Why did you make that decision?"

Nath shrugged. "I sold my adventure cargo and purchased the teak ship I sailed home. She's a sound ship and gave me a chance to increase my profits." He smiled ruefully. "Since I couldn't sail two ships at the same time, didn't think it prudent to separate the *Benjamin*'s crew, and knowing my attention would be divided, I decided to leave your employ. There would be no harm to you since business matters were settled, and Richard was qualified to bring her home."

"I see." Hasket steepled his fingers.

Nath fought down the urge to fidget and kept a calm expression on his face.

"I understand you encountered privateers as you neared Boston?" Hasket raised his eyebrows.

"We did. Both our ships sailed alone, so we were evenly matched in that sense. After we released a volley of cannon fire, the privateer broke off our engagement." Nath shrugged. "The remainder of our voyage was uneventful."

"Excellent. These times require a cool head such as yours has proven to be. Captain Silsbee, I have a proposal for you, if you'd like to hear it."

Nath smiled. "I'm always open to your ideas."

"I've enjoyed watching your career in my employ. You have skill, ambition, and a clear head—all attributes I look for in my ship's captains. I'm building a new ship for the India trade. Not so large as the *Grand Turk* was, but able to carry a substantial cargo. I'd like you to accept her command. Alternatively, I can offer you part ownership in any other ship you sail for me."

Nath's jaw dropped in shock before he quickly closed his mouth. *What an opportunity! But is it what I want? Now that I've had a taste of owning my own ship, do I want to go back to percentages in someone else's?*

Hasket waited for Nath's response.

"You do me great honor, sir," Nath began. "I must admit I've given such a possibility some thought."

"Did you reach any conclusions?"

"I did. I concluded on the basis of my last two successful voyages that I can better serve my own and my family's interests if I establish my own business ventures."

Hasket chuckled. "You have ambition, Captain Silsbee, and the means to make your ambitions reality. I admire your courage. Many men would choose the safer route."

Nath shook his head. "I have discovered that what looks like a safe route often fails. So, one loses nothing by taking a risk."

"I hold the same perspective."

Hasket stood and held out his hand. "I'm confident we'll do business together in the future."

"Yes, sir. I look forward to it."

Nath hardly noticed descending the stairs or putting on his coat before going outside to the wharf. *I did it. I settled my father's debts and made a stake for my own business. When people hear the name Nathaniel Silsbee, they will think of me and my success, not my drunken debtor father.*

# Captain Jacob Crowninshield

*December 1795*
*Calcutta*

"The elephant will not be happy."

Jacob glanced at his banian. The *America* was almost loaded. Extra casks of water filled the upper deck. Bales of straw filled the hold. Only his adventure cargo was left.

"Are you really doing this?" Benj asked. "If the beast gets loose, it could sink your ship."

"I'm confident we can keep her penned. Once she's loaded, we'll engage a sling."

"The elephant will not be happy, sir," the banian repeated. "It will need fresh air."

"We can open the gunports. Don't distress yourself. The beast is my entire adventure cargo. I won't lose it."

The banian nodded implacably. "Very well. I'm sure you know best."

"I don't share your confidence, Jacob," Benj said.

"You could have come in with me." Jacob laughed. "It's still not too late to invest half the cost. It will be the first elephant in America. Someone will pay a fortune for it."

Benj shook his head. "I don't know how you'll feed it, let alone have enough water to keep it alive."

The normal chatter of dockworkers reached a crescendo as the elephant, with her mahout mounted behind her ears, made her way forward to the ship.

"*Aghath,*" the mahout called.

The elephant swayed from side to side to avoid obstacles of men and carts. Eventually, she stopped by the gangplank. The mahout scratched her ears and dismounted.

"It's not as large as I expected. In fact, I've seen larger oxen," Benj said.

"Yes, but you've never seen an ox with a trunk. People will pay to see her. More importantly, someone will buy her, and my fortune will be made."

"No one can accuse you of low expectations. Does the fellow with her speak English?"

"He will by the time we arrive in New York. I've assigned a crew member to him." Just then, another man approached. "Ah, Thomas, there you are. Show our passenger into the hold and secure her. From now until we reach home, you are in charge of keeping this beast alive. And if you are successful, you'll have a bonus in your wages."

The burley sailor towered over the mahout. "Excuse me, Captain Crowninshield, sir, do we have anything for him to wear besides that loin-cloth? He's going to be cold."

"Excellent point. Dress him out of the slop chest. Now, let's get the beast loaded so we can be off with the tide."

Jacob held out his hand to his banian. "Until we meet again, sir." The man shook Jacob's hand before putting his palms together and making a slight bow.

Jacob watched the mahout guide his charge with a short hooked pole. The elephant turned her head with a wide side eye but continued forward into the hold. Crewmen quickly lifted the lower gangplank.

"Right." Jacob extended his hand to Benj. "The next time we meet ashore, we'll take on supplies at Cape Town."

"Good luck with your cargo, Brother."

"Luck has nothing to do with it. For a small investment, I shall reap great profits, marry our lovely cousin Sarah, and set up housekeeping." Jacob winked. "The world is full of possibilities."

Benj clapped his brother on the back as Jacob mounted the *America's* gangplank.

"I'm sure you'll earn your fortune, provided the elephant survives. On the other hand, Sir won't appreciate having to clean up your ship after a six-month voyage with an elephant on board. I'll stick to traditional adventures like silk, bohea tea, and coffee."

Jacob chuckled and mounted the gangplank. *Slow and steady. That was Benj's motto.*

# Captain Jacob Crowninshield

*April 1796*
*New York City*

The ship *America*, under the leadership of Captain Jacob Crowninshield of Salem, Massachusetts, commander and owner, has brought home an elephant from Bengal in perfect health. It is the first ever seen in America and is a great curiosity. It is a female, two years old.

Standing at the ship's rail, Jacob slapped the newspaper on his knee and lit a cheroot. The taper flared as he drew on the small cigar. He threw the ember over the side and watched it float down to the water.

"Excuse me, Captain Crowninshield, sir."

"Thomas." Jacob smiled. "You got our charge here in reasonable health. Congratulations."

Jacob held his hand out to his crewman.

Thomas cleared his throat. "There might be trouble getting the elephant off the ship. She's . . . um . . . drunk."

"Drunk? Why?"

Thomas shifted his feet. "We didn't take on enough water at Saint Helena, but we had plenty of beer. I didn't think you would want the crew to overindulge, so I gave the beast beer instead of water. And . . . now she prefers it. In fact, we brought water on board for her yesterday, but she wouldn't drink it."

"And?"

"She took her usual ration of beer this morning, and it went to her head. I'm sorry, sir. Perhaps we can off-load her tomorrow."

"Look below. The reporters and sketch artists are here today. We need to take advantage of their enthusiasm. Can the beast walk?"

"I think so. She'll sway a bit."

"The crowd won't know any different. Anyway, all elephants sway. You just need to get her to our warehouse on the wharf. The mahout can get her there, I'm sure."

Thomas scratched his head. "I'll get them to the warehouse, sir. Never you fear."

Jacob waved his hand to dismiss Thomas and then called him back. "Thomas, is the beer in a barrel, or does the beast drink it from bottles?"

"Bottles, sir. She drinks thirty quarts every day."

"And do you open them for her?"

"I did at first. But she figured out how to pull out the cork with her trunk. And then she tips the bottle into her mouth. It's quite funny to watch, sir."

Jacob quirked his lips. "Give her slightly less than what she needs today. Tomorrow, take her to the exhibition area at the corner of Beaver and Broadway. Leave her inside with the mahout and sell tickets. I'll introduce her myself."

The following day, Jacob found himself at the exhibition area, which was on a busy corner of the entertainment district in New York City. The novelty of an elephant was too much for newspapers to resist. A crowd of curiosity seekers gathered, hoping for a glimpse of the beast, but Jacob kept her under wraps at the back of the exhibition tent. The animal was thirsty and nervous from the noise.

Jacob was pleased at the size of the crowd. At twenty-five cents a ticket, he would soon recoup his purchase price of $450. Disappointed at being able to hear the beast but not see it, men began to buy tickets. Thomas stood at the door to keep out freeloaders. Men sat on benches inside, smoking and spitting, until Jacob judged the venue full. He noticed a garishly well-dressed man standing behind the benches and smiled to himself. He could almost see the man counting heads and doing his sums.

Jacob, dressed immaculately, motioned Thomas to prepare the elephant to move and walked into the center of the exhibition area.

"You are indeed fortunate to be here," Jacob began. "You are the first Americans to see this remarkable, fantastical beast from farthest India. What you are about to see is a young elephant who came here in the hold of my ship the *America*. She traveled belowdecks, feasting on one hundred thirty pounds of vegetation every day. Unlike my crew, the creature prefers greens."

Jacob waited for the rustle of laughter to subside. "But there's nothing interesting about an elephant that eats vegetation. You could watch an ox eat for the same effect, except for the extraordinarily long nose the beast has. A protrusion that picks up her food and places it in her mouth the same way we use our arms."

As if on cue, the creature trumpeted behind the canvas.

When the crowd gasped, Jacob cocked his head. "Ladies and gentlemen, I present to you the first elephant ever to set foot in America, and her Indian mahout."

"*Chai*," the mahout called, touching the elephant's left flank with a long pole. When the elephant reached the center of the viewing area, the mahout stood on its left front toe and began stroking the elephant's trunk.

Thomas tossed the mahout a quart bottle of beer. The mahout held it out at the end of the elephant's trunk. Delicately, the creature removed the cork and tossed it aside. The mahout then placed the bottle so the elephant could balance it at the end of her trunk, which she then turned to pour the bottle's contents into her mouth before tossing the container aside.

The audience broke into laughter and applause. Thomas tossed the mahout another bottle, and the performance continued.

"The beast can drink thirty bottles of beer a day with no visible effect."

The audience laughed and clapped each time the elephant tipped another bottle into her mouth. When half the bottles lay scattered on the ground, the mahout turned the elephant and led her away.

Audience members broke out into cheers and made their way out of the venue.

"That's quite an amazing sight, Captain Crowninshield. When does she get the rest of her beer?"

Jacob turned to see the strangely dressed man he had noticed before. "At the next show, of course."

"My name is Owen, and I'd like to buy your elephant. Is it for sale?"

"My dear sir," Jacob beamed. "Everything is for sale, provided the price is right. Shall we adjourn our conversation to the tavern across the way?"

Jacob led Owen past the line of people waiting to purchase tickets for the next performance. It wouldn't hurt to show the man that exhibiting an elephant was lucrative.

In the tavern, men who had been in the audience regaled their companions with the tale of an elephant who could essentially open a bottle of beer with one hand, which was more than most men could do.

Owen brought two glasses of whiskey back to the table.

"To your health," Jacob saluted. "Do you know anything about elephants?"

"I know enough to hire his handler to take care of the beast."

Jacob grunted his agreement.

"I'm offering $10,000 for the elephant, provided I can take delivery after the next exhibition, and the stable hand comes with him."

Jacob almost spit out a mouthful of whiskey. The man was offering twenty-two times what he'd paid for the creature.

"I will send word to my agent at Bailey & Bogart. Once you deposit certificates for the $10,000, he will give you ownership papers and send word to me. You can pick up the beast at the warehouse we're using. If I don't hear from him by close of business tomorrow, our negotiation is void. You'll have to talk directly to the mahout, but I'm pretty sure he doesn't want to be separated from his charge."

Jacob held out his hand, and Owen clasped it with both of his. "It's a pleasure doing business with you."

As Owen pushed out the door, Jacob motioned the barmaid for another whiskey, lit a cheroot, and puffed contentedly. *Benj will rue his decision not to share the investment. But I'm glad to keep it all for myself. Once I get the money, Sarah and I can marry. And then I shall enter politics.*

# Captain Jacob Crowninshield

*April 1796*
*Salem*

"Whoa!"

The stagecoach stopped with a lurch in front of the Salem Inn. Six horses stamped their feet and blew out their nostrils.

Jacob nodded to the driver as he dismounted. "Thinking of a good feed, no doubt."

"Aye." The driver threw down Jacob's small chest.

"Enjoy a drink on me." Jacob tossed a coin up, hoisted the chest to his shoulder, and walked down to his father's house on Derby Street. It had only been a year since he sailed the *America* over to Calcutta, but his entire life had changed for the better, thanks to the elephant and people's enthusiasm for exotic entertainment. Soon he would be a married man with his own house.

Jacob rapped on the front door.

"Captain Crowninshield, sir! Welcome home." Marcus took Jacob's coat and picked up the chest. "I'll take it to your room. The family is just sitting down to dinner."

Jacob held a finger to his lips. "I'll announce myself."

In the back dining parlor, Jacob's parents and sisters sat around the wooden table his mother had brought with her when she set up housekeeping. She said it reminded her of sharing meals with her brothers and sisters. The curtains were open to the afternoon light. Jacob paused in the doorway, taking in the scene before entering the room.

"Can you lay another place for dinner?" Jacob smirked. "I haven't had a chance to change yet."

"Jacob!" Mary Crowninshield jumped up from the table and rushed to hug her son. She grabbed each side of his face as if to be sure he was really there. "You're home."

Jacob extricated himself. "Did you doubt me, Mame?"

"Of course not, but I worry when my sons are at sea, and now that you've returned, I have one less to worry about. Here, come sit by me. Move down, girls. Abigail, bring another chair to the table—and a place setting."

George stood and reached around his wife to shake Jacob's hand.

"Welcome home, son. Sit. Your mother wants you to herself, but we'll speak after dinner when we have a bit more room."

Just as Jacob sat, Molly and Sally came to either side of him and grabbed his hands.

Jacob laughed, stood up again, and hugged them both.

George cleared his throat. "Girls, there'll be time enough for that after our meal. Please take your seats. Jacob, what's this you wrote about an elephant?"

In between bites of ragout and fresh bread, Jacob told tales of keeping an elephant alive at sea.

"It all went remarkably well, though she now prefers beer to water, which her new owner may find a bit expensive."

"And you got a good price for her?" George asked.

"Ten thousand American dollars." Jacob grinned.

George slapped the table. "Well done, son."

"Thank you, Sir." Jacob preened under his father's praise.

"And what are your intentions now?" George asked. "Do you have plans for your next voyage?"

"Before we discuss Jacob's future," Mary interrupted, "let's be more comfortable in the drawing room. I told Abigail to serve coffee and biscuits. Molly, Sally, please clear the table before you join us."

Molly immediately began clearing plates. "Hurry up, Sally. I want to find out what Jacob's going to do next."

The diamond windowpanes in the drawing room glittered with rays from the setting sun. Abigail placed the silver coffee service and porcelain cups next to a plate of ratafia cakes on the low table in front of the sofa.

Mary poured coffee into her son's cup. "Still three spoonfuls of sugar?"

Jacob nodded and watched his mother spoon sugar into the thick liquid before passing the cup.

"How long will you stay in Salem?" George asked. "You can assist me with a number of business arrangements."

Jacob stirred his coffee several times before taking a sip.

"While at sea, I spent a lot of time thinking about my future."

Alarm crossed George's face. "You're not thinking of striking out on your own?"

"Most assuredly not, Sir. My future is with our company. No. I was thinking of another aspect of my future."

"Were you thinking of Sarah?" Mary asked. "You've been seeing each other quite a bit when you've been ashore."

*How shall I phrase this? It's always best to be straightforward.* "You always have good intuition, Mame."

Mary nodded. "Go on."

"Before I left with the *America*, Sarah and I reached an understanding of sorts. She's presently staying with her father, and I shall call on her tomorrow."

Molly and Sally rushed into the drawing room.

"Have you said anything important?" Sally demanded.

Jacob chuckled. "Not yet."

"And he won't if you women don't stop interrupting him," George growled.

"Tell us," Molly demanded.

Jacob swallowed a sip of what was now lukewarm coffee. "Yes, but first, promise me you won't say anything before I confirm Sarah and I are agreed."

Mary was so close to the edge of the sofa, she looked as if she would slide off the cushion.

"Stop stalling, Jacob. Say what you have to say."

"Yes, Mame." Jacob took a steadying breath. "When I call on Sarah tomorrow, I shall formally ask for her hand in marriage."

Mary's eyes filled with tears. "I can't tell you how much this means to me. Since the day my sister died, I've prayed Sarah would one day join our family."

Mary reached for her son's hands and squeezed them tightly. "Jacob, I'm proud of everything you have accomplished, but your decision about Sarah brings me more joy than I can describe."

Jacob felt a flood of emotion. Ever since he was a boy he yearned for his mother's affection and approval, and now he had both.

"Well, er, I don't know if she'll accept me. I've left her to her own devices far too long."

"Nonsense," George said. "We've been family friends and relations for years. It's a wonderful match. Good for the family and good for business. I have no doubt there will soon be a wedding."

Jacob's sisters squealed. "We must have new dresses," Molly said.

"I'll consider it," Mary replied.

George poured out three glasses of brandy and two very small glasses of Madeira.

"Are you certain?" Mary asked.

"It's not every day a son of mine proposes marriage to a lovely young woman. Such an event deserves a toast. To your success, Jacob—in business and in life."

# Sarah Gardner

*Captain John Gardner's House*

Sarah clutched Jacob's note to her chest and danced around the garden. *He'll call tomorrow and then . . . What?* Her smile dropped.

Heavy footsteps crunched on the gravel. "Sarah, are you out here?"

"Yes, Father." Sarah abruptly stopped dancing and shoved Jacob's note into her pocket. "I'm just by the kitchen garden."

Captain Gardner rounded the corner. "I heard the front door close. Did someone call?"

"Er, not precisely, but Jacob will call tomorrow. The *America* arrived in New York two weeks ago, and, I can hardly believe it, but he brought back an elephant and sold it."

"Did he get a good price?"

"I don't know. But he must have sold it for more than what he paid for it."

Captain Gardner grunted. "That's usually the Crowninshield way. Any particular reason Jacob wants to call? You'll have to have one of the maids as chaperone."

Sarah's heart thudded in her chest. "Of course. I'm sure Jacob is just calling out of friendship. We are cousins, after all." Sarah nervously smoothed her dress.

"According to your Aunt Elizabeth, your relationship is a bit deeper than family ties."

"I don't know how she can say that. What other reason could there be?"

Captain Gardner stroked his chin. "I'm thinking that if there is another reason, it would have something to do with the enormous fruitcake aging in our kitchen."

Mary dropped her head and blushed furiously. "Perhaps."

"And a bridecake by any other name is a fruitcake."

Sarah made a choking sound.

"Speak up, daughter. I can't quite hear you."

"You are, as always, correct, Father," Sarah said with a brittle laugh. "Bridecakes and fruitcakes are much the same. Though the size varies . . ." Her voice dropped off.

"You've never been much good at spinning stories, Sarah. And if I wasn't already an observant man, your aunt supplies me with plenty of information about your comings and goings. So here is what I think. Although Jacob Crowninshield never asked my permission to court you, you spend time together whenever he's in Salem. I can understand if you don't wish to speak of Jacob because the situation makes you look foolish. But perhaps you could explain more about the fruitcake."

*Does Father approve of Jacob? Is he trying to discourage me? It doesn't matter. I'm of age. I can make my own decision. I'll just tell Father my expectations. Yes, that should work. Maybe.*

Sarah squared her shoulders and took a deep breath. "Ah, yes, the cake. Well, Jacob and I have an understanding of sorts. Um, I agreed not to accept suitors while he's away, and um, we write each other."

"I'm aware."

"And I am of age now. I don't need your permission," Mary said with an edge of defiance.

Captain Gardner held out his arm. "Since we're in the garden and it's a pleasant evening, we may as well stroll about."

Sarah placed her hand on her father's arm and followed his lead as he guided them toward the box hedge at the rear of the garden.

"I know you are of age, and I can't forbid your choice of suitor, though I may offer advice." Captain Gardner smiled. "I've known Jacob Crowninshield all of his life. His mother was your mother's sister. And I've had business dealings with George Crowninshield, carried his cargo on ships I sailed. If you make a match with young Jacob, I certainly have no objection. But you should have mentioned your connection sooner."

"Jacob wanted to keep things quiet until he could declare himself."

"Which you think he will do tomorrow?"

Sarah nodded. "I hope so. If he made enough money from the elephant."

Captain Gardner grunted. "*Now* will you tell me about the fruitcake? Are you hoping to serve it at your wedding?"

Sarah laughed nervously. "Yes, you've found me out. I didn't want to delay my wedding to Jacob because I had to wait for the bridecake to age."

"So you started it early. I understand your thinking, though Jacob may find it presumptuous."

"I don't know what he'll say, but I'd like to marry as soon as the banns are read. We're both twenty-five years old, and I see no reason to wait."

The following afternoon, Sarah tried to calm her nerves by focusing on her appearance. Sitting at her dressing table, she peered into the tarnished mirror. *Possibly the most important day in my life, and I can't properly see what I look like.* Sarah pinched her cheeks. The bedroom door cracked open.

"Shall I come in now, miss? I have your dress."

*Is it that late already?* A flutter flew up from Sarah's stomach.

"Yes, yes, come in Louisa. I'm just finishing my hair. I can't decide. Up, or slightly down, or . . . ?"

"Allow me, miss."

Louisa pulled up Sarah's hair, looped curls down the left side of her face, and attached a silver hair clip to keep them in place.

"Thank you so much!"

Louisa pursed her lips. "You'll want to pinch your cheeks again and bite your lips before you greet your guest, or you'll look too pale."

"And you'll be in the drawing room with us?" Sarah confirmed.

"Yes, I'll be in the far corner to give you privacy. Marion will bring in the tea things, so nothing will call attention to me."

Sarah swallowed. "That sounds excellent. Yes." She nodded.

"Now step into your shoes and let me adjust your clothing."

Louisa dropped the white muslin gown into place and adjusted a broad ribbon under Sarah's bustline.

"Yes, that will do," she clucked. "I don't much like the new fashion. Too much white, if you ask me. But I'm sure your guest won't be taking fashion notes."

When she went downstairs, Sarah made a final check of the drawing room.

"You look very attractive, Sarah. Captain Crowninshield is sure to be smitten, if he isn't already."

"Father!" Sarah gasped. "I didn't hear you come in."

"I'm not surprised. You've had your head in the clouds all day. I'll be glad when things are settled between you and Captain Crowninshield."

"Yes," Sarah squeaked.

Captain Gardner cupped a hand by his ear. "I hear a horse outside, so I'll leave you to it. If Captain Crowninshield wishes to speak to me, I'll be in my study. Good luck, my dear."

Captain Gardner kissed Sarah's forehead and left the room. Five minutes later, the housekeeper escorted Jacob into the drawing room.

"Captain Crowninshield is here, miss. I'll tell Marian to bring the tea things."

"Yes, thank you," Sarah said. "Captain Crowninshield, how very nice of you to call." She curtsied as Jacob bowed. "Please sit near me on the sofa."

"Miss Gardner," Jacob said softly, "it is an honor to call upon you. Since other than your chaperone we are alone, may we dispense with formalities?"

Sarah giggled. "We are cousins, after all. There's no need to be formal."

Marian arranged the tea service on the low table and departed.

"Tea?" Sarah offered and added sugar to the cup of hot liquid. "We also have biscuits if you like. So, tell me all about your voyage on the *America*, especially the elephant. Did you let it loose on the deck?"

Jacob shook his head. "We had to keep her in the cargo hold for the entire voyage, but we kept the gunwales open, so she had fresh air."

"Oh. Did her legs cramp?"

"I don't know. I think the mahout had her stamp her feet from time to time."

"And is it true she drinks beer?"

"Every day. Do you want to spend our entire visit discussing elephants?"

"I suppose not, except, did you sell her for enough money to . . . um?"

"Set up my own household? I did indeed." Jacob put his untouched cup onto the table, winked, and picked up Sarah's hands. "I've kept you waiting a very long time. You've been patient with me, and now I can reward your endurance."

Sarah felt her heart rate speed up.

"Sarah, we've known each other all our lives. Our mothers were sisters. We are, I think, very compatible. And we would make a good match."

"Yes?" Sarah asked.

Jacob pulled his cravat away from his neck. "I . . . I'm feeling a bit shy all of a sudden."

*Shy?*

Jacob cleared his throat. "Sarah Gardner, will you do me the honor of becoming my wife?"

"Yes. Absolutely," Sarah blurted before blushing deeply.

"Wait, before you answer, I should tell you that I plan to make my way in politics. It's time to take the Derbys down from their dominance of Essex County. It could mean I have to be away while I fulfill my duties for elected office. You would have to take care of our affairs when I'm gone."

Sarah bobbed her head. "I don't mind. I can always ask my father for help if I need it, or yours, I suppose."

"The idea doesn't frighten you?"

"I know you'll look after me, even if you're away. And it won't be for long, will it, if you are?"

"No, no. Of course not. So, your answer . . . ?"

"Is still yes." Sarah smiled broadly. "And I don't want a long engagement. I want to marry as soon as the banns are read. We can have the wedding here, and I already started the bridecake, so it will be ready as soon as may be. And Uncle John says he has a house we can live in."

Jacob laughed. "How could you be sure I would ask?"

Sarah reached out to touch Jacob's cheek. "I suppose because you asked me not to take other suitors, and I wanted you so much. So, I thought I'd start the cake, and if things didn't work out, well, fruitcakes can last a very long time. I think it's all the brandy."

"Possibly." Jacob chuckled and leaned in for a kiss. "May I?"

Sarah lifted her face. Jacob bent down.

"Hello? Good afternoon."

Sarah's face flamed. "It's Father."

"Don't panic." Jacob winked, stood, and held his hand out.

*I've never been so embarrassed in my life. He promised to wait until I sent Jacob to him.*

"Captain Gardner, your arrival is most timely," Jacob said, shaking the older man's hand.

"Sit, sit." Captain Gardner waved his hands toward the sofa. "You haven't touched your tea, and it's gone cold. Marian! So, Captain Crowninshield, what's all this about an elephant? Is it the monster I've heard it is?"

Marian rushed into the room. "Yes, Captain Gardner?"

"Bring a fresh pot of tea. This one is cold. You can leave the biscuits."

"Of course, sir." Marian picked up the tea tray and left the room.

"The elephant is still young, so she isn't very large yet. But some elephants grow quite large."

"I'm aware. I've been in Calcutta myself."

"Of course you have, sir." Jacob sat up straighter. "I'd like to speak to you on another matter, if I may."

Sarah shifted her eyes between her father and Jacob, her face still red. "Father, you said for me to send Jacob to your study."

"I did, but then I became peckish and decided to come in search of biscuits. Ah, Marian is back with the tea."

While Marian busied herself with the tray, Louisa drifted out of the room. Marian curtsied and left Sarah with her fiancé and father. Under her skirt, Sarah clenched and unclenched her hands.

"Would you pour out the tea, Sarah?" Captain Gardner asked. "When do you expect the *America* to return to Salem?"

"She'll be coming back as soon as our agents in New York take charge of the cargo," Jacob said. "In fact, I expect her in the next few days."

The conversation drifted to business matters. *Jacob, say something about us. Don't let my father lead you into business.* Sarah glared at Jacob, but he didn't respond. She drank two cups of tea and walked over to the windows. *Why doesn't Jacob speak up?*

"Is there something of interest outside?" Captain Gardner asked.

"No, Father."

"Is there something of interest inside? Any news you would like to share with an old sea captain?"

Jacob put down his cup. "Captain Gardner, there is a matter I must discuss with you. Sarah has accepted my proposal of marriage, and we hope for your blessing."

Captain Gardner slapped his knee and laughed. "Welcome to the family, young man. I was beginning to wonder if you'd ever get to the point. Sarah, bring the Madeira and three glasses."

"Then you approve?"

"I do. And your mother, God rest her soul, would be so pleased. Shall I arrange to have the banns read? Sarah told me that if you proposed, she didn't want to wait any longer than necessary."

"And she told me she already made the bridecake."

The men laughed.

"It's taking up so much space in the kitchen, I think she plans to feed it to all of Salem," Captain Gardner said, his face jovial.

Jacob grinned. "I don't care as long as she gives a piece to me."

Sarah picked up Jacob's hand. "The first piece is already yours."

# Captain Jacob Crowninshield

*June 5, 1796*
*Captain George Crowninshield's House*

Mary adjusted her son's white linen cravat so it covered his entire neck.

"Stop fussing, Mame."

"I've been waiting a long time for this day, and you are going to look your best."

Mary tapped Jacob's cheeks. "My sister would be so pleased. We talked about whether any of our children might marry each other. And after she died . . ." Mary paused. "Well, I thought it unlikely our dream would come true, especially after my brother John took her in. I thought she'd end up with one of the Derbys. So you've made me very happy."

"Anyone care for a glass of Madeira before we depart?" George held up the decanter. "And where are our daughters?"

"I'm sure Captain Gardner will have plenty of drink on hand, and Molly is doing Sally's hair. They'll be down shortly."

"Gardner won't serve anything but tea until after the ceremony. And Jacob's wedding deserves an extra toast. Especially as it's taking place in what must be record time. How did you persuade your bride to forgo the usual engagement parties, Jacob? In my observation, most young women like to stretch out the process. Will you share a glass with me or not?"

Jacob chuckled to hide his unease. "It's all Sarah's doing. And since we'll be staying at her father's farm in Danvers until her uncle readies our house, there isn't any housekeeping to set up. You're right about a glass of Madeira. I'll definitely join you."

"As will I," Mary said with twinkling eyes. "Since Edward didn't share his wedding with us, you, Jacob, are the first of our children to marry properly. Though, perhaps I should thank your elephant instead of you."

While George laughed and began to tease his wife about her knowledge of elephants, Jacob made his way to the front windows. The carriage awaited their departure, and he was more than ready to leave his parents' home. He had packed only a few things to take to the farm in Danvers, because he didn't expect to stay long. *I want my own house, not the use of another person's farm, even if he is my father-in-law. I'm the one who should be providing our house. Why did Sarah insist we accept her uncle's offer? People won't see me as my own man until I have my own household.* Jacob sighed. *That's a question for another day.*

Jacob's sisters finally arrived downstairs. It was comical to see twelve-year-old Sally in a hairstyle fit for a young woman.

"What do you think, Sir?" Sally twirled for her father. "Did Molly make me look pretty?"

George squeezed Sally's shoulder. "You always look pretty, though sometimes you have grass stains from playing outside. Come, girls, it's time for us to be off before Jacob changes his mind."

While Mary guided her daughters into the hall to pick up their shawls, George walked over to Jacob and clapped him on the back.

"Are you ready to change your life, Son?"

Jacob looked at his father with pensive eyes. "I am, Sir."

"Good. May I offer a word of advice?"

Jacob swallowed the last of his wine and nodded.

"Sarah's family sheltered her. She doesn't have your experience with the world outside Salem. Cherish the different perspectives you bring to the marriage. Make it a true partnership such as your mother and I have. Let her into your life and decisions. Do that, and you will both be happy. Do ye ken?"

"Yes. And you're correct. I don't want an ornament. I want a wife who shares my ambition for a public life."

George pursed his lips. "If you love each other, she will. And one other thing. Take things slowly this evening." George winked. "Now then, let's get you married."

# Captain Jacob Crowninshield

*Captain John Gardner's House*

Sarah warned him she would have to invite all her family connections to the wedding, but Jacob didn't expect so many people to accept the invitation. Surely, they had better things to do than witness the marriage of a poor relation. Jacob looked at his mother in bewilderment.

"Who are all these people and why are they here?"

Mary squeezed Jacob's hand. "They are your family. You follow your father's lead and think of the Derbys as enemies and rivals, when the truth is, we are related by marriage. Hasket Derby is my brother, so naturally, he wants to see my son properly married. Now, paste a smile on your face and act like you're pleased to see them. You don't want them to snub your wife because of your rudeness. Now, if you'll excuse me, I have to remind your father this is a wedding, not a business exchange."

Jacob glanced around again and saw Elias Derby weaving his way through the crush.

"Jacob! Congratulations on your successful voyage and happy courtship. One would be a triumph, but two victories so close together is noteworthy. Come, I'll take you round the back. Otherwise, you'll be exhausted by well-wishers before you see the bride."

Jacob accepted Elias's offer. The Gardner house was on the small side, and soon Jacob found himself at the kitchen entrance.

"Where to from here?"

"I thought we'd go through the kitchen and make our way into the large drawing room, where the ceremony will take place. It wouldn't do to accidentally see the bride before her grand entrance." Elias chuckled.

The kitchen was stifling. Sarah said she would serve a cold supper, so why was the cooking fire burning so high? Near the door, bits of laundry slapped Jacob's face. Elias laughed.

"I can tell you don't go through the kitchen very often. You'll have to duck until you get to the wooden table."

Jacob shook his head in annoyance. Smelling like a kitchen fire wasn't his idea of how to greet Sarah. But it was too late to go back outside. Elias led him through the back parlor and into the drawing room, where gentlemen helped themselves to tea and biscuits.

"How did you become familiar with the back of the house?"

Elias shrugged. "I have occasionally been called upon to enter Father's house with a certain amount of . . . discretion. And these houses are all very much the same."

Elias handed Jacob a cup and saucer. "Drink up. You don't want a dry mouth when you say your vows."

"Jacob!"

"Captain Gardner." Jacob bowed his head.

"What a happy day! I've seen the bride, and she is astonishingly beautiful. She looks exactly like her mother. The resemblance brought a tear to my eye." Captain Gardner paused. "The magistrate hasn't arrived yet. After he does, we'll invite the ladies to join us, and I'll escort my daughter to your side. Please excuse me. I must greet Mr. and Mrs. Derby."

*I hope you already greeted my father. He'll be quick to see a snub today.* Jacob looked around the room and was relieved to see his father engaged in conversation with Captain Nathaniel West.

# Sarah Gardner

*So many guests.* Sarah felt a bubble of anxiety. *What if I trip? What if my throat dries up? What if Jacob comes to his senses and realizes he can do so much better than me?*

"Sarah, are you ready?" Her sister-in-law tapped on the door. "May I come in?"

"Yes, of course." Sarah turned toward the door and smoothed down her dress. "It sounds like guests are still arriving."

"The parlors are filling up nicely. It's lucky to have so many well-wishers."

"Do I . . . look presentable?"

"You are a picture. Captain Crowninshield is a lucky man to have you for a wife. Do you have something borrowed to carry?" her sister-in-law asked.

Sarah's face fell. "I forgot about that."

"I'm glad you did. Would you like to borrow the lace handkerchief I carried when I married your brother John?"

Sarah's eyes welled with tears. "Yes. That would be wonderful."

"Allow me to speak to you, one Sarah to another. Don't look back, and don't doubt your decision. You are a beautiful bride, so take a deep breath and let me escort you to the bridal parlor until the magistrate arrives." Sarah's sister-in-law held out her hand.

Sarah gripped it, and they went downstairs, taking an immediate left off the hall and into the bride's parlor.

"Oh!" A strangled cry greeted them at the door. Jacob's mother came forward with tears streaming down her cheeks. "You look exactly like your mother on her wedding day. I can't believe it."

Mary Crowninshield grabbed Sarah's hands. "I can't express my happiness." Molly put her arm around her mother's shoulders.

"She's been thinking about your mother ever since Jacob told us he planned to propose. They were close."

"I know." Sarah nodded. "Mrs. Crowninshield, I can't tell you how much it pleases me to have you for my mother through marriage. You have always been so kind to me."

Mary wiped her eyes. "Yes, yes. Never mind that. You are a beautiful bride, and my son is a lucky man. And if he ever gives you the slightest difficulty, you come to me, and I'll set him straight."

"Ladies, I'm sorry to interrupt," Captain Gardner said, "but if you will make your way over to the drawing room, the magistrate has arrived, and there's a very nervous young man anxiously awaiting his bride."

Captain Gardner patted his daughter's arm. "You look lovely, my dear. If your mother was here, she would be proud."

Captain Gardner held out his arm. "Shall we?"

# Captain Jacob Crowninshield

The room was too small for so many guests. Jacob wondered again why so many people wanted to witness his marriage vows. Did they think he would run away? His cravat felt too tight and sweat trickled down his back, but Jacob forced himself to stand calmly in front of the magistrate. He didn't ask his father to stand up with him. He would have asked Benj if his brother had been in port. But he was perfectly capable of standing on his own.

The drawing room double doors opened. Sarah stood there with her hand on her father's arm. Jacob watched her take a deep breath before her eyes locked on his and never wavered until her father placed Sarah's hand on Jacob's arm and nodded. Jacob relished Captain Gardner's unspoken approval more than a glass of celebratory wine. *He trusts me to take care of Sarah, and I will.*

The magistrate spoke quickly. Suddenly, the man gave Jacob a meaningful look.

"Ring," he whispered.

Jacob removed the ring from his watch pocket, slid it on the third finger of Sarah's left hand, and began to murmur the required words. "With this ring, I thee wed, with my body I thee worship, and with all my worldly possessions I thee endow."

Jacob looked into Sarah's eyes. "And I mean that with every fiber of my being."

Sarah smiled so broadly that Jacob thought there would be no need for candles.

The magistrate motioned for Jacob and Sarah to face the wedding guests. "Allow me to introduce Captain and Mrs. Jacob Crowninshield. May their marriage be long and fruitful."

Everyone applauded. Servants circulated with trays of glasses filled with Madeira.

"Are you happy, Mrs. Crowninshield?" Jacob asked.

Sarah gave Jacob another dazzling smile. "With every fiber of my being."

# Captain Nathaniel Silsbee

*June 1796*
*Madras*

Nath and William held on to the surf boat's bouncing sides. The trip from the *Betsey* to shore was as uncomfortable as a squall. Large waves billowed until they crested and dropped into foaming surf, bearing the boat closer to the beach.

"Pity we couldn't sail straight home from Calcutta," William said. "I truly hate bobbing to shore from the *Betsey*'s anchorage."

Men waiting on shore pulled the boat onto the sand and offered to assist the two passengers slinging their legs over the rail.

Nath waved them away and slid down the side of the boat until he felt sand suctioning his feet. He grimaced as he slogged to firmer ground. Behind him, two men grabbed William's shoulders, lifted him a foot above the sand, and carried him to firmer ground. William gave each of them a few coins and waited for his brother. Nath shook his head and kept his pace through the wet sand.

"You must like having sand stuck to your boots." William grinned.

Nath shook his head and motioned for the bearer with their belongings to follow them. He led the way past the beachside warehouses and across the ditch into town.

"We'll call into Ross's London Tavern to make ourselves presentable," Nath finally said. "Then stop at Perry's offices. Hopefully, he's sold the wine we left here, and we can be on our way tomorrow."

"Why are you in such a sour mood?" William asked.

"Not sour, just apprehensive. Did you notice the British frigate anchored near the *Betsey*? I've a bad feeling the captain is looking to impress a few sailors into the British navy, and our ship is closest to theirs. The sooner we wrap up our business and sail out of Madras, the more likely we'll keep our crew."

Nath led the way into London Tavern and ordered breakfast and a newspaper before taking a seat near the fire. Few patrons occupied the great room just after dawn. William held out his hands to the flames.

"What are you thinking, Nath?"

Nath stretched. "We'll eat, wash, doze, and then be off to collect our profits."

Sunlight streamed into the upstairs bedroom, when Nath awoke to loud knocking.

He reached for his trousers. "William, answer the door."

"What do you want?" William asked the dark-skinned man in the hallway.

The man handed him a folded note. "Just here."

William nodded and closed the door.

"A note addressed to you," he said. "Looks like Richard's writing."

Nath tore open the note and read it quickly.

"Damme!" Nath swore.

"What happened?" William demanded.

"It's as I feared. The British boarded our ship and seized Edward Hulan."

Nath shrugged into his coat. "William, settle up here, conduct our business with Perry, and get back to our ship. I'm off to the *Betsey* to find out what happened and get Hulan released. Do not dally. I want to be away from Madras as soon as possible."

First Mate Richard Smith met Nath as he swung his leg over *Betsey*'s rail.

"Tell me what happened," Nath growled.

Richard handed Nath a spyglass and took him to the forward bow.

"Just after I set the lads to their tasks, a jolly boat pulled aside us with an officer and four marines from HMS *Beaver* over there. Said his name was Lieutenant Beverly and demanded to come aboard."

"And you approved?"

"Didn't see as I had any choice. She had her guns trained on us, and Madras is British territory. So I piped 'im aboard. He ordered me to assemble the crew. Sent a man to walk through the ranks. He pulled Hulan out and accused 'im of being a British deserter. Course I set 'im straight. But he took 'im anyway. That's when I sent the note."

"Did they board other ships?"

"That they did. And off-loaded at least one sailor from each, sometimes two."

Nath gritted his teeth. "I've known Edward Hulan all my life. Bloody Jack Tars. I'm going over there. Lower the longboat and prepare to weigh anchor once this affair settles."

"Aye, sir."

Nath sat in the longboat's stern, watching four oarsmen maneuver the small boat to the *Beaver*. When he was in range, Nath hailed the watch captain.

"Permission to board."

"Who's askin'?"

"Captain Nathaniel Silsbee of the *Betsey*, an American merchant ship. I demand you return my sailor."

An officer nodded, and the watch captain threw a rope ladder over the side. Once on deck, Nath waited for the officer to approach.

"Allow me to introduce myself. Lieutenant Beverly at your service. How may I be of assistance?"

Cold fury coiled up Nath's spine. "Captain Nathaniel Silsbee of the American merchant ship *Betsey*," he spit out. "You boarded my ship without permission and kidnapped one of my crew. I want him returned. Now."

"There seems to be a misunderstanding. Your mate granted me permission to board your ship. I had no reason to think he wasn't authorized to do so."

"Your guns were in position to fire."

"A training exercise. Apologies if your man misunderstood." Beverly gave a slight shrug. "In any event, it's a moot point. My orders were to visit every American ship in port and remove one or more of their seamen."

"On what grounds?"

"Captain Cook holds the opinion that every American seaman is a British deserter."

Nath took a deep breath. "The man you took, Edward Hulan, is an American. We grew up together in Salem, Massachusetts."

"I see. Well, perhaps you could exchange him for one of your other men. Unfortunately, I've already entered him on our roster and cannot remove him without Captain Cook's order."

Nath clenched his fists at his side. "And where is Captain Cook?"

"He's ashore at a bungalow in town. You'll have to call upon him there."

"Very well."

Nath descended the rope ladder and ordered the oarsmen to take him ashore.

Above the waterline, Nath hired a gig to take him to the residential area. The driver guided the gig through an area lined with European shops, hotels, and churches. Nath spotted Perry's mercantile and hoped William had concluded their business and gone back to the *Betsey*. He wanted to grab Hulan and sail with the tide, but first he had to confront this Captain Cook.

The gig wound up a long drive lined with palms. A slight breeze rustled the fronds. Arriving in front of the bungalow, Nath told the driver to wait. The man nodded and pulled into a small patch of shade.

Nath squared his shoulders and climbed four steps to the broad veranda that surrounded the bungalow. A man sat in a cane-back chair, smoking a cigar and reading a newspaper.

"I'm looking for Captain Cook of the HMS *Beaver*."

"For what purpose?"

"That's between us. Is he here?"

"I am Captain Cook, and you are?"

"Captain Nathaniel Silsbee of the American merchant ship *Betsey*. Your men took an American member of my crew. I want him returned."

"Do you indeed? According to British law, every man aboard an American vessel is presumed to be a British deserter unless he can prove otherwise."

"I vouch for him. We grew up together."

"Proof requires documentation. Do you have any?"

"I give you my word," Nath huffed.

"I'm sure your word is good, but documentation requires a proof of residence. Do you have any?"

"I've never heard of such a thing. I shall appeal to the governor."

"By all means, but I can save you the trouble. British naval ships aren't under his jurisdiction."

Captain Cook stood. "And your petition for your countryman's release is denied."

The British captain threw his cigar into the shrubs outside the veranda and entered the bungalow.

Nath swallowed several times and returned to the gig. *This is insupportable!*

Back in the business district, Nath called at Thomas Perry's office, which was situated above his mercantile. A punkah wallah stood outside the office door, pulling the rope that operated the punkah fan inside. Rays of the afternoon sun slipped between the loose shutters, illuminating the dust motes stirred by the punkah.

Nath pulled out his handkerchief to mop the sweat from his face and neck. Thomas Perry handed him a tumbler of whiskey.

"From what your brother told me earlier today, I'm sure you could use this. And if you're here, I presume you're looking for a way to get your man back. I'm sorry to tell you, nothing can be done."

"There must be something! It's nothing short of a kidnapping."

"Not according to British law."

"I need a letter of introduction to the governor."

"I can write it, but even if it gains you entrance, it won't change the outcome. The British navy is a law unto itself. Civil authorities have no jurisdiction, and they know it."

Thomas topped up Nath's glass.

"You won't like my advice, but I'll give it to you anyway. The best thing you can do is give your man his wages so he can survive and accept the reality of the situation."

"I shall appeal to the officers' board. I want it in the log, and as a ship's captain, I have a right to that courtesy."

"I thought you'd say something along those lines. Keep a civil tongue in your head, or you may lose another sailor."

After the two men shook hands, Nath went back to the beach and boarded the *Betsey*'s longboat. Too restless to sit in the stern, he exchanged places with an oarsman and encouraged the men to an increasingly fast pace.

At four o'clock the next day, Nath boarded the *Beaver*. Lieutenant Beverly shook hands with him and escorted Nath into the captain's cabin. Officers from two nearby British vessels lounged around a long table. Captain Cook sat at the head of the table.

Cook glared at Nath with hostility. "As a courtesy, we've humored your request for a board. State the nature of your complaint."

Nath's jaw pulsed. "My complaint is that you have kidnapped an American sailor and accused him of desertion from a British ship without any witnesses or proof. I am here to testify on his behalf. Hulan was born and bred in Salem, Massachusetts. He has never been a British subject, nor sailed on a British ship. I demand his release."

"Can you prove your claims?" Captain Cook asked. "Do you have documents of residence? Do you have proof that the man we have in custody is not simply impersonating the man you claim is American?"

Sparks flew from Nath's eyes. "This court is a farce. It is entirely illegal."

"I shall note your concerns in the ship's log." Cook looked to the other officers. "Gentlemen, do you have any concerns relating to our retrieval of a known deserter?"

No one spoke.

Nath banged his fist on the table. "This is a travesty!"

Cook sneered. "When a man comes aboard my ship, he does not leave it before peacetime. Lieutenant Beverly, please escort our guest off the ship."

Nath shook off Beverly's attempt to grab his elbow but allowed the officer to escort him to the outside deck. Hulan stood near the rail.

"Edward!" Nath embraced his friend. "I'll get you out of here yet. I shall write the State Department and demand their intervention. I'm sure Mr. Derby will lend his support. I won't leave you without an appeal for justice."

The burly sailor clapped Nath's shoulder. "You did everything you could. No one else spoke up for their men. It means a lot." Edward cleared his throat.

Nath felt what seemed like tears behind his eyes and willed them away. *I refuse to show any weakness here. My anger weakens me enough.*

"This isn't over, Edward." Nath reached in his pocket. "But, um, in the meantime, I have your wages here."

"Just give me ten dollars and save the rest for my mother. She'll need it. I meant what I said. You're a good friend and a fine officer. Someday we'll sail together again."

"That we will." Nath turned to Lieutenant Beverly. "I accept that I have no choice in this matter, but I commend Mr. Hulan to your protection."

"You've done everything in your power. Rest assured, I shall do what I can. I accept your testimony that Mr. Hulan is an American citizen, but nothing will induce the captain to release him. Perhaps your government can intercede. If asked, I shall support your case as best I can."

Nath nodded curtly. "Thank you. Call upon me if I can be of any service." Nath reached for Edward's hand. "Well, Edward, it's goodbye for the moment, but we'll see each other again. I'll be sure your mother is cared for."

When Nath boarded the longboat without Edward Hulan, the men were quiet.

*To my dying day, I shall never forgive myself for failing to bring my man home.*

# Captain Elias Derby

*July 4, 1796*
*Outside Ezekiel Derby's House*

"My, my. You're up early."

Elias scowled and kicked an unattended brick near the entrance to his brother's house.

"Here." Zeke passed Elias a flask of whiskey. "I'm most surprised to see you in my front garden."

"It's the best spot for viewing Mother's folly." Elias gestured to his parents' mansion across the street. Workmen on scaffolds applied plaster to the Corinthian columns rising next to the second- and third-story windows.

"It's the most impressive building in Salem, and it's not even finished. Carriages pass by every day to catch a glimpse of Derby Mansion and pay no attention to my own house across the street. But let us speak of more interesting topics."

Elias turned to face his brother. "Such as?"

"I heard from Mother's acid tongue that you attended Jacob Crowninshield's wedding. Whatever possessed you to bless our mother's sworn enemy with your presence?"

*It's too early to listen to Zeke's gibes.*

Elias shrugged. "I wasn't the only Derby in attendance. Even Father stopped in to toast the bride, which caused quite a rustle among the guests."

Zeke laughed. "Well, Jacob learned his trade in Father's counting house, and he's our cousin. But why did you attend?"

"I'm not sure anymore. Perhaps to see someone marry for something other than a business connection. The Gardner girl doesn't have much beyond what our uncle John gives her.

"And Jacob's not a bad fellow, though he can be opportunistic. He was clever with the elephant." Elias paused. "I should have brought one back."

"But you didn't think of it." Zeke laughed and snapped his fingers. "Perhaps you could take a ship to Calcutta and come back with something equally exotic. A tiger, perhaps? Then you could sell it and clear your debts."

Elias took another swallow from Zeke's flask. "I shall find another way to make my fortune."

"Doing what?"

"I didn't come here to be insulted."

"Then why did you come? At such an early hour too. Is it to admire my unfinished house?" Zeke stroked his chin. "Probably not. Let me think again. Will you ask me to stand up for you at your wedding? That can't be it. You aren't courting anyone. Wait a moment." Zeke gave his brother a speculative look. "You've made several trips to Boston in recent weeks."

"Business with our brokers. Nothing more." Elias grunted. *The opportunity to visit Lucy has nothing to do with it.*

"If you must know," Elias said in annoyance, "I came here to view the cupola across the street."

"It's astonishingly pretentious, don't you think? Mother hired Mr. McIntire to alter Bulfinch's design and create a Greek temple to sit on top of her Georgian mansion."

"You're not planning a mirror image for your house, then?"

"Certainly not," Zeke scoffed. "I don't want a house full of columns and curlicues. Look," Zeke said, pointing, "someone's come out on the cupola. I should have brought my spyglass. What are they doing?"

Elias shaded his eyes from the rising sun.

"What do you think, sons?" Hasket put out his hand for Zeke's flask.

"Damme, Father." Zeke gulped. "You shouldn't sneak up on us like that. Why are you in my front garden and not your own?"

"I have a better view of my cupola from here. I've ordered a telescope. You both must join me on a clear night after it's installed."

"I shall look forward to it," Elias said. "Is that what you came across to show us?"

Hasket handed Elias his spyglass. "Have a look for yourself."

Elias focused in on the workmen, who were shaking fabric over the cupola railing.

"I don't believe it. That's the largest American flag I've ever seen."

"Yes. I'm hoping we'll have some stiff winds today, especially when the militia is doing maneuvers. I've also arranged for a few fireworks. It's time for people to notice our new home."

"Are you perchance referring to the Crowninshields?" Elias asked.

"Among others. A house serves many functions, and one of them is to inform observers that the inhabitants are people of substance. Now then, Ezekiel, perhaps you'd be good enough to invite your brother and I inside for breakfast."

# Captain Jacob Crowninshield

*Crowninshield Counting House*

George pursed his lips. "Why do you hesitate? I'm perfectly capable of supplying you and Sarah with a house."

"I can supply my own house," Jacob said through gritted teeth. "It's Sarah. Her uncle John Derby promised her a house, and she has her heart set on whatever he provides."

"Then where is it? It's not practical for you to live in Danvers, and on her father's farm, no less. It's inconvenient for business as well as politics. You can't establish yourself in Salem if you aren't able to meet with people. You need to be seen. You need to entertain. And you need to take your proper place in our business. We're adding ships and investments all the time. The *Belisarius* should be in soon, and we'll need to refit her."

Jacob let his father's rant wash over him as it shifted into fury over the Derby mansion on Essex Street, Ezekiel Derby's house going up across the street, and the fact that his brother John would probably take over the Washington Street house. *And I live on my father-in-law's farm in Danvers. It's humiliating.* Jacob drummed his fingers on the desk. "There's nothing for it. I shall speak to John Derby directly."

"And we need to extend our wharf," George continued. "The *America* is too large to come into our present pier—"

"You are correct, Sir," Jacob interjected. "I'm sorry to cut our discussion short, but I need to confer with my wife's informal guardian about our housing situation."

# Captain Jacob Crowninshield

*Captain John Derby's House*

Jacob walked up the stone walk in front of Captain Derby's residence on Summer Street. It was a bit out of the way from the wharf and counting house, but Sarah was fond of the location, though she had stayed with her father when she was in Salem. Perhaps Captain Derby had another property nearby.

Jacob rapped soundly on the front door.

A bemused housekeeper wearing a dark dress and mop cap opened the door.

"Captain Crowninshield to see Captain Derby."

The woman raised her eyebrows. "Is he expecting you?"

"I come on a matter respecting his former ward, Mrs. Sarah Gardner Crowninshield."

"Come into the drawing room. I'll see if Captain Derby is available."

Jacob stood gazing out the drawing room windows into the street, until a middle-aged man appeared at the door.

"Captain Crowninshield? Please sit down. I've been meaning to call on you and your bride. Make yourself comfortable." Captain Derby gestured toward the sofa. A slight breeze ruffled the curtains by the open window.

Jacob nodded. "Captain Derby, forgive me for visiting unannounced."

"Not at all, Captain Crowninshield. I should have called on you and your bride before this, but I don't get to Salem much, and Danvers is rather far out of my way. Please accept my apologies. My wife and I very much wanted to attend your wedding, but . . ." Captain Derby spread his hands. "Well, it all happened quite quickly."

Jacob chuckled. "Your former ward didn't wish to wait any longer, and I concurred."

"Of course. By the way, my wife and I enjoyed the bridecake you sent us. Very thoughtful."

"Did it come through in one piece? I thought it rather a long journey for a piece of cake, but Sarah assured me all would be well."

"And so it was."

The conversation lapsed. *I can't just demand he give us a house.* Jacob unbuttoned his coat.

"My wife would be pleased if you paid her a call. She speaks of you often, with great fondness." Jacob cleared his throat. "Allow me to express my gratitude for the many favors you and your wife gave her over the years."

"Nonsense. She's a delightful young woman, and my wife and I have no children to lighten our days. Since Sarah's father is often at sea, it was our pleasure to offer her a place to live during his absence. Next time I'm called to Salem, I shall bring my wife, and we will definitely call upon you. Of course . . ." Captain Derby paused, "you and your wife are always welcome at my home in Boston."

Jacob accepted a glass of whiskey from his host. *Insufferable man.*

"I regret I can't stay long if I'm to arrive home in Danvers at a decent time." Jacob swirled the amber liquid in his glass. "I've come on a matter of some delicacy. My wife is adamant that we forgo making our own housing arrangements in Salem, because you assured her you wish to provide us with a residence. We have been in Danvers over a month, and I've heard nothing about your plans in this regard. I'm quite happy to make our own housing arrangements, but I thought it only fair to discuss the situation with you first."

Captain Derby smoothed his sparse hair. "Well, this is awkward. Here's the way of it. I am in the process of wrapping up my affairs in Salem and removing to Boston on a permanent basis. But, as you may imagine, there are many odds and ends that need attention. I expect to vacate this house next year. When Sarah first spoke to me about her possible future, I thought your engagement would last at least a year."

Jacob clenched his jaw.

"And, though I'm pleased on your behalf as you embark on your career, I really can't change my plans."

*Of course not.* "Understandable. That being the case, I shall move forward with my own arrangements."

"Actually"—Captain Derby held his hand up—"I have another property that may be suitable. Give me a week to make arrangements. Sarah has brought my wife and I a great deal of joy over the years, and my wife will never forgive me if I don't follow through on our promise. Give me a week. I'll be in touch."

"A week, then. I look forward to your note."

Jacob stood and shook hands with his wife's informal guardian. He hoped the man was as good as his word, because he and Sarah were moving into Salem by the end of July.

# Sarah Gardner Crowninshield

Sarah watched Jacob with a bemused expression as he guided Pompey and Cicero in front of a small but pleasant house on Summer Street. He'd pulled her out of bed just after dawn, urged her to dress quickly, and helped her into the gig. With a rap of the reins, the two horses trotted into the still-cool morning. Sarah pulled her light shawl around her shoulders. With the whisper of a smile on his full lips, Jacob refused to tell her where they were going, and now it appeared they had arrived.

"Whoa!" A lanky boy came out to take the reins. "This is Isaac, our outside lad."

"How do ye do, ma'am."

Sarah shook her head in surprise. "Er, well, thank you. Jacob, what do you mean Isaac is our stable boy? Where are we?"

"At our new home, and about time too." Jacob held out his hand to assist Sarah up the steps to the doorway before opening the door and swinging her over the threshold.

Sarah shrieked in surprise. "Our what? Jacob, put me down."

"Not yet. I'm giving you a tour. We are in the hall, and over here, on our left, is the dining parlor."

Jacob walked through the open door into a pleasant room furnished with two dining tables, twelve chairs, and a sideboard cupboard filled with a porcelain dining service, tumblers, wine glasses, and decanters.

"What? Jacob put me down."

"Not until I finish our tour." Jacob crossed the hall through the double doors leading into the drawing room, with a sofa, a rocking chair, a dozen bamboo chairs lined up along the walls, and a card table near the windows.

"Jacob, please put me down. I'm starting to feel sick from the motion."

"In a minute. I just want to show you upstairs. The rooms aren't all furnished yet, but I want you to see our bedroom." Jacob bounced up the stairs and into a room with windows facing down into the street before setting Sarah on her feet. "What do you think of our new bed? The ticking holds eleven pounds of feathers. And there's a dressing table over here." He pointed to a side window.

Sarah turned in a circle as she took in the room, with its high bedstead, full looking glass, and comfortable chair. A counterpane covered the bed. She looked around in consternation.

Jacob looked at his wife with a wide grin. "What do you think?"

"I hardly know what to say. I thought you said my uncle couldn't give us the house until next year, and we shouldn't waste money on a lease when we can stay at my father's farm. Please tell me you didn't rent this house."

"I didn't." Jacob folded Sarah's hand over his arm and guided her back downstairs and into the drawing room, where a young girl was laying out tea things on a low table. Sarah noticed that the cups had a brown rose pattern.

"Sarah, this is Becky. I engaged her to do light chores until you select a housekeeper to organize things."

"Hello, Becky."

Becky bobbed her head. "Pleased to meet you, ma'am. If you need anything else, just call."

"You can go, Becky," Jacob said. "Now, serve me a cup of tea, and I'll explain everything, starting with your uncle."

Sarah's hand shook slightly as she passed Jacob his cup.

"You told me he didn't expect to give us a house until next year."

"That's true, but he also said he would see if he could come up with an alternative. And he found this house and paid the rental fee for the first year."

"And then what happens?"

"Nothing. If we like it here, we stay. If we don't, we move. It's quite simple, really." Jacob grabbed Sarah's hands. "You keep forgetting that I have enough funds to provide for us now and in the future. Have a little confidence in me, Sarah." Jacob winked.

"And the furnishings?"

"Your father provided them, as is appropriate. He isn't able to provide everything we need. You'll need to buy carpets and furnish the other rooms, and a library. And, I don't think the kitchen is anywhere near complete. But my mother will help you sort the house out."

Sarah gave her husband a puzzled look. "I did hear that Mrs. Abbot is selling a Brussels carpet that would look well in the entry hall. Is that what you mean?"

"Yes, exactly." Jacob smiled. "Our life as a couple starts today."

"Today? We don't have supplies in, or servants. I can't possibly . . ."

"Mame and my sisters will be here shortly to get things started, and our things in Danvers should arrive this afternoon."

Sarah's eyes lit with excitement. "And I can arrange things as I wish?"

"Of course. This is our home." Jacob leaned over to kiss his wife's forehead. "I'll let you organize it yourself. I have work to do at the counting house, and I need to return Father's gig and horses so Mame has transportation. Don't forget to tell Becky you'll need a fresh pot of tea when Mame arrives."

Jacob grabbed his hat, gave Sarah a cheerful grin, and headed toward the barn. Sarah walked back into the drawing room and squeezed her arms around her midsection.

A smile broke out on her face, followed by joyful giggles.

*I have a new husband, a new mother, and a house—I'm not a poor relation anymore.*

Sarah dropped her arms and twirled around the room, unaware of Becky's envious gaze through the doorway.

# Captain George Crowninshield Jr.

*September 6, 1796*
*Union Wharf, Salem*

Geordie adjusted the wheel to match the incoming tide and smiled broadly when his crew threw out the ropes to secure the *Belisarius* to Union Wharf. Once the wheel was secure, Geordie ducked into the captain's cabin to change into more formal attire. He still wore an old-fashioned lacy cravat, though he replaced his breeches with the new style of pantaloons. *Pity. I'm rather proud of my legs.* Geordie tucked his logbook under his arm and went on deck to join John.

"I don't believe it." John pointed to the wharf. "Sir and Jacob are both here to welcome us."

*Glad I changed my clothes.* "Come on, then, no reason to keep them waiting. We need to congratulate our brother on his good fortune."

Geordie strode down the gangplank like he owned it.

"Sir." Geordie shook his father's hand. "I present you with my log chronicling our many endeavors as well as our accounts. It's been a successful voyage—despite the fact we didn't return with an elephant."

Geordie smirked at Jacob, who merely raised his eyebrows.

George Crowninshield passed the logbooks to his clerk and clapped his son on the back. "Welcome home. I hope we can persuade you to stay ashore. But that's a conversation for tomorrow."

*Stay ashore?* Geordie nodded as his father greeted John.

"John!" George slapped his younger son's shoulder. "Good voyage?"

"Yes, Sir. We have enough coffee, sugar, and indigo to fill our warehouses for a year at least."

"Well done," Jacob said in a flat tone that made Geordie wonder if his brother was being sincere.

"You've done well yourself, Jacob. Congratulations on your wedding. I'll bring gifts ashore tomorrow." Geordie grinned.

"Instead of blocking access to our ship, let's go to the house. Your mother ordered me to bring you two home immediately, and she has her own spyglass, so she'll know if I dawdle. And you can meet Sarah, Jacob's delightful wife."

"She makes me a happy man," Jacob said.

"You're still living at the family house?" Geordie asked.

"We have a house on Summer Street to which you are invited once Sarah finishes settling in."

"Clever location, Brother," John said. "She won't be able to watch everything like Mame does from her perch in the cupola."

Jacob laughed and touched the side of his nose. "I'm clever like that."

Geordie followed behind his father and brothers, stopping to greet colleagues and sailors after two years away. *Two years. My daughter must be . . . could she be three?* He felt a twinge of regret he hadn't seen his child in so long. But the same was true of any other man who lived off the sea. The thought of remaining in Salem and visiting his daughter more frequently appealed to him. And it would be nice to spend time with Lizzie, if she hadn't found herself a suitor. *I'll visit them tomorrow.*

The family's brick house, with its cupola and the statue of a man holding a spyglass at the top, hadn't changed. Presumably, Mame would put him in the smaller second-floor bedroom overlooking the harbor. The view was nice, but Geordie would spend the night aboard the *Belisarius* and find somewhere else to sleep tomorrow. *Perhaps with Lizzie? No, that's a bad idea. She'll think more of it than she should.*

Mary pulled open the front door. "It's about time you got here. I saw you dawdling on the wharf, talking to everyone you passed. Geordie, John, come greet your mother like the good sons you are."

John immediately walked into Mary's open arms.

"You've grown taller," she said, looking up at her son's face.

"It must be the sea air, Mame." John chuckled before kissing his mother's cheek. "It's good to be home again."

Jacob walked around his brothers to greet Sarah.

"Mame, please excuse me. My brothers haven't met the new Mrs. Crowninshield yet."

"Cousin Sarah." Geordie stepped forward. "You are doubly part of our family now. Though I think Jacob may have bamboozled your acceptance."

Sarah blushed and accepted Geordie's hand. "I assure you, Jacob is the most forthcoming of husbands."

Geordie winked. "May it ever be so. And this lanky lad behind me is John, whom I'm sure you remember."

Geordie noticed that Jacob kept his arm around Sarah as if to remind both him and John that Sarah was now his.

Mame returned to her conversation with John, patting his sleeve to get his attention.

"Your room is waiting for you, and you must come and go as you please while you're ashore. We'll have a drink before supper to celebrate your return.

George, take everyone into the drawing room. Molly and Sally are already inside. Geordie and I will join you shortly."

"I'll have your glass ready." George nodded to Geordie.

"Aye." Geordie heard his sisters' high-pitched voices exclaim at seeing John again. *I hope they save some of their joy for me.* Reluctantly, he turned his attention to Mary, accepting his mother's embrace without encouraging it.

"It's good to be home." Geordie kissed Mary's cheek. "You'll note that, unlike my brother, I haven't gotten any taller."

"He hasn't either." Mary winked. "But I like to tease him. Otherwise, he'll shrink into your shadow. Tell me, do you think John can manage the *Belisarius* on his own? Your father thinks it's time he took more responsibility, and after sailing with you for two voyages, there isn't much more you can teach him."

Geordie drew his eyebrows together. "I naturally assumed I'd stay with the *Belisarius.*"

"Perhaps you will, but the business has grown, and your father . . . well, shall we join the others?"

*What isn't she telling me? That's the second time I heard I may stay ashore. There must be another ship. There has to be. After over ten years at sea, surely Sir won't beach me. What would I do ashore?*

Geordie listened to the drawing room clock tick past another hour. After long months at sea punctuated by crowded wharves in humid climes, his parents' house felt small and oppressive. John happily shared stories about sourcing coffee at Isle de Bourbon, to his sisters' delighted response. *Surely, Jacob told them plenty of stories already. Why do the rest of us have to listen to what we already know?* Jacob played with his wife's fingers.

"So," Geordie said when John paused for breath, "do we have a timetable for the *Belisarius?* She'll need a month or so for refitting."

"She should be ready in October." George's voice faded from Geordie's ear. *Two months ashore then. Perhaps I will stay with Lizzie.*

"And there's work for you to do here." Abruptly, Geordie realized his father was still speaking.

"Sorry, Sir. I don't think I heard you properly."

George glowered his impatience. "I said the *Belisarius* will go out in October with John as her captain. There's work to be done here, and it's time for you to follow Jacob's example and find a young woman willing to accept your courtship."

Geordie nearly spit out the whiskey he'd just swallowed. *The* Belisarius *going out without me! Mame suggested it, but I didn't think she was serious.*

John's face filled with shock. "You trust me with the *Belisarius*, Sir?"

"Why wouldn't I? You know the ship. You're familiar with the market. Who better to take command? I would have given you it this sail, but your mother likes it when you boys sail together."

John's eyes shone. "I won't let you down, Sir."

George nodded as if he expected nothing less. "I know. Now then, Geordie, I need you and Jacob to help me with the business end of things. I'll continue to work with merchants and markets, but I need you to manage our vessels and advise me on shipmasters. Jacob here will work with me in the counting house, as well as joining me in challenging the political stranglehold Hasket Derby has on our county. It's past time to take him down a few pegs. I've also decided to lengthen our wharf to better accommodate our larger ships, so you'll be busy with that as well."

"Is that all?" Geordie smirked. "Anything in mind for your other sons?"

"In due course. Benjamin, Richard, and John will be sailing for the next few years. We make a better profit when we master our own ships."

"But Sir," Molly interjected. "I thought my brothers were supposed to come home."

"They have to earn their way just like everyone else. There's no special treatment for an owner's son. You wouldn't want to marry someone who hadn't earned his own way like your brother Jacob, would you? How could you count on him to support a family? You couldn't."

Molly's face fell at her father's rebuke.

"I'm sure you can help Sarah with her new house and introduce her to any of our friends she hasn't met yet," Geordie offered.

Sarah smiled. "I truly welcome your assistance, Molly. I spent so much time in Boston, I don't have much of a social circle in Salem."

"Yes. I can definitely help you with that. I'll call tomorrow afternoon."

Geordie answered Jacob's raised eyebrows with a shrug. "Well, I'm too old to squire Molly about. I'm sure Molly and Sarah will soon be inseparable. In any case . . ." Geordie rose and bowed to his family. "If you'll excuse me, I'm going to spend the night aboard the *Belisarius*."

"But Geordie, your room is ready," Mary protested.

"Thank you, Mame. But I left my things on board, and I have more to pack up than I anticipated. I also want to give the crew my final orders for the voyage."

"Shall I come with you?" John asked.

Geordie waved him away. "Please indulge me. I want a final night as master of the *Belisarius* before consigning her to your more than capable hands."

John grinned at the compliment.

Geordie made the rounds, shaking his brothers' hands and kissing his mother and sisters on their cheeks. George walked him to the door with his arm around Geordie's shoulders.

"I look forward to working more closely with you. Your attachment to your ships does you credit."

"Indeed." Geordie shook his father's hand. "Good night, then. I'll be in the counting house once I get things sorted on the *Belisarius*."

Outside, Geordie took deep breaths of the late-evening air. Darkness would descend soon. He had expected to remain with the *Belisarius* until she went out again, but she was lost to him. Geordie shook his head. *I'll just have to make a life on shore.*

## *The Next Day*

Toby, a bay gelding, wasn't the best horse for riding, but he was the best one available at the stable. With Pompey and Cicero presently residing in Jacob's barn, Geordie would see quite a bit of the gelding. He took Toby into a trot and stood in the stirrups to stretch his legs. The horse responded well, though he had an unusual gait.

*Probably the result of too many riders who don't know what they're doing. I suppose I'll have to purchase my own horse and saddle. And perhaps a gig? Or maybe a carriage? Yes, definitely. I'd enjoy driving through Salem with a handsome pair of horses and a freshly painted carriage.*

Geordie turned onto the road that led to Lizzie's cottage. *I didn't think to send a note. What if she isn't home?* He dismounted and led Toby around to the shed at the back of the cottage. After settling the horse, Geordie turned toward the cottage and caught his breath. Lizzie was hanging linens on a rope line stretched from the edge of the cottage to a nearby tree. Gazing at her from behind, he saw Lizzie had pulled her skirts up a bit for ease of motion as she stretched to toss fabric over the rope.

"Do you need any help with that?" Geordie called out.

"What!" Lizzie shrieked and dropped her linen into the dirt. "How dare you sneak up on someone? Who are you?"

Geordie stepped farther into the yard.

"Get away! My husband will be home any minute."

*Husband?*

"Lizzie, don't you recognize me?"

Her hands were fisted at her sides, and her eyes were wild with fear. "No! I'm asking you to leave now before my husband arrives. He gets jealous quickly, and he's a violent man."

Geordie's heart sank. He'd never considered that Lizzie might have married someone. And now they lived in the cottage he paid for. Anger quickly replaced disappointment. Geordie reached for Lizzie's elbow.

Lizzie shrieked. "Let me go, you brigand!"

"Elizabeth Rowell," Geordie said through clenched teeth. "Stop acting like you don't know who I am."

"Release me this instant. My husband . . ."

"Yes, I heard you the first time. Your husband is a violent man. At the moment I'm even more so. How dare you bring a man into the house I pay for. The house where my daughter lives."

Lizzie stopped struggling. "Captain Crowninshield?" She looked into Geordie's tanned face. "Geordie?"

Geordie snarled. "I take it you weren't expecting me."

"Usually you send a note," Lizzie whispered.

"Actually"—Lizzie's voice picked up in volume—"for all I knew, you were dead. I've not heard one word since your ship left two years ago. Not a word. And now you show up unannounced? Get out!"

"You thought I was dead? And you grieved for me so much you married someone else and invited him to live in my house?"

"What would you have me say when a stranger comes into my garden?" Her rage seemed to be replaced by something else. *Resignation?* "Sit down inside and I'll bring you something to eat."

Geordie glared at Lizzie before rubbing the back of his neck. *She has a point about my manner of arrival.*

"I concede. You have a right to be angry. I should have sent a note. But I'm here to visit you and my daughter."

Lizzie nodded. "Come inside. I have to feed Sophia her dinner."

The one-room cottage was much as Geordie remembered it. Lizzie left the doors and windows open to catch whatever breeze blew by. There was a small bed near the fire with what appeared to be a trundle bed halfway under it. A corn husk doll lay on the bed. The main room had a table and two cane-back chairs. One of the chairs had cushions on it.

*I never realized what a dismal place this is.*

Sophia sat on the rug, stacking blocks until they fell down. Geordie draped his coat over the back of a chair and squatted down next to her.

"Hello?"

The child looked at him with dark eyes.

"She won't remember you," Lizzie said. She poked coals in the fireplace before scooping porridge into two bowls.

"There's porridge if you're hungry. Can you bring Sophia to the chair with pillows so I can feed her? Unless you'd like to do it?"

Geordie looked at his tiny daughter and held out his arms. "Would you let me carry you to the table?"

Sophia looked up again and held out her hands. Geordie grabbed Sophia under her arms and swung her around the room before placing her on the topmost pillow.

The girl squealed with delight.

Lizzie tied Sophia to the chair with a length of rope and placed a bowl of porridge in front of her. She handed her daughter a spoon.

"Can she feed herself?" Geordie asked.

"After a fashion. I let her get the feel of it, and if she has difficulty or makes too much mess, I feed her. There's a bowl on the table for you if you want it."

"You added molasses but no nutmeg."

Lizzie shrugged. "We live simply, because I didn't know how long I'd have to rely on the funds you left. I have enough coin for another half year or so."

Geordie thought back to the purse he left Lizzie. She had more money left than he thought she would, which explained the threadbare linens and lack of rugs, aside from the one he gave her before he left.

Sophia started mashing her wooden spoon into the porridge.

"That's enough of that," Lizzie said, taking the spoon.

"Shall I feed her?"

Lizzie shrugged. "If you like. Are you going to eat your porridge?"

"Help yourself." Geordie focused on feeding Sophia.

"You've got more on her face than inside her mouth." Lizzie wiped Sophia's face and hands before lifting her out of the chair and taking her across to the bed. She handed Sophia the corn husk doll and smoothed back her daughter's hair before kissing her forehead. Sophia yawned, clutched her doll, and snuggled into a flat pillow.

"Go to sleep. Mama has to talk to Captain Crowninshield."

Lizzie washed the bowls in a bucket, poured out two cups of water from the pitcher on the table, and handed one to Geordie.

"We would be off better drinking cider or small beer."

"Probably. Bring the chairs by the door. It's cooler outside."

Lizzie sat silently, her gaze on the linen that still lay on the dirt. Geordie knocked back his cup of water.

*I need to send for more supplies, especially if I'm going to stay here. In fact, we need a bigger cottage, with proper furniture. If I decide to stay.*

The idea of staying with Lizzie was more appealing than previously.

"How long will you be in Salem?" Lizzie asked.

Geordie shook his head to clear his musings. "Longer than you might think."

"Oh?"

"I'd like to know Sophia better and spend time with you."

"Meaning what?"

Geordie cleared his throat, rolled up his sleeves, removed his cravat, and opened the top button of his shirt.

Lizzie dropped her jaw. "I hope you aren't expecting me to embrace you just for the honor of your presence."

"It's a hot day, and there's no shade."

"If you're looking for a garden, you won't find it here."

Geordie ran his hand through his hair, dislodging his queue. *I deserve her ire. I'm going about this the wrong way.*

Geordie drew in a deep breath. "The thing is, Lizzie, my circumstances have changed."

# Lizzie Rowell

Lizzie looked at Geordie briefly before turning her gaze back to her linen, still sagging off the line from where she had dropped the edge.

"I need to brush off the dirt before it sets," she muttered.

Geordie grabbed Lizzie's elbow before she could stand. "I need to talk to you."

She yanked her elbow away. "Well, I don't need to talk to you."

Lizzie stomped over to the rope line, attached the linen she'd dropped, and slapped her hands on it to remove the dirt off the edges.

*How dare he? He's been gone for two years with nary a word, and now he thinks I should be pleased to see him! Pleased to see another purse for Sophia, more like.*

Geordie placed his hands on Lizzie's shoulders.

"Will you stop sneaking up on me?"

"Lizzie, please hear me out."

"Nothing you say is of any interest to me. You made it quite clear before you left that my sole purpose was to keep you warm, and since it's a hot day, you have no reason to be here."

Geordie shrugged. "My child is here."

"Are you planning to acknowledge her?"

"I . . . can't."

"That's what I thought."

Geordie put his hands in his pockets. "My situation is . . . complicated."

"Not from where I'm standing. Your family is rich. You come and go as you please, with nary a thought to people forced to depend on you. You visit our daughter when it suits you and ignore her when it doesn't. I've had enough. Next month, I'm going back to the Ship. You can visit Sophia there when you're in Salem. Now, please leave."

Geordie's face contorted. For a moment, Lizzie thought he might cry. *How is that even possible?*

"Please listen to me. I was wrong to say we only kept each other warm. I didn't want an entanglement, and I couldn't think of another way . . ."

Bile rose in Lizzie's throat. She swallowed it down. *I will not humiliate myself.* "You didn't need to."

"Please," Geordie begged.

Something in Geordie's expression gave Lizzie pause. It was desperate. Heartbroken. Terrified.

*I'm going to regret this.* "Let's sit in the shade," she suggested. "You'll have to be quick. Sophia doesn't nap very long."

Geordie turned the chairs to face each other and gestured for Lizzie to sit.

"Lizzie, I've had a lot of time to think about what happened between us. I took advantage of you and treated you badly. But, in my defense, I took responsibility for your situation, and provided food and shelter for you both."

"I already had food and shelter."

"Your cousin treated you like a skivvy. I took you away from that."

"Aye." Lizzie nodded. "But Cousin Anna would have softened after a few months. So you didn't do me any favors. Not really."

"But you went with me."

"I thought you wanted us. You thought you were settling an account."

Geordie hung his head. "That's true. But I didn't want a family then."

"And you do now? I'm not the girl fresh from the country anymore. I know your kind don't marry women like me."

Geordie dropped his head. "I'm not saying things the right way. Let me try again."

Lizzie snorted, but Geordie plowed on. "I went to sea before I was twenty, more so after Sir started our family business. I was never ashore long enough to have mates. And I didn't want any ties. I'm like my brother Edward, but without his courage. He left the family. I expected spending my life at sea would serve the same purpose but still allow me to come home. I couldn't take on family responsibilities then. I still can't, not really. Not the way you would like me to."

Lizzie scoffed. "What . . . ?"

Geordie held up a hand. "Please let me finish. I may never have the courage to speak to you again. My circumstances have changed. Sir told me I'm to stay in Salem and manage our company's ships. As an unmarried son, I can't set up a separate household, but I can make informal arrangements to spend my free time elsewhere. That's what I was doing when we met."

"So you're going back to the Ship? My cousin won't have you after what you did, and rightly so."

"No, wait. I'm not quite finished. I want to stay with you and Sophia. I'll get us a bigger cottage, and you can hire servants. It will be better for Sophia."

Lizzie's jaw dropped. "And what do you want in return?"

"I want something that looks like family life. I want to spend time with our daughter . . . and with you. I want to be your true friend. I'll be here as often as I can, but I have other calls on my time. And, I have to be honest: no one can know about our arrangement."

"You can't just come in here after two years and turn my life upside down."

Geordie reached for Lizzie's right hand and started drawing circles in her palm. Lizzie gave in to the feeling of warmth the simple motion gave her. If Geordie lived in her house, she wouldn't have to worry about money or anything else. It wasn't as though anyone would want to take on a woman with a child, and she didn't want to spend her life working at the Ship.

*This could blow up in my face.*

"If I agree to your suggestion, when would our new living arrangement begin?"

"This very moment."

"You'll have to eat porridge for supper, and sleep on a straw mattress that I barely fit on myself."

"I can do that. And tomorrow I'll arrange for supplies and make arrangements for a bigger cottage. And then you can order furnishings to fill it. Will you give me a chance?"

*Despite everything, I still want him, and when Geordie looks at me like that . . .*

Lizzie nodded. "I accept your offer. Don't make me regret it."

"I promise you won't." Geordie kissed Lizzie's forehead. "Thank you for giving me a chance."

Lizzie cupped Geordie's cheek. "In truth, I'm not strong enough to turn you away."

The next morning, Geordie was surprised to wake up with his arms around Lizzie. *Probably trying to keep us both in this tiny bed.* Despite the fact his bunk on the *Belisarius* was more comfortable, Geordie couldn't remember sleeping this well since being with Lizzie at the Ship.

On the trundle bed, Sophia was awake and playing with her doll. She bounced it up and down a few times and pulled a few strands out of the doll's husk stuffing. Geordie slipped out of bed and reached down to lift up his daughter. Putting his finger to his lips, he carried her into the main part of the room, settled her on the rug, and began rolling a ball back and forth for her. A feeling of deep contentment settled over him.

"I'll make this work," Geordie vowed to himself, "and Lizzie will never regret taking me in."

# Lucy Brown

*September 1796*
*Reverend Clarke's House, Boston*

"It's so humid I can't keep hold of my embroidery needle," Lucy muttered. She dabbed her forehead with her handkerchief and offered a self-deprecating smile to her friend Esther Clarke.

"In that case," Esther said, "I suggest you put your needlework aside. I'll go for some cider, and then we can talk about your future."

Lucy pretended not to hear and kept her eyes focused on the floral embroidery pattern she was adding to the bottom of what would become a white muslin dress. As Lucy pulled blue thread through the fabric, she dropped her needle. It dangled at the end of the thread in what seemed like a silent rebuke, until she grabbed it and folded her project back into its basket.

"Here we are." Esther placed a tray with two clay beakers on the table.

Lucy immediately grabbed the closest one and let the cool liquid flow down her throat. Esther picked up her own beaker and took several swallows of the liquid.

"At least it's refreshing." Esther put the beaker back on the tray. "I'm compelled to speak to you about your future. Several young men have sought your favor, but you dash their hopes before giving them a chance."

Lucy flushed. *Esther's about to pester me again about marriage prospects and my lack of suitors. If only Elias would speak up!*

"In fact, I felt no attraction to the men who have called on me. It wouldn't be fair for me to give them hope when there is none."

"My dear, you haven't spent enough time with any of them to discern an attraction or lack of one. I'm not trying to force you into anything, but do you intend to spend the rest of your days as a spinster?"

Lucy chewed on her lower lip. "As it happens, I've had a note from Captain Derby. He has business in Boston and will pay a call today." She fanned her face and glanced at the porcelain mantel clock. "In fact, I expect him at any moment."

"Am I correct that you have an attraction for him?"

"Yes. Yes, I do," Lucy said with some emphasis. "And I believe he has also taken an interest in me. I wonder if . . . when he arrives . . . you could give us some privacy? We leave the drawing room doors open now to circulate the air, so there's no risk of impropriety. It's not as if I'm an untried maid without common sense."

Esther tapped her chin in consideration. "Very well. After Captain Derby arrives, if he arrives, I shall withdraw to the dining parlor and leave both sets of doors open. The maid will be in to offer refreshments, so you won't be entirely unattended.

"But I must remind you that Captain Derby may never declare his intentions in a formal manner. He's remained unmarried for some time, and my husband Reverend Clarke confided in me that he has substantial uncleared debts. If that's the case, it seems unlikely he's in a position to offer you marriage, and I don't think a life of spinsterhood would suit you."

Lucy wrinkled her forehead. *Is that why he won't declare himself? Why didn't he tell me? Does he think I won't wait for him?*

"Esther, Captain Derby's situation is not easy," Lucy said, beginning her excuses. "Mr. Derby is such a dominant force in Salem that it is difficult for Captain Derby to establish himself."

"Doesn't Mr. Derby employ his sons? And surely, Captain Derby makes investments in the Eastern trade?" Esther paused. "In fact, from what Reverend Clarke tells me, Captain Derby is the last son in the family still at home."

"I thought clergymen didn't gossip," Lucy deflected.

"Well, if you want gossip, I can tell you the Derbys employed Mr. Bulfinch to design their new mansion. And it seems it is a massive structure for just two people. Clearly, the Derbys aren't planning to hide their financial light under a bushel. In that, I'm just stating what is clear for anyone to see.

"Captain Derby's parents aren't likely to pay down his debts while constructing a mansion. Therefore, he cannot marry you. When you meet him today, think about your future. If he doesn't state an interest in moving forward, I advise you to turn away from his potential courtship so another gentleman can form a friendship with you."

Lucy's head began to pound. "I know you have my best interests at heart. And you only want for me the contentment you have with Reverend Clarke and your children. I'm aware of Captain Derby's situation . . . well, not so much about his indebtedness, but I know his position in the family firm.

"In his letters, he pours out his heart, perhaps more than he should. He cares deeply for me and wants only my happiness. I believe his declarations are sincere, and I completely reciprocate his desire to establish a home and begin a family. Captain Derby is everything I want in a husband. I don't care about his financial issues."

Esther shook her head. "You will if he can't sort them out."

Just as Lucy was about to speak, she heard boots stamping outside the front door. Someone rapped with the brass door knocker. The doorknob squeaked when the housemaid opened the front door.

"Captain Derby. I believe I'm expected."

Esther picked up her embroidery basket. "Remember what I said," she whispered as she left the room.

Lucy managed to stand, smooth her skirts, and pinch her cheeks in the moment before Elias entered the room. Her heart pounded so strongly she imagined it throbbing out of her chest.

Seeing Elias standing just inside the doorway, Lucy felt suddenly dizzy. *I'm not going to faint. I don't swoon at the sight of a man. Though, if I was that sort of woman, I'm sure I would faint.* Lucy waved her hand in front of her face to move a bit of humid air past her nose.

Elias stood tall in a well-fitting suit of clothing that accented his broad shoulders. His light hair was pulled back into a queue. He smiled broadly as he approached Lucy. Lucy's heart pounded harder.

"Miss Brown, it has been too long since we last met."

He bowed to her curtsey and reached out his hands for hers. Lucy trembled slightly. *I hope he doesn't notice.*

"It's wonderful to see you again." Lucy gazed into Elias's blue eyes. "Um, perhaps you'd like to sit?"

Lucy gestured to the seat next to her on the sofa. Elias raised his eyebrows and seated himself in the cane-back chair on the opposite side. Lucy blushed. *I shouldn't have invited him to sit next to me. He'll think me forward.*

Elias smiled. "Miss Brown . . ."

The maid entered the drawing room with a tray containing beakers of cider and a plate of biscuits.

"Cider," Elias exclaimed. "The perfect beverage for such a warm day."

"Yes. I'll call if we need anything more, Clara."

Lucy fell silent watching the maid leave the room.

"Thank you for the letters you sent," she said at last.

"You don't think them too bold? When I think of your understanding nature, I am inclined to share my innermost self with you."

"My mind is much the same when I reply. However, propriety requires me to be less direct in case my letters go astray."

"I meant what I wrote. I will do anything I can to promote your happiness."

Lucy hesitated. *If I press him for a declaration, I could lose him. But Esther is right. I need to know his true intentions.*

She took a deep breath and cleared her throat. "Captain Derby, we've been friends since your brother's wedding. We meet socially and exchange letters. I think it is time for us to speak plainly."

Elias suddenly started coughing, his face turning red from the effort. Lucy jumped up to help him stand and pound his back. Elias covered his mouth with a handkerchief and sat down again, though he continued to lean forward. The spasm passed, leaving him breathless.

"What can I do to help you?" Lucy wrung her hands.

"Nothing, really." Elias held out his hands. "I'm almost recovered. You..." He cleared his throat and swallowed. "You took me by surprise."

Lucy felt instantly contrite. "My behavior was shocking. It's no wonder you lost your breath. Pray forgive my intrusion. Shall I send for tea? Perhaps to settle your digestion?"

Elias shook his head. "No, please don't. And your behavior wasn't shocking so much as honest. Your honesty and compassion are the traits I admire most about you. You have been nothing but honest with me since we met. I, however, have been less forthcoming."

Lucy shook her head. "No, not at all. You don't owe me any explanations."

Elias grimaced. "Most of the time, I mask my true self because I fear that if anyone sees me truly, I will lose everything. I've never been fully honest with my brother Zeke, and he's my closest confidant.

"The truth of the matter is that I've entertained great affection for you since the day we met. I feel you are the only person who would never reject me if you knew everything about me. And despite my confidence in your compassion, I still find myself unable to tell you everything. But I can tell you this—"

Lucy shook her head and reached for Elias's hand. "No, truly you are my friend and do not owe me any explanation."

Elias rubbed his neck and scrunched his eyes before raising them to look at Lucy's face.

She felt her heart thump again.

"Lucy?"

"Yes?"

"I can't make you a formal offer for your hand, but . . ." Elias swallowed before moving to sit next to her on the sofa. He picked up her hands again. Lucy stopped breathing.

"Could you find it in yourself to spend your life with me? Wait." Elias held his hand up. "Don't answer until I finish. Joining your life to mine may not be what you envision. It's true, my family is wealthy, and I invest in shipping and trade. However, my investments are not always successful, and if I were any other merchant, my standing would be more modest."

Elias and Lucy began leaning toward each other, until Lucy felt the light sheen of his sweat when their foreheads touched.

Lucy whispered softly. "I don't care about your wealth. I care about you."

"That's a dangerous commitment. I could easily fail your trust."

Elias wrapped his hand behind Lucy's neck and brought her lips closer to his. Lucy thought she might float away on a cloud.

"Lucy." An acerbic voice cut through the moment. "You didn't tell me Captain Derby was here."

Esther looked at Lucy with daggers in her eyes as the couple sprang apart.

"How are things in Salem, Captain Derby?" Esther barreled on. "I understand your parents are building a new house."

Elias coughed into his hand. "How kind of you to ask, Mrs. Clarke. The exterior is nearly done now."

*How did Elias recover so quickly?* Lucy gulped in large breaths of air until her heart slowed. From a distance, she heard him speaking.

"I've taken up rather a lot of your time, Mrs. Clarke. Allow me to take my leave."

*No!* Lucy bolted to a standing position. "I'll walk you to the door, Captain Derby."

"I'm sure he can find his way," Esther said acidly.

Lucy walked to the door with Elias and handed him his hat.

"I didn't have a chance to answer your question," she said.

"About what?"

"You asked if I could find it within myself to spend my life with you."

Elias grimaced.

Lucy placed her hand on his arm. "The answer is yes, and *when* you make a formal offer, my answer will still be yes. I only ask that you don't wait much longer."

Elias grinned and kissed the back of Lucy's hand. "I promise you a formal declaration very soon."

Elias crossed to the pavement and waved his hat to Lucy.

Lucy raised her hand in farewell. *Please don't disappoint me.*

# Lizzie Rowell

*November 1796*
*Danvers*

To Lizzie's surprise, Geordie kept his promises. Within a week, he leased a small house farther out of Danvers. Instead of one room with a fireplace, it had two bedrooms upstairs, a kitchen, a dining parlor, and a drawing room. Geordie discarded everything from the cottage, except the rug Lizzie insisted on keeping, and ordered furnishings. A dining table, cane-back chairs, a sofa, a four-poster bed with a feather mattress. Porcelain plates and cups. Candles. Wall coverings and rugs in every room. Food and someone to cook it. Madeira wine. Lizzie had never seen such luxury, let alone been surrounded by it.

"It's too much," Lizzie protested. "It's more than I deserve."

Geordie shook his head. "It is less than you deserve. When I'm with you, I'm content. You are my true wife in every way, and a wonderful mother to Sophia. You nourished and protected her despite every adversity."

"But . . ."

Geordie kissed Lizzie's cheek, and Lizzie returned his affection.

Soon a pattern of life emerged. When Geordie stayed at the house, he rose early so he could be at the counting house by ten o'clock. Some days, he returned home late in the evening. Lizzie always had a hot meal ready for him, but she didn't wait up for his arrival, because there was no certainty he would arrive.

"You could send a note," Lizzie suggested.

"No, I couldn't," Geordie replied. And that was that.

When September slipped into October, Lizzie became increasingly nervous. Geordie was quiet and moody. He had little to say, and when he spoke, it was often to complain.

*It's his ship,* Lizzie thought. *It will be leaving soon, and he won't be on it. Or will he?*

During the third weekend of October, Geordie stayed in Salem. Lizzie busied herself sewing soft woolen winter dresses for Sophia and pressing apples into cider. Monday night, she tucked Sophia into bed with an extra quilt before going back downstairs to stare into the fire.

*Geordie wasn't serious after all. He's gone out with his ship without even a farewell note.* Silent, fat tears slid down Lizzie's cheek. *Tomorrow someone will deliver a purse.* Lizzie pushed a poker into the fire to bank the coals and went upstairs. When she peeked behind the door, she saw Sophia sleeping soundly. *What will I tell her when she asks about Geordie?*

Lizzie kicked off her shoes and crawled into bed, too depressed to remove her clothing. She pounded her feather pillow until she had the perfect hollow for her head and then curved her body around it in a ball. Light from the harvest moon streamed through the window. An owl hooted. Lizzie closed her eyes and slept fitfully.

# Captain George Crowninshield Jr.

*Captain George Crowninshield's House*

"Will you sleep aboard the *Belisarius* tonight?" Geordie asked.

John raised his glass. "That was your habit, Brother. It won't be mine when there's a soft feather bed waiting for me."

Jacob slapped his hand on John's shoulder. "Time to establish your own method of command. The crew needs to see you as your own man."

Geordie listened to Jacob and his father offer suggestions to John as if his brother hadn't already learned what he needed to know from sailing with him the past few years.

A soft hand touched Geordie's forearm. "Jacob is only trying to calm your brother's nerves," Sarah said. "It's not easy knowing Sir will judge him against you."

Geordie shrugged. "My brother is as ready as he's going to be. If he weren't, we'd be sailing together as we have before."

"It must be hard to let go of the sea."

Geordie gave Sarah a quizzical look. "Why do you say that?"

Sarah led Geordie across the room to the front windows and pointed toward the wharf.

"Jacob likes to walk the wharf in the early morning. He likes to hear the gulls and watch their acrobatics. He fills his lungs with wet, salty air. And then he walks back home to have breakfast with me and prepare himself for a day in the counting house.

"I should imagine it's the same for you. Sir calls you and Jacob ashore to the life you always wanted. But now that you have it, you realize the sea will never leave you alone."

*How embarrassing for my cousin to know me so well when I know little about her.*

"And do you think this longing will pass?"

Sarah smiled sadly. "No. But I think you will learn to live with it as Jacob has."

"What are you two whispering about over here?" Geordie's mother asked.

"Nothing of importance." Geordie shrugged.

"Will you see off the *Belisarius* tomorrow? We could walk down to the wharf together."

Geordie bowed over his mother's hand. "Regretfully, I will not be on the wharf tomorrow."

Mame nodded. "It was much the same when your father came ashore. The first two or three times ships he knew sailed out, he couldn't bear to watch."

Geordie tapped John on the shoulder before pulling him in for a hug.

"Fair winds and following seas, Brother. I look forward to your return."

John clapped Geordie on the back but didn't say anything.

Geordie tapped John's cheek, saluted him with one finger, and went into the hall to put on his outerwear. Shorter days meant more chill at night.

"Going out, sir?" the footman asked.

"If anyone asks, tell them I'll be gone a few days."

"I will. Have a good evening."

Geordie walked to the stable to pick up Toby. The horse nickered a greeting before Geordie led him out of his stall and slung a saddle over him.

"Ready for a ride out under a harvest moon, Toby?" Geordie tightened Toby's cinch, mounted his companion, and headed toward Danvers.

Arriving at the Danvers house, Geordie threw Toby's saddle on the rack and hung his bridle over hooks in the wall. *Maybe I'll build this stable out properly while I'm here. Establish my new life.* He filled a bucket from the well outside and poured the water into the trough before tossing a few oats into the feed manger.

"That will do for now, Toby. I'll take you out tomorrow." Geordie gave the horse a few pats on his rump and walked through the moonlit path to the house.

Inside, remnants of the kitchen fire glowed in the open fireplace, keeping a small cauldron of food warm. Geordie pulled it away from the fire.

The house felt incredibly still. Geordie left his boots in the kitchen and loosened his cravat as he climbed the stairs. He peeked into Sophia's room to see his daughter sleeping with her thumb in her mouth. Geordie smoothed her hair back from her face and kissed her forehead. He put Sophia's corn husk doll on the pillow so she could see it when she woke up and made his way into the bedroom he shared with Lizzie.

Geordie slipped off his breeches and stockings before lifting the blankets and crawling in next to Lizzie. He came up behind her and reached his arms around his partner's middle in an effort to release her from her tightly curled position. Lizzie wrapped herself back into the cramped pose. Geordie stroked her arm.

"Relax, Lizzie. You're safe. I'm here," he whispered.

After about half an hour, Lizzie released her limbs so Geordie could spoon his body behind her and let thoughts of his family and ship drift away.

All too soon, Geordie heard Sophia push the bedroom door open.

"Mam?" she called before padding over to the bed.

Geordie opened one eye and sighed. He grabbed his banyan from the wardrobe and picked up his daughter.

"Come on, Sophia. Let's get you bundled up and feed you breakfast."

Geordie found Cook busy in the kitchen. She gave him a friendly smile. "You're home, Captain Crowninshield. I have fresh bread and porridge for you and young miss."

"Did you add molasses and nutmeg?"

"Yes, sir. Let's put young miss in the tall chair. Will you be feeding her, or shall I?"

"I will, Cook."

Geordie enjoyed Sophia first thing in the morning. She was awake, with lots of smiles, and she giggled every time she managed to get the porridge into her mouth.

"This is far better than putting out to sea," Geordie told himself. But he didn't believe it.

## Lizzie Rowell

Lizzie rolled over onto her back and reached up to rub her pounding head. *Serves me right for crying half the night.* A gust of wind rattled the windowpane. She used the chamber pot and reached inside the wardrobe for her banyan. *Odd, I don't see Geordie's robe.* Lizzie shook her head. *No, it can't be.*

She shoved her feet into slippers and went to Sophia's room. Her daughter's bed was empty. *Geordie takes her downstairs sometimes, but . . . No, I'm dreaming.* Lizzie's heart began to pound. *But maybe?*

Lizzie held on to the banister to stop herself from tripping on the stairs. She ran into the kitchen, and there they were. The only people in the world who mattered to her.

Sophia crowed happily as she shoved porridge in her mouth. Geordie dabbed at the blobs of cereal on her nightdress.

"I big girl." Sophia giggled.

"Yes, you are, Sophia. But perhaps you could aim the spoon more directly into your mouth," said Geordie.

A feeling of pure joy filled Lizzie.

"You're here."

Geordie turned with a smile. "I am. When I came home last night after seeing my brother off, you were both asleep. Well, Sophia was. You looked like you fought a ghost and lost. It took a long time to unwind your body so I could lie with you. What happened?"

Lizzie glanced at Cook, who kept her eyes on the chopping board.

"Cook, could you help my daughter finish breakfast?" Geordie asked.

"Of course, sir."

Geordie led Lizzie into the small parlor near the kitchen.

"Sit down, my dear."

Lizzie looked at Geordie, her face stricken. "When you didn't visit us, I thought . . . I thought you went out on your ship. I thought you didn't want us after all," she whispered.

Geordie lifted Lizzie's left hand and kissed the inside of her wrist. "You mustn't jump to conclusions. I told you I would often stay in Salem. I only promised to come when I could. I never said I would be with you all the time."

Lizzie shook her head. "I know that. But I also knew your ship was nearly ready to sail. And when I didn't hear from you . . . I naturally thought you'd had enough of us."

"Lizzie, you added two plus two and decided the answer was five. I have been busy. The *Belisarius* sailed today with my brother John as master."

Geordie rubbed the back of his neck. "I'll be honest with you. I hoped the circumstance would change. That John would ask me to sail with him again, or Sir would decide John wasn't ready to sail alone. But my hopes were foolish. John deserves his chance, and Sir is right to give it to him."

Lizzie nodded. "So, um, will there be another ship for you?"

"I doubt it. Jacob's wife told me something last night that helped me understand things better."

"What did she say?"

"She said she understood it's hard to let go of the sea. And she's right. I don't know who I am when I'm not on a ship. And she told me my brother walks the wharf every morning and then prepares for his day at the counting house."

Lizzie stroked the back of Geordie's hand. "And how did her words help you?"

"Jacob and I will never speak of this because that's not how we are. But I understand that the sea will never leave us, and also that I'm the lucky one. At least I'll be around ships, keeping them fit and designing improvements. He'll be stuck with letters and account books."

"Does this mean you'll stay with us?"

"It does. I will stay with you and Sophia, and though we won't have a conventional home, I'll be here as much as I can, and give you as much of myself as I can."

Geordie smiled gently. "You've no need to worry. There will never be another woman for me. And I will care for you as much as I am able. Do you believe me?"

Geordie stroked Lizzie's cheek, and Lizzie felt herself open up to whatever regard Geordie could give her.

*I won't know what Geordie is doing most of the time, but I'm sure he will look after us. There are wives who are held in less regard.*

Lizzie smiled and nodded. "I believe you, Geordie."

He lifted her chin. "And you know in your heart I won't abandon you?"

"I do."

Geordie took a deep breath. "Well, I'm glad that's settled. Shall we have our morning tea in the kitchen with Sophia?"

Lizzie felt a broad smile crease her face. "There's nothing I would like better."

# Hasket Derby

*December 1796*
*Hasket Derby's House*

Eliza sat on the sofa in the drawing room with a fire crackling in front of her. Her daughters surrounded her, commenting on wallpaper samples before passing them to their mother. Eliza placed a few of the samples beside her on the sofa for further consideration. Others, she tossed onto the floor. Observing their concentration, Hasket thought they looked like colorful budding crocus flowers forcing their way out of seemingly frozen soil in the spring, which could not come soon enough for his taste.

He stood in silence for several minutes before Betsey glanced in his direction.

"Father?"

"Ladies." Hasket inclined his head. "I have a matter of some importance that needs to be discussed."

Eliza glanced at the mantel clock before turning her attention to Hasket. "It's past ten o'clock. Why are you here? I thought you were at the counting house."

"Father, are you unwell?" Betsey asked in alarm. "Shall we send for the doctor?"

Anstiss and Patsy simply stared at his unexpected presence.

"I fear you'll have to move your samples, because I asked Mrs. Smith to serve us coffee."

Anstiss began gathering the bits of wallpaper into separate stacks so she could transfer them to a nearby card table.

"But why are you here?" Eliza asked again. "Did you go to the counting house and come back again?"

"In point of fact, after breakfast, I went to my study, because I saw no reason to be out in this morning's chilly fog. And I needed to think about family matters."

Eliza jumped up. "Are you unwell?" she demanded. "Is it your breathing?"

Hasket pushed Eliza's hand off his chest. "It's nothing to do with my breathing. I'm perfectly fine."

"You would tell us?" Eliza asked.

Hasket felt a flash of irritation. *My health is my own business, and if they need to know something I will tell them.*

"I want to speak to you all about Elias."

"But he left for the counting house. Shouldn't he be present if we're going to talk about him?" Patsy asked.

"No. I'm merely gathering information, and I would appreciate it if you would keep this conversation to yourselves. I need your opinions on what Elias requires in a wife." Hasket took a seat next to Eliza. "What do you think, my dear?"

"I think . . ." The footman opened the door to admit three maids. One with the coffee service. Another, with porcelain cups and saucers, and a third, with biscuits and small cakes artfully arranged on two serving plates.

"Almond wafers," Anstiss exclaimed. "My favorite."

Eliza busied herself pouring coffee so Betsey could distribute the cups and saucers.

"You started to say something, Eliza?" Hasket said.

Eliza pursed her lips. "You asked what Elias requires in a wife, and I think the first requisite is a social standing compatible with ours. Our other sons selected appropriate young women, but they brought no particular benefit to the family. In fact, Anstiss is the only one of my children to make an advantageous marriage."

"That's a bit harsh, Mother," Betsey protested. "Nate is a well-respected merchant."

"He is now, but he was a mere ship's master when you willfully married him." Eliza gave her daughter a long look and sniffed. "I admit he's done well for himself, but as our eldest daughter, that didn't make your selection appropriate at the time."

Hasket put down his cup before he lost complete control of the conversation.

"Your mother is correct that barring an extreme passion, such as she and I had, marriage is about social and business compatibility." Hasket winked at his wife.

"Humph," Eliza said. "I recall compatibility and advantage more than passion, extreme or otherwise."

"Mrs. Derby, shall I lead you out in a minuet such as we danced at our wedding? Perhaps that will jog the gaps in your memory." Hasket held out his hand, only to have his wife slap it away.

"I've forgotten nothing about our marriage." Eliza smirked.

Hasket inhaled a short breath. *Every time I try to talk to my wife and daughters, the conversation pulls off track.*

"To return to the original topic of a marriage for Elias . . ."

"He can't marry." Betsey spoke up. "My husband tells me he's in debt to merchants all over Salem."

Anstiss nodded. "Mr. Pickman says the same. So, even if you gift him a house when he marries, he probably won't be able to furnish it beyond what his wife's family donates."

"Elias travels to Boston frequently," Patsy observed. "But he hasn't mentioned forming an attachment to anyone. And at thirty years old, he's a bit elderly for marriage."

"You're older than he is," Betsey jibed.

Patsy tossed her head. "But I'm not the family heir. I may never marry. I'm sure Anstiss will take me in, won't you?"

Anstiss bounced her head up. "What did you say?"

"I said if I'm left an orphaned spinster, you and Mr. Pickman would take me into your home."

"I suppose?"

*I've lost the conversation again. It was a moment of madness when I decided to confer with them about Elias.*

"Ladies, we need to discuss Elias and his prospects."

"And what might those be?" Eliza asked.

"You won't approve. Our agents in Boston tell me Elias is courting a young woman named Lucy Brown, whose parents are deceased. She resides in the home of Reverend John Clarke. By all accounts, she is a personable, well-bred young woman with family ties to our son John's wife. Elias appears to be smitten with her."

Betsey's cup rattled on her saucer. And then the room fell silent for several minutes.

"But who is she?" Betsey asked.

"It appears she has the same social standing as your other two sisters-in-law."

"Then she's not acceptable," Eliza said. "Elias is our heir, after all."

"In point of fact, we cannot forbid the marriage. And having a wife might make Elias take more responsibility for his decisions. He's too much at loose ends and makes rash choices because he doesn't have a family to support. I think marriage will settle him down. At least that is my hope."

Hasket sighed. He didn't like admitting he had no useful authority over Elias. *I had such expectations when he returned from Isle de France, but he's never settled into the business or even his own life.*

"Elias's debts will break him," Patsy said. "Father, you must cover them so he can start fresh."

# Captain Elias Derby

*January 1797*
*Boston*

"January is a brutal time to travel," Reverend Clarke observed. "Your business must be important for you to brave the elements."

Reverend Clarke handed Elias a glass of brandy.

"Come, sit by the fire and warm yourself before we get down to business."

Elias leaned toward the fire, cradling his glass between his palms. Slowly the fire's warmth thawed his frozen limbs. Reverend Clarke's study was designed to hold in heat, with heavy curtains over the windows and a thick rug on the floor.

Elias sat back in the wingback chair. "Thank you for seeing me, sir. I realize I requested this meeting on short notice, but I don't know when I'll next be in Boston."

"It's always a pleasure to meet with Miss Brown's friends. She speaks very highly of you and enjoys your visits. My wife tells me that your visits amount to an informal courtship. Is she correct?"

Elias considered Reverend Clarke's genial appearance. By all accounts, he was a generous man who laughed more than he chastised. *He deserves an honest answer to his question.*

"Yes, sir, she is. Though between Miss Brown and myself, matters have proceeded a bit beyond the informal state." Elias swirled the brandy in his glass before setting it on the table.

"I hope you are not trifling with her affections. Her nature is far too generous for her own good."

"And I would never take advantage of it."

Elias took a deep breath. "I don't know if you're aware of it already, but I've been in a certain amount of financial difficulty."

"Indeed. Word of your dilemma has reached Boston."

"How?" Elias blurted.

"I have my sources," Reverend Clarke said. "Perhaps you'd like to apprise me of your current status?"

"That's why I requested this meeting," Elias said stiffly. "I want to advise you formally of my situation and request your blessing when I officially propose to Miss Brown."

"Continue."

*He's not going to let me off easily, but I have to try.*

"I make no excuses for myself. My investments have not done as well as I hoped. And I play cards, without an adequate amount of luck. In short, I have a great deal of debt. However, out of their goodness, my father and brothers forgave my debts so that I have the means to provide for a wife. Also, my father will provide housing for me after I marry. This means I'm well placed to provide for Miss Brown." Elias paused. "If she accepts me."

He kept his eyes on Reverend Clarke, who let the silence between them grow until Elias found it unbearable and dropped his gaze. The reverend couldn't refuse his marriage to Lucy, but would she defer to his judgment? Sweat beaded on Elias's forehead. Finally, Reverend Clarke cleared his throat. Elias released a breath.

"I have a question for you, and I want you to answer honestly. Have you repented of your past behavior?"

Elias rapidly went through his worst memories. He could think of several events that could answer Reverend Clarke's question but saw no reason to volunteer the information.

"What do you mean, sir?"

"I refer to your gambling." Reverend Clarke gave Elias a stern look. "Many a man falls into disrepute through debt. A man with gambling proclivities will likely lose everything he possesses. I do not want my ward tied to such a man."

"I give you my word," Elias said. "I have sworn off cards."

Reverend Clarke gave Elias a long look. "You renounce this vice without reservations of any kind?"

"I do. But without Miss Brown beside me, I don't know if I can succeed."

"Miss Brown cannot save you from your vices. Only God can do that."

"I understand."

"Do you?"

*Not really, but I'll promise whatever you need to hear.*

Elias smiled ruefully. "If I slide, I'm sure Miss Brown will remind me."

Reverend Clarke stood. "It took courage for you to face me today, and I respect that. You have the ability to live an honorable life if you choose to do so. Miss Brown holds you in high regard and is of age to make her own decisions. Under the circumstances, if she accepts you, I will give you both my blessing."

*Thank you, Lord!*

Elias stood abruptly and extended his hand.

"Thank you, sir. I won't betray your trust in me." Elias enthusiastically pumped Reverend Clarke's arm until the man withdrew his hand.

"Come. Miss Brown will be with the family."

Elias followed Reverend Clarke into the drawing room. Two women and several children were occupied in a game of hunt the slipper.

"Lucy, you have a visitor who wishes a private word."

When Lucy's gaze fell upon Elias, her face lit up.

"Captain Derby, how good of you to call."

## Lucy Brown

Lucy stood without thinking, the words of greeting leaving her mouth automatically.

"Lucy," Reverend Clarke said, "why don't you take Captain Derby into my study. I believe he has a private matter to discuss with you. Leave the doors open, and don't be gone more than ten minutes. I don't want the heat to entirely escape the room."

Reverend Clarke gave Lucy a small smile. "Go on, then."

"May I show you the way, Captain Derby?" Lucy said softly.

"If you would be so kind."

Elias offered his arm to Lucy. "Have you had a pleasant day?"

Lucy thought she detected a slight crack in Elias's normal, confident voice. *Is he nervous?*

She placed her hand on his arm. "We should walk more quickly if Reverend Clarke expects us to return within ten minutes."

Lucy opened the study door, guided Elias to a wingback chair, and took a seat on its mate.

"What did you and Reverend Clarke talk about?"

"You, but it was mostly about me and my prospects. I told him my family will clear my debts and that I would stop gambling. I asked his blessing to offer you my formal proposal of marriage."

Elias clutched Lucy's hands. Lucy felt her heart leap into her throat. *Can this finally be happening?*

"What . . . what did he say?"

"He said that if you accept me, he will give us his blessing. After all this time, I'm finally able to ask you the most important question of our lives."

Elias dropped to one knee in front of Lucy. "I want to do this properly, so please hear me out. Miss Brown, Lucy, you know my faults, which I have not hidden from you, and you know I am the best version of myself when you're by my side. I care for you more than I thought it possible to care for anyone."

Lucy held her breath.

"Lucy Brown, will you accept my hand in marriage? Will you build a family with me so we may go through life together? And, will you take a breath before you answer the question, because I don't want you to faint."

Lucy took a sudden inhalation as laughter bubbled through her body.

"Yes, Captain Derby, Elias. I will marry you and build a family with you. I will cherish you throughout our life together."

With tears of happiness streaming down her face, Lucy flung her arms around Elias's neck.

"Darling Lucy, I didn't know it was possible to be this happy." Elias kissed Lucy's forehead just as a knock sounded at the open door.

"Your ten minutes are up," Esther announced.

Lucy giggled. "Come in and share our happiness. Elias proposed to me, and I accepted."

Esther hugged Lucy. "I am truly happy for you, dear Lucy. And if Captain Derby fails to live up to his promises in any way, you will always have a home with us."

Lucy withdrew from Esther's hug and gazed at Elias. "From the time we say our vows, my home will be with Elias."

# Captain Nathaniel Silsbee

*July 1797*
*Salem*

Leaving his brother William to oversee the *Betsey*'s arrival back in Salem, Nath strode down the gangplank with a determined expression that discouraged people from greeting him. He walked along the tide flats until he reached Edward Hulan's lane. The moment had arrived. He had to tell Edward's mother he lost her son to a British press-gang in Madras.

Nath took off his hat and rapped at an open door.

"Mrs. Hulan? Are you at home?"

Edward's mother came into view with a broad smile. "Captain Silsbee, you're back."

Mrs. Hulan peered to either side of Nath. "Where's Edward, then? Have you left him aboard the *Betsey*?"

"May I come in? I . . . I have news of your son."

Mrs. Hulan's breath caught. "News?" She gestured for Nath to enter her cottage and sit on a cane-back chair that caught a breeze through the open door. "Please sit. I'll make tea for us."

Consumed with guilt over the news he had to share, Nath watched Mrs. Hulan pour water from a kettle over the fire into an earthenware teapot. She carried the teapot and two cups to a small table next to Nath's chair before seating herself across from him.

Nath opened his mouth to speak, but Mrs. Hulan held up her hand. "Wait until I pour out our tea. I find a cup of tea very soothing when I hear unexpected news."

Nath took a deep breath and watched his hostess fill his cup.

"I'm sorry I don't have any sugar to offer you."

"That's quite all right, Mrs. Hulan. I prefer strong tea."

"You're kind to say so. My funds are a bit low, just at the moment. I expected to replenish supplies after Edward returned, but he isn't coming back, is he."

"Rest assured, he will be back."

Mrs. Hulan put down her tea. "You'd better tell me what happened."

*Shall I tell her the long story or the short? Does it matter?*

"Yes, ma'am. We were anchored at Madras. My brother William and I went ashore to conduct business, and while we were in the city, a British press-gang boarded the *Betsey* and took Edward."

"Does the ship have a name?"

*Why does that matter?*

"She's the HMS *Beaver*. I immediately crossed over to her, but her captain refused to release Edward. I appealed to the British officers' board . . ." Nath shook his head. "To no avail. I cannot tell you how deeply I regret I couldn't obtain your son's release. I . . ."

Nath cleared his throat. "In our last conversation, Edward asked me to give you his residual wages. I've taken the liberty to add the wages he would have earned if he'd been able to complete the voyage."

Nath pressed a purse into Mrs. Hulan's hand. "And if you find yourself in need, you have only to request my assistance."

Nath watched Mrs. Hulan nod in agreement, her drawn features testifying to grief without despair. Her gray eyes glittered with unshed tears.

"It's the way of the world, Captain Silsbee. You mustn't blame yourself. You did your best, and the British will always plague us. There was nothing more you could do. Edward will come home as quick as he can. And I shall pray for his return and good health every day. I'm sure he'll find a way back to us."

Nath stumbled on, trying to reassure Mrs. Hulan he had done all he could.

"I've written the State Department. I'm sure they will take up Edward's case. And I'll be in contact with anyone who can plead for his release." Nath rubbed the back of his neck. "I—"

Mrs. Hulan gave Nath a stern look. "Captain Silsbee, you must stop this nonsense. Edward knew the risks when he signed on to the *Betsey*. He was proud to sail for you. I thank you for your continued support, but now it's time for you to get on and let things progress as they will."

Mrs. Hulan stood, walked Nath to her open door, and handed him his hat.

"I won't forget your kindness, but I know enough about ships to know you have things to do now, so you best be doing them."

# Captain Nathaniel Silsbee

*September 1797*
*Ship Tavern, Salem*

"I signed on with the *Betsey* again. I'll have a larger adventure this time," Richard Smith said.

Nath nodded at his former first mate and drank some of his coffee. Sounds of clattering crockery and the grunts of dockworkers taking advantage of the Ship's breakfast options drew Nath's attention.

"It don't seem right to go out in her without you and your brother."

"You'll do fine."

"And yourself, sir. Do you have another ship?"

"Not at present. My attention has been on selling my share of the *Betsey* and the adventure cargo William and I brought back with us. The profit was less than I hoped after everything that happened."

William took a seat on the other side of the table and sat down in front of his full plate.

Nath winced. "You've become a bottomless pit, William."

"Growing boy and all that." William winked. "Good to see you, Richard. I just heard you signed on with the *Betsey* again."

"Aye. Well, I'll be off, then. Hope to sail with you again, Captain Silsbee."

Nath stood and held out his hand. "I hope the same."

William put down his spoon. "Are you second-guessing your decision to sell your shares in the *Betsey*?"

"I've been thinking over our options."

William swallowed a mouthful of ale. "And?"

"I received a letter from Ebenezer Preble. He invited me to call at my convenience. Fancy a trip to Boston? We could catch the morning stage."

William grinned. "Count me in."

# Captain Nathaniel Silsbee

*September 21, 1797*
*Edmund Hartt's Shipyard, Boston*

"There she is." Nath pointed to a three-masted frigate stuck in the tide flats. "The first ship in our navy stuck in the mud."

"Look at all the copper sheeting below her waterline," said William. "She's too heavy for the ways. Looks like they're trying to cut a deeper angle."

William and Nath joined a crowd of people watching crews use picks and shovels to dig out a channel deep enough for the ship to be towed into the harbor until she could float freely.

"I hear they're going to try and launch her again tomorrow," William said.

Nath shook his head. "They'll have to dig deeper than that. The *Constitution* will be a fine ship once they float her. *If* they float her."

Nath clapped his brother's shoulder. "Come. We need to find Ebenezer Preble's counting house."

The men pushed their way out of the crowd watching the workmen and turned toward the wharf where Preble's counting house stood. To Nath's surprise, it turned out to be in one of the smaller warehouses, indicating that the man moved his cargo quickly. Entering the structure, he inhaled the familiar fragrance of coffee with an overlay of cinnamon and other spices.

Nath proceeded to the head clerk's desk. The grizzled man lifted his head above the document he was reading but didn't say anything.

"Captain Nathaniel Silsbee and William Silsbee to see Captain Preble."

"He be expectin' you. Up the stairs and turn right."

Nath rapped on the door twice and walked into Preble's office. Preble stood in front of the window with a spyglass to his eye. He turned and set the glass aside.

"Captain Silsbee, please take a seat. And this is your brother, I presume."

"Yes. William sails as my partner and supercargo."

"Did you stop by the works?" Preble asked. "Plenty of excitement yesterday. President Adams and the governor were both in attendance to see the great ship launch. Flags flapping. Militia marching. And she didn't make it to the harbor. Quite a lot of embarrassment for Mr. Claghorn. They'll try again tomorrow, but I doubt they'll have better luck. They'll have to dig a deeper channel than they can achieve in one day."

Nath allowed himself a small smile. "My former employer had a similar experience with one of his large ships."

"Oh, yes? Was that Mr. Derby's *Grand Turk*?"

"It was."

"She was a fine ship. I'm surprised he sold her. Speaking of selling assets, I understand you sold your share in the *Betsey*. I have an investment proposition for you if you're interested. Did you notice the *Portland* alongside my wharf? I'm preparing her for a voyage to the Mediterranean. Profits are lucrative for ships that can get through. The *Portland* weighs in at two hundred ninety-eight tons. She's an efficient ship. Are you interested?"

"Perhaps. As I understand it, conditions are tense between French and British naval forces and their privateers."

"They are. But when cargoes get through, the profits, as I said, are large. I propose to send the *Portland* with a cargo of sugar, coffee, and spices. She'll be ready to sail at the end of the year."

Nath stroked his chin. "Go on."

"I can offer you one-third ownership of the *Portland*, the position of captain and supercargo for you and your brother, facilities for generous adventure cargoes, and full authority over cargo dispositions and sailing destinations within the Mediterranean, and elsewhere, if needed."

Nath shifted his eyes sideways to his brother, who gave an imperceptible nod.

"Your offer is generous."

"The risk is high. French corsairs are active in the area, but the demand for luxury goods brings a good profit. Are you willing to take the risk?"

Nath clenched his jaw. "I have no aversion to risk, be it personal or financial. However, my decisions are based on hard facts. Today I'd like to look over the *Portland*. Provided you send over the financial figures and a projected cargo inventory tonight, I'll have an answer for you tomorrow afternoon. We have a room at the Bell-in-Hand. You can send the documents there."

Nath stood and offered his hand. "I look forward to a favorable outcome."

"Indeed. I like a man who measures a risk before he takes it." Preble opened his office door. "Henry," he called out in a voice reminiscent of his own years at sea.

A skinny boy appeared at the top of the stairs.

"Escort Captain Silsbee and his brother to the *Portland*. Tell Mr. Grimes they have free rein to inspect the ship."

"Aye, sir. This way, gentlemen."

"Until tomorrow, Captain Preble."

"I look forward to it."

# Lucy Brown Derby

*March 1798*
*Captain Elias Derby's House*

Lucy counted out the coins in her purse and decided which servants she could do without before calling her lady's maid into the drawing room. Lucy had taken in the fourteen-year-old girl on behalf of the Female Charitable Society to train her as a lady's maid. Bessie proved a quick student, and Lucy was sorry to let her go.

Lucy opened the drawing room door.

"Come in, Bessie. We have several matters to discuss."

Bessie followed Lucy to her desk near the window and curtsied, her dark curls escaping from under her mop cap. The girl looked nervous.

Lucy inhaled to create a sense of calm within herself. "Bessie, you've been an excellent student, but it's time for you to take a more permanent position so I can train another girl."

Lucy placed several coins in Bessie's palm and folded the girl's fingers over them.

"Put those in your pocket so you don't lose them," Lucy instructed. "I'm also giving you an excellent reference. Mrs. Bascomb's daughter is in need of a lady's maid, and I've arranged an appointment for you tomorrow afternoon."

Bessie's face fell. "What have I done wrong, Mrs. Derby? You've only to tell me, and I'll correct it. I want to remain in your employ."

Lucy sighed. "My dear, you've done nothing wrong, which is why it is time for you to seek permanent employment so I can train another girl. I would like you to stay until the end of the week, by which time you should have a place with Mrs. Bascomb. Try not to worry.

"In the meantime, go about your duties as usual."

"But . . ."

Lucy held up her hand. "There's nothing more to say and no reason to speak of the situation further. Run along now and be about your duties."

Bessie turned and slowly walked out of the room.

*She's such a sweet girl,* Lucy thought. *Elias's selfish actions affect more than just his own life.*

"Mrs. Derby?" The housekeeper bustled into the drawing room. "You asked to see me?"

*And now this.*

"Please sit down, Mrs. Weston. I'm afraid I have unfortunate news to share with you."

"Judging by Bessie's face, I think I can guess what it is. Captain Derby is in a pickle again, is he not? I've watched you trim the household budget for several weeks now and made arrangements to stay with my daughter in Beverly until I secure another position."

Lucy's shoulders dropped. "I see. I shall pay you through the end of the month for your inconvenience, and there's no rush for your departure."

"I shall be gone by the end of the week. Are you letting anyone else go?"

"I thought one of the housemaids and the kitchen maid," Lucy mumbled.

"I suggest you keep the kitchen maid. Otherwise, Cook will leave, and you don't know your way around a hearth fire. You might be able to release one or two of the outside men, but you won't be able to prepare for spring. I presume you want to keep the situation quiet?"

Lucy nodded and gave a purse to Mrs. Weston. "I've also written you a reference."

"Thank you, Mrs. Derby. It's been a pleasure to work in your household. I'll leave my address with you in case your situation changes."

Lucy shook her head. "I fear we shall be in straitened circumstances for some time."

Mrs. Weston nodded and closed the door softly behind her.

Lucy stared out the window before dropping her head into her hands.

*We haven't been married a year, and already Elias is gambling again. Now his creditors call here, and soon everyone will know I'm reducing our household staff. How can he hold his head up? How can I?*

## Hasket Derby

*Derby Counting House*

"Mr. Derby, thank you for seeing me."

Hasket looked at the tradesman while he waited for the pressure in his chest to relax.

He waved his hand. "Sit, Mr. Thomas. Have you come to invest in adventure cargo?" Hasket wheezed softly.

"Are you quite all right, sir?"

"It's no secret I take a turn once in a while. I'm right again soon enough." The pressure eased. Hasket leaned forward and steepled his fingers. "What is so important that you've left your shop to visit my counting house?"

Mr. Thomas pulled a handful of invoices from his breast pocket and laid them across Hasket's desk.

"I represent your son's creditors. As you can see from these invoices, Captain Derby has accumulated serious debts that we have carried for almost a year. Clothing, horses, furnishings, household supplies. We have applied to Captain Derby many times and sent him copies of the invoices in case he mislaid them. I regret that he never responds."

Hasket glanced at the invoices but didn't read them.

"Why come to me? Captain Derby is an independent householder responsible for his own debts. I am not his financial sponsor."

Mr. Thomas gestured to the invoices again. "Please advise us where we should apply. Captain Derby refuses to receive us. The accounts are in arrears."

"As I said before, my son is an independent householder. He enters into his own contracts."

Mr. Thomas cleared his throat. "We thought that since he is part of your business concerns, you might see your way to clear these debts to . . . ah, improve your investment opportunities? Did you not do so before Captain Derby wed last year?"

"Mr. Thomas, you overstep. Your business is with my son and not with me." Hasket gestured to the invoices at the edge of his desk. "Please see yourself out, and take your documents with you."

The tradesman gathered his invoices and tucked them back in his jacket. "You leave us no choice but to sue in court."

Hasket ignored the threat and turned his attention to an account ledger.

# Lucy Brown Derby

*Captain Elias Derby's House*

Lucy watched her husband throw his unopened letters into the fire, his lips set in a hard line as the edges of the paper curled in the flames. *If only he could burn his debts as easily as he destroys their evidence.*

"They won't disappear, Elias," Lucy said. "Your creditors will send more invoices. If you don't respond, they will drag you through the courts."

Elias loosened his cravat and ran a hand through his hair.

"What would you have me do, Lucy? I'm at my wit's end. Everyone I've ever done business with demands payment."

"Then we'll sell this house," Lucy said with a note of desperation. "Surely, that will bring enough funds to pay your debts."

Elias smiled bitterly. "Unfortunately, that's not an option. My father gave us the house to live in but retained ownership. I asked him to help me, but he refused. Said he'd already done enough. How I wish I'd been born a simple farmer."

Lucy placed her hand on her husband's arm. "Come sit. I'll bring in tea, and we can discuss this calmly."

Lucy watched realization dawn on her husband's face. "You've been dismissing staff. I wondered but didn't realize. Why did you dismiss the maids?"

Lucy shrugged. "You didn't give me enough funds to run this big house. Even if we can't sell the house, we can move somewhere less costly."

"You miss the point. If we move, we'll have to pay our own expenses, and I don't have the money."

Lucy shook her head. "I don't miss any point, especially the point that you promised Reverend Clarke and myself that your gambling days were behind you. I'm sure you meant it at the time, but you didn't follow through. It's no secret you attend games at the Salem Inn. We have to sort things out, even if you must beg your father for assistance."

"Dear Lucy, I'm afraid we're at an impasse." Elias stared at a picture of cows in a meadow for several minutes before suddenly jumping up. "I shall inflict my own punishment by shutting myself up in my study. I shall not be at home to anyone. My meals can be delivered through the window at the back. If I need anything, I'll pass a note through the window. Beyond that, I shall speak to no one, including you."

"But . . . what can you hope to accomplish?"

"Oblivion, sweet wife. I shall break myself of my addiction through lack of company. And when people no longer see me, they may write off my debt as one made by a madman."

"Elias, you can't be serious. This isn't the way."

"Actually, it's the only way. Give me a farewell kiss, and then send necessities to my new abode. Never doubt my love for you. I shall make this right."

"You aren't making any sense."

Elias held Lucy's face and kissed her deeply before releasing her. "I hope to see you sooner rather than later."

For the next two weeks, Elias kept his word, with no signs of faltering. Meals and chamber pots were passed through the window. Lucy told callers her husband was not at home. Letters addressed to Captain Derby overflowed from two filigreed baskets by the front door, until the day Lucy carefully balanced a new note at the top of the letters in the second basket. The note slipped, taking the stack of paper at the top of the basket with it to the floor. Lucy looked at the papers on the floor, burst into tears, and went upstairs to change into an afternoon dress. She was going to pay a call.

# Lucy Brown Derby

*Hasket Derby's House*

"Mrs. Derby," the maid announced.

Eliza and Betsey rose from their seats by the tea table. Lucy walked forward to greet them. The women curtseyed to each other.

"Please be seated." Eliza gestured to a side chair. "Clara just left with the teapot. She'll bring in a fresh pot and another cup. How good of you to call."

Lucy looked at her mother-in-law and her husband's sister while she removed her gloves.

"I meant to call sooner, but Captain Derby has been . . . indisposed."

"Locked himself away, more like," Betsey observed. "Can he really expect to escape his obligations by making his family a laughingstock?"

Clara came in with the tea dishes. "Shall I pour, madam?"

"Please," Eliza said. "I've forgotten how you take your tea, Lucy."

"Two spoons of sugar. No milk."

Lucy accepted the cup and poured tea into the saucer to cool.

"How is your new house coming along, Mother Derby?" Lucy asked.

"With alacrity." Eliza smiled broadly.

"Is that why Father Derby has been unable to assist Captain Derby?"

"No," Betsey interjected. "Before you married, Father came to us and asked us to forego some of the profits from our husbands' investments in order for my brother to cover his debts and marry you. We agreed that if Elias fell into such a situation again, we would not assist him. It is hardly Father's responsibility to pay Elias's expenses, or yours." Betsey gave Lucy a pointed look.

Lucy's face flamed. "I assure you the expenditures are not mine. I have, in fact, instituted several household economies. Mother Derby, I've come to beg for your help. Elias has been shut up in his study for two weeks. This morning, the pile of letters addressed to him grew so high it tipped onto the floor. I can only imagine he must have a similar amount of correspondence at the counting house. I'm sure his creditors will sue him in the courts. Think how embarrassing that will be for the family."

"He brought it on himself," Betsey observed. "I'm not inclined to offer him assistance."

"Elias is the heir," Lucy blurted. "He cannot be left in this state."

Eliza tapped her chin. "I have an idea. The only time Elias has been successful is when we sent him to Isle de France ten years ago. Since his return, he has worked with his father, but also on his own account. That's where the problem seems to be. And the gambling, of course. And the overindulgence. Tell me, Lucy, are you capable of keeping him at home in the evenings?"

"I can only try."

"His brothers can also be of assistance. And perhaps a role in the militia."

Lucy listened as her mother-in-law laid out her plan to cover Elias's debts and prevent him from accruing more, at least in the short term.

# Hasket Derby

*Captain Elias Derby's House*

"Are you well, Hasket?" Eliza asked as he assisted her out of their gig and passed the reins to a stable boy.

"I'm well enough for the task, Eliza. But listen well. This is the last time I bail Elias out of his difficulties, and I do so now as a favor to you and his innocent wife."

Hasket rapped his brass-topped cane on the door.

Lucy opened it with a tentative smile. "Come in, come in. All is in readiness."

Lucy assisted her guests out of their wraps and laid them on a bench near the door.

"Where is your footman?" Eliza asked.

"I had to let him go. I mentioned making household economies. It's just a housemaid, kitchen maid, and cook now. But we get on well enough."

Eliza patted Lucy's cheek. "I'm sorry, my dear. I didn't realize finances were so tight."

"Please take a seat on the sofa. Shall I serve the tea, or wait until Elias joins us?"

"I'll pour," Eliza said. "Hasket, you can invite our son to join us."

"It's best to reach him by knocking on the back window outside," Lucy murmured.

"I'm not creeping around your house like a derelict. Elias will walk through his study door and into this room like a normal person. Lucy, if you would be so kind as to direct me."

"It's down the hall, the door opposite the kitchen parlor. I can take—"

Hasket held up his hand. "You ladies enjoy your tea. Elias and I will join you shortly."

Walking down the hall, Hasket noticed that the runner rug stopped just past the drawing room. *Why is Elias so determined to drag his wife into ruin? No wonder she has yet to give him any children.*

Hasket knocked on his son's study door. "Elias, it's your father. I want to speak with you."

Silence.

"Elias?"

"Go round to the window," a reedy voice replied.

"I'm not going to stand outside like a common workman. Open this door."

"Father, go to the window. You'll be glad of the fresh air. This room is rank."

"If it is, it's because you choose to live in filth. Open the door."

"It's not locked. If you're determined to see me, come in."

"Your mother is waiting with your wife in the drawing room. We need to discuss how you can free yourself from your delusions—or at least pay your debts."

"I assure you, Father, my debts are no laughing matter."

"I am aware. But hiding in this room won't solve your problems. You have to come out."

Silence.

Hasket felt his chest squeeze. *I need to sit down.*

"Elias, I'm going back to the drawing room. I expect you to join us within the next five minutes. I'm pulling out my watch. Your five minutes start now."

Feeling slightly dizzy, Hasket returned to the drawing room and accepted a cup of tea from his wife.

"Where is he?" Eliza asked.

"I told him he has five minutes to meet us here." Hasket looked at his watch. The second hand ticked off the time.

"You don't have to check your watch, Father. I'm here."

Lucy jumped out of her chair and flung her arms around her husband.

"Elias, I've been so worried about you." She stroked her husband's cheek. "You're so pale."

"That's what happens when you shut yourself inside," Eliza said acerbically. "Sit down and drink some tea. Your father and I have a proposition for you. It may be your last chance."

# Captain Elias Derby

Lucy pulled Elias into a chair by her side. Her small hands patted his shoulders and arms. She kissed his fingers.

"Leave off," Elias said, more harshly than he intended, and hung his head in his hands.

"Did you come to gloat, Father? To see me at my worst?"

Hasket rubbed his chest. "I take no pleasure in viewing your present state. When did you last wash?"

"That's none of your affair."

"What your father means," Lucy interjected, "is that you don't look like yourself. After we have tea, you can bathe and put on fresh clothing. You'll feel much better then."

"Tell me," Elias said, "do I still have a manservant?"

Lucy took a breath. "No. But I can assist you."

Elias grunted. "Humph."

"Have you finished your tantrum, Elias?" Eliza asked. "A man of your age hiding in his study. It's a disgrace. But out of the goodness of our hearts, your father and I have devised a way for you to clear your debts and have useful employment. Would you care to hear our thoughts?"

"It appears I have no choice."

"That's the point, Son," Hasket said. "You always have a choice. For the sake of your wife and our family, I hope this time you choose wisely. Are you interested in what I have to say?"

Elias gave his father a long look. The man was not without guile, but he seemed sincere. Lucy looked at him with pleading eyes. Eliza sniffed and busied herself with pouring more tea, though it was probably lukewarm by now.

Elias rubbed the back of his neck.

"Very well. Let's hear what you have to say."

"I don't know how closely you've been following events overseas. The British and the French are at loggerheads again. Between them, they have closed off ports in the Mediterranean. French privateers hunt freely in the waters just past Gibraltar. Demand is high for sugar and coffee with commensurate profit."

Elias shook his head. He had no desire to put himself in harm's way. He'd done that enough at Isle de France.

Hasket raised his hand. "Hear me out, at least."

Elias twisted his lips. "Very well. Continue."

"As you know, I've laid down a keel for a new ship. The *Mount Vernon* will be four hundred tons with twenty guns and a crew of fifty. She'll be more than ready to outrun privateers or defeat them as needed. When she is ready to sail, I'm going to fill her cargo hold with sugar and send her into the Mediterranean. I want you to oversee her construction, and I want you to sail her. She will surpass even the *Grand Turk*, and I want you on her decks."

Elias's jaw dropped open. "Father, I haven't been at sea in years. I'm not qualified to sail her under such conditions."

"Which is why you will have a sailing master to take care of the details, as well as a supercargo to handle the business side of things. But you will be her master."

Elias shook his head. "Once, I might have been pleased to command such a ship, but not now. I'm not a sailor, and I'm not good at taking risks."

"You are my son," Hasket replied. "When the ship is ready for her sea trials, you will take her out. And when she's ready to sail, you will be in command. I'll have it no other way. Consider your portion as ship's captain and the size of adventure cargo you can take. This one voyage can set you up for the rest of your life."

Elias looked at his wife's huge eyes and picked up her hand. "I would do it for you, Lucy. But Father, in all likelihood, when the *Mount Vernon* sails, I'll be in debtors' prison."

"Elias Hasket Derby, you will not speak that way." Eliza's commanding voice cut through the room. "You are our oldest son. Our heir. You will *not* disgrace yourself in such a way. And from the moment you take responsibility for the *Mount Vernon*, you will be paid an amount that will allow you to clear your debts and bring your household back in order. For goodness sake, you've put your wife in the position of having to brew her own tea. It is insupportable that any son of mine could be so selfish. You will do as your father asks, pay your debts, command our ship, and take your proper position in our community. I am still your mother, and I demand that you accept these terms now."

Eliza's face was so red, Elias thought she might faint.

Hasket patted his wife's hand. "Calm down, my dear. There's no point giving yourself apoplexy. Here, have a fresh cup of tea." Hasket pushed a cold cup into his wife's hand. "Drink."

Eliza took several deep breaths, and her color returned to normal.

Elias looked at his parents and his wife. *I disappoint them all, and yet . . .* Despair gave way to a glimmer of hope.

"Please, Elias," Lucy said.

The room fell into a silence punctuated by the ticking mantel clock. Elias kissed his wife's fingers.

"Lucy, do you believe I can sail Father's ship and restore our fortunes?"

"With all my heart."

Eliza started to say something, then closed her mouth when Hasket touched her shoulder.

Elias rubbed his chin. *Looking after the ship will keep me busy, and if I come directly home, perhaps I won't be tempted to engage in risky activities. Let this be my final gamble.*

Elias stood and stretched out his hand to his father. "I accept your offer."

Hasket took his son's hand. "I shall advance your wages to cover your debts. I expect you at the counting house at the opening of business tomorrow."

Hasket didn't say this opportunity would be his last, but Elias knew it was.

"I won't let you down."

Hasket nodded. "We'll take our leave now. Come, Eliza."

Hasket went outside, calling for the stable boy.

Eliza and Lucy curtsied to each other as if forging an alliance.

Elias stood in the drawing room, his future stretching before him. He couldn't determine if the path led to success or failure, only that he had to take it.

# SNEAK PREVIEW: SALEM STORIES, BOOK 3

## Captain Nathaniel Silsbee

*April 1798*
*Aboard the* Portland, *Alboran Sea*

"We've passed Gibraltar but we're not home free yet. Keep our ship steady in the middle," Nath ordered his helmsman. "We'll add more sail and push into the Mediterranean."

"Aye," Ezra answered. "And we'll keep her clear from the coasts."

"Good man." Nath cupped his hands around his mouth. "Hoist the sails!"

"Hoist the sails!" The echo bounced to crewmen on the rigging. Quickly the sails unfurled and filled with the easterly wind coming off the Atlantic. The *Portland* began picking up speed.

"Sail ho!" a sailor shouted from the crow's nest.

"Add more sail!" Nath ordered before raising his spyglass. He swept the open sea before him but didn't see any sails.

"William, what can you see?" he called to his brother on deck.

"Nothing yet."

"Port side!" the lookout shouted down.

*Damme and blast!* "Crew to battle stations!" Nath ordered and jumped down onto the deck.

William kept his spyglass in position and pointed with his left hand.

"Looks like she's coming out from Málaga, moving fast."

Nath lined up his spyglass, sweeping it over the intruder's deck. *Too many men on deck for an honest ship, and they're holding grappling hooks.*

"More sail!" Nath ordered.

Even with all his canvas unfurled, Nath felt exposed. The interloper continued her swift approach.

"We can't outsail her!" William shouted.

The attacking brig gained more distance and turned to expose her gunports.

"Nath, she'll sink us with one volley. We have to yield."

Nath clenched his jaw. Distance between the ships continued to close.

"*Bonjour! Frappez vos couleurs. Préparer l'embarquement.*"

"He said—" William began.

Nath snapped his spyglass closed. "I know what he bloody said. Give the order to strike our colors and order the crew to stand down. I'll be in my cabin."

Nath opened the *Portland*'s logbook, noted the date, time, and ship's position, and recorded *Portland*'s capture.

*As I write, French corsairs board the* Portland*. They have no grounds to sequester our ship. They will discover nothing on our ship of British origin. Nevertheless, we are on our way to the prize court.*

Nath closed out the entry as the invaders attached grappling hooks to his ship. The *Portland* shuddered as men crossed onto her decks. He heard William order the crew to take positions on the main deck. Nath closed the logbook, put on his coat and tricorn hat, and went on deck to meet his adversary.

A man wearing an elaborate uniform with gilded epaulets soon stood before Nath.

"*Je suis Capitaine Moreau*, and your ship is now ours. Pleased to see your cargo and crew manifests."

"Captain Nathaniel Silsbee," Nath responded. "I place the strongest possible objection to your intrusion, which is entirely illegal. We have nothing on board of British origin."

Moreau glanced at the papers Nath handed him and put them in his pocket.

"Your response is noted. Please to join the others on deck. We'll sail the ship."

The prize crew raised a French flag over the *Portland* and sailed toward the Spanish coast. Nath joined his men, who lounged near the starboard rail under a watchman's indolent gaze.

"They don't seem concerned about us," William whispered.

Nath shrugged and swallowed his anger. *Better to save it for the prize court.*

"No reason they should be," Nath calmly replied to his brother. "We're outnumbered, outgunned, and can't subdue them quickly enough to escape. Especially since the corsairs are escorting us. Now you understand the precautions we took to remove British products."

Nath gestured to French sailors going belowdecks. "No matter how hard they look, they won't find anything to support sequestering us. And our crew will never admit being aboard before we loaded our cargo. We'll be on our way soon enough. It's the loss of time I object to."

A shout went up from the French crew when a school of dolphins passed by the ship, their graceful leaping arcs drawing everyone's eyes until the *Portland* turned into the natural harbor at Málaga.

Dozens of American and other neutral ships flying French flags bobbed offshore. A castle loomed behind the shoreline, its walls matching the dry, sandy soil around it. Nath felt his stomach plummet. *Are all these ships awaiting a hearing?*

Men turned the capstan, releasing *Portland*'s anchor chains. When the longboat from shore arrived, the bosun dropped a rope ladder down for Captain Moreau. Nath grabbed his hat and rushed to join his captor.

Moreau turned in surprise. "*Non.* Remain here."

"I demand to see the American consul."

"*Non.*" Moreau flicked his fingers, shooing Nath back toward the deck. Three members from the prize crew took positions around Nath.

"Wait," Nath said. "Let me write a note. You can read it."

"*Non.*" Captain Moreau swung his foot onto the ladder. "*Au revoir.*"

At twilight, the French cook brought stew for the Americans. Nath thought about throwing it over the side.

"You should eat," William said, scraping out his bowl. "It's tasty."

"It's French."

"That too. We don't know when we'll have our next meal, so you should take advantage of this one. You'll need to be sharp tomorrow."

Nath nodded, the stew sticking in his throat.

Darkness descended over the harbor. A few lights twinkled from town. Glimpses of cooking fires from the surrounding ships were visible. Ropes and anchors creaked and moaned. Small waves lapped against the ship.

"Nath," William whispered. "What do you think will happen tomorrow?"

"Nothing. Moreau will file his report and we'll sit here, wasting time."

The next day, no one came to the ship. Nath paced the deck in a clockwise direction before reversing to pace the opposite direction. The crew played cards or slept.

On the third day, a longboat came out to the *Portland*. The French first mate dropped the rope ladder over the side and motioned for Nath to get off the ship.

"You're in command," Nath muttered to William. "If you find a way to escape, take it. I'll catch up to you when I can."

"Aye. Keep your temper, Nath."

"Humph."

When Nath reached the last link on the ladder, burly arms pulled him into the boat and slammed him onto a seat. Four soldiers kept him anchored while sailors rowed the longboat ashore. After they beached the boat, the soldiers marched Nath to the French consul's office. The room had plain whitewashed walls. Bright sun poured through large windows. A clerk sat to the side, away from the sun. He gestured toward a bench. *"S'asseoir."* Nath remained standing.

At nine o'clock, the outer door opened and a well-dressed French official entered, followed by several men. Nath recognized Captain Moreau.

"Consul Dannery," the clerk announced.

"Sit, Capitaine Sizbee. There is no reason to stand. You know Capitaine Moreau."

Nath nodded.

"This is Monsieur Bachelot, owner of the *Hercule.* I have your papers. According to government decree, any ship with cargo from Britain or her possessions is considered a good prize. You understand? We will keep your ship."

Nath took a slow breath. "We have not violated the decree."

Dannery handed the *Portland*'s cargo manifest to his clerk.

"Etienne will read out each item on the list. In five words, explain where the articles were produced, who brought them to the États-Unis, and how they came into your ship's possession."

Nath bristled but held his temper. "Monsieur Dannery, there is no reason to prolong this investigation. May I suggest you ask about items that cause concern. You will see that everything is correct and release the *Portland*. But I must judge the length of my explanation, not you."

"Monsieur, you are not here to make demands."

"You are correct, but neither can I be denied the opportunity to fulfill my duty to the owners of the property I supervise."

Consul Dannery drew his lips into a thin line, leaned toward Nath, and said, "I suggest you remember your place. I have no reason to regard anything you have to say."

Nath's temper began simmering to the surface. "The innocence of my ship and her cargo is evident. We have no British goods of any kind, a fact that is so clear you could decide it in less than an hour."

"I am the one to decide when your case is decided. I advise you to remember that. And also that I am losing patience with your claims."

"I am aware of your power. But I shall not leave your office until the matter is decided."

"Gentlemen," Captain Moreau interrupted, "perhaps we can return to the matter at hand. I observed several navigational instruments with no marks to indicate their origin. I suggest they are British."

"But you have no proof," Nath growled.

"No instrument is made without a mark," Moreau retorted.

With nightfall, the office grew darker, but the interrogation continued, until Consul Dannery pulled out his pocket watch.

"Enough. It is the middle of the night, and I want my dinner. Guards, escort Capitaine Sizbee back to his ship."

"I told you before, I will not leave this office until the *Portland* is restored to me. I have violated no laws of France, and I demand my hearing."

Consul Dannery sighed. "You try my patience. Very well. Stay here tonight. It's not as if you can escape. Come, gentlemen, we will return tomorrow."

"Why waste time?" Captain Moreau asked. "It is standard practice to condemn neutral shipping. Every one of them carries contraband."

"*Non.* We are leaving. *Bonne nuit*, Capitaine Sizbee."

The clerk picked up the papers on his desk and followed the mariners out of the office. The guards yawned and gave Nath one-fingered salutes, stretching their arms as they left. Porters came in and began cleaning. A watchman sat in the consul's chair and gestured for Nath to take the bench on the opposite wall.

Mentally going over the day's events, Nath doubted he could persuade the consul to release the *Portland*. He could appeal the decision to the civil court at Aix-en-Provence on lack of definite evidence. But an appeal would take months, possibly years. Unsettled, Nath lay down on the narrow bench with his arms under his head and listened to the watchman snore.

Eventually, the long night ended. Nath swung his feet to the floor, wincing when his back complained about the bench's narrow, hard surface.

"I might have done better to sleep on the floor," he mused.

Nath's stomach grumbled. He walked over to the desk and shook the watchman. "*Bonjour.* Time to wake up."

A guard entered and waved the watchman away. Nath walked around to get some feeling back in his legs.

The clerk walked into the room with his sheaf of papers. When he saw Nath, he raised his eyebrows but said nothing.

"*Quelle heure?*" Nath asked.

"*Neuf.*"

*Nine o'clock, then. The consul should arrive soon.*

A few minutes later, Consul Dannery, impeccably dressed and groomed, entered.

"Capitaine Sizbee, you are still here."

"I told you I won't leave until my case is decided."

Dannery took a seat behind his desk and steepled his hands. "Very well. Write an order to your crew. I will send men to examine your ship. They will look at everything on board and record their origin. Then we shall know the truth."

Nath rubbed his chin. "I can write such an order, assuming your men will make an honest account."

Dannery bristled. "I give you my word."

Nath gestured to the clerk for writing material and gave the written order to Dannery, who passed it to the guard.

"*Bon*. It is done. There is no reason for you to remain in my office. I have other business to conduct."

Nath sat back down on the bench, folded his arms over his chest, and leaned his head against the wall. Petitioners came and went. The consul left for lunch, coming back in the late afternoon.

"*Bon après*," Nath said.

Dannery slapped papers on his desk. "I have the report on your ship. You have not been forthcoming with the truth. Every article on the *Portland* is a product of British colonies. Your ship is condemned without any appeal. What have you to say to that?"

Nath shrugged and spread his hands. "The outcome is as we both expected. How could it be otherwise? I sincerely hope that a man such as yourself serving in such a high office will not allow himself to be influenced by a report filled with falsehood. What British colony, for example, produces the spice called mace? Please tell me."

Dannery blanched. "I assure you I am a man of honor. I will get to the bottom of this affair."

The consul sent his clerk out with a note. Nath sat down on the bench again. Outside, a few stars twinkled in the twilight.

To Nath's mild surprise, Captain Moreau entered the office with Monsieur Bachelot, the privateer's owner. Dannery called for brandy. The men talked and smoked while Nath watched. The conversation became heated at times with what sounded like protests, until Dannery slapped his hand on the desk.

Nath straightened in anticipation. Dannery wrote out a document and handed it to Captain Moreau, who signed it and passed it to Monsieur

Bachelot, who also signed. Dannery signed at the bottom of the page and gestured to his clerk, who handed him a sheaf of papers.

"Capitaine Sizbee, please take all your papers. Here are your cargo inventories. Here is permission to take your ship and go to the devil with her, or anywhere else you please. And here is an order for the prize crew to depart from your ship."

A sense of relief flooded Nath's body. *I can hardly believe it.*

"*Merci beaucoup*, Consul Dannery. You restore my faith in justice." *And the arbitrary seizures of neutral shipping.*

Three days later, with a favorable wind and in company with a Danish convoy, Nath watched Málaga recede like a nightmare dissolving in the light of day.

*Aboard the* Portland
*Near Genoa*

Nath squinted through his spyglass. Following a storm, the *Portland* peeled off from the Danish convoy and set a course for Genoa. Nath was sailing under cover of darkness to avoid capture, but he had still encountered several small privateers. Evading them, Nath now heaved a sigh of relief when, like a mother's embrace, the two peninsulas jutting out from Genoa's harbor beckoned his ship into a secure oasis. The *Portland* scooted by the fortified *molos* on either side to enter the protected waters and tie up on the wharf.

"I don't mind admitting I'm almost as relieved by our safe arrival as you are," William said.

Nath laughed ruefully. "Only *almost* relieved?"

"Well, while you held our fate in your hands at Málaga, I was safe on our ship with a French cook and only had to keep the men's spirits up."

Nath shook his head. "I doubt you were as relaxed as you sound, but thanks for giving me the credit. I had my share of embargoes at Isle de France, but this business at Málaga was something I never expected to experience. I don't mind admitting to you I had no confidence we would succeed. There was no logic to the charges, no honest investigation."

"There was from the consul's perspective, I suppose."

"More like theft. I don't know why Dannery changed his mind, but I'm glad he did. Anyway, in the interest of protecting our investors, I've decided not to go on to India. We'll deliver the cargo we consigned in Cádiz here, sell supplies we don't need, and take on a cargo of wheat for Barcelona. I'll arrange to pick up a cargo of brandy at Reus, and then we're off toward home."

"I like the sound of that." William grinned. "We'll have a tidy profit, and as you often say, we're merchants, not fighters."

Over the next several days, Nath and William visited various business agents to arrange cargoes, while an increasing number of French transport ships entered the harbor. French troops arrived and established a headquarters office for the general staff. Soon after, the military general announced an embargo on any ships leaving the harbor.

"Something is definitely afoot," Nath mused. "Come with me, William. It's time to collect rumors."

Nath and William walked along the wharf, looking for taverns catering to dockworkers.

"That one, I think." Nath gestured to a run-down building nestled in the shadow of a large warehouse. Inside, most of the light came through the doorway. Nath and William settled by the bar and watched patrons pass by. Dockworkers drank quietly with morose expressions. Nath scanned the room for a likely source of information.

"*Signori?*" the barman asked.

"Grappa."

Nath placed a coin on the bar. The barman scooped up the coin and returned with two beakers of clear liquid.

William swallowed, coughed, and hit his hand on the bar. "I wasn't expecting it to be so strong," he said, gasping.

Nath shrugged and took a small sip from his glass. "Let's make friends," he said and led the way to a table where two grizzled dockworkers drank in silence.

"Captain Nathaniel Silsbee. I'm with the American merchant ship *Portland*. May we sit?"

"*Certo. Io sono Antonio.*" Antonio held out his hand.

"*Inglese?*"

"*Sufficientemente.*"

"*Bene.* What's going on in the harbor?"

Antonio's eyebrows shot up. "You don't know? The French army is here. They need ships. Supplies."

Nath cringed. *The* Portland *is the best-looking ship in the harbor. They'll come after us. It will be worse than Málaga.*

"The ships." Nath gulped. "They are buying them?"

"No." Antonio waggled his fingers. "They take them, and the crew. Sail to somewhere." Antonio shrugged.

*The rumors must be true. Napoleon is going to invade Egypt. If I don't have something to bargain with, I'll lose my ship.*

"William, do we have salted meat we don't need?"

Nath's brother looked up in surprise. "About forty barrels. Why?"

Nath turned his attention back to Antonio. "I have work for you if you can keep a secret."

"From the *Francese*? *Certo.*"

"Come to the *Portland* at midnight. I need to hide cargo outside the city."

Nath palmed a purse from his pocket and passed it to Antonio. "More when the job is complete," Nath said.

Antonio weighed the purse in his hand and smiled. "I will be there with my men. *Sii pronto.*"

Nath made a show about carrying out his business. He obtained the cargo of wheat he needed for Barcelona. During the day, dockworkers loaded bags of wheat, but under cover of darkness, Antonio and his men took off the salted meat. Nath watched troops continue to requisition ships until the day a lieutenant with a small escort boarded the *Portland*.

Nath took a breath and mentally prepared to defend his ship.

The lieutenant's uniform was less than immaculate. His epaulets had a greenish tinge, and his boots were scuffed.

*"Bonjour, je suis le Lieutenant Gaspar."*

*"Oui,"* Nath replied. "I am Captain Silsbee. What is your business here?"

Instead of answering, Lieutenant Gaspar handed Nath a document and ordered his men to leave the ship.

"What's that?" William asked.

"If I'm not mistaken, the French army just requisitioned our ship. I'm going to the general's office to decline. Dress in your good suit and come with me."

The French army headquarters was near the palace inside the walled city. Nath and William entered a large, mostly empty reception area with several desks and cane-back chairs. Nath walked to the clerk's desk and handed the subaltern the requisition document.

*"Capitaine Silsbee pour monsieur le général. Anglais?"*

The subaltern looked at the document and smiled. "We take your ship. *Oui.* A great honor for you. *Portland* for staff officers."

"It is no honor for us. It is theft."

"Monsieur, you insult us."

William put his hand on Nath's arm.

*"Le général?"* William asked.

*"Attendez."* The subaltern knocked on the door behind him and entered the next room. A few minutes later, he returned and nodded to Nath. *"Entrer."*

Nath entered the general's austere office. One large desk with a comfortable chair. Two straight-back chairs. A standard with a regimental flag leaning against a wall. The general was a man of medium height. He was wearing a white wig and riding boots, but Nath didn't think he spent much time on a horse.

"*Bonjour, Monsieur Général. Anglais?*"

"*Oui. Je suis le général Cartier. Quel est le problème?*"

Nath held out his hand. "I am Captain Silsbee of the American ship *Portland*. Your men confiscated my ship, and I demand her immediate return."

Cartier shrugged. "Our army needs your ship and crew. *Merci* for your cooperation."

*Not so fast.* Nath held up his hand. "I'm told Genoa can't provide enough provisions for your army. I can sell you salted meat."

The general smiled. "*Bon.* How much salted meat do you have, and at what price? You know I have the power to take it at whatever price I choose, so don't make it too high." Cartier chuckled without mirth.

*Here's my moment.* "I have forty barrels of fine American salted meat, both beef and pork. I'm happy to sell it to you at whatever price you set—or no price at all. Simply release my ship. Otherwise you shall not have the meat."

The general narrowed his eyes. "Who are you to dictate to me? I can take your ship and your provisions and throw you in jail for your insubordination to a French general."

Nath smirked. "The provisions aren't on my ship. You need them, and I'm the only one who knows their location. I'll let you consider my proposal."

Nath turned his back and left the office.

"What happened?" William asked.

"Back to the ship," Nath growled softly. "If my gamble works, we'll keep the *Portland*."

Images of every nautical disaster he'd ever experienced flashed in Nath's mind. He'd come so far from his penniless days in Hasket Derby's counting house. But even with insurance, he could lose everything he'd gained with a stroke of a French general's pen.

"Don't second-guess yourself," William said. "The general needs what we have—he just doesn't know it yet."

Two days later, General Cartier summoned Nath to his office.

The office looked exactly the same, except there were four soldiers at the back of the room. The subaltern sat at a small table ready to take notes. Nath felt the tension in the room and barely restrained himself from loosening his cravat. General Cartier gave him a cold stare.

Nath kept his voice steady. "*Bonjour.* You summoned me?"

"Monsieur Sizbee, you were not honest. My men wasted valuable time looking for the forty barrels of salted meat you said you stored. I do not believe you ever possessed it. You insult me, yet I honor you by taking your ship for the army staff. If you have the meat, tell me where it is."

Nath spread his hands and shrugged. "I assure you I have the meat, but it is hidden where you will never find it. To be honest, I recognize the honor you give me, and if the *Portland* was mine alone and the cargo likewise, I would be gratified by the honor of commanding a ship taking the staff of such an army on such an expedition.

"But neither the *Portland* nor her cargo is entirely mine. I am obligated to others and must discharge my duty to them before assuming any new duties. As a man of honor, I'm sure you understand my situation. If I cannot exchange the salted meat for my ship, I shall abandon her to the city of Genoa, and every man on my ship will quit."

By the time Nath stopped speaking, the general's face was an alarming puce color. Cartier stood and pointed at Nath. "In the name of the French Republic, I can order you to perform any and every duty I assign you," he said coldly. "You, your officers, your crew, and your ship are all requisitioned. No person can thwart the Republic."

The subaltern leaped up. "*Oui, mon général.* Suppose God had one ship here and the Republic wanted it; he must give it."

Nath's mouth dropped open. The subaltern, as if embarrassed by his own outburst, sat down and arranged his papers.

Nath gritted his teeth. "I assure you, Monsieur General, that the only way you will gain those provisions is if you release my ship."

Nath executed a sharp turn and left the office. Once outside army headquarters, he walked with a firm step to the wharf.

Boarding the *Portland*, Nath retreated to his cabin, removed his jacket, and stretched out on his bunk. He listened to water splashing against the side of his ship and stared at the ceiling. Would Cartier carry out his threat? Everything rested on how badly the French army needed his salted meat.

After a restless night, Nath completed his log entry from the day before. How long would he have to wait?

William knocked. "This just came for you. It's not from General Cartier."

Nath looked at the embossed seal. "No, it's from Signor Rossi, the merchant who arranged our wheat cargo. He asks me to call at my earliest convenience." Nath felt a sense of relief and raised his eyebrows. "I think the general wants the salted meat after all."

"But Rossi doesn't have it."

"No, but the general won't offer me a deal with his men looking on. He'll be at Signor Rossi's. I'd put money on it."

It took half an hour to walk to Rossi's mansion near the center of town. Nath rapped with the brass door knocker.

Moments later, a footman opened the door.

"Captain Silsbee for Signore Rossi."

"*Accedere.*"

The footman led Nath to a well-appointed drawing room. Signore Rossi rose to greet Nath.

Out of the corner of his eye, Nath spotted a familiar figure. *I was right; my deal was too good for the general to pass up.*

"Welcome to my home. I think you know General Cartier."

Nath nodded. "It's good to see you again."

"Shall we have coffee?" Signore Rossi gestured toward a low sofa.

The men agreed and all took a seat as the coffee was promptly served.

"Monsieur Sizbee," Cartier said coldly. "I have given your offer considerable thought. I would like to pay you the cost of the salted meat and return your ship in exchange for the salted meat you have sequestered."

Nath wanted to cheer but kept a straight face. "Of course, Monsieur General. Have you brought the documents to release my ship?"

"*Oui.* You may leave when the embargo is lifted next week, after the fleet sails. And now tell me the location of the provisions."

Nath reached a hand in his pocket to retrieve a small piece of paper.

The general raised an eyebrow. "You've been carrying the location with you?"

"No." Nath shrugged. "I hoped you'd had a change of heart and brought it for you today."

Cartier took the slip of paper. "*Merci.*" He stood and gave a slight bow. "Forgive my departure. I have matters that call for my attention."

Nath silently waited until he heard the front door close. "*Grazie,* Signore Rossi."

Rossi winked. "The general needs provisions. You need your ship. And the Genoese need the French to leave. In a good negotiation, everyone wins. Now, join me in another cup of coffee, and tell me more about your adventure in Málaga. To best the French twice is quite an accomplishment."

# AUTHOR'S NOTE

*Sea Tigers & Merchants: A New American Generation* is the second book in the Salem Stories series. It is a work of historical fiction inspired by the Derby and Crowninshield families of Salem, Massachusetts. The names of individuals in these families refer to real persons, and the story is based on primary research materials.

The term *sea tigers* does not refer to a specific organism. The term *tiger*, however, is often used to refer to a fierce, determined, or ambitious individual—attributes readily applied to Captains Nathaniel Silsbee, George Crowninshield Jr., Jacob Crowninshield, and John Crowninshield. They and others of their generation went to sea while still in their teens, risking natural and naval dangers to secure their fortunes. Quick wits, unabashed courage, and pure luck brought great success. The reverse was also true.

Elias Hasket Derby, sometimes referred to as "King Derby," was the first American millionaire. Though Hasket's father founded the family business, Hasket increased his fortune through privateering and extensive trading networks in the West Indies, Europe, and East Asia. Politically, the Derby family supported the Federalist Party.

Captain George Crowninshield founded George Crowninshield & Sons in 1790, though several of his sons continued to work for Hasket Derby until 1799. Throughout the 1790s, the Derby and Crowninshield families continued to be business and social rivals. Politically, the Crowninshields allied with what became known as the Democratic-Republican Party.

During the eighteenth century, families used similar names for their children and often named an infant after a child who had died. To clarify the characters, I used nicknames popular at the time. Thus, I refer to George Crowninshield Jr. as Geordie, Elizabeth Crowninshield Derby as Eliza, Eliza's daughter of the same name as Betsey, Martha Derby as Patsy, Sarah Crowninshield as Sally, and Mary Crowninshield as Molly. I also refer to Elias Hasket Derby Jr. as Elias. Elizabeth Rowell, known as Lizzie, became Geordie Crowninshield's secret domestic partner. Nathaniel Silsbee later married Molly Crowninshield.

In 1789, President George Washington embarked on a one-month tour of New England, both to acquaint himself with the region and make a visible statement about the existence of the new federal government. Washington's itinerary included Fairfield, New Haven, and Hartford, Connecticut; and Springfield, Worcester, Boston, and Newburyport, Massachusetts. The stopover in Salem occurred on the route from Boston to Newburyport.

During the 1790s, the first American political parties appeared. The Federalists, led by Secretary of the Treasury Alexander Hamilton, advocated a strong central government with an emphasis on manufacturing and fiscal security. In contrast, Secretary of State Thomas Jefferson advocated against a strong central government, with an emphasis on self-sufficient farmers. In this context, he favored the rights of the states above those of the central government. Advocates of this position became known as the Democratic-Republicans.

In 1796, George Washington declined to run for a third term as president. Vice President John Adams ran for president on the Federalist platform. Thomas Jefferson ran as leader of the Democratic-Republicans. After a bitter campaign, Adams was elected president.

At the time Adams became president, the ongoing War of the First Coalition pitted the new French Republic against the alliance of Britain, Russia, Prussia, Spain, Holland, and Austria. Though the United States followed an official policy of strict neutrality, mitigating factors led to an undeclared naval war between France and the United States. In 1794, the United States signed the Jay Treaty with Britain, which, among other things, led to the withdrawal of British army units from the Northwest Territories. Americans were also granted rights of trade in the British West Indies.

The French Republic viewed the Jay Treaty as a violation of the Treaty of Amity and Commerce negotiated in 1778. After diplomatic efforts failed in 1796, French privateers began attacking all merchant ships sailing in American waters, as well as American ships at sea.

Relations between the United States and Great Britain were strained by the British impressment of American sailors. The United States denounced the practice of impressment as an international right and further asserted the rights of neutral shipping on the high seas, stating that belligerents did not have the right to seize enemy goods, contraband, or personnel. Britain and other nations at war asserted that they had the right to stop and search neutral ships. The United States argued that while neutral ships might be boarded, no one had the right to seize neutral civilians.

The British countered that they had the right to remove British deserters from American or other neutral ships. The similarity of culture and language between Britain and America often led to wrongful impressment. In 1796, Congress passed legislation to investigate incidents of impressment and pursue the release of those unlawfully taken. This, however, was difficult to enforce.

The most important aspect of my research was the Derby and Crowninshield papers and letters in the collection of the Phillips Library of the Peabody

Essex Museum (PEM) in Rowley, Massachusetts. Jennifer Hornsby, reference and access services librarian, and her staff at the Phillips Library reading room extended me every courtesy during my visit.

William Bentley's diaries, from his arrival in Salem as minister of the East Church in 1783 until his death from apoplexy in 1819, were a key source regarding events in Salem during those years. Bentley supported the Crowninshields' political aspirations. The Essex Institute of Salem published Bentley's diaries in four volumes. These can be accessed online.

*Sea Tigers & Merchants: A New American Generation* is a work of historical fiction inspired by the Derby and Crowninshield families. It is not a work of biography or nonfiction.

# ABOUT THE AUTHOR

Sandra Wagner-Wright holds a doctoral degree in history and taught American and women's history at the University of Hawai`i for over twenty years. She lives in Hilo, Hawai`i. *Sea Tigers & Merchants* is Sandra's fifth work of historical fiction. Connect with Sandra on social media and at www. sandrawagnerwright.com. Subscribe to her newsletter for updates on blogs and future projects.

**CONNECT WITH SANDRA:**

Facebook: https://www.facebook.com/SandraWagner-Wright

Pinterest: https://www.pinterest.com/sandrawagnerwri

LinkedIn: https://www.linkedin.com/in/sandrawwright/

X (formerly Twitter): https://twitter.com/SandraWWright

# GLOSSARY

baccarat—Popular card game originating in Italy in the fourteenth century.

banians—Local trading partners for Euro-Americans in Calcutta who sold and acquired cargoes and raised funds as needed for short- or long-term loans. Banians also supplied linguistic skill and knowledge of the local market.

banyan—Loose dressing gown worn at home. Sleeves and body of the garment were cut as one piece.

bed ticking—A cloth bag the size of a modern mattress that enclosed bedding materials, such as feathers. The fabric was strong and tightly woven.

betel nut—Or areca nut, is the fruit of the areca palm. In small doses, betel nut produces a sense of euphoria and can function like an antidepressant. Prolonged use creates an addiction and can be carcinogenic. For chewing, betel nut is wrapped in the betel leaf with spices for flavoring. Consumers chew the betel nut and spit out the red residue.

black pepper [*Piper nigrum*]—A flowering vine cultivated for its peppercorn fruit. The peppercorn is a stone fruit, with the stone surrounding a single pepper seed, which is ground to produce the spice.

brig—Two-masted sailing vessel. Square rigged on both masts. Brigs have been used as cargo ships and as small warships with about ten guns. Length measures between thirteen and seventy-five feet, with tonnage up to 350 tons.

burgoo—Ground oatmeal boiled on ratio of three parts water to one part oatmeal. Can be boiled with salt beef fat made from what comes to the

top when boiling the beef or pork rations. Molasses and/or nutmeg may
be blended in.

capstan—Drum-shaped device used for hoisting weights or winding a ship's
anchor cable.

careening—A method of gaining access to a ship's hull without the use of
a dry dock by pulling the ship onto a beach in order to clean, caulk, or
repair it.

carmine rouge—Bright-red pigment derived from carminic acid extracted
from scale insects, e.g., cochineal scale.

duff—A steamed pudding made of flour, suet, and currants or raisins put
into a bag with a tied top.

flip—A popular warm tavern beverage. See Eighteenth-Century Recipes.

Governor Vigoureux—Jean-Baptiste Vigoureux du Plessis (1735–1825).
Governor of Isle de Bourbon (1792–1794).

*Grand Turk*—Three ships bore the name *Grand Turk*. Two were owned by E.
H. Derby and the third by a group of investors during the War of 1812.

- The first *Grand Turk* was built in 1781 as a privateer with twenty-eight
  six-pounder guns and a crew of 140 men. In 1784, Derby sent her to
  open up the China Trade at Canton. In 1787, the first *Grand Turk*
  sailed to Isle de France, where Captain Elias Hasket Jr. sold her.

- The second *Grand Turk* was built for Derby in 1791 by Enos Briggs.
  She was a larger ship with three decks. After three successful voyages, E. H. Derby determined the ship was too large and sold the
  vessel in 1795.

- The third *Grand Turk* was built by thirty investors in January 1812
  to serve as a privateer.

hair bun—Hair attachment made of wool in a color matching the natural
hair. Attached with pins at center back of hairstyle so the style could be
built around the bun.

Hessian boots—Military riding boots popular during Regency era (1811–1820). The boots featured polished leather with ornamental tassels. The boots have a low heel and semi pointed toe to allow easy access to stirrups. Decorative tassel at top of the boot shaft with a V notch at the front. Later evolved into Wellington boots and cowboy boots.

Hugli River—Also known as the Hooghly River, flows from Calcutta into the Bay of Bengal. The Bengal Pilot Service navigated ships up and down the Hugli River to avoid shifting sandbars between Calcutta and the Bay of Bengal.

Isle de Bourbon—Now known as Réunion, a French department in the Indian Ocean, southwest of Mauritius.

Isle de France—Located in the Indian Ocean. Now known as the Republic of Mauritius.

Jack Tar—Slang for British sailors who often kept their long hair in a queue smothered in tar to keep it stiff and out of their eyes. They also sometimes covered their clothes in tar as a type of waterproofing.

lambkin—A term used by Shakespeare in the Henry plays that can be applied to a small child or a lover. One who is cherished.

leading strings—Pieces of fabric attached to the shoulder of a small child's garment to support learning to walk.

mace—A spice made from the seed covering of the nutmeg seed. Mace and nutmeg are indigenous to the Moluccas Islands.

Madeira wine—The primary luxury drink of the eighteenth and early nineteenth centuries, Madeira was produced on the volcanic Portuguese island of Madeira. British consumers preferred the sweeter version of new wine. Americans drank a vintage fortified with brandy for a drier, more acidic taste.

Madras—A city in India on the Coromandel Coast in southeast India. Now known as Chennai.

oilskin—Waterproofed cloth garments in use from late eighteenth century. Made by coating sailcloth with a layer of tar, or coating canvas duck with applications of linseed oil and paint.

Pelu Penang—Now called Palau Pinang, a Malaysian Island in the Strait of Malacca. Acquired by British East India Company in 1786 and developed into a free port with the capital city of George Town.

pipe [of wine]—A barrel that will hold from 95 to 108 gallons of wine.

Press-gang—An organized group [gang] that forcibly conscripts [presses] men into naval service.

ratlines—Lines tied between the shrouds on a sailing ship to form a ladder. They are part of the rigging for square-rigged sailing ships because crews have to climb up to the sails in order to stow them.

"reef the sails"—An order to "reef the sails" means to tie down the sails, exposing the bare masts.

saltpeter—Or potassium nitrate, a key ingredient for black-powder gunpowder. Sulfur and carbon act as the fuels while saltpeter is the oxidizer. Alternative spelling: saltpetre.

schooner—A sailing vessel with two to seven masts that can sail closer to the wind than a square-rigged sailing vessel. Schooners were a favorite vessel in America and Canada in late eighteenth and early nineteenth centuries.

ship—A squared-rigged sailing vessel with three or more masts, as well as jibs, stay sails, and a spanker sail on the aftermast.

ship gallery—Also, a quarter gallery. A type of balcony in the stern of ships from the sixteenth to nineteenth centuries. Located behind the officers' quarters, it served primarily as a latrine for the ship's officers.

ship's stores—Supplies and equipment needed for the upkeep of a ship, including food and water. Ship's stores also included turpentine, tar, and pitch sourced either from American pine trees or the Baltic region, as well as cordage and sailcloth.

Siege of Nijmegen—October 27 to November 8, 1794. This was part of the Flanders Campaign during the War of the First Coalition. On November

8, Nijmegen fell to the French. From there, it was only 122 kilometers to Amsterdam.

skittles—A lawn game similar to nine-pin bowling.

sloop—A single-masted vessel with fore and aft rigged sails.

slop chest—Clothing and other supplies carried by merchant ships that could be issued to the crew as needed. Usually charged against their wages at the end of the voyage.

Stage Point—Located in Salem, Massachusetts, a relatively flat point of land between South River and Salem Harbor where fishing "stages" were built. The stages were wooden frames where fishermen could unload, clean, cure, and dry fish. Enos Briggs's shipyard was located here. Located off present Congress Street, encompassing Peabody and Ward Streets. About a half mile south of Essex Street.

# EIGHTEENTH-CENTURY RECIPES

From *The New Whole Art of Confectionary* by W. S. Steveley, 1828.

### Funeral Biscuits

Take twenty-four eggs, three pounds of flour, three pounds of lump sugar, grated, which will make forty-eight finger biscuits for a funeral.

### Bride Cake

Take four pounds of fine flour, well dried, four pounds of fresh butter, and two pounds of loaf sugar. Pound and sift fine a quarter of an ounce of mace, the same of nutmeg, and to every pound of flour, put eight eggs, well beat. Wash four pounds of currants, pick them well and dry them before the fire. Blanch a pound of sweet almonds, and cut them lengthways, very thin. Take a pound of citron, a pound of candied orange, the same of candied lemon, and half a pint of brandy. First work the butter to a cream with your hand, then beat in your sugar a quarter of an hour. Work up the whites of your eggs to a very strong froth.

Mix them with your sugar and butter. Beat your yolks half an hour at least and mix them with your other ingredients. Then put in your flour, mace, and nutmeg, and keep beating it well till the oven is ready.

Put in your brandy and beat lightly in your currants and almonds. Tie three sheets of paper round the bottom of your hoop to keep it from running out and rub it well with butter. Then put in your cake and place your sweet-meats in three layers with some cake between every layer.

As soon as it is risen and colored, cover it with paper and bake it in a moderate oven. Three hours will bake it.

## A Recipe for Flip

From *The Cook's Oracle* by William Kitchiner, 1836.

To make a quart of flip:

Put ale on the fire to warm and beat up three or four eggs with four ounces of moist sugar, a teaspoonful of grated nutmeg or ginger, and a quartern* of good old rum or brandy. When the ale is near to boil, put it into one pitcher and the rum and eggs into another. Turn it from one pitcher to another till it is [as] smooth as cream. [Plunge a hot iron into the mixture to warm it.]

* A quartern is one-fourth of a pint, or half a cup.
** The term *flip* refers to pouring the mixture back and forth into the pitchers.

# QUESTIONS AND TOPICS
## FOR DISCUSSION

1. What was your first impression of Lizzie Rowell? Did your opinion of her change over the course of the book? Does she make good decisions?

2. The Derby and Crowninshield families are closely related through marriage, yet they function as business and political rivals. What were their family dynamics?

3. What type of future does Captain George Crowninshield envision for his sons? Do the young men have the same goals?

4. How would you characterize Captain George Crowninshield as a parent?

5. What was the relationship between Captain George Crowninshield and his wife, Mary?

6. What type of businessman is Hasket Derby? How do his decisions compare with those made by Captain George Crowninshield?

7. What is your impression of the relationship between Captain Nathaniel West and his wife, Betsey?

8. What sort of person is Eliza Derby? What is her relationship with her children? Her husband?

9. How would you characterize Eliza Derby's ambitions? Are they the same as her husband's? Is Eliza an effective social leader?

10. In January 1791, Captain Elias Derby returns to Salem after spending three years at Ilse de France and India. How well does he adjust to being back in Salem? What is his relationship with his father?

11. In 1791, Captain Nathaniel Silsbee sails for Hasket Derby aboard the *Betsey*. He is eighteen years old. How well does he cope with his first command? Does he make good decisions?

12. Why does Hasket Derby build the *Grand Turk*? Why is this ship important to him? Does his son Elias share Hasket's attachment to the ship?

13. How does Captain Nathaniel Silsbee react to news of his father's death? What effect does it have on Nath's future plans?

14. Do you think Captain Nathaniel Silsbee made the right decision to bring the *Sally* back to Salem? How does his decision affect his future career?

15. Why does Captain George Crowninshield visit his son Edward? What is Edward's response?

16. As things turn out, do you think Geordie Crowninshield and his brother Edward had similar discomfort with their situations within the Crowninshield family?

17. Captain Nathaniel Silsbee's command of the *Benjamin* included severe challenges. Under crisis conditions, did Nath make good decisions?

18. What sort of person is Jacob Crowninshield? What are his aspirations? How does he compare to his brothers?

19. What do you think about Jacob's risk in bringing back an elephant from India to America?

20. Why do you think Jacob wants to marry Sarah Gardner?

21. Does Geordie treat Lizzie fairly before he leaves on the *Polly & Sally*? Do you think her situation was unusual?

22. Is Hasket Derby pleased with the *Grand Turk*'s performance?

23. How would you characterize Hasket Derby's relationship with his wife and children?

24. When Geordie returns, how does he treat Lizzie and his child? Did he behave responsibly?

25. Why is Captain Elias Derby attracted to Lucy Brown? Is it just her appearance?

26. What affect do the wars between Britain and France have on American merchant vessels?

27. Did Captain Silsbee's decision to lose the money he had won at baccarat surprise you?

28. How did Geordie respond when British marines boarded the *Belisarius* and impressed one of his men?

29. Compare Geordie's decision with Nath Silsbee's response to the impressment of his crew member at Madras. What motivated their decisions?

30. Does Geordie make a smooth transition to life ashore? If his father hadn't removed Geordie from his command of the *Belisarius*, do you think he would have made the same domestic arrangements with Lizzie?

31. Any thoughts on why Geordie doesn't propose marriage to Lizzie?

32. What is your impression of Captain Elias Derby? Do you think Lucy made the right decision when she married him?

33. Who is your favorite character in the story? Why?

# OTHER BOOKS BY SANDRA WAGNER-WRIGHT

**Fiction**

**Salem Stories Series**

*Ambition, Arrogance & Pride: Families & Rivals*
*in 18th Century Salem* (Book 1)

**Women of Determination & Courage Series**

*Saxon Heroines: A Northumbrian Novel*
*Two Coins: A Biographical Novel*
*Rama's Labyrinth: A Biographical Novel*

**Nonfiction**

*Ships, Furs, and Sandalwood: A Yankee Trader in*
*Hawai'i 1823–1825* (edited journal)

*History of the Macadamia Nut Industry in Hawai'i:*
*From Bush Nut to Gourmet's Delight*

*The Structure of the Missionary Call to the Sandwich*
*Islands 1796–1830: Sojourners Among Strangers*